CELEBROMANCY

MICHAEL R. UNDERWOOD

PRAISE FOR MICHAEL R. UNDERWOOD

"If *Buffy* hooked up with *Doctor Who* while on board the Serenity, this book would be their lovechild. In other words, *Geekomancy* is full of epic win."

— Marie Lu, author of the Legend trilogy, on *Geekomancy*

"Michael R. Underwood just keeps getting better and better. We need more urban fantasy like this."

— Seanan McGuire, New York Times bestselling author of *Discount Armageddon*, on *Celebromancy*

"This is truly a unique spin on the typical Urban Fantasy story and one of the most genuinely fun stories I have read in a long time."

— KristenD, Bitten by Books, on *Attack the Geek*

"Come for the geeky world and fun storyline, stay for the fabulous characters, relationships, and action. I thoroughly enjoyed the whole series; I simply loved *Hexomancy*. I commend it for your reading pleasure. Seriously, pre-order today."

— Joe's Geek Fest, on *Hexomancy*

"Heroes, villains, and a world like no other."

— Joe's Geek Fest on *Shield & Crocus*

" . . .a bright and exciting space opera in the cosmic comic book style of Marvel's *Guardians of the Galaxy*. In a galaxy that has been dominated by the mollusk-like Vsenk for a thousand years, three treasure hunters stumble across an artifact that will shake the foundations of an entire empire . . .Underwood's prose is brisk and funny without ever sacrificing his skilled sf world building. Highly recommended for fans of action-packed space opera and anyone else looking for a fun and fast-paced read.

– Booklist (Starred Review), on Annihilation Aria

"In this entertaining space opera from Underwood (the Genrenauts series), a married couple—one an affable archaeologist from Earth who was accidentally transported across the universe with no way home, the other a warrior woman from a devastated alien culture who utilizes songs to enhance her combat skills—becomes embroiled in a mess of galactic proportions after they "liberate" a dangerous artifact from a long-lost temple . . .This is a rollicking good time."

– Publisher's Weekly, on Annihilation Aria

"*Annihilation Aria* is the found family space opera you've been waiting for."

– Adam Rakunas, author of Philip K. Dick Award-finalist Windswept

"*The Younger Gods* is a solid urban fantasy with an interesting premise and characters you can't help but get invested in."

– Bibliotropic

"This is fun . . . Readers will be looking forward to Leah and company's next trip to a story world."

– Library Journal, on *Genrenauts: The Shootout Solution*

"This is one of those high concepts so irresistible, you can't believe no one has come up with it before. This first install- ment is a rollicking exploration of western tropes, with hints of a larger conspiracy afoot. Underwood has plans for a lot more of these, and I can't wait to read them."

– Joel Cunningham, Barnes & Noble Sci-Fi & Fantasy Blog,
on *Genrenauts: The Shootout Solution*

"A Tardis of a novella, *The Shootout Solution* is packed full of ideas . . . The possibilities are endless . . . Tor.com contin- ues to blaze a bookish trail in terms of both originality and diversity. More like this, please."

– Geek Syndicate, on *Genrenauts: The Shootout Solution*

"*The Shootout Solution* is Genre blending fun."

– Fangirl Nation

"A clever, exciting, and seriously fun twist on portal fantasy that sends a geeky stand-up comedian into the Wild West. Sign me up to be a Genrenaut, too!"

– Delilah S. Dawson, NYT-bestselling author of *Star Wars: Phasma*

"I have this sinking feeling that the Genrenauts series, with its raucous meta-commentary upon the stories of pop culture, is going to say important things that I might not be clever enough to catch the first time around because I'm too busy enjoying the books."

– Howard Tayler, Hugo Award Winner and creator of *Schlock Mercenary*

"My favorite new TV show of 2015 isn't on TV, it's in the pages of Mike Underwood's Genrenauts. Deeply funny and creative, shrewdly insightful, and thrillingly paced, every pop culture diehard will want to keep living vicariously through the characters in this series."

– Matt Wallace, Hugo Award winner and author
of the Savage Rebellion and Sin du Jour series

"*Born to the Blade* is the best Fantasy Epic NOT on TV"

– Inverse

"a complex and fascinating world that is filled with cool shit."

– Liz Bourke for Tor.com, on *Born to the Blade*

2nd edition
Copyright © 2013, 2022 by Michael R. Underwood
All rights reserved, including the right to reproduce this book or portions thereof in any form whatsoever.
For rights inquiries, contact info@morhaimliterary.com
ISBN: 9780998060644 (Paperback)
        9780998060651 (ebook)

Cover by Deranged Doctor Design (derangeddoctordesign.com)
Also available in audiobook

First edition by Simon & Schuster Pocket Star Books July 2013
1st edition ISBN 9781451698145

MORE BY MICHAEL R. UNDERWOOD

The Ree Reyes Geeky Urban Fantasy Series
Geekomancy
Celebromancy
Attack the Geek
Hexomancy

Genrenauts
#0 -The Data Disruption
#1 -The Shootout Solution
#2 - The Absconded Ambassador
#3 -The Cupid Reconciliation
#4 - The Substitute Sleuth
#5&6 - The Failed Fellowship
#7 - The Wasteland War

The Space Operas
Annihilation Aria

Other Books
Shield and Crocus

The Younger Gods

Born to the Blade
(with Malka Older, Cassandra Khaw, and Marie Brennan)

CHAPTER ONE

Confirm & Deny

Ree was late to her first public appearance as a screenwriter, and she couldn't even blame it on a monster attack.

Ree Reyes (Strength 10, Dexterity 14, Stamina 12, Will 18, IQ 16, Charisma 15—Geek 7 / Barista 3 / Screenwriter 2 / Gamer Girl 2 / Geekomancer 2) was already on the bus talking with her father and one-man cheerleading section when she got the *Where are you?* text from Yancy Williams, director, executive producer, and her new boss as a screenwriter.

"The fuck?" Ree said unconsciously as she read the text.

"What's up, Ree-bee?" her dad asked.

"I'm late. I was supposed to be there half an hour ago." Her pulse pole-vaulted straight past nervous all the way to freaked-the-hell-out.

"How far out are you?" her dad asked, his voice level. Ree's dad was an ex-marine and had all of the calm. She tried to borrow some, consciously slowing her breath.

It's not like your writing career is hanging on this or anything.

"Five minutes," Ree said. "But no one told me there was a makeup team!"

"It'll be fine. You can't make the bus get there any faster, so just remember why you were invited. Because you earned it. You'll be great."

"Gotta go. Time for a media power-up," Ree said.

"Love you," her dad answered.

A smile wiped away her worry for a moment. "Love you, too, daddy-o."

Ree hung up, looked at the text message again, sent her *ETA 5 min* response, and then queued up one of her power-up videos.

The bus would get there on its own time, so she did her best to concentrate on "The Late Shaft" from *Castle*.

For most new writers, watching a single scene of a TV show would be as useful as cramming French before a Medieval German exam. But Ree wasn't just any writer.

When they arrived at her stop, Ree practically dove out of the bus, and rushed into the hotel, brushing past fancy people in furs and suits that cost as much as her entire DVD collection.

One of Yancy's assistants, a young Chinese-American woman, was waiting in the lobby. *Was her name Patricia or Vanessa?* Ree wondered. She'd met most of the cast and crew all at once, and her brain's capacity for new names was about four at a time, max.

Patricia/Vanessa spotted her and said, "Thank God." She grabbed Ree's wrist and started off like a roadrunner. "Come with me, there's no time."

Ree imagined the woman speaking in the Terminator voice.

Come with me if you want to live . . . or look good on camera.

⋅✕ˣ⟨⊕⟩ˣ✕⋅

They rushed to the bathroom that One Tough Mama had commandeered for their makeup prep. As Ree stepped inside, she saw a small handful of makeup artists clustered around Jane Konrad, the owner/executive producer of One Tough Mama and the star of *Awakenings*. The bathroom had been jury-rigged into a dressing room with extra lights, a clothing rack, and three Avon ladies' worth of makeup. The room smelled of hair spray and BPAL. And in the hot seat was Jane Konrad, (in)famous actress and producer.

Jane Konrad (Strength 8, Dexterity 13, Stamina 12, Will 15, IQ 16, Charisma 17—Performer 5 / Child Star 3 / Producer 2 / Philanthropist 2 / Party Girl 1 / Geek 1) was about Ree's height, had a currently-limp mane of chestnut-red-brown hair, and had starred in many happy dreams of Ree's over the years. She wore simple sweats, which hung loose on her diminished frame.

Just two years ago, Jane had been a world-class superstar, but her career had recently gone the same way as a famous young redhead's. The Jane of now was much skinnier than when she'd last been in a movie, which the tabloids blamed on drugs but Yancy denied fervently. She'd also collected more than a few citations and DUIs, and starred on the gossip sites ONTD and WTF on a regular basis.

Ree didn't know how long Jane had been in the chair, but she still looked pretty rough. Makeup failed to cover huge bags under her eyes, her hair was thin and lifeless, and her skin was wan. And then there were the things makeup couldn't touch.

Skinny could be sexy, but on Jane, it just didn't work. The actress looked empty, used up, like she'd gone nine rounds with a wight. She was operating far below her normal +3 Charisma bonus.

One of the makeup artists ushered Ree to a foldout chair in front of a sink and mirror, then started working.

"Glad you could make it," Jane said. Even her voice was hollow. *Are we in trouble with this show?* If her first pilot bombed, getting another job would be all that much harder.

Ree tucked a stray lock of hair behind her ear, still a little gun-shy around the star. "Sorry, I missed the call-time message."

Jane managed a weak smile. "It'll be fine. There's no need for writers to be glamorous. They'll want it anyway, since you're a woman, but you'll be fine. Just let Brendan do his magic."

Ree's nostrils flared at the comment. She knew it was true, and the double standard of it all stuck in her craw like a jagged chunk of popcorn.

Brendan was the man with at least four hands starting her makeup, if Ree had to judge just by the speed of his work.

"Can you see without these?" Brendan asked, indicating her thick-lensed glasses. If the money from selling the script hadn't all gone to overdue bills, credit cards, and paying back her roommate, she might have been able to replace the specs she'd worn since college, or afford new contacts. But that would have to wait for a series pickup.

"Not in any useful fashion," she said.

He tutted disapprovingly and said, "Then we'll work around them. Go ahead and take them off for now."

Ree obeyed and Brendan set to work, first removing the meager makeup she'd put on herself, then starting to rebuild her look from the base up. Thanks to an Irish-American mother and a Puerto Rican–American father, Ree had the "ethnically indeterminate" look, which in Hollywood would mean she'd generally be cast as the wise-cracking friend.

Brendan highlighted the light brown in her complexion, but also drew attention to her eyes. While he did that, Jane's hairdresser did a drive-by, untying Ree's functional shoulder-length braid and giving her a quick comb and treatment with some hair spray that nearly made Ree choke in her seat.

The door to the bathroom opened, and Yancy poked his head in. "Looking good, folks. Jane, how are you feeling today?"

Jane sat up, looking at Yancy in the mirror. "I've got this. You keep them on topic, draw attention to our new star writer, and it'll be great." Jane turned and smiled at Ree, who tried to restrain a blush. Her reflection told her she'd failed, even with the makeup.

"All right. We're on in ten," Yancy said, then disappeared behind the closing door.

Brendan flashed back and the hairstylist continued to work wonders.

Ree caught Brendan's eyes in the mirror, then waggled her phone as she asked, "Do you mind if I zone out with a show while you work? It helps me calm down."

Brendan shrugged. "Just listen for my instructions when I need you to move your head."

"Got it," she said, and restarted the scene.

Since becoming a Geekomancer, a magician drawing power from her love for science-fiction/fantasy/horror/etc. media, Ree had made the executive decision to become more organized.

Her part of the apartment was still a pigsty, but she had gotten her shit together for her new Urban Fantasy life. Over the last few months, she'd made playlists of videos to watch for short hits of genre emulation and had tagged her video collection by gleanable skills.

The short clips, she'd found, were only good for ten, maybe fifteen seconds of magic, usually just one trick. But the right trick at the right time could be a lifesaver. And with the screen only ten inches away, she could see well enough.

Genre emulation was the most powerful (and rare) form of Geekomancy, and it was her best chance to not freak out and wretch during her first ever press panel.

Re-upping her connection to the feel of *Castle* could give her the cocksure charm of author Richard Castle and help her waltz through her first press conference. She got through the scene three times, trying to talk along with Richard Castle as he charmed the reporter with his spiel about *Dead Heat*, the first novel based on Lieutenant Kate Beckett.

During her fourth watch-through, Brendan said, "That should do it," handing back her glasses.

Ree put her specs back on and looked up to see herself in the mirror.

She blinked and felt her jaw drop. *Who's the hottie?*

The woman in the mirror was far more put-together and glamorous than Ree had felt in years. Her hair had shape that wasn't braided, and, dare she say it, volume. She had blush, eye shadow, and lashes long enough to use the D&D natural attack rules, and generally looked entirely unlike herself. It was a total violation of her residual self-image in the most flattering kind of way. She beamed, her pride boosted by the *Castle* energy buzzing in her mind.

"Wow" was all she could manage. "Wow."

Brendan's smile was as wide as the room. "Not bad, eh? You better get used to it. This is Hollywood standard."

Jane leaned over to her. The star looked better herself, her fatigue concealed behind masterfully done makeup, her hair voluminous and healthy. She still looked under the weather, but the hollow look was gone, leaving the star undeniably gorgeous.

Changing into a skirt and gauzy top helped as well, focusing attention on her (diminished) curves.

Ree stood and cracked her neck, happy to not have to hold her good posture anymore. She resisted the urge to reach up and fiddle with her face. *Stay cool*, said a Nathan Fillion–esque voice in her head.

"Do we wait in here or beside the stage?" Ree asked.

"Out there." Jane stood and hugged Brendan. "Great job, hon." She turned to Ree. "Now it's our turn."

The two joined Yancy outside. Yancy Williams (Strength 13, Dexterity 10, Stamina 14, Will 16, IQ 16, Charisma 14— Scholar 2 / Director 5 / Producer 4 / Kingmaker 3 / Dad 3) was an impish kind of fiftysomething, with well-earned laugh lines, a full head of white hair, and a whiskey-barrel chest. Yancy lead the group down a short hall to the entrance of the Washington ballroom.

Yancy ducked his head into the ballroom for a second, then said, "They're almost ready for us."

Jane took Ree's hand and gave it a squeeze. "Talk slowly, and give short answers when you can. Let them ask the follow-ups.

Don't answer anything you don't want to. Except the basic stuff. If you don't answer the basic stuff, we look bad." Jane gave a lopsided smile that made her look like a normal person, not one burdened with fame or plagued by her recent past. Just one woman giving advice to another.

All right, Ree. Don't fuck this up. It's just another kind of performance, like talking to customers, pitching a script, or a first date.

Set mode to Ree Reyes, Screenwriter.

Another minute later, a young man with a headset opened the door and waved them in.

Yancy went first, then Ree. Jane would go last. Ree followed Yancy up the three steps to the stage and tried to pretend there weren't fifty reporters standing in the front rows, that there weren't another couple of hundred people behind them clapping and cheering.

Stay cool.

Ree put on her best smile and tried to look confident as she took long steps, stopping at the seat next to Yancy. There were a water bottle, microphone, and a name card, which announced her as Rhiannon Reyes, at the space.

As she turned to take her seat, the room exploded. Ree saw Jane step up onto the stage, waving to the crowd. Whatever last-second touch-ups and costuming tricks Brendan had done in the hall made a world of difference.

Jane was stunning, a L'Oreal commercial crossbred with a red carpet parade and unleashed on the room. Her hair flowed like a waterfall as she worked the stage like a runway.

She practically glowed from within; the star looked like she'd had a month's worth of yoga and good diet. Her famous curves were back, filling out her clothes and accentuating the confident sway of her hips.

Di-damn. Whatever Brendan made, he deserved a raise.

The flash of cameras was nearly blinding, and the roar of the crowd was primal, enthralled.

Jane reached her seat, gave another big smile, and took her seat. Ree remembered that she was still standing and was probably staring. She took her own seat and grasped for her water bottle with a smile, eager for a chance to clear her head as a storm of thoughts bounced around her mind like a game of *Arkanoid.*

Yo. Get a grip, she told herself. Remember the you-have-to-talk-to-people part? The screenwriter thing?

She answered the voice in her head. *But . . . pretty!*

Ree took a long swig of water and turned to the press, which had sat down as the roar of the crowd faded. She tapped into the *Castle* magic, thinking *What Would Rick Castle Do?* and her shoulders relaxed, her smile brightened. Her connection to the power wouldn't last, thanks to the radioactive butterflies in her stomach burning away her concentration, but she'd milk it for all it was worth.

Yancy held his hands up, and the room settled. A few moments later, he leaned in and started talking.

"Good afternoon. I'm Yancy Williams, executive producer and director of *Awakenings.* I'm honored to be joined by the one, the only, Jane Konrad." He paused for applause. Facing the audience, Ree saw the enraptured look on many of the audience's faces. The press seemed less enraptured, but they were still fascinated, attentive, and sitting on the edge of their seats.

Jane smiled and nodded to the crowd for a few seconds, then raised a hand herself. The cheering died out like an orchestra, with Jane as the conductor.

Yancy started up again. "And I'm especially pleased to introduce to you the creator of *Awakenings,* the woman behind the next big television hit, Ree Reyes!"

The applause for Ree was a fraction of what Jane had gotten.

But it's for me. Not anyone else.

Ree beamed, waving to the crowd.

Oh, yeah. Who's the shit?

A few moments later, Yancy spoke again.

"We're very happy to speak with you about *Awakenings*. We're starting the second week of principal photography, and things are going splendidly. I'm sure there are many questions, so let's launch right in."

A young Latina with long silky hair wearing a West African shawl as a scarf stood, raising her hand. Patricia/Vanessa rushed over to hand her a microphone.

"Kelly Dominguez, *Pearson Patriot*. Ms. Konrad, what attracted you to this project and the choice of an unknown screenwriter for your return to the screen?" Kelly was a local video-blogger who had parlayed her positive but probing video reportage into a full-time gig. Ree'd been a fan for years, and it was fun to see her in the flesh.

Jane pulled her mike in, nodding to Kelly. She spoke with warmth and poise wrapped together in a perfect braid. "Hello, Kelly. That's a lovely shawl. I told Yancy that I was looking for fresh blood on the project, a new voice that I could introduce to the world, the way that he helped me break in to the industry.

"I started with a stack of manuscripts selected by our interns, which must have been three feet tall." Jane paused to laugh, drawing the audience in even more.

"There was a lot of good material, but when I came to *Awakenings*, I knew this was it. Ree has a crisp, humorous voice, and the script is one of the best pilots I've read. Television is the perfect medium for combining entertainment and social commentary, and *Awakenings* is the right show for the right time. There are a lot of shows that entertain, but precious few that go deeper, tackling real issues, and none that do it the way Ree has in *Awakenings*."

Several reporters nodded like bobblehead dolls, hanging on to Jane's every word. The star gestured to Ree, shifting the spotlight of attention. "But let's hear from the genius herself. I'm sure she'd be happy to tell you more about the show."

That's me. She felt a hundred eyes lock onto her movements, their attention as intense as a spotlight. Ree was used to performing in small crowds—stores, parties, and the Midnight Market. This was a whole different world.

Ree cleared her throat and pulled in her own mike, calling forward the *Castle* energy again.

Keep it cool.

"Thanks, Jane. I wrote *Awakenings* for a number of reasons. The biggest one is that ever since *Battlestar Galactica* went off the air, there hasn't been another show, for me, that tackled social issues in the way I wanted to see. So I had to write it myself.

"I grew up reading Ursula LeGuin, Frank Herbert, Octavia Butler, and New Wave SF. It's hard to do social science fiction on TV, because many viewers are expecting the eyeball kicks, explosions, and constant jokes. But I wanted to take a risk, trust that an audience would go with me on something that took the time to dig into issues between fight scenes."

Another reporter took up the mike, a thirtysomething white guy with a shaved head and big plastic glasses. He was dressed in the traditional garb of his people, the black turtleneck, as well as a finely-crafted air of self-importance.

"Alex Walters, WTF. Given the crash-and-burn failure of shows like *The Event*, *Mutant X*, *Inhumans*, and others, what makes you think that a show that seems to boil down to a mashup of *The Incredibles* and *The 4400* can succeed in today's television market, especially with a washed-out flight risk as the star?"

Ree knew this guy. He was hipster royalty online, and prided himself on eviscerating everything in the world as soon as it started to smell of success, predicting failure everywhere he went. And since he had a million Twitter followers and headed one of the biggest gossip sites this side of TMZ, when he did his doomsaying, a whole lot of people listened.

Yancy looked to Ree, and she nodded, trying to indicate, *I got this.* Though she had to restrain her first instinct, which was to pull the lightsaber out of her purse and take a Dark Side point.

Ree adjusted the mike and said, "The fact that companies keep putting on shows like the ones you mentioned means that the execs and others believe that there's something to it. And concept isn't destiny. Execution matters more than originality." *Look at me being diplomatic,* she thought, when all she wanted to do was drop-kick the smarmy bastard out of the zip code.

Ree continued. "Only a handful of them have hit it big, but does that mean the others are doomed to fail, or that just because a couple of them aren't great means the others are crap? Of course not. Each show deserves to be judged on its own merits, don't you think?"

Do not engage, she told herself. *That way lies viral fail videos.*

Alex shifted his weight, eyes narrowed. "That's easy to say, but if we're supposed to judge your show on its merits, will *Awakenings* actually have any?"

Because you're the God-given arbiter of taste, right? Ree thought, restraining the growing urge to jump the table and strangle the bastard.

No one will care if I clobber him, right? The media ecosystem will survive with one less parasite.

Yancy leaned in to answer. "Ree has a wry, crisp voice, and she's given us a great world to bring to life for audiences. Our special-effects team is going to deliver amazing visuals, and Jane is putting in some of the best performances I've seen in the fifteen years I've worked with her."

Ree gave Yancy a smile, waited for him to continue or Jane to hop in. After a beat, Ree spoke again. "I can give you the basic concept, just to put everything on the table. In the might-as-well-be-now future, magic returns to the earth, and people around the world awaken with magic powers. People flip out, and all of a sudden, there's a brand-new way to be stigmatized. *Awakenings* takes the one-family lens approach to tackling social issues, while always staying personal."

Ree stopped there, remembering Jane's suggestion to keep it brief, or at least brief-ish. Plus, she felt the *Castle* energy starting to run low, and wanted to keep some magic back for other questions.

Her hands were shaking, and she took a long swig from her glass as she calmed herself down, mentally grasping onto the magical energy.

She looked to Alex, bracing for another *gotcha* or snide remark. But either he was satisfied or he was going to save the rest of the bile for his article. A half-dozen other hands stood in the air, and Ree looked to Yancy, who nodded.

The next reporter was a shorter, curvy woman with tightly curled black hair. "Vlada Janczuk, StraightDope.com. One Tough Mama has had a difficult few years. How important is it that this pilot succeed, and why shoot a pilot on spec instead of pitching to studios right away?"

Yancy's response was a guarded grin. "Every project is important, and right now money is tight for everyone."

Ree had asked this question when the production company made their offer to buy the pilot. So she knew that Yancy's answer read as *This is the last of Jane's money, and if the pilot bombs, the production company will go belly-up.*

Announcing, *Hey, we're screwed if this fails, so please watch us!* wasn't exactly a way to get people to tune in, not for a brand-new show. Some series needed "Save Show X" campaigns before they hit the air, but no one wanted to be that show. Plus, first they needed to find a network to bite.

Yancy continued, "As for why to dive right into shooting a pilot, Jane has always tried to innovate with our efforts at One

Tough Mama. After the success of independent productions from *The Guild* to The Lizzie Bennet Diaries, Jane wanted to get the pilot in the can before making presentations, which will give us more flexibility. If the networks pass for whatever reason, we still have a product, and we can go direct to the fans and use Kickstarter to raise funds for a full season."

Yancy'd said part of why they were doing the press conference this early was to help drum up interest, as well as to dispel the myths that Jane was too far gone to get through a production.

From where Ree sat, they were doing all of that and more, thanks to Jane's charm and Yancy's tact, and maybe even her own fu.

The press worked through a few more questions, getting into details about the production schedule and their hopes for the series' home (any major network, plus Syfy, TNT, HBO or one of the streaming services, etc.). Ree let Yancy take the lead, and Jane answered the softball personal questions with grace and waved off the inflammatory ones from Alex and others. Eventually, the PAs got the message and stopped giving the mike to the muckraker. After the third time he was ignored, he got up and made a big production of storming off.

Good riddance.

"That's all the time we have for today," Yancy said finally, an hour into the press conference. "Thank you for your time, and I hope you'll continue following our progress with *Awakenings!*"

They stood to another round of applause. Jane played to the crowd on the way out, and Ree heard the roar continue even through the door and down the hall as they left.

"We've got a car in back," Yancy said.

Jane shook her head, grinning wide. "No, we're going out the front. Give them a minute to gather." She looked like the cat who'd caught the canary.

A shadow passed over Yancy's face. "Careful, Jane."

Jane stretched, cracking her back. "I'll be fine. And we need every bit of press we can get."

Yancy took a halting step toward Jane, a worried, paternal look on his face. Jane raised a hand, and he stopped.

"It's going to be a hit, Yanc. And then we'll be back on top."

They waited for a minute.

Why am I getting a foreboding vibe off of this? It isn't just the worry of maybe people will throw fruit instead of cheering—it was something bigger.

"I've got a bad feeling about this," Ree said without getting the chance to censor herself.

Jane looked to Ree and smiled big.

Why worry? Ree asked herself. It'll be fine.

"Follow me and stay close. This is going to be a great ride."

Jane nodded to her bodyguard Danny, who had appeared from nowhere to take the lead, engaging his not-to-be-fucked-with look.

Danny Park (Strength 15, Dexterity 16, Stamina 14, Will 15, IQ 13, Charisma 10—Laborer 2 / Security 3 / Martial Artist 5 / Bodyguard 4) stood only five feet and change, but he was ripped, the muscle shirt he wore under his jacket showing enough skin to make that fact abundantly clear. He wore a short ponytail tied back, and his jeans were well worn without being patchy.

Ree followed, and as they walked through the hotel, Ree couldn't help but envision the group in their very own Badass Walk: the last or next-to-last shot of a TV credits sequence or film trailer where the main characters stride with purpose down a hallway, alley, or battlefield. Bonus points if something explodes in the background.

Her mind played a made-up theme song in the style of Nerf Herder as they walked. Danny reached the front of the hotel, and two men in suits opened the doors for them.

The crowd outside was even bigger than it had been in the ballroom by at least 50 percent. *Where are all these people coming from?* Ree wondered.

Jane sauntered through the crowd wearing a modest smile.

The air was tight with excitement and the flow of energy as the star held court, soaking it all in like an emotional vampire. *I sure hope Dresden's White Court doesn't really exist. If they do, we're all fucked.* According to the model that Eastwood gave Ree during her brief stint as a snarky apprentice, there might be individual vampires that followed the model from Butcher's novels, feeding on emotion instead of blood, but probably not enough to be their own society. If they did, Ree had no doubt that they'd have Hollywood wrapped around their sexy alabaster fingers.

Some heroines got simple universes, with monsters and magic that followed consistent rules. As far as she could tell, magic in her world was as inconsistent and dynamic as real life, so just when she thought she understood what was going on, something would change for no discernible reason, like fashion, pop music, or Facebook.

Ree headed straight for the waiting town car, sliding in beside Yancy. Jane took several minutes to sign, schmooze, and soak up the love.

Yancy kept an eye on his star, and Ree watched out of the corner of her eye.

Jane waved goodbye to the crowd and slinked into the car with deliberate grace, proving Ree's point. She beckoned Ree in next, and Yancy took shotgun as Danny closed the door to the car, interposing himself to keep the crowds away.

Jane leaned in to speak to both of them.

"See, wasn't that fun?" Her eyes were wide, like she'd just taken a hit of something high-grade.

Yancy harrumphed. "Back to the set, please." The driver, an older Middle Eastern man in an aviator cap, nodded, and the car pulled out into the street.

"Actually, can you drop me somewhere?" Ree asked. "I've got a lunch."

Yancy nodded. Jane frowned. "I thought you were going to be on-set this afternoon?"

"I will," Ree said. "When I say 'I have a lunch,' what I really mean is 'I have work.' My boss has been good about being flexible and giving my work here priority, but I do have to help out for a few hours." *That and take a meeting that could really go well, or really really not.*

"Just tell the driver," Yancy said, the car already in motion.

Ree gave directions to an office building across town.

Of course, that wasn't where she was actually going.

CHAPTER TWO

Like Cheers, but with Dice

You can't find Grognard's Games and Grog unless you're meant to, or with someone who has been.

Proprietor Grognard (First or last name? Don't ask) is a veteran of the world of Geekomancy and an expert brewer.

Find rare memorabilia, play in tournaments with bizarre prizes, but just don't get on Grognard's bad side.

Be sure to chat with new employee Ree Reyes, a novice Geekomancer who has made a splash with her signature snark.

—Not For Mundanes: Pearson

Grognard's Games and Grog was a full block underground, and the front door was disguised as a maintenance door inside the sewer.

As far as Ree could tell, it was mostly because Grognard didn't like being bothered.

The shop was split into two sections: the bar, and the great sea of merchandise.

It'd only been six months since she started at Grognard's, but she'd taken to the job like a tomcat in an aviary. And until the show took off, the checks for *Awakenings* were enough for her to catch a breather on her bills, but not to quit her job. It had all the hustle and bustle of her old job at Zombie Café, plus it kept her right in the middle of Pearson's magical underground.

Other than the Midnight Market, Grognard's was the #1 meet-up destination for the city's magical Geekomantic community, with practitioners prowling the aisles for just the right back issue or action figure for their rituals or just whiling away an evening over pitchers arguing about which Star Wars was the best and why.

That afternoon, the shop was empty, except for Grognard, who stood at the bar with a stack of paperwork.

Grognard—*Just Grognard. Like Logan.*—(Strength 14, Dexterity 10, Stamina 15, Will 18, IQ 15, Charisma 10—Geek 7 / Collector 4 / Geekomancer 3 / Brewmaster 5) was tall, bald, and thick. He looked somewhere between thirty and fifty and wore black, black, and more black.

Grognard topped off his look with the kind of beard that took constant cultivation: full, long, but perfectly groomed and easily stroked with one hand while haggling over a rare back issue, action figure, or game supplement.

"Hey," Ree said as she approached.

Grognard chuffed. "You just missed Eastwood."

"Pudu," Ree said, frustrated and relieved all at once. They'd made plans to plot over beer.

For all of two days, Eastwood had been her mentor in the weird world of Geekomancy, until she discovered that he was aiding and abetting a demon that pushed teenagers to suicide.

He had been doing it to try and rescue her mom (aka his girlfriend) from hell, a geeky Faustian bargain, but in Ree's book, no level of good intentions could really justify sacrificing kids—not even for her mom, who had left a planet-sized hole in her and her dad's life when she'd disappeared.

These days, the only time she saw Eastwood was when they were trying to figure out how to spring her mom from hell. This generally involved a lot of mutual frustration and tense stares across a table at Grognard's, ending with one or the other of them storming off.

Eastwood was stubborn, grating, and probably unhinged, but he was as committed to Ree's mom as she was. Probably more.

The enemy of my mom's enemy is my grudging ally. Working with him meant taking a trip through guilt, anger, betrayal, shame, and usually landing back at anger.

They'd pushed back this meeting twice already. What the fuck was he up to?

Ree massaged her temples, the pent-up anxiety about the meeting clustering in her head. "He leave a message?"

"Not as such. He complained about your lack of dedication and said something about 'If she's too busy playing Hollywood to do the work, then I can do it on my own.'"

"Sounds like he was in a great mood."

Grognard chuckled in his grunting, huffing kind of way. "Right in one. Hope you two kids kiss and make up" was all he said, showing just how much he didn't care about Ree's drama.

"While you're here, can you reorganize the card singles? Uncle Joe sorted them by artist again last night while I was doing liquor inventory."

Oh, Joe. Uncle Joe was one of the regulars, a Geekomancer with an inner Order Muppet that would make Ernie look like a Jack Black character.

"As long as you put on some Lacuna Coil to help me stay chill," Ree said, making her way to the collectible card game binders.

First she reminded herself which folders were which, presorting the piles so she could start sorting them in earnest.

After spending a couple of minutes' prep work and shaking off the Eastwood/Mom grump, she hopped on her phone and used the store wireless to send Drake a text.

Swing by Grognard's. We haven't gotten to hang in a while.

She got a little spike of happy when she thought of Drake, but the taste finished sour.

Things with Drake were . . . weird. They hung out, patrolled together, went out to movies as Ree tried to catch him up on pop culture, and she hung out in his apartment while he tried and failed to blow himself up with one or another Steampunked experiment.

But nothing had happened. And she could not buy a frakking clue as to what was going on with their relationship. Last Halloween, there'd been all this . . . something, but after that, when the weird magic world became her new normal, they hadn't taken that next step, the smooching one, where things stopped being awkward and got awesome.

But she had no idea if he really liked her like that, given the weirdness of his background. And she was pretty sure that if she just planted a big smooch on him, Roger Rabbit-style, he might self-implode from the catastrophic impropriety of it all.

So instead, they were stuck in a frustrating purgatorial almost-maybe.

Ree pulled a three-inch binder out of a huge stack and set it atop the row of comic longboxes with a thud.

This at least makes sense.

The binder probably contained $3000 worth of cards from *Magic: The Gathering.* For a pro tour player, it might contain just the right card to take their deck to the next level. And for a Geekomancer, it might have the final ingredient for a ritual, an enchantment, or the panic button to save their ass from a hungry troll. Ree had picked up more than a few choice singles for her own magical sideboard.

Ree opened the binder and sighed. All of the cards on the first page had art by Miao Aili. She flipped several pages, where they changed to Rob Alexander.

This was a crap detail, but it had to be done or customers would complain. Geeks were marvelous, creative, and fun, but were also often picky bastards who loved to pick nits.

Not that Ree had ever been guilty of nitpicking. Nope, not once. Certainly not when discussing obscure Expanded Universe Star Wars continuity or back-talking to a guard at a secret magical market. Nope.

She daydreamed about the press conference, *Awakenings*, and how fucking awesome her life was at the moment while she pulled and reorganized the cards in the binder. She checked her phone every few minutes, expecting a message from Drake.

When she'd re-sorted half the binder, she checked her phone again: 3:15. She needed to get back to the set if she was going to be able to give notes on anything.

She checked her messages again and, on a whim, tapped out the message she'd been wanting to send for months:

Dear Drake,

So, here's the thing. I like you, and I really need to know if you like me or if this is just you being a courteous and generally affable guy who thinks of me as that madwoman with a foul mouth and a mean right hook.

Can we meet up sometime so you can tell me what's what and we can get to smooching or not?

Kisses,

Ree

She stared at the message, her finger far away from the send button. She sighed, and deleted the message.

Instead, she sent:

Done at Grognard's. Headed back to set. Catch you later?

She sighed, restacked the binders, then called over to Grognard.

"I've got to get back to set. I'll get the rest of these next time."

Grognard gave her the stink-eye as she packed up.

Luckily, he had many stink-eyes, and this was the one that meant *I'm grumpy you're going, but there won't be any notable repercussions. Mmm, beer.* Though pretty much all of his stink-eyes ended with *Mmm, beer.* Dude was a brewer, after all.

Ree stared at her phone the whole way back to set, checking Twitter and her Google Alerts for the postpanel scuttle-butt. It was mostly bland recap, a couple of complimentary notes about how together they thought Jane was for a change, plus Alex Walters's usual character-assassination tripe.

"Washed-up Mickey Mouse Club reject turned failed auteur."

Wow. Harsh. Does this guy eat his cereal in the morning with Haterade?

CHAPTER THREE

Talk the Talk, Walk the Walk

In less than a year since the new city initiatives, Pearson, Oregon, has become the new Hollywood North, stealing productions away from Portland and Vancouver both.

Tax credits, cheap rentals, and unprecedented access have helped make Pearson home to seventeen TV and film productions last year, and it looks like we're set to double that this year.

Good for the economy, good for writers, actors, and for reporters like yours truly, who suddenly finds herself getting to report a Hollywood beat on Oregon rents and with a more relaxed dress code.

This year's big productions include Cosmic Studios' Blog Wars and One Tough Mama's Awakenings, written by local writer Ree Reyes. Props to a local girl done good, and for Jane Konrad for bringing some indie charm to Pearson and helping balance out the Big Hollywood.

So I say, let the show go on.

—Kelly Dominguez, ThePearsonPatriot.com

One Tough Mama's production campus was a half-dozen trailers parked in the alley of Douglas Street, as well as a handful of trucks that contained costumes, props, and all the other bits that made a production run. They were close enough to the wharf to be cheap, but not so close that they had to worry about shady "import/export" guys and 3 AM deals.

All the crew commentaries and TV episodes about TV hadn't prepared her for what being on an actual production was like.

Especially since she'd gone from unknown to working with a superstar in four months flat.

Ree stood at the edge of the hustle and bustle while people shuttled back and forth with gear, props, and clipboards. She took a breath, smiled, and headed inside. As the screenwriter, it seemed like she needed to always be around, but at the oddest times. She imagined it was a lot like being an on-call doctor or IT lead, except your emergencies ranged from *What's my motivation?* to *We need a whole new scene. In an hour.*

One Tough Mama was renting a former office building, which they divided into several sets for the production, with room for cameras and equipment on each side. Ree was re-minded of a middle school she'd gone to in Maryland, where they had fold-away dividers between classrooms so that they could connect several rooms for "integrated learning."

The set was abuzz, with crew members dressing the sets and climbing through the rafters in precarious positions to make adjustments to the lighting, and a small army of pro-duction assistants buzzing back and forth.

Yancy controlled the room, managing crew and staff alike, almost all of whom Ree had been introduced to and then promptly forgotten all of their names. She could distinguish Bifur from Bombur perfectly, and tell you all about the mis-adventures of the *Real Teen Titans*, but real people names? Those were harder.

Yancy waved her over to the director chair beside him, which awesomely said REE REYES, WRITER. She'd already asked if she could keep the chair (yes), if someone could take a picture of her in the chair (which they did), and if this was all really happening (yes, and we need to get back to it).

"So, what are we up to today?" Ree said, taking off her bag and sitting in her chair.

"Jane wants to chat with you about her character. She has some questions about the dinner scene today."

"She'll be in her trailer?" Ree asked. Yancy nodded.

Ree hopped off the chair, picked up her bag, and headed for the craft services table on her way back out to Jane's trailer. Ree picked up a muffin and started noshing even as she grabbed a plate.

Perks of being a real screenwriter #24: Free food.

Ree took her time winding back through the pop-up city, taking it all in and trying once again to convince her brain that it was all really happening and was not the most epic April Fool's joke ever. Her life had gone from normal-twenty-something-adrift-in-life to madcap-Urban-Fantasy-lifestyle, but this recent jump to showbiz was almost as estranging as becoming a Geekomancer and integrating herself into Pearson's occult underground.

She reached Jane's trailer, which had her name in yard-tall cursive script painted on the side. Ree nodded at Danny, who stood watch outside. "How's it going, Danny?" she asked, extending a hand to shake.

Danny met her hand and smiled, which looked even cooler under his shades. "Not bad. Go on in, she's expecting you."

Ree pulled open the door and adjusted her eyes to the dim light inside as she closed the door behind her.

It was posh for a trailer, but not as ridiculously gaudy as she'd seen on "behind-the-scenes" shows over the years, with stars whose trailers were both larger and super-way-amazeballs-better-appointed than her apartment. The main room was filled with a Comfy Couch™, a never-been-used kitchenette, and a media setup.

One whole wall next to the media nook was filled with bookshelves, holding bound scripts, DVDs (Konrad's projects, Criterion Collection films, and some film from the category Ree referred to as "Beloved Schlock"), some classical lit, and a selection of SF/F novels that, when Ree had first seen them, had made her reevaluate her opinion of the star.

It was hard for Ree to dislike anyone who had *We*, *A Wrinkle in Time*, *Parable of the Sower*, *The Hundred Thousand Kingdoms*, *The Left Hand of Darkness*, and *The Lies of Locke Lamora* on their bookshelf.

Jane reclined in the papasan chair that flanked the Comfy Couch, holding script pages above her head and speaking in a soft voice. Jane saw Ree out of the corner of her eye and smiled, leaning forward and tilting the papasan into a more chair-like shape.

"Good, you're here." Jane stood and held the pages out to Ree. "I think we need to take another look at this scene—I feel like it doesn't hit the thematic notes we need for my character to pop."

Ree took the pages in hand, though she knew the scene by heart. She was still a little stunned every time Jane talked to her—the *holy crap, you're Jane Konrad!* effect wearing down over time. Ree had been a fan of Konrad since the start and had had more than a few not-pure thoughts about the woman during their shared teen years.

Clearing her throat (and her mind), Ree took a seat on the Comfy Couch and said, "Sure thing. I was trying to convey the claustrophobia of her family's disapproval bit by bit, but I can totally ramp it up if that'll give you more to dig into. It'll make the parents less sympathetic, though. I can have them contrast a bit more, with maybe the mom more scared of the Awakened and the dad suffering silently, not making waves. How's that sound?"

Jane's eyes lit up. "Sounds perfect. Are you sure this is your first pilot?"

Ree tried not to blush. *Is she just flirting to flirt? Stay cool, girl, you are a professional.*

"Just glad that we're on the same page. I can tweak those this morning and we'll be set for the afternoon, if Yancy's all right with springing sides on folks later."

Jane shrugged. "I've done worse. And we don't really have time to delay things any more."

Ree pushed on the side of the Comfy Couch, since trying to escape it without your full effort was a doomed effort (which she'd learned the first time she visited Jane in her trailer).

"Great. Do you need anything else?" she asked.

Jane smiled her broad, unselfconscious smile, considering for a moment as she looked Ree up and down. "Not right now."

The star wasn't glowing as much as she had at press panel, but she still shone. Jane held Ree in her gaze as the screenwriter left the trailer.

Ree chuckled nervously as she walked past Danny and back to the set.

Danger, Will Robinson.

✕✕✕

Ree spent an hour or so tweaking the scene, writing out three versions and playing them in her brain, until she decided on a winner and emailed it to a production assistant, who brought printed copies a few minutes later.

She sat in her chair as Yancy held court, answering questions and issuing orders like a sea captain in a storm.

Rekindling your crush on Jane Konrad will not help your career. Well, it might, but it's just as likely to sink you if she self-destructs again. Do the work, listen, and learn. Do not dive into the Hollywood Zone, land of fame, fortune, and all flavors of eccentric.

They shot an interstitial scene while the main cast memorized the new sides, and more crew dressed the dining room set for the afternoon's big blowout. They were scheduled to spend several hours on the blowout, which was the prime rib of act two.

Ree kept on the outskirts as Yancy led the crew through the shoot, nibbling at the craft services table and snatching up a sandwich before the rest of the production swooped down over the dinner break.

Jane emerged from makeup and wardrobe dressed in a black halter dress that looked even better than the one Ree had imagined while writing the script. The star's hair was up and back, braided in a just-barely-SF-inal way that suggested *We're in the future, but not so much in the future that you don't care.*

The set for the room was larger than the room itself, with only two walls, the other sides open to the world and making room for cameras, lights, and more. The table was set for six with fine china but not too much else. The Richmonds were supposed to be upper-middle-class, as white-middle-American as she could figure while still being close enough to areas of cultural conflict to make them a good core for her story.

Ree joined Yancy at the edge of the set. "How are we doing?"

Yancy eyed the set. "It needs something else." He turned over his shoulder. "Georgia! Can I get a slight blue filter on the overhead for tone?"

"Got it!" came a call from above. Ree looked up and saw a woman crawling around in the scaffolding fifteen feet in the air.

"We're fine. Just hang around in case the lines need tweaking in practice."

If rewriting the scene over an hour was bad, then having to hold up the production because her rewrite was crap in action would probably be akin to the USS *Defiant*'s cloaking field dropping in the middle of a Dominion fleet.

But as of yet, her impostor syndrome existed only in her head.

Ree moved her chair and watched as the TV-making machine spun up into high gear to run through the scene. Thankfully, once the new lines were in place, Ree got to sit back and watch as Yancy worked his magic, a cinematic conductor coordinating the orchestra of people, gear, blocking, and sound.

For all the "TV about TV" that Ree had seen, the experience of actually being on-set was still something else. When she'd tried to do a webseries a couple years back, it had been a tiny production, with no professional anything, just some friends and digital camera. This was small by Hollywood standards, but it was still the Big Leagues.

Jane brought a huge amount of energy to the scene, capable of filling up the room with the smallest movements; even a slight nod of the head or furrow of the brow said as much as any of the words Ree had written.

That was the real magic of film and TV. Ree knew her script was good, but when Jane and the other actors brought it to life, it was amazing.

No wonder Cinemancers get lost in the little moments.

Ree's magic worked off of a personal connection to the characters, to the world, but Cinemancers were both more general and more specific. They used celluloid and AVIs to do cinematic alchemy. Ree had met a few through Grognard's, and they were obsessive fiddlers to the last.

What will they do with this show when it's made? Ree thought, a wave of pride carrying her off into a *how awesome am I* daydream.

She came back down when the take ended, and stood up to stretch while the crew reset.

The scene took over three hours, between the reaction shots, over-tos, and all of the coverage that it took to be able to piece together a multicamera show. And with the destructible set pieces for Allison's blowup (the props for melted plates and burned chairs were awesome), every run-through left a lot of work to do to refresh the set.

After the twelfth take, Yancy nodded to the director of photography, then said, "That's a wrap! Take five and then we head outside for scene twenty-three!" Yancy returned to his chair. A PA handed him a water bottle on the way, which he opened and swigged.

Yancy turned to Ree. "Good work. Can you stick around for the next one?"

Ree held back a shit-eating grin. He might as well have said, *Would you like a free margherita truffle oil pizza from Turbo's and a bottle of 2007 Silver Oak Cabernet Sauvignon?*

CHAPTER FOUR

Dining with the Stars

Jane Konrad's career has been one filled with exceptions to the rules of Hollywood. Most child stars don't make the transition to adult fame, but the star of the then-edgy remake of My Two Dads *(with gay parents instead of romantic rivals) and* Mermaid High School *weathered a few shaky years in her late teens, including the critically-praised but instantly-cancelled* 42 Heinlein St. *and a short run of middling romantic comedies—* Eyes on the Prize, Rudolf's Return, Love At First Bite—*Jane returned to work with Yancy Williams, the director who discovered her for* My Two Dads.

Jane's career is thought of as peaking in her twenties, when she found commercial success with deeper films. From her fan-favorite role as Ms. Marvel in the Marvelman *film to her Golden Globe nomination for the Sundance hit* Young Love.

Three years ago, the twenty-eight-year-old Konrad dropped out of the spotlight, then fell back into it with a series of DUIs, topless candid shots, and a much-televised revolving-door year of rehab and counseling.

—Staropedia, "Jane Konrad"

×X×⬡×X×

Shooting for the day wrapped up around eight. Ree had the night off from Grognard's, so she was waiting at a bus stop three blocks away from the set when her phone played her text-message sound file, straight from *Monty Python and the Holy Grail*: "Message for you, sir!"

Ree pulled out her phone and read the message from Drake: *Apologies for not responding sooner. And for my absence today. I've been waylaid. Do not worry, all is well.*

Ree looked at the message, cocked her head to the side to try to decode Drake-speak, then read it again.

Waylaid? But not something dangerous? she wondered.

Something explode in the apartment? she texted in response.

The bus still hadn't arrived when his response came several minutes later.

Not that kind of waylay. More later.

Huh. Drake wasn't the sort to blow her off.

But a minute later, she got another message and thought—hoped—Drake had reconsidered, but then she read:

Want 2 do dinner? Love to chat about Act 3.—Jane

Either someone else named Jane had mistakenly texted her with a plausibly applicable message, one of the Rhyming Ladies was pranking her, the universe was being really cruel—

Or she had just been invited to dinner by Jane Fucking Konrad.

Before realizing that she'd moved, Ree was out of the bus stop enclosure and halfway down the block back toward the set.

If a movie star asks you to dinner, you say yes.

Even if they turn out to be creepy, you get an expensive dinner and a story. This aphorism is void where prohibited (i.e., Scientology compounds).

Ree nodded to Danny as she approached, then took the steps in one bound before knocking on Jane's door.

"Come in!" Jane shouted from inside. Her response came fast enough that it jolted Ree a bit.

She stepped inside to see the trailer, which was bigger than her first two apartments out of college. But her eyes slid instantly to Jane.

The star had changed out of her character outfit from the shoot into a club-ready getup, one that was way more Warrior-era Ke$ha than *Awakenings'* Allison Richmond: short (but not mini) skirt, a shoulder-less top held together by a steel ring above the chest, and about a dozen bracelets on her left arm. Her hair had about three times the volume it had that morning.

Di-damn, Ree thought.

Jane smiled at Ree. "Great work today. Do you like sushi?"

"Sure," Ree said, wondering if she'd missed the start of the conversation. Ree gestured at Jane's outfit. "If that's the dress code, I'm a little underprepared."

Jane shook her head. "You'll be fine. Those glasses with that outfit mean you totally own the artist look. But if you want, feel free to raid my closet." Jane pointed over her head to a closed door near the hallway-that-goes-to-a-bedroom part of the trailer.

Ree scratched her chin in an exaggerated gesture and made for the closet. She opened the door, and when she saw the assortment, her brain's jukebox played the *you just opened a treasure chest* stock music from a dozen games, triumph and discovery in all the majesty of MIDI.

She started at the bottom, looking past what must have been tens of thousands of dollars' worth of shoes and boots, with heels that started at two inches and went up from there, all the way to a set of boots that she was pretty sure should be classified as stilts.

From there, she saw a small pile of designer jeans, most artfully distressed, with washes from light-dark-blue to blacker-than-obsidian. And most of the closet was taken up by a small army of hangers and a rainbow of tops and skirts.

Ree took a moment to appreciate the Warehouse 23 of clothes before her, then realized she probably shouldn't stare. She scanned through the tops for a few seconds and pulled out a couple of pieces she thought would work. Ree didn't have Jane's build, but they were close enough in stature that it should work. Plus $300 tops looked good on nearly everyone.

Turning, Ree held them up to Jane, eyebrow raised. Jane nodded. "Bathroom is the first door on the right."

You could be getting yourself into trouble, kiddo, a voice in her head warned. *It's one thing to sell scripts to hot, self-destructive movie stars. It's another to dine with them when they're dressed to kill.*

Ree walked to the restroom and flipped on the light as she closed the door. The inside of the door had a full mirror, which she used to try on the tops. The first was a loose, gauzy, and sheer white top. The size worked, since it was intentionally big, but the fact that it showed Ree's bra did not.

Luckily, Jane had another shirt of the same cut, but in red. Much less with the *here's my bra* effect.

Ree adjusted the shirt, fiddled with her hair, and stopped as she looked at herself in the mirror.

What am I primping for? A dinner with my employer? Clubbing with a movie star? Or a first date with a known hot mess?

Ree had the Advanced Gaydar feat (+5 bonus), but that didn't mean she automatically knew if someone was actually interested in her. That was still a moving target of a Sense Motive check. Guys were usually really freaking obvious, at least to her (DC 10 or less). Some women were just as obvious, thankfully. And the four enbies she knew weren't enough to make a generalization.

But between the heterosexual default setting that society tried to inflict on everyone, the normalized feminine homosociality that comes with it, and the celebrities-make-their-own-rules factor, Ree had no fucking clue where she stood (DC 40).

So just go have dinner and see what happens. It's not like a Schrödinger's date with a movie star would be more dangerous than chasing were-suited monsters down alleyways, fighting off feral gnomes with a tanto, or dogfighting through high-rises while desperately trying not to look down.

Buckle up.

Ree took a long breath, tucked her hair over her ear, and opened the door.

Jane was holding a snifter of booze in her hand, and took a sip as Ree emerged.

Jane's smile carried more than a hint of sultry. "Very nice. Care for a pregame?" Jane offered the glass.

Ree shook her head as she crossed the hall back into the living area, wall-mounted entertainment center to her right, along with a Comfy Couch™ and love seat.

"You have a place in mind?"

They continued through the room, past a kitchenette and small round table with chairs posh enough that they'd scoff at anything from Pier 1. Jane said, "I've heard that Yoritomo's is good."

"I've heard it is," Ree said, nodding. "It's also a little rich for my barkeep-and-baby-screenwriter blood." Ree focused on opening the door in front of her, a bit embarrassed to have to admit her near-bankruptcy to the star as she stepped down out of the trailer.

"Not for mine." Jane took a swig of her drink as her heels touched down on the concrete of the alley. The star offered Ree her arm, which she took.

"Just be warned that I've been known to run up a pretty good bar tab," Ree said. *Though should I be enabling the woman who got three DUIs in a month? No, I don't want to answer that.*

Jane nodded. "Not too much, though. We both have to work tomorrow."

Ree matched Jane's nod hastily. "Of course, but, well, in general." Jane's flop back to professional mode broke Ree's rhythm, and she felt like she was back in college, her early years of endless awkwardness.

As they approached the street, Ree looked over her shoulder to see Danny following behind.

"Shouldn't we wait for him?" she asked.

"I think I can handle a cab ride with company. He'll catch up. Plus, I remember from your bio that you have a black belt."

"Touché," Ree admitted.

Less than ten seconds after the pair reached Douglas Street, a cab pulled up and stopped.

Let's hear it for fame, Ree thought as Jane opened the door to slide in. Ree joined her as Jane said, "Yoritomo's, please."

Ree closed the door behind her, seeing Danny walk at a slow, confident pace, his hand up for another cab. Ree felt a bit bad for him, having to alternate between demanding lots of attention to warding people off or hiding in plain sight, all at Jane's whims.

Note to self: Cross bodyguarding off of list of fall-back professions.

P.S. You will probably have to do this anyway.

Since, you know: Magic, scary people, monsters, etc.

Jane cleared her throat, and Ree looked back at the star, confused. "Sorry?"

"I asked how you were liking the job so far," Jane said.

"Ah, sorry. My brain decided to take a joyride for a minute."

Jane leaned back in the seat, a warm smile on her face.

"It's awesome. Watching Yancy in action is pretty amazing. And I've been fans of pretty much the whole cast since I was a kid."

"Way to make me feel old," Jane said.

"But you're like my age."

"Does that make me wrong, or does that make you old?"

"Let's plead the fifth," Ree said.

They chatted amicably for a few minutes until the cabbie deposited them at the restaurant.

Yoritomo's was named for Minamoto no Yoritomo, founder of the Kamakura Shogunate. Ree liked to think it was named for the *Legend of the Five Rings* Mantis Clan Champion, but the restaurant's distinct lack of giant kama meant it was probably just wishful thinking on her part.

Jane walked in like she owned the place as an eager-looking East Asian young woman held open the door for the two of them.

"Welcome to Yoritomo's," the woman said. She stopped for a moment, presumably recognizing Jane.

Jane gave her a generous smile and said, "Thank you," as they entered.

The restaurant had all the stock artifacts of a P.F. Chang's, but from Japan instead of China. And about five times as spendy.

The suit of armor in a display case in the lobby looked about as expensive as the prize at Grognard's from last night.

Ree had a momentary twinge of guilt. Before the *Awakenings* deal had come through, she'd spent many of her nights off patrolling, Batman-style. She'd tried to keep her finger on the city's magical pulse. But now, she had other priorities.

The city got by without Ree Reyes, Geekomancer, before last fall, so it could deal for a few weeks. Drake was somewhere mysterious, and Eastwood had been in *Thunderbolts*-level Redemption Mode since Halloween.

Enjoy the ride, she told herself.

Jane sauntered up to the hostess, the same eager young woman who'd held the door open. She had her hair back and loose over a kimono-inspired black shirt with short sleeves.

"We'd like a table for two. Somewhere private, if possible. And a table for my bodyguard."

The woman had a really-well-dressed deer in headlights moment, looking at Jane, down to her board, back to Jane, then over her shoulder. Ree followed the woman's gaze and saw Danny standing in wait. He gave her a quick nod of acknowledgment.

The hostess considered Danny for a moment as he took up a casual stance. She scanned out the room, looked down at her table plan, then said, "Just . . . just one moment, Ms. Konrad."

The woman left in a hurry, crisp steps echoing on the polished tiles.

"Do you get that reaction everywhere?"

Jane shrugged. "Pearson isn't quite like L.A., at least not yet. When I go incognito, I can sometimes act like a person, but even then, I usually just get outed by paparazzi and then there are a ton of bad pictures of me all across the tabloids."

"Damned if you do, damned if you don't," Ree said.

"Yeah, but at least it comes with embarrassing stacks of money that can make good things happen . . . at least when the work is flowing."

Jane had signed on to several projects since her self-implosion, but dropped out of each of them, citing "creative differences" or "health concerns." But Ree wasn't about to pry about that, at least not yet.

Several other people walked into the restaurant, and each and every one of them stopped for a second when they recognized Jane. She nodded to them politely, while Danny kept them all in his gaze, nonthreatening but clearly present. One group had a fourteen-ish-year-old girl who walked up to the star and said,

"I loved you in *Mermaid High School!*" The smile that inspired was broader, warmer, more genuine. The girl couldn't have been more than two when *Mermaid High School* was canceled, but thanks to the wonders of DVD, all shows were eternal.

Ree faded back, letting Jane deal with the attention. *I don't really need any of this fame-by-association, not unless the show actually lands and does well.*

She leaned over to Danny and asked in a soft voice, "Any last-minute advice for chatting with the boss?"

"Stay away from the bad luck she's been having and you'll fine. Don't worry, she likes you."

"Thanks, man." Feeling just a bit less nervous, Ree stepped back to join Jane when the girl returned to her family.

The hostess guided them through the restaurant, around and through until they reached a private room, closed in by rice-paper sliding walls. *What are those called?* Ree wondered.

The room had five tables, all empty. The hostess set them up at a small circular table for two, and Danny crossed several tables over to sit at another two-top by himself.

Ree considered asking Danny to join them, but thought better of it. *If she wanted him to sit with us, she would have asked.*

And he's on the clock. The *Upstairs Downstairs* of it all was more than a little uncomfortable. *Deal with it or ignore it. Focus on the movie star that thinks you're interesting.*

Jane settled in and the hostess presented them with the faux-worn scroll menus. She rattled off some specials, but Ree was busy thinking about the script and questions Jane might have as a way of distracting herself from being nervous that this might turn out being a date.

The hostess was walking over to Danny as Jane said, "So, how about we just get one of these daimyo platters and have fun with it?"

Ree looked at her menu, then up at the star. "Sure, sounds good."

"And some sake. I hate eating sushi without sake. And those bottles are awesome."

"I'm game. So what did you want to talk about for the show?" Ree asked.

Jane waved her hand through the air, brushing off the question. "That was just an excuse to go out. I want to hear more about you. Are you still bartending?"

Ree nodded. "Yeah, it's a private club. The owner's really secretive, but it pays pretty well and it's a fun scene."

Ree heard someone approach as Jane continued. "Sounds great. I'd love to go sometime, if it'd be allowed."

"I'll check with the boss. He has . . ." Ree paused as she

tried to think of a way to explain Grognard and his place that didn't spoil everything about her whacky magic life, failed, and defaulted to the vague. " . . .odd tastes. Not creepy, just odd."

A woman appeared to Ree's left. She was short-ish, with delicate features. She looked more Chinese than Japanese, but then again, one of the other servers they'd passed had been tall and blonde, so it was all good. She wore her hair back and up, held in place by jade chopsticks.

"Welcome to Yoritomo's, Ms. Konrad. I'm Susan, I'll be taking care of you, but let any of our staff know if you need anything. Will you be having sushi tonight?"

"The daimyo platter, please. And we'd like a bottle of White Crane."

Susan looked over to Ree, then back to Jane. "Will that be all?"

"Good by me," Ree said.

"That'll be great, thanks."

Susan nodded and then walked over to Danny's table, repeating her spiel.

Jane picked up the conversation just where they'd left it.

"Your boss sounds like an interesting guy. I'm sure he could be convinced to make room for little old me. We could do guerrilla marketing."

Ree raised her hands placatingly. "I'll ask. He's prickly. But I am definitely getting word out to everyone I know. My dad threatened to fly out and watch a day of taping."

Jane beamed. "That'd be great, he should totally come."

So where's the self-destructiveness?

Ree had spent time with Jane on and off camera, and she didn't sense any of the kind of behavior that had gotten the star spreads on all the tabloids with horribly unflattering photos and DUI and Drunk & Disorderly charges. Maybe the booze would bring it out. But then why did she preempt the drinking by talking about how they had to be good?

It's almost like she was a complex person who behaves in a variety of ways depending on her decisions in the moment. Preposterous!

"I'm not sure you know what you're asking for. I love him to death, but he could medal in parental embarrassment. It's really impressive."

They continued on throughout the dinner, Jane poking and prodding (with good humor) at Ree's life, a gracious and curious interviewer. Ree turned things around a couple of times, hearing stories about Jane's early acting work and some horror stories from movie sets. They got louder as the sake poured, and Ree lost count of how much sushi she'd put away. Between the two of them, they'd demolished most of a twenty-four-piece platter.

Jane polished off the last of the sake and said, "So, you up for some dancing?"

"What happened to 'We have to work tomorrow'?" Ree asked.

The star waved off her question. "I'll be fine. If you can't keep up, then you'll miss out on the fun."

Ree scoffed. "I have a +10 to Save vs. Peer Pressure, I'll have you know."

"Save what?" Jane asked.

"Never mind." *Not that kind of geek. Noted.*

"Don't worry, I'll have you home before midnight, Cinderella," Jane said.

Susan returned with the check. Jane slipped the server a black-on-black credit card that looked like the Mega-Elite-Bonus-Person card that George Clooney's character had in *Up in the Air*.

Once they settled up, Danny shadowed them as they left Yoritomo's. It was a warm night, the heat of the day lingering far better than it had even two weeks previous.

"So, do I have to twist your arm again?" Jane asked as she walked to the street to grab a cab's attention. Moments later, a cab pulled up to the sidewalk.

Ree asked, "How do you do that?"

Jane winked. "Magic."

Danny opened the door and kept an eye on the crowd.

A Police song started playing in Ree's head, but she cut it off before the earworm could take hold. *Not every little thing . . .* Ree wondered as she piled into the cab.

This trip, Danny joined them in the same cab.

"Infinity Club, please," Jane said.

The cabbie leaned over his shoulder. His brown skin showed the results of years of too much sun.

"You're Jane Konrad."

Danny leaned forward. "That she is. Be discreet, and you'll have a great tip at the end of the ride."

The cabbie considered for a second, then turned back to the road. "We're cool. Nice night for a drive."

"When we get there, follow my lead," Danny said to Ree. "This could get interesting."

Jane said, "A fancy restaurant is one thing. Where I have in mind, there will be a lot more attention."

Ree said, "I've survived the crowds at Comic-Con, I can handle a club full of fans."

"I'm not worried about the fans," Danny said, his carefree expression gone. It was game time.

"It'll be fine," Jane said with a self-satisfied grin. "Plus, a little transitive fame can't hurt your career, can it?"

True story. It could be a huge bonus for her screenwriting.

And she was already running the risk of becoming some weird walking talisman, a Geekomancer who could also become a famous writer.

For that matter, that brought up the possibility that if the show hit it big, she might be able to use Geekomancy with her own writing.

That was a scary-awesome thought. *What if Guillermo del Toro, Felicia Day, or, hell, George Lucas and Steven Spielberg, were Geekomancers? What if the iconic films of geekdom were iconic as much for the fact that they were created by practitioners*

And if they were, what did that mean for fans?

Ree filed that away for later consideration.

One thing for sure: Being a magician and a minor celebrity would put her on the radar for various practitioners around town. Ree had no idea what part of the magical underground in Pearson was in control of the clubs, if any of them were.

As far as she could tell, the real world wasn't like in *World of Darkness*, where supernaturals owned the entire city. But she was certain the big-time practitioners had their fingers in many pies.

Danny may be the bodyguard, but if something comes along from the hinkyverse, it would be up to Ree to intercede.

CHAPTER FIVE

They Can Have Their Diamonds

CATFIGHT IN THE TWITTERSPHERE!

In an uncharacteristic display, critical darling Jane Konrad showed her claws on Twitter this morning, laying into superstar Rachel MacKenzie, calling her a "money-grubbing studio stooge." MacKenzie responded, calling the ex–Cosmic Studios' star a "washed-up former child actress" who was "looking to steal the spotlight."

The spat was quickly tagged #DivaFight, which trended world-wide throughout the day.

Neither star has released an official statement about the argument.

—Plugged.com

Infinity Club was three stories tall and was identified only by the ten-foot-wide infinity-symbol light that flowed and shifted across the colors of the rainbow. Even muted by the doors, the music and feel of bass thumped on Ree's sternum and called to her. The busy smell of perfumes and colognes wafted through the spring breeze, hitting Ree's nose all at once as she stepped onto the sidewalk.

Infinity Club wasn't the biggest, most exclusive, or expensive club in Pearson, but it was at least #2 or #3 in each category.

Ree had only been there once, a couple of years back, before it made its reputation. Priya had been showing pieces from her first Steampunk clothing line at a local fashion show, and they'd gone out afterward to celebrate.

Infinity had been cool then, but it had been an outsider cool, the kind that said *I know I'm not cool by your standards, but I don't give a crap.* Jane ignored the large crowd waiting behind the velvet rope, hip youngsters pleading with the six-foot-twenty bouncer.

"It's Jane Konrad!" someone shouted, and the jig was up. The crowd whipped itself into a froth faster than Ree could pour a pint, people shouting Jane's name and waving. Dozens broke out of line to rush her, but Danny stopped them. His wingspan wasn't even six feet, but he could have kept them all at bay with the force of his stare.

Ree felt the energy of the crowd like a gust of wind in her face.

Not just the sound, but the feeling.

Magic senses tingling! She'd felt magic a few times since picking up the lightsaber and becoming a Geekomancer, experiencing various styles' different flavors. The magic sense was always synesthetic, reminding her of the smell of purple or the taste of police sirens.

The question was: Was there someone using magic—a lot of it—or was this just raw energy of the fans' excitement, and just felt like magic?

Ree's question was answered as she looked over to Jane, who stopped, smiled, and pulled off her sunglasses. Beaming like she was professionally lit, her features became warmer as Ree watched. Ree blinked. It was like someone had taken Jane and turned her up to 11: her energy, her smile, the smoothness of her features, the shape of her curves.

For a second, Ree doubted herself, wondered if she'd been mistaken, that Jane had made herself up already, and she was just beaming with the attention. *Because . . . damn.*

Wait. Ree paused to look around the crowd, which had locked onto Jane like she was a living oasis. She felt and saw the energy flowing from the fans to Jane, then an energy rolling out, creating a feedback loop. If this wasn't magic, she'd eat a week-old burger. And if Jane was using magic, then there was likely a lot more going on that no one had bothered telling her.

Ree looked around to people on the edge of the scene. *Did anyone else notice what happened, or does the Doubt cover it up?*

The Doubt, Ree had discovered, was a magical force of disbelief that helped keep the magical world under wraps. But once you were in the magical world, the Doubt rolled off you like pop-up ads off a digital native. It shouldn't be affecting her. *But if it's not the Doubt, what gives?*

Ree crossed her arms and stood by, watching the scene playing out. *How is she doing this?* She knew a few styles that made a glamour, but which one?

Ree wished she could just text Eastwood to ask. But that would be crossing a line in their already-too-murky relationship.

Instead, she made a note to do some research on the matter.

Jane approached the crowd, produced a pen from somewhere, and started signing whatever she was handed. Danny kept the crowd from trampling her, but just barely. They broke around him in ones and twos, raised voices and strained hands seeking a chance to connect with a living legend.

Farther back in the crowd, Ree heard some jeers, some filthy epithets. Not everyone loved her, especially not lately. But the true fans had beaten them to the punch, at least this time.

After a few moments, the bouncers waded into the insta-mob, making a wedge that funneled people back toward the club. The six-foot-twenty guy wove through the crowd and plucked out the hecklers, pointing them to the back of the line.

One of the bouncers approached Jane, saying, "Ms. Konrad, if you'd like to come with me. . ."

Jane lingered for a few moments, signed another couple of hands, napkins, and even a shoulder then nodded to Danny, who covered her as she walked to the door. Ree saw a dozen smartphones up, some snapping pictures, others doubtlessly tweeting up a storm. She imagined what they would say:

"*OMG* Jane Konrad @InfinityClub!"

"J-Rad about to get smashed again @InfinityClub"

"Who's the hot chick with J-Rad?"

Well, maybe not that last one.

And when those tweets hit the gossip circles, Infinity Club was about to get a lot more crowded.

Jane extended her arm to Ree, and she joined the star as they walked inside.

"How often do you get mobbed like that?" Ree asked.

"A couple times a day back in L.A., depending on how incognito I go. Sometimes it's fun to just soak it all in."

I bet it is, Ree thought, looking at the still-charged star.

Confidence rolled off of her like radiation. It was all Ree could do to not just stop and stare. Now that she'd pegged Jane's magnetism as magic, she couldn't not see it. She held in a knowing smile.

Infinity had one main dance floor, with a sixty-foot-long infinity symbol beneath the reinforced glass. It changed colors through the rainbow like the symbol on the outside, in sync with lights from the side walls, which cast the whole room in a shifting array of color.

The floor was half-full, most of the dancers clustered in a circle above the X-cross of the floor symbol. The air was cool and clean, missing the trademark musk she expected from smaller or less super-over-air-conditioned clubs. Ree couldn't place the music, but she could feel it, heavy bass reverberating off her sternum. Jane pulled her by the hand as she cut a corner of the dance floor to pick a booth decked out in crushed velvet, with a table that looked like crystal but was probably made from heavy plastic. Infinity wasn't that ritzy.

A gorgeous server on three-inch heels intercepted them as Jane set her purse down on the cushion. The woman looked closer to sixteen than twenty-one, but a bar like Infinity wouldn't be careless enough to tempt Excise like that. She wore locs in the style of the club's logo, braided on the back of her head with another infinity symbol and a matching pin. She wore a silver sequined dress that was long enough to be respectable but short enough to be intriguing, a great compliment for her brown skin with amethyst undertones.

As she approached, Ree noticed that the woman looked nervous, fingers fidgeting by her side. "Welcome, Ms. Konrad. I'm Lacey, and I'll be taking care of you tonight."

Jane greeted Lacey with a slight inclination of her head. She purred her response. "Hello, Lacey. This is Ree, and you should treat her the same way you'd treat me. Let's start with a bottle of Grey Goose and see where that takes us."

Lacey nodded, then looked to Ree. "Welcome. Please let me know if you need anything tonight."

After Lacey left, Ree raised an eyebrow. "They work all night in heels like that? My calves would murder me."

Jane shrugged. "If they couldn't hack it, they'd work somewhere else. You pay a price to get to the top, but once you're there . . ." Jane extended her arms to the club, indicating her proof.

"What happened to not going overboard tonight?" Ree asked, returning to the star's earlier warning.

Jane leaned back and spread her arms out on the couch.

"If it's too much, you can always go home." Jane winked, then leaned over to adjust the strap on one shoe, giving Ree just a bit of a look down the star's shirt.

Is it hot in here? a voice in her mind asked mockingly. Jane stood back up and turned, walking to the dance floor. Jane looked over her shoulder, hair catching in the light. The star beckoned Ree to the floor.

Another voice answered, presenting the eternal dilemma of the queer girl: *Is she actually hitting on me?*

Jane had been romantically linked to women before, but she was also notoriously friendly with everyone, and flirty enough for the tabloids to speculate endlessly.

It's just dancing, she told herself, heading for the floor. *I'll be fine if I keep ahead of the booze.*

Another internal voice, this one contrary, said, *She ordered a bottle. Are you going to drink a forty of water to stay on ahead of the booze?*

Ree laughed at the notion, imagining the dozen restroom trips that would require.

On the floor, Ree was reminded of the clubs from the Mass Effect series. This one had a distinct lack of war-like lizard-cricket people and blue-skinned aliens.

However, it did have ample supplies of neon, flashing lights, and crowds of dancers gyrating with planted feet. She hadn't been clubbing much, unless you counted Vampire LARPs. Bars were one thing: a good night out at Trollope's Trollops with the Rhyming Ladies, a few pitchers, and some good conversation.

But even when you weren't pretending to be a fangy child of the night, clubs were really only good for three things: Drinking, Dancing, and the Hook-Up.

Jane grinned as Ree joined her on the floor, dropping to a low crouch and standing slowly, her arms stretching to the ceiling as she rose, locking Ree in her gaze the whole time.

Ree rocked back and forth for a few measures, testing out the music and sinking into the feel of the dance. Then she matched Jane, the two circling each other, trading moves, looks, and grins as they went. The crowd parted around them, and Ree heard a rising burble of murmurs as people took note of the star.

For a short while, Ree pushed all of the worry, selfconsciousness, and uncertainty to the back of her mind, diving deep into the glorious oblivion of music and motion.

Two songs later, Jane wiped a sheen of sweat from her brow and walked back to the booth, where a bottle of Grey Goose in a silver iced bucket awaited them, along with two highball glasses. Lacey stood off to the side, waiting for them as they returned.

VIP service doesn't suck, Ree thought. Lacey was a heavy pour, and handed each of them a glass that must have held four regulation shots apiece. She was calmer this time. Maybe she'd taken a drink of her own, or the bout of starstruck-itude had simply passed.

Jane raised the glass to Ree. "To *Awakenings.*"

Ree toasted, then took a shot from the glass. As Ree lowered her glass, Jane's was already half-empty, resting on the table.

Ree flashed back to the star's very public DUIs and Drunk & Disorderly charges. It'd be up to her and Danny to keep Jane from going down that rabbit hole again.

Jane leaned back into the couch, resuming her leonine lounge and projecting her voice over the thumping bass. "What's your favorite novel?"

Ree could smell the star's perfume, which had settled into a new note: chocolate and chile, poured over something musky and enticing.

"*Dune,*" Ree said, after a beat. Not because she had to decide, mind you. She'd had to defend her literature preferences to boyfriends, customers at Zombie Café, and film agents with oddly specific taste. She just hadn't been expecting the question, especially given the setting.

"It's fantastic, isn't it? I like my art with a punch, something real. I especially loved *Children of Dune* and *God Emperor.* I know they aren't very popular in the sci-fi crowd, but I just adored Saint Alia of the Knife. And I love how Herbert shows us a religion forming in real time, around a leader with the force of personality to lead an entire people into the future, a leader that uses their fame for all of humanity, not just for themselves."

The drinks were forgotten as Ree listened, rapt.

"But the power and the story he makes becomes a prison as well. He gets wrapped up in his own myth, trapped by the society he fought for millennia to create. He's so trapped that in order to push humanity forward, he has to take himself out of the story." Jane stopped, shaking her head as she looked up and out to the lights window. "It's amazing."

Ree nodded, impressed. Woman knew her SF. "I could have done without the whole turning-into-a-worm part, but Alia is awesome. I was pleasantly surprised by the Sci-Fi miniseries they did."

"Anything to replace the David Lynch film in my brain," Jane said with a toss of the hand. "I mean, the costumes and sets were amazing, but the editing was a travesty!"

"I hear that," Ree said. "What's yours, then? *God Emperor of Dune?*"

Jane raised her glass. "Right in one." She made the *ooh, ooh* sound, and set the glass down rather than drinking. "But growing up, I was all about *A Wizard of Earthsea*. LeGuin writes like a dream. I got to meet her once, a few years back, when I was trying to get Yancy to remake *The Lathe of Heaven*."

Jane's voice was softer, and Ree scooted forward, leaning in.

"Really? What was she like?"

"Sassy, kind, and too smart by half. I could barely keep up with her, and I came away with a to-be-read list as long as my arm."

Ree nodded her head vigorously. "That fable she did about unemployment was such a fantastic kick-to-the-teeth. Nobody else could have written something so on the nose and gotten away with it."

Jane sat forward and put her hand over Ree's, resting on the table. "Stick with me, and you'll meet anyone you want."

She's definitely hitting on me, Ree decided. The sexy eyes, she could deal with. The look down the shirt at the cream-clear cleavage, well, that was hard. The dancing even more so. But the electric current that ran up her arm, her hand in Jane's . . . that was something else.

Will checks were something games never quite got right.

When they come along, you really, really want to fail in the short-term, even if you know it might cause a giganto mess in the long-term. More of them should incentivize giving in to get the real sense across.

But all of that rumination was just her trying to distract herself from the temptation.

It'll be fine, said a (horny) interior voice. *You're both grown-ups, and she's surface-of-the-sun hot. Are you going to pass up an opportunity like this?*

She felt her heart pounding in time to the techno, and picked up her glass of vodka for an excuse to take a break from Jane's spotlight of attention. Ree took a sip and saw something move through the light cast by the exit sign above a door.

Granted, there were plenty of people moving around, but club patrons didn't usually set off her personal Spider-sense, and this figure had.

Ree stood, keeping an eye on the exit. "I'll be right back," she said, grabbing her leather jacket and setting off through the crowd. She was glad she'd stuck with her flats, even if it meant that Jane in heels was three inches taller than she was, which put her own head much closer to looking at her marvelous . . .

Focus. Something's hinky.

Ree donned the jacket and surreptitiously pulled out the switchblade it held as she wove through tables and slinking club-goers. She hadn't had time to power up with anything, and busting out her lightsaber in the club would be asking a lot of the Doubt. She scanned the crowd for whatever it was that was setting off her radar.

She reached the exit and leaned up against the wall just to one side of the door. She scanned the room again, wishing she had a BTRS or tricorder or something other than intuition for threat assessment. But a night on the town didn't exactly call for DEFCON-1 in terms of preparation.

Danny emerged from behind a waiter and took a place beside her.

"What are you doing?" he asked. His tone was more intrigued than accusatory. She imagined cops in a world with supers might use the same tone when they came upon an unidentified hero at a crime scene.

"I got a weird feeling."

Danny hrmed, nodding. "Me, too. You can go back to Jane; I'll take care of it."

Ree shook her head. "You're the bodyguard. I've got this."

Danny shifted his weight, evaluating her. "We could just call security."

Ree winked. "What fun would that be? But yeah, do that, too. They can be my backup."

"No offense, but if there's something out there, what's a skinny writer going to do about it?" Danny asked, a half-concerned, half-amused look on his face.

"A skinny writer with two black belts and a switchblade can handle herself, thanks." Ree held out the handle of her knife and looked Danny square in the eyes, trying to convey her martial-arts-y-ness like people did in kung fu movies.

The corner of Danny's hard-set mouth twitched into a half-smile, and he took a step back and started toward Jane's table.

Ree scanned the room again, then took a sidestep and pressed on the bar to open the door. She left it open a crack, waiting to listen for conspicuous sounds like guns cocking, creatures snarling, or something equally terrifying.

Not hearing anything particularly scary, she leaned out the door and looked into the alley herself.

The alley outside Infinity was clean, well kept, with a Dumpster ten paces down to one side, allowing patrons to step out for a smoke without inhaling yet another kind of deadly fume.

Ree stepped out, scanning down the side of the alley to the street in the distance. It might have been the strobe light on the club walls, but she thought she saw a form disappear around the corner.

Did they give me the slip? she wondered. With skills honed by years of Taekwondo, Ree took one step in pursuit while simultaneously pushing a *Don't get locked out* rock between the club door and its frame.

She hurried a few steps toward the mouth of the alley, but her eyes quickly found something far more pressing.

Atop one of the plastic recycling bins leaning against the opposite building hunched something that looked like a panther crossed with a dragonfly. It had iridescent black-and-green scales, honeycomb eyes, and big, big claws at the ends of muscled feline forelimbs.

Where the fuck did you come from? Ree asked in her mind. *You sure as hell don't look like the thing I saw by the door.*

Ree pulled her knife out and flipped it open. She circled out and around, trying to get the far wall at her back.

The panther-fly tracked her movement, shimmering wings flapping every few moments the same way a person might blink.

"If you promise not to hurt anyone, I might just let you leave. What do you say to that?" Ree asked.

In response, the creature's wings unfurled, and it lifted off the ground, hovering forward. The creature's forelimbs spread, as if getting ready to gather her up and rip her head off. Or maybe to give her a hug.

She wasn't betting on the hug part.

Ree shrugged her jacket off, wrapping it around her left arm, then took the knife in her right hand. A couple layers might not stop those claws, but they couldn't hurt.

What is it doing here?

Ree had learned that there was a baseline level of weird in Pearson, and that sometimes, creatures were just around. They lived on the fringes, in alleys and sewers and hidden away in parks. They seemed to mostly prey on smaller animals, but sometimes they went for bigger game. *Lucky me.*

The panther-fly zipped forward, slashing with one paw. Ree ducked under the shot, lifting her jacket-padded arm as a shield and aiming for the creature's elbow with her knife. She felt the blade tear through flesh, and rushed forward at the diagonal to get under the beast and avoid any retaliatory claw raking.

Ree lashed out again as she turned, guessing on a shot at the creature's thorax-abdomen-ish area.

She missed, then took another step back and looked up, seeing the creature turn in place like a helicopter. It swiped down at her, so Ree faded back and dodged out of the way of the cuts.

When the creature hovered forward, Ree spun the knife around and slammed it into the back of the panther-fly's left paw.

The creature shrieked with a tinny voice, rearing back and flailing. Ree pulled the knife out of its paw and stood back as the creature flew upward. Ree checked the nearby terrain (trash bags, Dumpster, fire escape) and saw that she couldn't chase the thing down without ridiculous effort, and watched as the wounded creature climbed into the sky, wavering in the air but eventually passing out of sight.

"Huh, weird." Ree checked the alley, wishing that real-life random encounters yielded loot the way they did in RPGs. She did her best to flick the sticky blood off of her knife, then walked out to the mouth of the alley to see if someone was standing around with magical puppeteer strings or the like.

What she did see was that the line to get into Infinity had at least tripled, but she couldn't see anyone who projected *suspicious*, so she headed back into the alley, unfolding her jacket to put it back on and return to club mode.

Note to self: Always bring plastic baggies for monster-goop control. Hand sanitizer as well.

Also: Figure out way to bring all of these things along without a purse. Jackets only go so far. See if Grognard can special order a portable hole.

Ree pulled the door open again and rolled the rock back out of the way. She caught a whiff of crisp-scented air, narrowed her eyes at the stray strobe lights, and stepped back inside.

Jane was waiting, perhaps even a little anxiously, when Ree made it back to her seat. The star brightened upon seeing her and lifted a full glass in greeting.

"Sorry, had to freshen up," Ree offered by way of explanation.

Off to one side, she saw Danny at his table. *He must have covered for me*, Ree thought. She gave him a slight nod of thanks, again trying for that martial-artists-communicate-volumes-with-simple-motions thing from movies. Mostly she hoped she didn't look silly.

"Let's get back to enjoying the evening. You owe me another dance for leaving me hanging when they played Florence + the Machine."

Aw, damn. Ree shook her fist. "Khan! Done and done." Then she jingled her glass, clinking the ice. "But if I have much more of this, the only dance I'm going to be doing is with the porcelain throne."

Jane stood and took Ree's hand, sending a not-at-all-unpleasant shiver down Ree's neck. "Dance first, then. I can nurse you back to health after I've had my way on the dance floor."

Twist my arm, why don't you. Ree walked with Jane to the center of the club. Jane worked her way through the crowd, dealing with a few touchy fans and one pushy drunkard who threw some choice curse words her way before the club's security pulled him off the floor.

The crowd parted, and Jane dominated the center of the floor. The star moved with even more energy than before, taking bounding jumps as she fused punk-y moshing with more classic rocking out. Ree had done her fair share of dancing off her demons, but Jane was putting Ree's old Goth days to shame, jumping, spinning, and grooving with intensity for one, two, three songs straight. And she wasn't showing any signs of slowing down. Instead, she was practically glowing, her own light layering over the strobes and spotlights of the club.

Jane had her own audience, dozens of club-goers staring at any given moment, all feeding the star's power.

Ree caught a glimpse of Danny at the edge of the floor. He looked worried. But not crowd-of-potential-threats worried.

Really worried.

Ree started back toward Danny, but Jane caught her by the arm.

"Where are you going?" Jane asked, pushing her voice to be heard over the din.

Ree looked to Danny again, who had clammed up, back to normal ready mode.

Step down the Red Alert. It's fine. Live life a little, Batgirl, she told herself.

As if on cue, the DJ put on "Airships" by VNV Nation.

That's what I'm talking about.

Ree dove headfirst into the dance, shutting out the world and submitting to the music. She flowed with the synth, adapting the flowing techniques of tai chi into the dance, her feet moving slowly as she gathered energy. Jane caught Ree's change in attitude immediately, ramping up even more and directing her attention at the writer, showing her off to the crowd, giving her room. They owned the floor for eight minutes and eighteen seconds of mainlined catharsis.

When the song ended, they quit the floor without a word, still in sync.

There were ice waters waiting at their table when they returned, though Ree didn't know if those were due to Lacey's thoughtfulness or Danny's protectiveness. Ree pounded the water and then collapsed into the chair, happily beat.

"All right, I'm calling it so I can go out on a high note," Ree said to a still-glowing Jane. She shimmered with sweat, wearing it proudly. She was, frustratingly, one of the women who looked hotter when they sweated.

Damned if I don't want to drag her home with me right fucking now, Ree thought, most of her wishing to just jump into the roaring river of her desire.

"Will you at least be a lady and escort me home?" Jane asked, mischief in her eyes.

Ooh, boy, she thought, considering all of the reasons why doing so would be professionally dangerous.

What the hell? The rest of her responded, carrying the vote.

Ree extended a hand to Jane and said, "But of course, milady."

⚁

Ree hoped that Jane had tipped the cabbie big-time for his discretion. Because . . . damn. *Scandalized* didn't start to describe what went down on the cab ride.

They'd spent the whole trip wrapped around each other, limbs intertwined in a lascivious Gordian knot that was only partially untied when they climbed out of the cab and stumbled their way to Jane's trailer, a four-legged smoochmoeba.

Jane closed the door of the trailer and Ree came up for air, disentangling herself for a moment to catch her breath.

Are we really doing this? She flailed mentally, grasping for the smart thing to do while wrestling her libido.

She'd had her hook-ups during college, and they were fun, but they weren't remotely responsible. She'd grown up since then, or at least tried to tell herself that she had.

"Are you sure you want to do this? We've had a lot of vodka," she said to Jane, who had kicked off her shoes and was curling her toes in the trailer's plush carpet.

Jane took two long, only slightly wobbly steps back to Ree. She breathed in, focusing. "We have, and I'm sure. Are you?"

Ree paused, the pleasant cloudiness of inebriation receding. *Well, am I?* There would be consequences, but there were always consequences. Jane was gorgeous, she was kind, and she was, according to all the tabloids, a total badass in bed.

What about Drake? a voice asked. She and Drake had been on tiptoes around each other for months, and the things left unsaid could fill a novel. But he hadn't made a move, even a charmingly overstated grand gesture or an understated request to call on her at her apartment, aka The Shithole.

"I am," Ree said, and Jane smiled. The star turned toward the bedroom and exaggerated her gait, drawing attention to the movement of her hips; she looked at Ree over her shoulder in a manner more pronounced than Bugs Bunny in drag beguiling Elmer Fudd.

Unf.

Ree drop-kicked caution out the window, then followed Jane to her bed. There, they shed layers in rapid succession: tops, bras, skirts, and more.

The world fell away, leaving only Ree, Jane, and the ecstatic joy of discovery.

Hours later, Ree woke to the sound of screaming.

CHAPTER SIX

Tinseltown Throwdown

*A new flame for Jane Konrad? Star seen partying downtown
with Awakenings screenwriter Ree Reyes. lty.bty/3gwoaj
—@WTFStars, 03:17, May 24*

*Hawt! I'd love to get in that lez sandwhch. MT @WTFStars
Star seen partying downtown. lty.bty/3gwoaj
—@ZachAttk96, 03:19, May 24*

*@ZachAttk96 Fuck off, creep.
—@RhiActUp, 03:20, May 24*

@WTFStars She's obv. in no condition to be working.

*@RealJaneK Sort yr shit out before U fuck this girl's life up 2.
—@MaddowsWife, 03:18, May 24*

Ree shot up in bed. She looked around in the moon-
light-gray room, going from sleeping-off-the-drunk
to wide 'tawake in a millisecond. Pawing her way around

the nightstand, she found her glasses and put them on the double. Her farther-away-than-her-nose-vision enabled, Ree searched the room for whatever it was that would cause someone to be screaming bloody murder.

Something hit her on the hip, and Ree saw Jane flailing in her sleep, looking like she was trying to wrestle someone who wasn't there, full-on night-terror-style.

Ree reached out and shook Jane's shoulder, shouting, "Jane! Wake up! It's just a dream!" Jane seemed to turn at her voice but continued fighting with the invisible terror.

And then something hit Ree in the shoulder and knocked her off the bed. Something that wasn't Jane.

Ree's voice and world wobbled as she conceded the point. "Not a dream! Definitely not a dream!"

A light turned on from the front room of the trailer, and then the bedroom door burst open, showing Danny, lit from behind, wearing boxers and a sleeveless shirt.

"Jane?" Danny called, holding a shotgun in one hand.

Ree righted herself, tried to ignore the fact that she was naked in a room of at least two (three?) people, only one of whom she'd intended to see her that way. Instead, she focused on the invisible thing that had just hit her. She narrowed her eyes and tried to see . . . whatever it was. The light from the living room should have been enough to see the attacker, but all she saw was Jane fighting for her life.

Ree reached down again to find her jacket, pulled out the lightsaber she kept on her always, and lit it. The blade leaped to life, blue light filling the room.

Fuck secret identities.

She still couldn't see Jane's attacker, so Ree stepped up and sliced horizontally where the creature should have been. The blade skipped off of an invisible nothing like it was a force field.

"The fuck?" Ree said, spinning the blade around and trying to stab it. The blade bit in, and Ree felt like she was holding a stick dipped in quicksand.

"Duck!" Danny said from behind her. Ree did so and saw that he was maneuvering for a clear shot. But it didn't seem like he could see the thing any better than she could.

Ree squatted on the floor, shaking Jane's arm.

"Wake up!" she shouted, but Jane was still locked in a dream, struggling and screaming with her eyes closed.

Ree cut through where the creature should have been again and felt the blade skip off like it was plated in adamantium.

The lightsaber wasn't working. Maybe some good old Hapkido would fare better. She dropped the blade, which extinguished and returned to being a lifeless plastic prop as soon as it left her grip.

She stayed low.

"All yours!" Ree said, letting Danny have a shot. The gun went off, almost deafeningly loud inside the trailer. She heard the impacts, but Jane still struggled. Danny fired twice more, but it didn't seem to do anything.

"My turn!" Ree said, waving behind her to get Danny to stop. She re-assessed where the thing should be, and dove forward. She slammed into something that was both heavy and insubstantial, like thick gas in a plastic case. Ree felt around for limbs, trying to use her sense of touch to figure out which way to wrench it to inflict damage. She smelled smoke, but not wood smoke. It had a sharp note to it, like burned plastic.

The thing reared, swinging her around the bedroom like a rag doll as she held on for dear-God-life.

As she struggled, the 50% miss chances and grappling penalties for invisible opponents rules from various RPGs all made a scary amount of sense.

Ree pulled on a maybe-arm, trying to catch her feet somewhere to give her more leverage. Danny made a calculated swing that produced a *thump* sound and stopped in the middle of the air. The invisithing recoiled, and Ree hauled harder, trying to tighten the circle of her move to maximize the effect on the joints. The thing lurched to the side, and Ree broke through the closet door with the invisithing crushing her.

The air in her lungs quit in a huff, leaving Ree clawing for breath without losing her grip.

The invisithing broke free of her grasp, and Ree took a vicious right hook on the cheek.

The pain let her gasp in air, and as soon as she had breath to use, she shouted, "Fucking A!" at the compounding pain. She kicked out at the thing as Danny jumped over the bed with an overhand swing of the bat. The thing caught Danny in the air and knocked him back into the doorway, then tore down the curtain covering the window in the corner, broke the window, and then, presumably, disappeared out into the alley.

Ree clambered over to the window, careful to keep her hands off the broken glass but not so careful she didn't step on it, and stared out into the night, looking for traces of the invisithing.

She took a half-step back and looked to Danny, who had picked himself off the floor and was at the bedside, hand on Jane's shoulder.

The star was awake again, eyes wide as a cartoon character's, filled with terror.

"Is it gone?" she asked, breathless.

"It's gone," Ree said as Danny said, "Yes."

Ree grabbed an errant sheet and wrapped it around her chest, stepping gingerly off of the shards of glass. Once again, she hoped the decade of callusing from Taekwondo had protected her. She sat on the bed, leaning into Jane. "It's gone. You're safe now."

Jane turned away from Danny and Ree and vomited on the headboard.

Yikes.

Ree looked to Danny and asked softly, "Has this happened before?"

Danny furrowed his eyebrows. "Of course not."

I smell something extra-fishy here.

Ree pressed the topic, asking louder, to both of them. "Has something like this happened before?"

Jane leaned into Ree and curled up into a ball, breathing inconsistently and sobbing.

Fucking hell. Ree's protective instincts dropped her onto the bed, and she wrapped her arms around the star before she realized what she was doing.

"We need to take her to the hospital," Ree said.

Danny shook his head. "No. She told me not to."

The hell? "She told you? She knew this would happen?"

Ree looked down to the terrified star, the woman who just hours ago had captivated an entire club, who'd had a whole room of fans and reporters eating out of the palm of her hand.

"What the hell is going on here, Danny?" she asked, point-blank, locking him in her gaze.

The bodyguard considered for a moment, looking at Jane, then Ree, then the broken window. "I'm going to go get Yancy. Stay with her, okay?"

Ree nodded, one hand caressing the star's sweat-slicked hair.

Danny stood, grabbed his gun, then nodded and left the bedroom. He closed the door behind him, leaving Ree with a sobbing superstar, the fading smells of sex and fear, and her own troubled thoughts.

×××⬡×××

Yancy showed up wearing a blue robe that screamed *anniversary present*, with his initials monogrammed in gold. He'd clearly just been asleep. Ree saw other lights on in the trailer camp, and far more activity than normal at whatever o' clock in the morning it was. It was too dark out to be anything later than four.

"How is she?" Yancy asked, his face drawn with worry.

Ree looked down to Jane by way of illustration. The star looked to be catatonic, occasionally twitching and sobbing.

"Are you going to explain what the hell is going on here?" she asked. Jane had become unresponsive, though she seemed conscious. Ree had no intention of leaving Jane unless it was at a hospital. This had happened on her watch, even if she didn't know she was on duty.

Yancy stood at the base of the bed, looking at Jane with patently paternal worry. "She'd talked about nightmares, had for months. I told her to take it easy, to get help, but it wasn't just withdrawal—at least, not normal withdrawal, from the drugs. This is something else."

"No fucking duh," Ree said, pointing to the broken window.

She paused for a moment, considering how many of her cards she should lay on the table. But subtlety had never been her strong suit.

Fuck it.

"Last time I checked, normal withdrawal doesn't include your actual demons appearing to carry out the night terrors, at least not in any cases I've ever heard of. She obviously does magic, and it sounds like you know that. I don't have a magician badge or anything, but I'm in the know, so it'd be great if you could spill the beans now."

Yancy raised an eyebrow. She imagined he didn't get challenged like that very often. But she didn't exactly have a lot of time to dance around the issue, since there might still be an invisible monster prowling around the neighborhood. He walked over to the window side of the bed and leaned in to push aside a stray strand of Jane's hair, a tender and familiar touch.

He stood and stepped back, fear crossing his face.

He sighed and said, "I need some coffee."

"Me, too," Ree said.

Danny brought over a chair, and Yancy sat. "How much do you know about Celebromancy?" the director asked.

Ree did a double take. "Say what?"

"Celebromancy."

"I saw the lightsaber, Ree," Danny said, pointing to the discarded prop. "You're not just anybody."

Fair enough. Not like it did me much good. What kind of monster shrugs off a lightsaber?

Not the point, she reminded herself.

She'd heard of the style, but only in passing. She'd seen Geekomancy, Bromancy, and Atavism (aka Furrymancy) up close, as well as whatever it was that the vindictive Rorikon Strega Lady Lucretia did. But she had only been in the game for six months and didn't know everything.

"Almost nothing," Ree said finally. "It has something to do with fame. So that thing with the crowds last night was Celebromancy?"

Danny nodded. "When the fans spotted her, she started to lap up the attention."

"I knew it!" Ree said, thinking back through the previous day, how quickly Jane had gotten her makeover before the press conference, and the way she reached epic levels of magnetism at the club, glowing like a gigawatt bulb.

Yancy continued. "When she gets that charge, she can enhance her looks, use some energy to get more attention to get more energy. It creates a feedback loop. But now she can't control it.

Once she gets going, she becomes erratic, uncontrolled. That's not how it normally works, not how it used to work."

Yancy took a breath of imminent exposition, and Danny turned to walk out of the trailer. *Please let him be getting coffee*, Ree thought.

"Celebromancy has been around for as long as I have, and probably long before that. It might even date back to the time of the Shakespeare, troubadours, or even the geisha, for all I know. But some people, the born performers in the world, can tap into the attention they're given, use it like fuel, then weave it into spells to look more beautiful, act more powerfully, hold a crowd's attention, or crush a rival."

Yancy took a breath. "It's that last one that got Jane in the situation she's in now."

If she can charm people, then how much of last night was real? Ree asked herself, a churning in her stomach as she considered the implications. Some of the night was a blur, but she very clearly remembered Jane stopping and asking her if she wanted to proceed with the sexytimes. *She could have used the mind-whammy, but I don't think she did.*

"Again, more with the explain-y," Ree said, circling a hand in a *go on* gesture.

Note for those in odd circumstances: When in doubt, get more information.

Yancy continued. "There are mantles in Hollywood, Bollywood, and anywhere with enough of a celebrity culture to have a hierarchy. There's The Most Handsome Man, The Elder Statesman, Idoru Ichiban, The Grande Dame, and here, we have America's Sweetheart." He pronounced the titles with capitalization, giving a clear sense that they each had their own weight.

A chill wind whirled its way into the trailer through the broken window, raising goose bumps on Ree's shoulders.

"Jane was a child star, but a few years ago, fresh off of her success with *Young Love*, she made a bid to seize the title of America's Sweetheart. It's a tremendously powerful mantle, belonging to the actress who transcended fame to become forever enshrined in American hearts, no matter her origin. The bid failed epically. As far as I can tell, the reigning Sweetheart, Rachel MacKenzie, got wind of what Jane was doing and cursed the ritual, making the power that Jane had accumulated backfire."

If there was anyone who could possibly be called America's Sweetheart, there was no denying that it was Rachel MacKenzie.

After her film *Downtown Girl* beat *Pretty Woman* to the modern-Cinderella punch and cinched her an Oscar, she'd gone from one charmed project to another. They were all fairly brainless popcorn flicks, but they made mad bank.

She'd aged gracefully from ingenue to mature beauty, though a magic-is-real world made a lot more sense than plastic surgery to explain why the fifty-ish MacKenzie looked even more gorgeous today than she had in her thirties.

Yancy ran a hand through his bed-mussed hair. "Now whenever Jane uses Celebromancy more than a tiny bit, it starts to color her judgment, overwhelms her, makes her seek out more attention."

"So all of those scandals and arrests were her drunk on magic?" Ree asked. That put Jane's last year in a way different light.

Yancy sighed. Ree took that as a yes. Ree ran through the last year of tabloid headlines, trying to imagine what the star had been through, her power tainted like Saidin in *The Wheel of Time*. Except just for her.

"It becomes a feedback loop, and it leaves a mark . . ." Yancy said. "And it's gotten worse. It used to just knock the wind out of her; she'd wake up the next day tired, a bit out of sorts, like she'd had a poor night's sleep. Then it was nightmares in earnest and hangovers in the morning. The worse it got, the more she needed to use Celebromancy to look the way she wanted, which just made things worse."

Yancy looked to the thankfully-sleeping Jane. "She talked about the thing in her nightmares, but this is the first time it was really here, as far as I know. I told her to take it easy, but she's been a star since she was fifteen. It's part of who she is, and who could walk away from that?" The director shrugged. "I know I couldn't."

Danny returned with two steaming mugs of coffee.

Score!

He handed a mug each to Yancy and Ree, then produced a brown bag filled with cream and sugar. Ree Tasmanian-deviled through the bag for a handful of natural sugars and tore them all at once to pour in.

She took a long breath, the caffeine hitting her system faster than The Flash imitating E. Honda's

Hundred Hand Slap. "So why haven't you done something about MacKenzie?"

Yancy took out cream and poured it into his mug, then grabbed a stirrer. "If we could have taken her on, we would have been able to counter her curse. My power is in proxies. I'm not at the auteur level of folks like Tarantino, Anderson, or Lucas; I don't get the power myself. I bring people's attention to my actors, namely Jane, and work with them. Jane's the real powerhouse here."

Ree took a sip of her coffee, which was just barely on this side of scalding. It would have been solidly on the other side if Ree hadn't burned off most of her taste buds in the caffeine-filled years before. Jane had indulged Ree's request to have her old boss Bryan Blin supply the coffee for the set. She closed her eyes and savored the familiar butter and hazelnut flavors of the Sunnydale Blend.

The director took a long swig from his own cup. "It was a risky move, but she was so sure of herself, thought it was the best thing to do. MacKenzie is just in it for the money. She only takes popular films, formulaic low-hanging fruit. She got more money and power, and just put it all back into getting more money and power."

Yancy's face was red with frustration as he spoke.

"But Jane, she was actually helping people. She was experimenting, bringing in new talent, trying to tackle real issues. Every project we do, Jane donates 30% of her take-home to women's charities, children's charities, used the attention she got to shine a light on inequity, and got people revved up about finding solutions."

Ree nodded. Up until last year, it seemed like Jane had spent a season every year somewhere in Africa, rural India, Haiti, wherever there was need that went unnoticed in the States.

"She was so eager to take that next step . . . see what good she could do with that power . . ." Yancy stopped again, his eyes locked on the young star.

"Do you know for sure that it was Rachel MacKenzie who did the whammy?" Ree asked.

"Not for certain," Yancy said. "But she's still got the mantle, so the rumors seem to be dead-on. Hollywood is one big rumor mill, and once you factor out the more ludicrous hype machines, we're pretty good at keeping apprised of what's going on, magically-speaking. It's an open secret in the biz, like the fact that a splinter sect of Scientologists are alien-worshipping sorcerers who have magical indoctrination camps out in the desert."

"I knew it!" Ree said.

Yancy raised his free hand, palm open and out to calm her response. "Not that we could take that evidence to the feds. At least one alphabet-soup agency is clued in, but they seem to leave well enough alone, at least as far as Hollywood is concerned. They learned their lessons at the end of House Un-American Activities Committee, when Reagan and Disney pivoted to clean house of the competition."

All fear the Mouse, Ree thought.

"The big multimedia companies have their own stables and their own agendas, fueling their ambitions with the star power harvested by their films and shows. That's why Jane and I went independent a few years back. But we made some enemies when we left Cosmic Studios."

"Well, that's not scary at all," Ree said, considering what it'd be like to have a megacorp in her rogue's gallery. "But how does that explain the invisible monster-hag-thing?" Ree asked, gesturing to the room and to Jane.

"She complained about nightmares, of something invisible attacking her in her dreams."

"Like Freddy Krueger?" Ree asked, shivering. She hadn't slept well for a month after seeing that movie as a kid. She took another sip of coffee.

"Not quite. And it's never come through into this world, as far as I know. This is beyond me, and it has me worried." Yancy leaned back in the chair, then turned to Danny. "Someone stays with her through the morning, and then at all times. She won't like it, but I'm going to insist." Yancy glanced at Ree. "Well, almost all times."

Ree nearly snorted coffee out her nose.

She took a second to reclaim her semblance of composure and asked, "Are we going to stop filming?"

Yancy nodded. "I can't in good conscience ask her to work like this. I asked her not to take the pilot . . . It was too dangerous, not until she had more control, could stop the flow of magic before it overtook her." He shook his head. "We need to fix this, and soon. I don't think anyone can convince her to take it easy if she doesn't want to. She'd much sooner burn out than fade away."

What have I gotten myself into?

Ree took a long swig of coffee, letting the marvelous mistress of caffeine have her way with her neurochemistry. "So we just have to find MacKenzie and get her to undo the curse, right?"

Like that will be simple, she challenged herself.

I'm trying to sound confident here, okay? she responded inwardly.

Yancy started pacing. "If anyone can undo it, it'll be Rachel. But getting to her is easier said than done," Yancy said, corroborating her doubt. "Rachel will be extra-wary with Jane in town, even if she's just letting the curse play out without any extra effort. She might not know you by sight, though, so you'd have a better chance at snooping around. Though she's not exactly accessible."

Ree couldn't say exactly how suspicious to be about Rachel, since more and more companies were filming in Pearson these days.

He stopped. "But you're not just a writer, are you? What are you, Cinemancer? Geekomancer?"

Ree was struck. She hadn't expected the magic world to be quite that small.

She nodded. "Geek. And I've got some tricks up my sleeve. But Rachel probably has enough bodyguards to run Danny and me straight out of town."

Yancy smiled, his eyes still sad. "Probably. But if you could get to her, or get information about the curse, we might be able to go from there."

"I know a few people. Not so much on the Celebromancy side, but they should know the field enough to point me in the right direction. Since the right direction tends to be straight into the mouth of danger."

"Isn't that the truth. I'll leave you to rest, if you can. We've called the police, as well."

Ree raised an eyebrow. "What are we supposed to tell them?"

"There was too much of a ruckus for us to be able to cover it up, thanks to the tabloids. They're camped outside, and the net has already gone berserk with rumors. I'll do damage control as best as I can. Say you didn't get a good look at the assailant, and that he left out the window."

Ree sighed. "This is going to be a big fucking mess."

"Don't I know it. I'll do my best to bury the story, but make sure I know what you told them. The best thing for us is for the press to write this off as a crazed fan and go on a wild-goose chase to find a person who doesn't exist."

"Don't they, though?" Ree asked. "Some invisible ninja attacker person? How many of those are there around?"

Yancy opened his arms up as if to indicate *how should I know?*

He said, "As many as you can think of, and probably several more." Yancy folded up the chair, stepped over the bed to kiss Jane on the crown of her head like a father kissing a child good night, then nodded to Ree as he left the trailer.

"Well, fucksticks," Ree said to the world in general. She slid carefully out of bed to collect the rest of her clothes and get ready to spin the tale to the police as well as the not-insubstantial chance of getting annoyingly knowing looks from the detectives.

Not the kind of fame I was hoping for.

The gods were kind and sent Ree a female detective to take her witness statement. Jane was still out when the police arrived at 4:13 AM, a half hour after the attack.

The detective reminded her of Kate Beckett (early season, not late—short hair). She was no-nonsense and patently ignored the wrapped-in-sheets form of Jane Konrad and asked only the most general questions about why Ree was there, what they were doing, and what they knew about the attacker and what had happened.

I won't scandalize if you don't, the detective seemed to say with her look. *Thank Sappho.*

Jane was still out when Detective Yao was done taking Ree's statement, so she gave Ree a card and left.

Ree checked her phone. 4:47. She could flop back in bed and deal with several stages of awkward in the morning, or duck out and head home at ass o' clock for a few hours of marginally-better sleep at home and deal with the awkward slightly later. But then again, Jane might freak out if she wasn't there in the morning.

Hell, she should freak out. And it's not like you're BFFs. One night out and a hookup do not a couple make—or even friends, necessarily.

Ree fell on the side of tired and returned to bed, curling up next to Jane. It took what felt like an eternity, as the hamster on a wheel of her brain dashed along like it was on speed. It wasn't even the coffee. That much had barely registered to her addict-level tolerance. But eventually, after much wheelspinning, she did get back to sleep.

The next time she woke, it was light outside, and she smelled the barest scent of perfume. Jane was still sleeping beside her, flopped on the bed in the exact same position she'd settled into after the attack.

Ree snuck out of bed, dressed, and tiptoed out to the main section of the trailer to scavenge for breakfast. As she clattered around the kitchenette, someone knocked on the trailer door.

Ree walked over and opened the door a creak.

It was Danny, holding two coffee cups.

"Bless you," Ree said, channeling her mom's Midwestern family. "Coffee?"

Danny held one cup up, then the other. "One's a cappuccino, the other is black, for Jane," Danny said. "Is she up?"

Ree shook her head as she took the cappuccino, then shouldered the door open to let Danny in. "I'll give her the coffee, but she's still out. How was the rest of the night?"

"Tense but silent."

Ree sipped some of the cappuccino, and took a long breath and imagined the *look, we have a CGI budget!* digital animation of the caffeine hitting her bloodstream, little tiny Rees waking up and starting to bounce around the vein.

"Much better," she said. "How long do you think she'll be out?" Ree asked, eager to get started doing . . . something.

Anything other than sitting and waiting in the place where she'd had her first naked fistfight. Her mind cued up a graphic for the milestone.

Achievement Unlocked: 25G — THIS IS SPARTA!

Danny leaned into the hallway and peeked down toward the bedroom. "I don't know, but if you want to leave, go ahead. I'm the one who gets paid to protect her, after all."

Fair point.

The bodyguard took a step back, putting him out of sight from the trailer door. "Geekomancer, eh?"

"So they tell me. I'm still pretty new to the game. You?"

Danny shrugged. "Just a guy."

"Vanilla mortal. More points for skills," Ree responded, as if it were the thing to say.

Danny didn't follow.

You're out of your element here. Stick to the movie references.

"I'll head out, then. Have Jane call me when she's up for it. Not that I'm slinking off or anything, it's just, you know. Stuff to do, magic, investigation."

Danny pursed his lips while the Awkwardness Monster critted for a special Condition.

Explaining to the bodyguard of a superstar you just slept with that you weren't trying to vanish after a hookup followed by a midnight magical fight scene: X4 Social damage multiplier with a lingering Embarrassment effect. Save ends.

Danny waited, patiently, while Ree shook off as much of the self-consciousness as she could.

"Take care of her. And yourself. I'll be around. Unless I'm dead. Hopefully I'll be around."

Ree picked up her coat from its resting place on the sofa and walked down out of the trailer into the early light of morning.

Step 1) Go home, take shower, reboot brain.

Step 2) Set mode to Detective and do some research on Rachel MacKenzie.

Step 3) Try to keep production clear of doom and personal life from spiraling into soap opera.

And . . . go!

CHAPTER SEVEN

Step One

Rachel MacKenzie's marriage on the rocks?

The Big Dish has exclusive pictures showing America's Sweetheart leaving her Malibu estate with luggage in tow, well in advance of the start of principal photography for Blog Wars.

— The Big Dish, May 13

Ur pic's broken, geniuses. U call that journalism?
—@MSTCHIEF96, Twitter, May 13

Both parties in the MacKenzie-Patterson divorce have filed for a closed-room hearing. Rachel MacKenzie is suing for full custody of their daughter, Amelia, but Patterson's counsel is "confident" that they will win custody, citing a "history of instability," which they will prove in court.

Court date is scheduled for June 7, immediately following MacKenzie's wrap on Blog Wars.

—SpiceOfLife.com, May 22

Unlike the rest of Ree's night, Step One was simple. She made her way home, showered, and made herself a pot of Bryan's Dark Dungeons roast. Her mind drifted back to simpler times at her old life working at Zombie Café as she sipped, a life where arguments about how X and Y magic systems would interact was all for fun, not to keep yourself from ending up dead in real life.

She resolved to spend several afternoons reconnecting with Bryan, Charlie, Aidan, and the gang when the pilot was done shooting, then she put her focus back on the previous night.

She noshed on a plastic bag of carrots that were headed from carrot orange to no-longer-food white. They still smelled like food, and they didn't have that sliminess carrots got when they had become mulch.

Researching Rachel MacKenzie's production was simple.

She was shooting a romantic comedy called *Blog Wars*, starring as a plucky food blogger trying to stand out in the L.A. food scene (All cities stand in for L.A., just as L.A. stands in for all cities. Most people don't notice. Except the tons who do.), when her path crosses with a brusque bar blogger (played by Ryan Gosling, who had become the new Actor Who Must Be in All the Movies).

In the film, Gosling's Gonzo-style video blog, Mulholland Drunk, completely eclipses the popularity of MacKenzie's blog, threatening her livelihood. Personalities clash, chemistry sparks, yada yada, smooching, misunderstandings, and then romantic reconciliation with swelling music by The Lumineers or the like.

As with most things, it would come down to execution, but Ree was getting a big scent of gold-plated crap off of the project.

The bar seemed to be low for romantic comedies these days, with big streaming companies focusing on quantity over quality. Though there were some gems, thankfully.

Cosmic was shooting the film a few miles south of the sets for *Awakenings.* Google and insider production stills showed scenes being shot all across downtown: the Wedge, Pearson Plaza, and the Orange Building. One Tough Mama was the plucky independent, and Cosmic was in the Big Leagues.

Well, it'll be easy to find them. Maybe not so easy to get in. But luckily, magic.

Ree looked over to her media wall. She used to be fairly laid-back about organizing her collection. It was where it was, and she knew more or less where everything lived.

Now that her media collection was part of her magical arsenal, she'd arranged the films by what she could get out of them.

General action movies went together—the ones that could give her movie physics dodging, leaping, and toughness.

Overt fantasies were another row—films that could let her fling fireballs or fight off a dozen orcs wearing nothing but skimpy leather armor.

Superhero movies went at the top, arranged in ascending order of power while she finished figuring out how to use them effectively—she'd tried to fly after a Superman marathon and had only gotten across one rooftop.

Watching a movie or show built up a certain amount of magical energy, depending on how much she loved the show in question, how popular it was overall, her relative experience as a Geekomancer, and how much of the show she watched before using the power.

And to make the math even more complicated, the charge faded slowly over time, even if she didn't use it. She had tried to create a formula to make things more precise, and decided to drink instead. It was all variables and no solid numbers. How do you put number rankings on your fandoms? Did she like Star Wars 3.75 times as much as Star Trek, or just 3 times as much?

Math aside, she was getting more efficient the more she practiced, that was certain.

But the big stuff, like flying, laser eyes, and the more reality-breaking stuff, was beyond her for the moment. It took more juice than she could hold at once. She'd learned to target the middle-level powers, tricks that were contextually instead of universally badass.

Unlike the one-shot tricks she used by tearing up CCG cards or comics, genre emulation was an infinitely renewable resource. She could go back and rewatch something to top off her magical charge. Trial and error were her friends, just as long as the errors in her trials didn't get her killed.

She had also grouped the horror movies together, but she'd been afraid to try most of them out, since she wasn't sure she qualified for Last Girl status, even with her just-now-broken stint of chastity-due-to-an-extreme-lack-of-dating. Plus, she'd just seen *Cabin in the Woods* and was now feeling uncertain guilt about consuming horror thanks to the fact that the film seemed way more plausible in a magic-is-real world.

What's going to work here? she asked herself. Something that grants invisibility would work, as would something that could give her an air of authority. (*I'm an associate producer, I'm supposed to be here!*) She could watch *The Usual Suspects* and try to bullshit her way in, or maybe *The Adventures of Lois and Clark* to get her Lois Lane on.

The prop One Ring that her dad had sent in one of the goody boxes from home would do the trick as well, though she didn't like using that in case it proved to be a little too realistic. Sure, Eastwood's rings worked, but he never mentioned where they came from, and she'd rather not take risks with repeated exposure. Ree knew women who could pull off bald, but no one could pull off the Gollum comb-over.

Ideally, she'd get something that wouldn't lead to instant fail when the magic ran out. She'd gotten much better at timing out how much power and time she could get out of various lengths of viewing. Geekomancy was actually not unlike D&D magic for some things. Now, if only she could see the dice rolls so she could know exactly how long a power would last. Duration: 6d10 rounds was quite a range in a three-second-round universe.

Ree stopped at her copy of *X-Men: First Class*, settling on the Mystique approach. She could impersonate a local reporter, and Ree knew just the one.

She took a lap around the Internet while the movie loaded up through five minutes of hard-coded trailers and advertisements, remembering something she'd seen in her Twitter feed on the way home.

There was a message from her dad, an email about some film blogger who wanted to interview her, and a Google Alert for her name.

Achievement Unlocked: First Tabloid Appearance.

Someone at Infinity had put two and two together with a short piece of technically-journalism captioned by a picture of her and Jane dancing.

Jane Konrad's Wild Night

Dancing and Drinking, then Screaming and Police: Has She Lost It Again?

Child actress turned hot mess Jane Konrad was spotted at Infinity Club, downing vodka and dancing up a storm with her apparent new playgirl, screenwriter Ree Reyes. The pair arrived together, split a bottle of vodka, and were seen leaving together making significant glances, and WTF has exclusive photographs of two female silhouettes in the star's trailer.

But did the night go bad? Police were called onto the set of Konrad's new pilot for Awakenings, written by Reyes. A lover's quarrel, perhaps, or another meltdown from the former child star? Is another trip to rehab far off for Konrad?

Ree read the article three times, wavering between anger and worry. *Just what I don't need: attention.* It'd be hard to snoop around the city with paparazzi following her hoping to get exclusive dirt or access to Jane.

She closed the message, scanned the rest of her email, and very deliberately didn't make the rounds through the TV-focused sites she followed.

One thing at a time, she thought. She looked up and noticed that the DVD menu had looped around again, so she put the laptop down and pressed play.

As the credits started rolling, Ree's mind was bursting with the magical energy of the film, the power of change, the metaphors made real. Ree controlled her breathing and focused on Raven's story for the film: her sense of alienation, her totally obvious crush on the equally oblivious Xavier, and her desire to truly belong.

She'd discovered that for emulating a character and their power, the more she empathized with the character, the better off she was. So watching the whole film was way more effective than just watching a Raven Darkholme badass reel.

Ree closed her eyes and held an image in her head that she'd had up on her laptop the whole time during the movie, that of *Pearson Patriot* reporter Kelly Dominguez.

She'd met Kelly once before the press panel, at a launch party for a web series a friend of a friend had been involved with.

Between that one meeting, the press panel, and Kelly's video reviews, she hoped she'd be able to do a passable enough job of impersonating the reporter to get onto the set and try to dig up some information, maybe even talk to Rachel MacKenzie in person. Any other magic on-set would be buck wild, so it'd have to be strictly recon, in and out. Plus, the charge wouldn't last long enough for anything else. Ree bet that a full-body change like this would drain the battery way faster than the kinds of powers where she just tapped the energy for bursts, like she did with *Buffy*, *The Matrix*, and the like.

Energy rippled across her body. Her hair grew longer, her face shifted, nose and mouth and jaw settling into new positions. Her torso shortened and grew more curvy, going from twig-like to Rubenesque. She walked to the bathroom and checked herself in the mirror.

Yep, it worked. Kelly Dominguez looked back at her from the mirror, complete in the media professional outfit she wore in one of the *Pearson Patriot* team profile pictures and a press badge dangling hilariously above her ample cleavage. Ree stretched out, feeling the differences and marveling at the weird awesomeness of being in someone else's body.

Note to self: Don't do this too much. It could get creepy.

Plus, if she wanted to, with this and some other tricks, she could be one hell of a criminal. Not that impersonating a member of the press wasn't already on the gray side, but it's not like she was going to take up a career as a cat burglar.

Though there are also the kinky possibilities, her libido offered.

Down, girl. Work now, play later, she told herself, trying to stay present in the moment.

The clock was ticking on her X-Magic, so she gathered up a purse (with a lightsaber, a sonic screwdriver, and *Magic: The Gathering* cards for escapes, counterspells, and assorted one-off fixes) and headed out.

After a twenty-minute subway trip, Ree turned onto the corner of Pearson Plaza and zoned in on the signs of the shoot. She power-walked her way over, annoyed that Kelly was the kind of woman who wore three-inch heels as a matter of course.

Ree kept her eyes open as she closed in on the production, futzing with the press badge around her neck.

A young Middle Eastern woman in a black T-shirt, sunglasses, and cutoff jeans stopped her at the edge of the shooting area.

Ree presented her press badge, trying to look like she'd done it a hundred times.

"Kelly Dominguez, *Pearson Patriot*. I have an appointment," Ree said, a bit surprised to hear someone else's voice coming out.

The woman seemed unimpressed. "What appointment?"

Ree let the magic guide her words, augmenting her memory of Kelly to keep the ruse going.

"Oh, great. So now the biggest paper in Pearson isn't important enough for Hollywood to keep our appointments anymore?" Ree turned up the drama. "My boss said this would happen. He told the mayor that if we let the production companies in, we gave them an inch, they'd take ten square miles, set up shop, and stop answering calls from the local press."

Ree locked the woman in her gaze to hit the point home. "This isn't Hollywood north, you know that, right? You're here as a part of our good graces. You blow us off, and my editor raises hell in City Hall. Then *poof* go your permits, your tax breaks, and who do you think they will blame?"

The probably-intern wilted under Ree's Scathing Reporter act and took a step back before saying, "Stay here, I'll go make sure they know you're coming." The woman vanished into the hubbub, leaving Ree unguarded.

Ree relaxed, feeling a bit bad for biting the woman's head off for doing her job. *So, do I wait for her to come back and escort me in, or barge in for more juicy info and try to push a reaction?*

If she did the latter, it'd come back to bite Kelly even more than what she was already doing. And the real Kelly would be around sometime today; Ree had gotten the whole idea off of Dominguez's Twitter feed when she had asked her followers for questions to ask MacKenzie during her set visit that afternoon.

Ree took several long breaths, maintaining her mental grip on the magic keeping her in Mystiqued mode.

The probably-intern came back, looking a bit less annoyed as Ree tried to greet her with a smile.

"Straight back, then the third trailer on the left. Her assistant says you're early."

"Better than being late," Ree said with a smile, trying to flip from Bad Reporter to Good Reporter as she walked by.

Slightly less effective than Bad Cop/Good Cop. The right photo could do more damage than a gun, but people didn't tend to die because of scandals.

Well, maybe.

Which brought her thoughts back to Jane. Ree promised herself she'd check on the star after her recon, fit that in somewhere between changing, checking in with her dad, eating something resembling food, then heading into work at Grognard's for the Midnight Market shift.

Ree kept her eyes open as she walked down the pathway heading to the shooting set and the trailers. The production campus for *Blog Wars* was like the one for *Awakenings*, but three times as big and fancy. A brigade of PAs buzzed around like underpaid bees, and she had to resist the urge to stop into the craft services tent, where she swore she could smell potatoes au gratin and roasted lamb.

She was still new to the reality of show biz, but there was no mistaking Rachel MacKenzie's trailer. It was 50% bigger than Jane's and had two burly bodyguards standing out front, each so top-heavy with muscle they looked like inverted Weebles.

Ree held up Kelly's press pass again. "Kelly Dominguez. I'm expected."

One bodyguard, a big Eastern European–looking guy with stubble-shaved head and a less-shaved beard, stepped forward and said, "Let me see your bag."

"Paranoid much?" she responded, trying to cover a wave of panic with snark. She had no idea if the magic would cover up the weird props in her bag. That wasn't discussed in the movies, and Mystique's *clothes are part of my shapeshifting* had always been a gray area, the kind of thing the films and comics asked people not to think about too much.

Maybe the Doubt would help her, but she wasn't counting on it. She reached into her bag and pulled out her phone and a microphone. "This is all you need to see, okay? I'm press, not some shady traveler at JFK."

She tried the withering look again, hoping it'd work on the bodyguards at least enough to get her in the door.

Her pulse quickened as she thought about all the ways that this could go really, terrifically wrong.

The bodyguard met her gaze, checked out the equipment, and then gave her a look up and down, leering blatantly.

The other bodyguard piped in, an older black man that had an ex-military look. "Go ahead."

Ree put her recording equipment away and walked past the bodyguards to open the trailer door and peek inside.

"Kelly Dominguez, *Pearson Patriot*," she said by way of announcing herself as she stepped into the trailer. It looked a lot like Jane's trailer, because really, how different could actresses' trailers look? Rachel's had more chrome and glass, but there were still some personal touches, lush carpet, posters on the wall of old projects, and a whole wall devoted to pictures of MacKenzie's daughter. And, of course, her Academy Award, which stood tall on a round table.

A prim, twentysomething blonde woman in slacks and a baby-blue sweater looked down at her clipboard, tapping a pen.

"You're early."

Ree tried to disarm the woman with a smile. "If she's free, might as well be done with it so she can go back to rehearsing, right?"

The young woman, who Ree was tempted to call Emma due to the ice-queen demeanor, narrowed her eyes, then spun on her heels (heels on carpet?) and walked out of sight, presumably to speak with Rachel.

Ree could feel the magic starting to fade in her mind, and her mental ticking clock got just a bit louder.

Okay, magic, hold together. We have to untangle this cluster-frak of a situation.

About two minutes later, Rachel emerged in what Ree took to be her costume for the shoot and full cinema makeup. Ree felt Rachel's energy before she saw the woman, as she was wrapped in more Celebromantic power than Jane'd used even at the height of the previous night's escapades. Now that she knew what to look and feel for, the magic was obvious. But no less seductive.

Damn, Ree said inwardly. *That's some force of personality. Like Impressive x5.*

Rachel would stand a couple inches taller than Ree even in her own body, so she towered above Ree-as-Kelly. She had a veritable mane of curly red hair, bright-blue eyes, and skin so perfect you could use it for a color swatch. Celebromancy at work, and from the magic radiation Ree was getting, it was Grade-A stuff.

Ree wondered just how far the rabbit hole really went. She'd been playing in the deep end of a small pond, but there were many other pools, and Rachel brought her own diving arena with her as she entered the room. Ree wondered if knowing about Celebromancy would help make her resistant to the mega-charm powers, or if the star would be able to wrap her around one perfectly-manicured finger.

"Hello. I have to be on-set in half an hour, so I'm afraid this will need to be quick," Rachel said.

Ree smiled again. "Of course. Thank you for seeing me early."

Was she lying about the set call, or had she never intended to see Kelly? Well, the real Kelly.

Rachel took a seat on the couch, comfortable but regal, more than a hint of royal graciousness in the look she gave Ree. Ree didn't know whether to be more scared because the woman clearly had Big-Leagues levels of magic or less intimidated because she was clearly using some of it to be scary. Ree split the difference and settled on wary, keeping the wall to her back.

Ree spotted a chair opposite MacKenzie's couch and took a seat, then pulled out the recording equipment, which she'd retrieved from a closet and hadn't been used since she'd abandoned her webseries. She turned on the recorder and put it on the glass table between her chair and Rachel's couch.

Ree spoke in full voice to pick up on the bidirectional shotgun mike. "This is Kelly Dominguez for the *Pearson Patriot*, here with the Academy Award–winning star of film and television, Rachel MacKenzie. Thank you for speaking with me today, Rachel."

Rachel flipped some internal switch, and her voice came out effortlessly warm and generous. "It's a pleasure, Kelly."

Ree rolled with it, going into interviewer mode, cribbing from questions she'd gotten herself and the hundreds of interviews she'd read online while the *Awakenings* deal was being solidified.

"First, for people who aren't familiar with *Blog Wars*, can you tell us a bit about the premise and your character?"

They went back and forth with the basic questions, Rachel answering with calm confidence. She was relaxed, in control, a queen on her throne.

Now for the real stuff. Ree asked, "*Time* magazine has proclaimed you America's Sweetheart, twice, over a decade apart. What does that mean to you?"

Ree saw a shadow pass over Rachel's eyes, but it didn't touch her smile or show in her response. "It's a great honor. All I can do to show my appreciation to my fans is to keep making good films, mentor and encourage young actresses, and do my best to inspire young women."

Sure, because taking role after role where her job was to show up, look pretty, and have plot happen around her thanks to the actions of men was being a role model. Ree bit back her snark, staying on-target.

"But last year in *Time*, Laurence Russell asked, 'Is Jane Konrad America's New Sweetheart?' shortly before her accident and hospitalization. Do you think those events were connected? What's it like to be held up to that level of public scrutiny?"

Ree caught another hint of something in Rachel's eyes at that question, and the star took a moment before answering.

"America is a big place, and there are enough fans for everyone. I think Jane hit a bad spell, and she made some choices I wouldn't have made myself. But I'm very excited to see her on her feet again and back in the game. I just hope that she doesn't take on too much all at once."

Ree watched Rachel MacKenzie like a hawk, and even with the magic-fueled confidence, Ree thought she detected unease in her answer, an artificiality in the star's well-wishing for Jane.

But she wasn't even remotely objective, and might have been making Lonely Mountains out of wight-less barrows.

As she prepared her follow-up question, Ree felt the magic fading in her mind. With her focus on coming up with questions, she was having a harder time keeping the magic active. She was used to the stress of combat or running while maintaining magic, but this was out of her comfort zone.

There was a momentary fluctuation, like her body skipped a beat as her sense of self hiccupped back into her old body.

Ree looked up with a start to see if MacKenzie noticed. The woman had folded her arms and was leaning forward, guarded but confident.

Time to go, Ree thought.

"Thank you, Ms. MacKenzie, it's been a pleasure. Best of luck with *Blog Wars*."

Rachel's face showed surprise, but her voice was still a clear and pleasant danger. "No, thank *you*, Kelly."

Was it just her, or was there more emphasis on Not-Her-Name than normal? Ree felt her hold on the magic growing weaker, and she snatched up the microphone, pressing stop on her phone's recording program.

"Excellent, thanks for your time," Ree said, stuffing the mike in her bag and heading for the door.

Rachel rose from her couch, moving like a lioness. She took a step forward. "If you have the chance to speak with Jane, do tell her to look out for herself. It can be nasty out there."

"Yeah, sure thing." Ree felt taller. Or, more properly, less short. She tromped down the steps and opened the trailer door, nearly charging by the bodyguards and back into the open lane heading out of the shooting area. She felt her center of gravity changing with each step, and felt muscle spasms around her side.

GTFO, girl. Red Geekomancer is about to revert.

She made a beeline for the entrance, hoping there wasn't some kind of sign-out/waiver/release that the young assistant would challenge her with at the exit while she comically reverted bit by bit, cartoon-style.

Instead, just as the woman registered her again, Ree felt the magical energy slip, and she toggled back to her normal body and clothes, arms tearing the too-small clothes, only to have the clothes then stretch and shift back into her own kick-around-the-house outfit she'd been wearing while watching the film.

Ree nearly fell as her stride length, shoes, and center of balance changed midstride. Ree caught herself on the stand-up metal fencing that served to block off the area and looked up at the woman, whose eyes had gone wide.

"What the hell?" the intern asked.

"Don't worry, you won't remember this in a few minutes. These are not the droids you're looking for." Ree waved her hand at the woman, trying to find calm in the familiar joke.

Nope, still not working.

She felt like a hundred eyes were on her at once, and knew that she couldn't count on the Doubt to make them all slide away. Someone would remember her, someone who could call the cops, point her out on a lineup, or at least recognize her from the tabloid pictures. Every production needed to have at least one person who kept up on all of that, right? If she were a producer, she'd put someone on that, at least.

Run now, worry later, she told herself, finding her footing again. Her real body, with its decades of Taekwondo training and several months of advanced Oh-God-Run-For-Your-Life masterwork, was more than up to the task of fleeing the scene of the impersonation.

"Someone stop her!" cried a female voice as Ree booked it across the street, running against traffic.

Not that Ree was an expert, but people didn't usually send security to chase someone leaving a film set, especially if they hadn't stolen anything. *That's not disconcerting at all.*

She dodged around cars as they tried to start accelerating across the crosswalk, and decided to slide over a hood rather than running straight into a car.

The car hood slide maneuver worked way better when one wasn't wearing boy shorts. She could practically feel the rash coming on as she hopped off the hood while listening to a soccer mom swear like a sailor from her green Dodge Caravan.

"Sorry!" she shouted to the road in general as she looked over her shoulder, trying to see if anyone had followed her.

Yep. Generic tough guy, probably production security judging by the blazer he's wearing. Him, I can lose. Ree looked back ahead of her, plotting a path through the walking crowd and trying to hold the map of the neighborhood in her head.

I could just pull out some cards, she thought, and registered the idea, putting it off to the side—still in reach, though. It'd be a better test of her skills to get away on her own, but she wasn't too proud to tear up a Black Dahlia card from the *Netrunner* card game to make her escape.

Ree tore down the street, dodging among the crowds of people, slowing to avoid knocking over a stroller. She turned to make sure the dad and toddler were fine and to check on her tail. Her tail was making his own way through the crowd, pushing people aside to shouts and complaints. She couldn't see his eyes thanks to thug standard-issue sunglasses, but he was locked onto her, no mistaking it.

Stay on target . . . actually, don't. You can bugger off.

Ree took the turn onto Park Drive, and started booking down the street, looking for the alley she swore was around here somewhere. An alley, complete with a fire escape that she was betting she could scale faster and more easily than the tough, who was broad-shouldered enough to have to be greased through the gaps in the escape.

People were parting to let her by, but she wasn't seeing any fire escape. *Where the hell is it?* she asked the city, as if it'd shift around to suit her.

Good idea, a little too late: Pull out Authority comics for Jack Hawksmoor God of Cities powers.

Hopefully that won't require being barefoot.

Ree was so busy daydreaming about how cool it would be to have Hawksmoor's rapport with cities that she nearly passed the alley and its fire escape . . . which was on the other side of the street from what she remembered.

Gorrammit. Ree evaluated the traffic, grabbed a light pole to swing herself around, and ran across the street in between a car trying to parallel park and the car idling behind it.

Or so she thought until she saw the oncoming car, which was arcing into the oncoming lane to pass both of them— and speeding to boot. Regardless of that, Ree had about one second to get out of the way of the Suburban or end up as a hood ornament.

She lowered her head and dove out of the street, tucking into a shoulder roll and hoping for the best.

The car hit her shin and sent her spinning. Instead of hitting the ground on her shoulder and rolling across her back, she landed flat on the concrete alley.

The impact knocked the air out of her lungs with a *PUH*, and the world kept spinning as she heard a too-far-away sound of a car horn and people's gasps.

Get up! she yelled at herself as the world spun. Usually

her senses and the *hey, body, do stuff* parts of her brain actually communicated with one another, but for long moments, all Ree could do was try to get her lungs to unfold from their upside-down umbrella position.

Someone stood over her, a woman in a pencil skirt and collared shirt silhouetted against the sun.

She asked something in a voice that sounded concerned, but the words didn't make it through the lag between her senses and the rest of her brain. Ree flailed for a hand and pulled herself up with the woman's help.

The world settled out of shaky-cam mode and Ree scanned for her pursuer. He was crossing the street, moving slow so he could fit in as a concerned bystander, or maybe because he knew he had her.

Joke's on you, buddy, Ree thought. She fumbled in her bag for the cards she'd brought, steadying herself with a hand on the side wall of the alley.

Ree thumbed through five cards before she realized that she hadn't processed any of the titles. She started over and heard the heavy footfalls of the tough getting closer when she found the right card.

"Jump" was a crap card in *Magic: The Gathering*, since there were so many other cards that could make you fly, and not just for one turn. But for Ree, it was just right. She tore the card, eyed the lip of the roof of the building closest to her, and pushed off as hard as she could, biting her tongue at the pain in her leg as she left the ground far behind. She looked down to see eyes filled with wonder quickly glaze over into disinterest.

Thanks, Doubt! she thought as she looked back up to make sure she was on-target.

Nope. The card was good for a thirty-foot jump, but that left her just short of the roof. Ree reached out and grabbed the lip of the roof to stop her fall, took a moment to focus, then hauled herself up onto the roof, glad to be her normal skinny-ass self again, so that adrenaline could boost her up while covering up the pain in her leg and back.

She flopped onto the roof and collapsed again, breathing hard.

Shit, that was way too close. Next time, no showing off. Also, track down that speeding Suburban and slash the tires.

But first, she had to get her *Assassin's Creed* on and sneak across these rooftops so she could get away. The Doubt would protect her to a degree, but in her experience, it wasn't exactly consistent. Sometimes people would just totally blank out unexplainable events like the folks in the alley had done.

Sometimes they'd recontextualize, like experiencing a monster attack as a mugging. And some people seemed to be immune to its effects entirely.

Ree pulled herself up to a sitting position and opened her bag. She had painkillers in there somewhere.

She found her bottle of naproxen sodium and dry-swallowed a small handful while she scoped out the neighboring rooftops.

After crawling a few yards toward the center of the roof, Ree stood up. Most of the buildings in the area were two or three stories tall, but the gaps between them were more than she figured she could take without magical assistance.

So, options. She could watch *The Incredible Hulk* to enable Hulk-like jumps, or she could watch *Spider-Man* and get crawling skills to scale down another alley wall and sneak off.

While the former sounded way more fun, the latter was a lot less dangerous (since her power cutting out at the top of a leap would make her three times as much a pancake than crawling straight down). And if she could find a nearby building with another fire escape, she might not need magic at all.

Ree borrowed a page from Marcus Fenix and did the roadie run in *ow my leg* slow-mo to the far side of the building. She hid herself against the lip of the roof and looked down the one story drop to the apartment building across an eight-foot gap. The apartment building had a fire escape, but she had to get across the gap first.

Ree was in the middle of accepting defeat and reaching back into her bag to pull out her stack of cards for a solution when she heard a totally incongruous sound from above and behind her.

"Skreeeee!" said an avian voice. Ree spun in place and looked up to see a dragon.

Well, not quite a dragon. Maybe a wyvern.

A wyvern(?) about the size of a large motorcycle with whiskers, dull brown scales, and no forelegs. Whatever it was, it was definitely angry and looking at her as it lofted in place, wings beating slow and deliberate.

Well, shit.

CHAPTER EIGHT

A Typology of Random Encounters

It turns out that it'd take more than ten Monster Manuals to even start to cover the total range of monsters in the world, plus another dozen to get all of the creatures that have gone extinct or passed out of the popular consciousness and faded away. I don't know which one it is; I leave that to the research guys.

But what it means is as much as you think you know, there's always something new out there.

General rules:

1) Fire is a good standby. Except when you're fighting ifrits, salamanders, and demons. But on most everything else, fire.

2) Not many things like getting decapitated. Except Hydras. Those frakkers love it. I hate Hydras.

3) If you don't know what it is, keep hitting it until it bursts into ichor. Your laundry bills will suck Bantha pudu, but you'll be alive to complain about it.

—Eastwood, Personal correspondence with Ree Reyes, January 11

Ree pawed through her bag and pulled out the lightsaber. She pushed a button, and the prop sprang to life with the trademark whoosh, a blue blade igniting in front of her. She tried to ward off the wyvern as she figured out how to handle the fight. She briefly flirted with despair as fear hit her stomach like a Double Down from KFC.

Dear Universe,

What's with all the random encounters just when I don't need them? Is this some kind of payback for pulling off the Tomb Of Horrors without losing a single party member? Or are you just a cruelly indifferent universe inexplicably populated with random shit that wants to eat people and sends monsters after them when they're already hurt?

No love,

Ree of the Rooftops

P.S. I have weapons now, Universe. Lots.

The universe neglected to answer. Or maybe the monster's scream was its answer as it winged forward.

Ree stood to a crouch on her left leg, protecting her right, which had so offended the Suburban as to get bruised to holy hell and maybe broken.

The wyvern leaned forward and dove at her, rows of teeth glistening with spittle and spattered bits of bloody something.

Ree pushed off of her good foot, diving to the side as she swung at the wyvern. Her cut clipped part of the beast's neck, and she saw steamy blood hit the gravel-covered roof at the same time she did.

A fresh wave of pain hit her mind from her bum leg and her back, which she used to push herself to her feet again, warding off the wyvern with the lightsaber in one hand as she picked herself up.

You know what would be really nice about now? she thought.

An appearance from my favorite temporally-displaced Steampunk dandy.

You work on Providence, right, Drake? Well, It'd be really damned convenient for you to show up right about now.

In a display that proved to Ree that only part of the universe was out to get her, a green burst of energy suddenly flashed from the behind the wyvern and blew a hole in its right wing as it turned to attack Ree again. The beast foundered and crashed into the ground, revealing Drake Winters standing fifteen feet back, his aetheric rifle still trained on the beast.

"You rang, mademoiselle?" he said, a rakish grin on his face.

Drake Winters (Strength 12, Dexterity 15, Stamina 13, Will 15, IQ 16, Charisma 15—Inventor 4 / Gentleman 2 / Steampunk 6 / Fae-Touched 3) was five-five and had sandy-blond hair he kept short and prim in a late-nineteenth-century style. His leather duster billowed in the wind as it flowed in and out of the alleys between buildings. He trained his rifle on the wyvern and fired again, the shot taking the beast full in the backside. Above all things, Drake was a gentleman, and second, he was thorough.

Ree gave the wyvern another look, and if it could come after her with a basketball-sized hole in its spine, it was welcome to try. When it failed to pull a Michael Myers and come after her for one more go, Ree deactivated her lightsaber and put the lifeless prop back into her bag.

"How do you do that?" Ree asked.

Drake shrugged, lowering his rifle. "As I've said, Providence. I rather imagine if I questioned its guiding hand, I might soon find myself bereft of its assistance. Are you well, Ree?"

Ree tried, very slowly, to stand, keeping weight off of her right leg. "Not really, but I was about to get a lot worse. Thanks for the save."

Drake hurried over to Ree, slinging his rifle back over his shoulder and offering his arm to help her balance.

Ree leaned against Drake as she limped a few steps forward.

Her right leg had about as much tolerance for weight as she had for bullshit.

The closeness felt good, even with the scent of burning flesh a few feet away. But the touch brought up memories of Jane last night as well as the close calls with Drake back in October, and an emotional pileup started in her mind as remembered pleasure T-boned unsettled crushes, then the both of them careened into old embarrassments to round it all out.

The confusing moment was interrupted by the sound of popping. Ree glanced over and saw the wyvern burst into a puddle of goop, which as far as she could tell was near-universal for monsters, beasties, and other things that rational people knew not to exist.

She'd never claimed to be rational.

Ree climbed up onto the lip of the roof to avoid the flow of goop, as her shoes were not rated for ichor. The fluid rolled over Drake's boots without his notice.

"Shall we away? I imagine there is a tale to tell regarding why it is you found yourself on a roof with a leg wound and faced with a wyvern."

"Nah, just an average Friday," Ree said, winking.

Drake raised a well-groomed eyebrow.

"Can I use your rifle as a walking stick, pretty-please-with-I-owe-you-a-milkshake on top?" Ree asked.

Drake unslung the weapon and handed it to Ree. "To the . . . what is that eatery called again?"

"Burger Bin."

Drake gave a wry smile. "To the Burger Bin!"

The lunch rush was in full swing when they got to the Burger Bin, so Ree would have had plenty of time to explain things to Drake in line. Chances were that anyone listening to her story would write it off as something from a TV show or a game, or would just forget it in a half hour, thanks to the Doubt.

But considering the . . . sensitive nature of part of the story, Ree wasn't about to risk that. She'd already found herself on the tabloid radar and didn't want to pour any fuel on that fire, even if it was just small bits of word of mouth.

Instead, Ree prompted Drake to tell what he'd been up to.

"Most of my time in the last month has been spent in the pursuit of refining my Tellurian Actuator."

Ree waited a second for Drake to continue, which he didn't. "Which does what?"

Drake nodded, speaking again. "My apologies. I have been endeavoring to not 'overshare,' as you say. The Actuator is a device that, when functional, will allow me to power mundane machines using the magical energies of Faerie."

"No shit, really?" Ree said, quickly regretting the curse with the passel of four-year-olds being corralled between the benches by a pack of overworked moms. (Or nannies. They were young, who knew?) She looked back at the line, which was still more than thirty people long. The Burger Bin employees were as speedy as ever, darting back and forth in their Grimace-purple aprons and hats, but the crowd was still ridiculous. The shakes were worth it, though, and it didn't hurt to take a cool dip in the pool of normal before heading back into the fray.

"I am currently having difficulties refining the processes that modulate the wattage necessary for each individual device.

I've thought of utilizing the adapters present in contemporary electronics, but the input to those adapters is still inconsistent due to the nature of the source power."

"Then why do the normal Fae devices work?"

Drake ran a hand through his hair. "I'm not entirely certain, to be honest. I tend to believe that each device has its own semiotic frequency, and that all of the energy of the device occurs at that frequency. I suppose then all I would have to do is create a system for converting the wattage necessary to the Fae system of semiotic frequencies. If only I had the annotated copy of the Aarne-Thompson motif index I had on the Mistress's Galleon!"

"I can get the shakes and meet you at your place, if you need to get back to it. Plus, easier to chat there than here." Ree gestured to the still-packed restaurant.

"That would be most advantageous, as I have a number of chemical processes under way to address my conundrum with the Actuator, but I would not wish to leave you on your own while you are still injured. Are you quite certain that you will be all right?"

"What's this cane made out of, Drake?" she asked, waggling the rifle-as-cane.

"The point is conceded. Then I will see you shortly. Do ring me on the mobile if you are waylaid."

"What about Providence?" Ree asked. If he'd dropped in to save her ass once already, why not again?

"We need not rely on Providence when the creator has given us the tools to enable our own salvation, my d . . . Ree." Drake had choked on the phrase, correcting himself, which set off a ping in Ree's brain.

More on that later, she told herself.

"Fair enough. See you soon." She shooed Drake away, and the adventurer excused himself from the line and headed out the door. His apartment was only a few blocks from the Burger Bin, as they'd headed across town to get away from the set and Ree's persistent thuggish tail.

Ree took a lap around the Internet on her phone while she waited in line, and discovered that her self-stalking Google Alert had gotten a dozen hits, almost all of them ping-backs on the original gossip rag story about her and Jane, along with several tweets.

Fan-fucking-tastic. This was not how she wanted to spend her fifteen minutes of fame.

Someone behind her coughed. Ree had followed the rabbit hole of the Internet long enough that she was at the front of the line. Ree dropped her phone in her shoulder bag and stepped up to order the shakes.

In her years of working customer service, she'd taken orders from people on cell phones, people who stepped up and just kept staring at their glowing screens, and from people blasting music in big earphones.

Ree had made a promise early on that she would never be one of Those People. She looked the employee straight in the eye and smiled as she made her order, saying *please* and *thank you* like a courteous human being.

As she waited for the shake, her stomach rumbled with anticipation of the chocolatey reward it was about to receive.

Sugar makes the happy go. I will put my trust in sugar and caffeine.

Her hands occupied by delicious shakes, Ree hit the intercom at Drake's front door with her elbow to get buzzed in. Ree had stayed good and only drunk out of her own shake, refraining from skimming from Drake's like she used to do with her dad's as a kid. (And still did anytime he saw her. It was tradition by now.)

Drake greeted her at the door with a notepad and fountain pen. He smiled at her and then stepped back to resume his writing. "Welcome! If you will allow me to finish taking notes, I will be ready for confections and conversation presently."

Ree stepped in and looked over Drake's apartment. The living room was dominated by his lab, with beakers and vials arranged in rows, stacks of gears and vacuum tubes and circuitry in assorted piles, and another half-dozen health code violations, all covered up by an elaborate ventilation system he'd installed along the roof of the apartment, which took the smoke, steam, and scent of oil and did . . . something. He had tried to explain once, but it came out like the teacher's voice from *Peanuts*.

She walked past a stack of gear-and-chrome-tube spheres that looked suspiciously like grenades and some kind of pneumatic jackhammer and turned the corner into Drake's kitchen. And as cramped as the living room was, the kitchen was nearly empty and spotless.

Drake was a bachelor of the classic type, which meant that he either couldn't cook, or just preferred not to. She imagined he must have cooked during his misadventures across the magical realms of Faerie that had been his life before he was unceremoniously dumped on a Pearson street corner a few years back, his illustrious Mistress abandoning him as she'd done with all of her other boy toys (the ones that hadn't died).

She set the second milkshake down on the counter and took the liberty of opening up Drake's refrigerator to check out his array of condiments or whatever gadget he was keeping cool that day.

There was, in fact, gadgetry sitting on the racks: a compass hooked up to a football-sized battery, with pair of bunny-ear antennae sticking out of the top, a row of beakers filled with various liquids, and an oversized revolver approximately the size of a breadbasket, with a valve showing settings like *agitate*, *stun*, and *maim*. The last setting was covered with a bit of masking tape that had *Do Not Use* inscribed in ink by Drake's hand. In addition, there was a small army of condiments and a two-quart Tupperware that held a savory dish that looked oddly familiar.

Ree heard Drake walking over, his boots making the distinctive walking-with-purpose sound. Ree closed the fridge and filed that little morsel away for later. *Curiouser and curiouser*. Ree picked the milkshake back up and handed it to Drake as he rounded the corner. He accepted the drink and took a long sip, topped off with a satisfied sigh.

"Magnificent, as always. I must say, only my patrols and evening constitutional have kept my waistline from expanding since we met, Ree."

Ree toasted with her own cup. "You're not the first, and you won't be the last. So here's what's going on."

Ree launched into a quick summary of her last twenty-four hours, starting with the panther-fly. She glossed over the sexytimes, though the blush and raised eyebrow Drake gave her made her suspect that he'd read between the lines.

Worry about the love triangle later. There's weird shit afoot. God, my life has become a CW drama.

When she was done with the story, she realized her milkshake was gone and she had a brain freeze. *Ow.*

Drake's face was locked in a pensive look, the gravitas of the situation totally undercut by fact that he was slurping a milkshake.

The inventor set down his shake to respond, taking a thoughtful pose with one hand at his chin. "That is an interesting situation." Drake took to pacing, which, in a kitchen this small, meant he took a tiny step to the left, turned, then took a tiny step to the right as he talked. "I must admit, I am not familiar with this Celebromancy. It was not so known in my age, and I have not had reason to confront or study it in this century."

Drake pursed his lips. "But if you are again in need of an associate, I would be most happy to assist you . . . tomorrow.

Or later tonight. I am afraid I am engaged for a portion of this evening."

"Oh, really? Got a hot date?" Ree asked, intentionally baiting.

If she was wrong, it was a reasonable bit of teasing.

Judging from the shade of pink he turned, Ree realized she'd guessed right, though it did not exactly make her feel like she'd "won" anything.

"Who's the lucky girl? Or guy," Ree said, pretty sure that Drake didn't swing both ways but trying to walk the bisexuality awareness walk.

Drake's pink turned a shade darker, and he coughed, straightening up. "I will be accompanying your friend Ms. Tharakan to a gallery opening this evening, preceded by dinner at Bites."

Aha! Ree knew she recognized that Tupperware of curry. And it would explain why Priya had been AWOL the last couple of nights the Rhyming Ladies had convened for beer and kibitzing at Trollope's Trollops. She was smart, had good taste in friends, and was neck-deep into contemporary Steampunk, so she and Drake shared a common fictional language, even if they came at it from literally different worlds. They even had a shared hatred of Steampunk model, essayist, and fashion snob Abigail Wickham.

It's not like Ree could be upset about the two hooking up, considering that she'd never made a move and had in fact just slept with someone else, but all of that trying to be reasonable wasn't stopping the clenching feeling in her stomach.

"Well, have fun. Priya knows the best parties. And get the southwestern egg rolls. Priya always forgets about them." She almost went ahead and asked how she and Drake had met, and stopped herself.

Oh, but this is a familiar place. And not one of the comfortable ones. She'd given dating advice to friends who she had crushes on when they were dating other friends more times than she cared to count, and it was a big, thick awkward sandwich.

Drake nodded, leaning back on his heels and taking a short breath before speaking. "Thank you. And do let me know if you find yourself needing assistance this evening. I have promised to return Ms. Tharakan by midnight to allow her to wake early in the morning for work."

Oh, yeah. Work. Ree was scheduled to close Grognard's,

since there was a tournament tonight, with a big prize.

Ree held up a hand, one finger pointing. "I am contractually required to tell you that if you hurt Priya, I will hunt you down and then use your innards for an art project. I expect Sandra and Anya will tell you this soon, if they haven't already. We made a pact."

Drake nodded, solemnly. "I swear I will do everything in my power to ensure that she enjoys herself, and will not harm her by malice or negligence."

Of course you won't. I almost wish you would. Not really, but maybe. Augh. Time to get out of here before emo music starts playing.

Ree picked up her empty milkshake cup. "In that case, I'll leave you to the Actuator and your date. Swing by Grognard's tonight, if you want . . ."

Drake sighed. "I do not imagine there will be time for a visit, but thank you for the invitation." Ree took a step forward to leave, and they did a short shuffle of a dance so Ree could exit without having to brush by Drake and pour more fuel on the awkward fire. Ree left in a controlled hurry, her stomach still held in a Force Grip.

Set mode to Calm the Fuck Down.

×✕×⬡×✕×

Ree hobbled her way home, thankful for the billionth time that Pearson's public transportation was speedy and safe.

She could have used her sideboard, pulled out a card to teleport home, but that would have been a waste of resources.

Plus, if she just God-Moded through everything, she'd be headed down Willow's path to Dark Phoenix. Magic didn't need to solve every problem. Plus, if she blinked into existence in her own room and Sandra was home, it'd take some impressive bullshittery to come up with an excuse as to how she'd apparated.

Plus x3, the slow walk gave her time to think.

Her apartment, which she shared with Sandra Wilson, another of the Rhyming Ladies, was affectionately called The Shithole. The name was meant to ward off evil spirits of make-the-apartment-crappy-ness. The Shithole was a fifth-floor walk-up, which normally meant Ree got a little extra exercise every day, but with a banged-up leg, it was torture—even with the painkillers.

Maybe I should have just used the teleport after all, she thought as she passed the third floor. *It'd be even more of a waste to use it now, of course.*

She shambled into the apartment and flopped over the couch to die for a few minutes and let her leg stop throbbing.

This is not okay, she thought. There was no way she could make it through a tournament night at Grognard's on a bum leg, so she'd have to burn some resources to heal up before she went in for work.

Ree fumbled through her bag for her stack of cards. Gritting her teeth as her leg continued to throb, she scanned cards at the lightning speed she'd developed over a year of card gaming, looking for something applicable. *Fucking hell.* None of the CCGs used damage points. Things got killed or they didn't. Damage doesn't linger like that.

But it does in Descent . . . she thought, limping back to her room to fetch the bag that held the main store of her Geekomantic resources. She pawed through for a small plastic bag and dug out a cardboard icon for a healing potion. They were coming out with a new edition anyway, and the potions would lose some of their power as gamers upgraded, their emotional investment in the potions switching to the new versions.

One-off props were the instant-gratification approach to Geekomancy. Artifacts had more staying power, with a light-saber working for minutes straight at times, but when their nostalgia batteries were up, they were just so much plastic and chrome.

The disposable-props model was the fast food of Geekomancy: quick, easy, and hit the spot, but it cost you in the end. Every single comic, DVD, RPG book, or other physical artifact of a cultural property held a bit of the world's collective emotional investment. It was the first kind of Geekomancy she'd seen, not that she had recognized it that breezy afternoon last October.

The problem was that each use destroyed the artifact in question. The disposable model was incredibly useful, but she felt a bit of her soul cry every time she did it.

Ree sat herself down on her bed and tore at the cardboard piece. It wasn't exactly easy to rip. *Damned sturdy engineering. This is why Eastwood uses real potions.*

At some point, the universe decided the tear was enough, and Ree felt a wave of magic rush over her. She focused the energy with the idea of a healing potion, the basic unit of explaining why fantasy adventurers don't all keel over after an hour, and felt the energy rush down her body to her back and to her leg.

In about as much time as it'd take her to chug a real potion, she felt her pain evaporate, and the already-mean-looking bruise on her leg faded away.

Ree exhaled, going limp with relief. *Thank Trogdor.* Ree savored the extreme lack of pain for a minute, then sat up and got back to business. Her apartment was in pretty bad shape, but not so bad that Sandra had declared martial law and called for a cleaning day.

She considered, then decided against, shower beer, as much as it would help the cleansing process and calm her down from the craziness of the day. But the shower was nonnegotiable.

After washing off the funk, she put on a new set of clothes, searching her geeky T-shirt drawer for the Wil Wheaton–designed Roots T-shirt from J!NX that she'd acquired as soon as it had become available. A tiny part of her hoped that she would one day get to meet Wil Wheaton, and that he'd invite her for a game on a show or whatever. She had invested emotionally in that happening about as much as she had in the idea of winning the lottery, but it still made her smile every time she wore the shirt.

She was taking a risk not wearing black, but she always kept spare shirts at the bar, so she'd be fine. She matched the shirt with might-as-well-be-black dark-blue jeans. She tied her hair back in a several-times-looped-over braid, one of the designs she'd started using back when she was a barista at Zombie Café to amuse herself and the fangirl customers.

Her stomach grumbled for something more substantial than a milkshake, and she headed to the fridge to see if Sandra had left her any delicious presents. Her roommate had gone to culinary school long enough to learn several marvelous tricks, which she used to fulfill her *feed people!* instincts. Ree was not above enabling her friend in this matter.

Seeing Tupperware in the fridge made her stomach clench again, but she deluded herself by insisting it was just her being hungry.

Goddamnit, heart. You could have made this clear before things got ridiculously complicated. Now the best I can hope for is that Drake and Priya live happily ever after and make brilliant, brilliant gadget babies together.

Fortunately, there was leftover pizza for Ree to use to improve her mood.

Turbo's pizza wasn't nearly as good reheated, but it was still a damned sight better than most of the pie in town, and plus, it was right there.

Ree tossed a couple of slices in the toaster oven and made herself some more coffee. As the percolator worked its magic, her phone started playing "Piano Man," the ringtone she'd assigned to her dad.

Ree scampered over to her phone and picked up.

"Dad!"

"Hey, Ree-bee. Are you all right? I've seen some scary news."

"I'm fine. Just doing my thing. Shall I be vague, or do you want to do the Encryption Tango?"

Ree cradled the phone between her face and shoulder as she poured a mug of coffee.

Her dad laughed on the other side of the line. "Sure thing. I'll call you right back." He hung up, and Ree waited. Her dad had been a communications tech, and actually kept up with the wild world of IT, so he'd taken to using encrypted lines when they needed to talk about her far-beyond-the-norm adventures.

She still hadn't told him about her mom—his wife—who had disappeared over a decade ago. It'd taken him years to get over her disappearance, and he was doing his best to move on with his life. Ree had decided to live with the guilt of withholding the secret rather than facing the emotional carpet-bombing sharing the truth would effect.

Holding back from him was getting a bit easier, and she didn't like that, either.

A minute later, her phone rang again, but the caller ID showed *Unknown*. She picked up again, saying, "Hello?"

Her dad answered, "The squid inks at midnight."

Ree bit back the same urge she felt every call to just go ahead and spill. Instead, she swallowed the bile of guilt and stuck to the latest bizarre thing in her life.

"Great. So, here's the story," she said, and launched into her latest travails, again skipping the sexytimes and focusing on the attack in the night and the trouble she'd gotten herself into since.

"So, are all stars Celebromancers or whatever? Is that how the industry works?" her dad asked.

"I don't think so. It seems like only the Big-Leaguers have that much power. Though maybe some producers and direc-tors do it for other actors. Yancy wasn't clear about that."

"How does that work with fans and your Geekomancy? Do they take away your power, like kryptonite?"

"Nope, not that I've noticed," Ree said. "I think that the fandom that powers my stuff isn't mutually exclusive from the power they get from fans."

"That's good. I'd hate to have to find and rip up your Jane Konrad fan club card."

"Dad!" Ree said in the same complaining tone she'd used since forever when he was embarrassing her. "It doesn't work like that. And don't you dare touch that card."

She'd remembered getting that sad piece of cardboard shortly after mom left, which only made her think of what she wasn't telling her dad. She half-started to speak again, her resolve going out like the low tide when her dad chuckled on the other side of the line.

Then he cleared his voice and asked, "So what are you going to do now?"

Ree grabbed ahold of his question and pushed back the guilt. "I'll need to come up with a different way to make a run at MacKenzie, maybe catch her off-set instead of going directly into the belly of the beast. Or find a different ticket in. Maybe I can borrow the psychic paper from Eastwood."

Her dad inhaled. "Isn't he still persona non grata in magic-town?"

"Yes, but he's also Hercules with labors left to complete. He's been paying off his karmic debt bit by bit, mostly by being a reckless cowboy and running around like Kick-Ass with a lightsaber."

"That sounds like a terrible idea."

"For sure. But he hasn't exactly been open to debate. He charges in, blows stuff up, then scowls and storms off."

Her dad waited a second. "So should I be worried by what I'm hearing about you and Jane? It seems like she's trouble." He said *hearing about* in that generous parental way that meant *I know perfectly well what's going on but will give you the chance to explain.*

Ree huffed. "Don't trust the paparazzi, Dad. It's their job

to make shit seem more dramatic than it is. And Jane's no more trouble than any other star. She's smart, generous, but has a bit of a self-control problem."

"I don't know anyone like that," her dad said knowingly.

Touché. Ree let the comment sit there and just kept going.

"She's got this magical whammy on her, and she hasn't figured out how to manage it very well. And I can handle myself. I know what I'm getting into. Or at least, I know what I don't know what I'm getting into."

"If there's one thing that I know, it's you can take care of yourself. However, I am genetically required to worry," he said.

Ree wished, for probably the bajillionth time, that he didn't live so far away, so she could give him a big hug and let the stress bleed off, the way it always did when he was around.

Except when he was meeting her significant others, at which point the stress called buddies over for a party in her sinuses and the back of her neck.

"Thanks, Dad. I'll keep you in the loop. If I drop off the earth for more than three days at a time, then you can worry."

"I'll hold you to it. Kick the bad guys' asses, hon."

"Yes, sir," she said, smiling as she hung up.

The world was a bit less scary all of a sudden. Ree checked the time on her phone and tried to budget out the rest of her afternoon.

She settled into the couch and let *The Daily Show* run while she pondered, poking around the Internet as she went. Another slew of Google Alerts had come in, most just pingbacks on the original story or re-skins of the same information. Plus, Alex Walters was continuing his smear campaign, ranting about how pathetic, embarrassing, and doomed the *Awakenings* production was.

But along with them, she had an email from Priya, CC'd to Sandra and Anya, asking for someone to be on standby for her date that evening. All she said about his identity was that the guy was "cute and smart, but more than a little weird" and that she was pretty sure he was harmless but wanted to have someone know where she was just in case.

It was standard *Are You a Murderer* date protocol, and if it were any other guy, Ree would do it without blinking. But since Ree knew for certain that Drake was, in fact, weird, and that going out with him could be tremendously dangerous, she was worried.

And none of that has anything to do with how you feel about him yourself? asked a voice in her mind.

Shh. I'm deluding myself here, she responded.

Ree popped off a quick Reply All, saying that her shift started at 6:00 and that she wouldn't be available. It wasn't often that she appreciated her job swallowing up her evenings, especially around the weekends, but this time, at least it saved her some angst.

Too full of nervous energy to do anything restful or productive, Ree stood with a start, grabbed her bag, and decided to fulfill her earlier promise to head down to Zombie Café to say hi to Bryan, maybe catch Charlie or Aidan if they were in. She hadn't been by more than a couple of times a month since her life had Gotten Weird and Bryan had let her go.

Which had been totally reasonable, considering she'd had to call off of three shifts in a week and he was within his rights to not want an employee who might draw a targeted monster attack at a moment's notice, but it still sucked. She'd rocked as a barista, even more than she did as a bartender, and the hours were generally kinder to her social life.

And at that moment, her phone rang again.

When it rains, it pours, she said to herself.

She only recognized the area code. It was a Los Angeles County number.

What's the over-under on this being a tabloid, paparazzo, or random creeper from the Internet? she wondered, and let it go to voicemail.

A minute later, the phone rang again. Same number. Ree

closed the call and dialed her voicemail instead.

"Ree? It's Yancy. Jane is up, but we're still holding off on production today. I have Danny staying with her, and I'm planning on restarting tomorrow. You're welcome to come over anytime. I think Jane would appreciate it. And I'm sorry for the tabloid blowup. I've got our publicists on firefighting mode, but there's only so much you can do these days. This is my personal cell, if you need to reach me. Take care."

Well, there's something to do before work.

Except that going back would mean yet another big serving of awkward to top her off before she had to go to work and be on for eight hours.

Ree leaned back and forth, considering. It'd take an hour round trip to visit the set, which she could make.

She felt pulled in a dozen directions at once, and knew that doing any one thing, she'd be thinking about something else the whole time. It was bad enough that she'd undoubtedly be off her game at work. A nap could reset her world, but she had about as much chance of sleeping now as getting an email out of the blue saying she'd won a MacArthur Genius Grant.

Torn by indecision, Ree did what she usually did in that position. She sat back down and fired up her Xbox to get her game on.

She mentally scrolled through her game library and settled on *Mass Effect 3*. She'd finished the campaign already, but the multiplayer was pleasantly engrossing, especially with the free DLC. She jumped through the hoops and slotted in her Geth Infiltrator, a masterpiece of sneaky.

Playing the Infiltrator let her take the annoyance of Geth Hunters, who snuck around invisible to shotgun your teammates in the head, and turn it against the enemy, running around the battlefield immune to detection and taking fool enemies' heads off at two hundred feet.

Ree's team was a mixed bunch. They had a sharp, conservative Turian Soldier who killed at medium range, moving effectively across the field and reinforcing other players, and a Quarian Engineer with a hell-on-wheels drone, but their fourth was an overaggressive Krogan Battlemaster who jumped around the battlefield like he was soloing the mission, leaving his team behind to pick fights on the other side of the map and then grousing on team chat when he died under a tag team by a Brute and a pair of Marauders.

Ree did her best to play guardian ninja for the Battlemaster, leaving the Engineer and Soldier to handle the rest of the heat.

She fell into the rhythm of the game. Cloak, sneak, shoot, hide.

Lather, rinse, and reload. In this game, she could look out for people, keep herself out of danger, and even if she failed, she could try again. Playing magic guardian angel in real life was a lot harder, and she didn't get any extra lives.

The team pulled it off despite the Battlemaster's apparent death wish, and when the mission was over, she hopped up to get herself more coffee, the troubles of the world seeming just a bit less impossible.

But kicking around at home wasn't going to cut it anymore.

She poured the new cup into a travel mug and retrieved her bag.

⨂

Zombie Café carved out its existence in Pearson's University District, a half block off the main drag, where the restaurants, coffee shops, bars, a few more coffee shops, and upscale clothing boutiques vied for college students' attention.

It was a small storefront, only 20x20 in the front, with a small back room and two cellars, one of which Ree hadn't known was even there until her former boss had taken her down to reveal his secret stash of Geekomancy-ready memorabilia.

Ree stepped into the café, the familiar theremin chime registering her arrival. A trio sat at one of the tables, several open packs of HeroClix open between them as they chatted.

Bryan had kept the same arrangement as when she'd left, with a wall of miniatures and RPG books on one side, graphic novels lined opposite, with tables for gaming and chatting dotting the front room as densely as possible without impeding traffic (much).

It looked like Bryan wasn't in, but Charlie, her former work BFF, was. He was crouched behind the counter, restocking their card game boxes. Charlie French (Strength 13, Dexterity 13, Stamina 15, Will 15, IQ 16, and Charisma 14—Geek 5 / Barista 3 / Social Media Ninja 4 / Trekker 2) was almost five-six, though his wavy mop of sandy-red-blonde hair added a couple of inches on top of that. Charlie had stepped into the role of head baker/barista after Ree left, keeping the café in fabulous nerdy baked goods and generally making sure that Bryan didn't lose his mind.

"Ree!" Charlie said as he looked up from boxes of CCG packs.

He shimmied out from behind the bake station and joined Ree among the tables to give her a big hug.

"Hey, Charlie. How's it going?"

Charlie shrugged. "Cardboard crack never goes out of season, and lattes sell." Charlie took a step back and reached behind the counter. Something rattled against ceramics, and Charlie pulled out two d20s.

"If I get high roll, I get to buy you a drink."

Ree smiled. "And if I win?"

"You can close for me so I can go home and play *Diablo III.*"

Ree fiddled with the die, rolling it around between her fingers.

"Bryan would love what that'd do to his insurance and payroll," she said. Ree blew on her die and rolled on the table nearest the counter. Charlie rolled as well, his d20 skipping across the table to catch hers. Charlie's die came up 14. Ree's, 8.

Charlie grinned, scooped up the dice, and snuck his way back around the counter. "You're losing your touch, bub."

"Maybe, but I can make a martini in thirty seconds flat . . . and I have a pilot shooting."

"So say the Twitters. Well, the pilot part. I still haven't figured out where you bartend."

"Private company, NDA, sorry." She shrugged.

By way of response, Charlie started steaming some milk to make a cappuccino.

"Just one shot today. I've already been hitting the go-juice hard," Ree said.

"Everything all right? The Twitter-sphere's been flooded with gossip about the production."

"Gossip is as gossip does." Ree looked sideways at the trio, who were deep in their discussion. She leaned on the counter to speak in a low voice.

"Got a question for you."

Charlie leaned in to hear her over the steamer. "Shoot."

"Can you do some research for me? It seems like Rachel MacKenzie might be screwing with the production, and I need to know the backstory. And it needs to stay Ultraviolet-Secret."

Charlie pulled the pitcher away from the steamer and crossed his heart as he started the espresso shot.

"Just you, me, and Friend Computer."

Ree and Charlie caught up on TV, comics, and Charlie's latest info from the land of transhumanism and weird body modification while Ree sipped the (marvelous) cappuccino.

"So I hear they've got the subcutaneous RFID install under a grand a pop now?" Ree asked.

Charlie nodded. "I've been saving tips. But there's still a 40% rejection rate, so we're still a ways off."

Some people feared the future, cringed at the thought of the Singularity, when intelligent computers would replicate and technological advancement would outpace our ability to keep up. Charlie waited for it with the eagerness of a five-year-old in late December counting the hours until Christmas.

Ree finished her drink, then checked the clock on her phone.

If she headed over to Grognard's now, she could eat real food rather than trying to convince herself that a milkshake and a slice of pizza counted as dinner.

She gave Charlie another hug, left him a two-dollar tip when he wasn't looking, then headed out to make her way to Grognard's.

Not for the first time, she grumbled about the old man's desperate need for secrecy.

Nothing like a nice stroll through a sewer to get her excited about work.

CHAPTER NINE

Help Me, Ree Reyes, You're My Only Hope

Drama hits the Awakenings *set, as Hurricane J-Rad has reached Class Diva-Five. Shooting is off today as director Yancy Williams is desperately holding the production together. Delays like this can be killer.*

Expect One Tough Mama to close up shop if the stoppage continues.

—Kelly Dominguez, Pearson Patriot, *May 24*

It was tourney night at Grognard's, so the bar was packed full while the rows of merch stood temporarily abandoned. The twenty seats at tables and booths were all filled, trench-coated, bespectacled, and other -ed geeks crowded around tables filled by pitchers, mugs, and their decks, which were protected from the drinks by magically-sealed sleeves.

Ree wove her way through the tables, a full tray of drinks and food on one arm, the other arm free for counterbalance and to gently nudge patrons so she could make her rounds. She'd intended to do her makeup, since it was a hit with the customers.

She'd been deciding whether to reprise the facial tattoo from Neil Gaiman's Death or the tat from *Mirror's Edge*, but Grognard had put her straight to work as soon as she walked in the door.

Tourney nights were always busy, and this was no exception.

This month, the game of choice was *Legend of the Five Rings*, a samurai epic fantasy card game that was nearly as old as *Magic: The Gathering*. Where most tournaments used the newest card sets, this tourney was a sealed booster draft from some of the oldest editions of the game: *Anvil of Despair, Crimson & Jade*, with *Imperial Edition* starters. Each player had put down $500 for buy-in.

But the prize was worth it: a real, live set of Tokugawa-era o-yoroi armor, well used and perfectly-maintained. Ree had almost wished she wasn't scheduled tonight so she could enter the tourney herself. But she was already exhausted from her new and even-more-ridiculous schedule, plus the folks playing were truly hard-core. Some were retired Magic Pro Tour players, others still ran the circuits: poker, *Halo*, *StarCraft*, and more.

Grognard wouldn't say who had donated the prize, but he always invited the competitors to witness his divination on the prizes before the start of a tourney to show that they were what he said they were and that everything was on the up-and-up.

Grognard's no cheat. Plus, if he gave out a cursed prize, his reputation as a magical vendor would be shot, Ree thought.

So she did her best to keep up with the snacking and drinking habits of the truly hard-core. Triple Scotch on the rocks for Randy, a tall blond with a Magic Pro Tour T-shirt. Barbecue wings and Urban Ale-ian for Thomas, a short Korean-American with a buzzed head, who wore his trench coat 24-7. And so on.

Dumping a now-filled-with-empties tray on the near counter, Ree took a second to shake out the growing pain in her calves and stretch. Grognard was moving as fast as Ree ever saw him move, deliberate but relaxed, as he poured a drink with one hand and mixed a shaker with the other, his large hands able to palm the shaker and keep the cap from flying off into the ice bin.

"How are we doing?" she asked.

Grognard didn't look at her as he responded, just kept making drinks, a thin sheet of sweat on his bald scalp. "Good, good. Just keep things flowing, and they'll stay happy. Any problems?"

Ree shrugged. "Thomas is downing beer like a drunk fish, and a few guys have given me the come-hither eye."

Grognard laughed. "Thomas plays better drunk. Just cut him off if he starts calling you Olivia."

Ree raised an eyebrow as she cracked her neck in a roll. But Grognard still wasn't looking at her. The big man slid a drink down the bar to a waiting gamer, then pulled out a lime to start chopping.

"Got it," Ree said. "Do I want to know who Olivia is?"

"Nope," Grognard said, reaching for more glasses.

Ree shouldered the tray again and hip-checked open the door to the kitchen. "Fair enough."

Around midnight, Ree got a call on her phone. Since she was on shift, she ignored it without checking. When her phone buzzed again two minutes later, she checked it after she finished collecting a trayful of empty pint glasses from the table where the top four from the tournament were ribbing the winner over her "lucky" break. Two missed calls and a voicemail from Jane.

She looked over to Grognard, who was cleaning the bar, and said, "Can I step out and take this real quick?"

Without turning to look at her, Grognard gave a grunt of assent, still cleaning.

Ree stepped into the back room, where the dishes piled up like Mount Everest and the cook, Mohammed, kept the grill running and pulled some fries out of the oil, setting them to cool on a rack.

She played the voicemail and heard Jane speak in a strained voice.

"Ree? This is Jane. I was hoping to talk. I wanted to thank you after last night, and I've been trying to sleep for two hours and I just can't. Every time I close my eyes, I feel those hands around my throat. It's terrible. Danny's just outside my room, we hired security, but it's not enough. Can you please call me back? I hope you're all right, maybe you're at work, I don't know. Please call, okay?"

Shit. That wasn't a just-a-bit-scared voice, or a clingy-one-night-stand-trying-to-get-you-to-come-back-for-more voice. That was the for-reals verge-of-panic tone.

Shit.

Ree called Jane back, glancing sideways at Mohammed, and walked back into the office, closing the door behind her.

Jane picked up on the first ring.

"Ree?" she asked, her breath short.

"Yeah, it's me," she said, her heartbeat picking up speed.

"Thank God. Are you all right? I don't know if I woke you or if you were free." She paused, taking a long breath. "Thank you for saving me last night. It's never been that bad, it's never been real, while I've been awake."

"You're welcome. I was more than a little freaked out. But lucky for you, you had a naked protector. And a real bodyguard who somehow managed to miss the dress code."

The star laughed. It was a soft, guarded laugh, but a laugh.

Ree took the win. Jane said, "Danny has always been a stick in the mud. Though his excuse is that it's hard to carry a gun naked."

"At least to do so comfortably," Ree said. "I'm at work right now, but I might be able to take off. Benefits of the job."

"I'd really appreciate the company, Ree. Doesn't need to be anything else. This isn't a booty call or anything . . . I just can't handle being by myself right now. Danny and Yancy need their sleep, since they've been taking care of me all day."

Ree nodded. "I'll see what I can do, and text you either way. Even if I can't get away, I'm done at 3 AM, so I could come over then."

Bob Saget's voice filled her head, using his *How I Met Your Mother* narrator tone: *Remember, kids, nothing good happens* after 2 AM.

Ree took one last tray back to the dishwasher and then grabbed her bag to leave, texting Jane that she was on her way.

Ree had the whole trip across town (a ten-minute walk to the right subway station, then a fifteen-minute ride, capped off with another short walk) to try to sort out her approach.

Was she going as Jane's friend? As her screenwriter? As a Geekomancer and resident magic hero of Pearson? As the girl Jane had just slept with? All of the above?

Ree stopped at the edge of the trailer city to show her ID to a security guard. It wasn't one of the guards she'd met during set visits, and the tall, thin man looked more hard-core than the folks on day shift.

Is he extra help brought in since last night, or are night shift always more spooky-looking? The guard waved her through, and Ree filed the question away in the section of her brain marked RESEARCH AND SETTING DETAILS.

She noted three more guards between the perimeter and Jane's cabin. Yancy was not screwing around. But the extra muscle and a missed day of production had to be expensive, and One Tough Mama was already scraping the barrel with this production.

No pressure, Ree. Just dozens of people's careers on the line.

Ree stepped up to the squat guard who stood in front of the door to Jane's trailer. He was shorter than Ree, but heavily muscled. Ree pegged him as probably Pacific Islander. He had a sweet tattoo winding up his neck and all the way to the top of his shaved head. He had a soft face but moved like a guy who'd seen his share of brawls.

"Hi, I'm Ree Reyes. Ms. Konrad is expecting me."

He gave her the once-over with narrowed eyes, then waited a moment, arms crossed.

Is this going to be a thing? Ree asked herself, ready to bring out her *no, seriously, I belong here* spiel.

The guard smiled, the hard-ass demeanor gone. "Just kidding. You're the writer, yeah? Local girl done good."

Ree nodded. "That's me." She extended a hand to shake.

He met her hand, squeezing tight. "I'm Kalolo. Go on in." Ree was glad she'd learned to shake from her dad, an ex-marine, otherwise she'd have come away with a mangled claw.

Inside, the lights were on in the living room and all the way back to Jane's room. Despite the light, Danny was dozing contentedly on the couch, baseball bat resting across his chest.

Ree stealth-moded across the room, trying to avoid waking Danny. When she hit three paces in, he sat up, grasping the bat and staring right at her. Recognition hit his face, and he nodded, lying back down and settling into the couch, instantly asleep again.

Nice trick. Ree walked through the trailer and knocked on the door frame to the bedroom, the door half-open already.

"It's Ree," she said.

"Come in," Jane answered.

Ree stepped in and saw Jane sitting in bed, over the covers, wearing her robe, a well-loved copy of *Idoru* sitting on the bed by her side. Jane's eyes were puffy, but she didn't have any smudged makeup, so Ree imagined she'd already removed the day's face. Or had skipped makeup entirely, given the glamour magic of Celebromancy.

Jane slid over on the bed and patted the space where she had been sitting. "Thank you for coming over. Join me?"

This wasn't sex-goddess Jane from the club, but it wasn't run-down Jane pre-makeup at the hotel, either. The way she was acting now was closest to sushi Jane—calm but burdened. Ree relaxed a little, feeling no tension or awkwardness from Jane.

Just be a person, Ree. She needs a friend.

"This place is buttoned up tighter than a chaperone at a Catholic school dance," Ree said. "You're as safe as can be."

"Except the thing that came after me didn't come through the window or the door or past security. It came right out of my dreams, Ree. And when I go to sleep again, it might be there waiting for me."

"Freddy was always scarier than Jason," Ree said.

That got a laugh.

Okay, so, comforting. That I can do. Except that her normal comforting mode, as employed with Sandra, Anya, or Priya, included hugging, lots of wine, and terrible movies. The TV was out in the living room, Ree didn't know if there was wine, and hugging could be a pretext for more, and then things would get even more tangled up than they already were.

"I'm not sure what to do here. Last night was . . ." Ree trailed off, stuck on phrasing.

"The night became another thing," Jane said.

It was Ree's turn to laugh. "Yeah, that."

Jane shrugged. "What happened between us can stay last night. But there's no way this show will make it off the ground if you and I have to tiptoe around each other. Plus, I have bigger fish to fry."

"Speaking of, I went to check up on Rachel MacKenzie today."

Jane leaned away from Ree with surprise. "What? Really? How did you do that?"

"Danny and Yancy told you about my *other* other job, right?"

Jane nodded.

"Turns out, *X-Men: First Class* makes for a great disguise. I went in as a reporter to interview Rachel. I didn't get much, though, just a sense that she's still holding a grudge. Yancy said you tried to pull off something big a couple years ago, and that's when things got bad."

Jane sighed. "I wanted it all. I thought I had the right to take the mantle, and that I had the power to pull that off.

I wanted to do so much, Ree. Thought I could make things better. Change the industry, focus on real issues, real stories."

The star leaned back, her eyes distant. "But for that, you need backing, power. Not just a great team, not just the flash-in-the-pan fame all the reality stars are raking in feast-and-famine-style by putting themselves into the X-rated *Truman Show*. Investors can smell the weakness of a career teetering on the edge, and they don't like to take risks. After we broke away from Cosmic, Yancy and I hit a ceiling. We could never break back into the Big Leagues, not without a game changer, either cash-wise or on the magic side."

She stopped. "Let me start over. You didn't tell me you were a Geekomancer, and that's fine. But I don't know what you know about my art."

"Celebromancy? Just a bit, plus what Yancy told me, which isn't much. It seems pretty close to the glamours and such the Fae use. Control, direct, cultivate, and use attention."

Jane nodded. "And not just attention: Obsession, jealousy, aspiration. You can turn yourself into a Role Model, urge others to follow in your path. You can be a shining example or a cautionary tale, depending on how things go. I don't know which one I am these days. Labels are very important in Celebromancy. Archetypes, titles, roles. The World's Sexiest Man, the Ingenue, America's Sweetheart. Those archetypes come with immense power." Jane stopped and smiled at Ree. "And with great power . . ."

"Great responsibility. So you tried to nab the America's Sweetheart title. What went wrong? And how does a ritual like that even work to begin with?"

Ree hadn't done much ritual magic and still didn't have a good handle on it. Her former mentor used ritual frequently, since he didn't have her knack for genre emulation. But the rituals he'd done only vaguely resembled what Ree thought of as traditional magic, even when you stripped away the geeky trappings.

"The ritual was supposed to be simple. I took prints from each of my films, magazines where I was the cover model, featured, or interviewed, tapes of *E!* guest spots, so on, and gathered them on an altar as a representation of the fame and power I'd already accumulated. Then I made an effigy of myself and one of Rachel MacKenzie, who had the mantle at the time. I had a friend make the dolls, including a crown for Rachel, to represent the mantle."

Jane cracked her knuckles, looking anxious, like a junkie yearning for a hit. "I tied that crown to an actual tiara I borrowed from the prop department from *Fairy Godmother* with standard sympathetic magic. With that all set up, I jumped on Twitter and started slinging mud with Rachel. I called out her terrible, lowest-common-denominator films, and stirred up a shit storm."

"Is that why?" Ree asked. "It seemed totally out of left field."

Jane hadn't been the Twitter-feud type, at least, as far as Ree and most of the reasonable journalists had thought at the time.

Makes a body wonder what kind of secret agendas are behind all of the other weird shit in Hollywood.

"It was the fastest, most sure way I could think of to get a boost. I thought I needed the extra attention from the fight, then moved the doll crown from Rachel, putting it on the doll of me as I donned the crown myself and released the power . . . and that's when something went wrong. Instead of the sympathetic magic connecting the miniature mantle to the magical one and syncing them both to me, it all rushed through me and back to Rachel, or somewhere else." Jane made a *poof* gesture with her hands and slumped against the headboard.

"And ever since, any time I use my power, I get the backlash. I didn't even notice it at first. A headache here, fatigue there. I just thought I was just running myself too hard, trying to build back up with One Tough Mama. So instead of taking a break, I pushed harder. And that led . . . that led to some things I'm not proud of. It was a crappy year, and it wasn't until after rehab and the community service that I started to get a real handle on what had happened."

"So why didn't you stop?" Ree asked. "It's clearly getting worse."

"Could you stop watching movies? Stop reading comics? Stop writing? This is who I am, for better or worse, and I can't just walk away from it. Not if I'm going to have any chance of doing what I want to in this industry: try to support real, compelling work and help people."

Jane smiled at Ree. "Like giving new voices a chance to shine. Or empowering women to have more of a voice in Hollywood and in this country. I can help make that happen, Ree, and I'm willing to pay the price to get there."

Ree narrowed her eyes, fighting the urge to just say *bullshit* like her mouth wanted to. But tact won the day. Mostly.

"That's great talk, but this is your life, Jane. Martyr is a powerful mantle, but most folks don't get to wear it very long before they buy the farm. What good can you do dead? You kick off now, and I'm sorry, but they aren't going to remember you for your feminism and your pluck. You can do a lot without magic." Ree stood, folding her arms. "And if you want me to keep helping on the magic side of this, there's no way I'm going to let you dig yourself even deeper into this curse."

Jane looked relieved at first, then shivered. She hugged herself, nostrils flaring as she held something in.

"It isn't something you can just walk away from. How am I supposed to work without it?" Jane shook her head, dismissing the thought.

"Unless every actor everywhere has magic, then you can live without it. If it's really that much like a drug, then you'll have withdrawal, but that's better than getting dead."

Jane gave a petulant look. "You ever kicked a habit?"

Ree laughed. "I quit smoking after five years."

"But you still drink coffee, right?"

Ree sat back down, her hackles resetting. "Of course. I happily dove into the arms of one addiction to escape another."

"Aha!" Jane said.

Ree held her hands up in surrender. "Yeah, you got me on that. So, pick a new shiny to distract yourself from the jonesing!"

Jane gave a knowing smile and scooted closer to Ree. "Are you volunteering?"

Uh-oh. I walked into that one. Ree leaned back, her heartbeat picking up speed. Being someone's methadone wasn't exactly a good premise for a relationship.

But look at how gorgeous she is! her libido said with a stating-the-obvious tone. Ree refrained from following the trail of smooth leg up toward the hem of the star's robe, but when she tried to look Jane in the eyes, her gaze slid down to where the sides of the robe overlapped, and the promise of soft flesh underneath.

Down, girl! she told herself.

Jane noticed Ree's lingering gaze and said, "It doesn't have to last after the pilot, or after the show if we get picked up. But I haven't had a lot to be happy about since the ritual."

"I don't know if that's romantic or sad," Ree said, regretting her Snark Impulse as soon as the words left her mouth. *Goddamnit.*

Ree mentally set her Snark Dial down a few notches, hoping it would stick. With luck, her libido would have her back.

Jane looked away for a moment, then shrugged. "Take your pick, but it is true. I've wallowed, lashed out, shut off, and your script was the first thing that really excited me, that broke through whatever fugue-self-destructive bullshit this ritual has done."

Jane winked. "Plus, you're pretty cute."

Ree raised an eyebrow. "Said the international superstar-slash-model with thirty cover spreads to her name."

"Thirty-one," Jane said, her tone turning coy.

"I'm sorry. I must have lost track somewhere that summer when you were on every cover in the universe."

Jane inched closer. She was close enough that Ree could smell the shampoo she'd used on her hair and what was probably lotion. A chill ran down her spine. A happy chill, not the *holy crap, about to die* chill. She'd had precious few of the former the last few months.

"That was a wild year," Jane said. "But I've had wild, and I've had rock bottom. And it's taught me to appreciate the now."

Jane reached a hand up to brush a lock of hair behind Ree's ear.

It was a familiar gesture, something for an old friend or well-known lover. It was all still new with Jane, but she made Ree comfortable and nervous at the same time. The implications were frightening, catching her in loops of overthinking. But she wasn't scared by Jane or what the star might do. Maybe she should be, but she wasn't.

Drake had made his choice, and so her mess of a situation had gotten a helluva lot clearer.

Ree leaned in and kissed Jane slowly, testing the waters.

Last night had been a whirlwind. This wouldn't be like that, one way or another. Jane's lips met Ree's, strong but not forceful.

Ree's shoulders relaxed, and she settled into the kiss, building momentum. Her bag slipped from her shoulder, hitting the floor of the trailer with a thump.

"Danny's in the front room," Ree said, breaking off for a moment.

Jane stood without a word, took the two steps to the door and closed it in a slow, smooth motion. She looked over her shoulder back at Ree, smiled, and said, "It's just us. We have all night. So, what do you want to do?"

"I think we were getting somewhere just a moment ago."

Jane smiled as she slinked back to the bed. "Oh, really? Where were we getting, again?"

Put up or shut up, she told herself, once again instructing her sixteen-year-old self to play it cool, despite very clear memories of spending quality time in her room with an image gallery and clips from Jane's films.

She high-fived her inner sixteen-year-old and chucked caution out the window.

Ree brought her hand to her chin, pondering. "My memory's a little foggy. But I think it involved you being over here." Ree gestured to the bed. "And I was here." Ree slid back a few inches.

"You better come over and help me remember."

Jane took the steps back to the bed slowly, drawing out the moment. Ree felt pulled, like two magnets held inside each other's range. Two pieces yearning to meet, shaking with anticipation. The star ran a hand through her hair as she settled back onto the bed.

Jane moved achingly closer and reached out to brush the back of her hand across Ree's cheeks. Ree flushed at the motion, leaning in and taking Jane's hand to keep it close.

Their lips met again, and for one night, they put aside magic, show business, mantles of power, and everything that wasn't touch, taste, and connection.

×✕˟⬡˟✕×

After a night of sleep uninterrupted by monster attacks, Ree woke up to the warmth of sunlight kissing her cheek. No, scratch that. Just kissing. Lips. Ree blinked her eyes open and saw Jane beside her, wearing a million-dollar *maybe it's Maybelline* smile and nothing else but the sheets.

"Good morning," Jane said.

Ree stretched and yawned, enjoying the half-awake state and enveloping sense of contentment. She was aware that Bad Shit was going down somewhere that she'd have to deal with soon. But nothing had happened in the night, so Ree made an executive decision that worry could bugger off, at least until the day was truly under way.

"Good morning," Ree yawned. "What time is it?"

"6 AM. I have call for makeup in thirty minutes."

Ree blinked, the threat of imminent no-hot-girl-in-bed-with-me-ness souring her mood.

"I roll to disbelieve. I say it's 5 AM and the sun is just an overachiever."

Jane ran a hand through Ree's hair. Her body tingled at the slight tugging on her scalp. The Brazilians, being some of the sexiest people around, had a word for the gesture: cafune. And it was one of Ree's favorite bits of affection. Familiar and sensual, but still simple, and acceptable in public. And since Ree was a card-carrying PDA fan, it was all kinds of win.

"Do you need some help with the shower?" Ree asked. "I hear the ones in these trailers can be tricky." Ree added her best knowing look, hoping to extend the closeness just a little while longer.

Jane sighed, then shook her head. "No time for that, sadly."

"But it saves time and water. You are a conservationist, aren't you?" Ree asked.

Jane took a pillow and thwapped Ree on the shoulder. "You're too much."

Ree melted back into the bed. "And proud."

Jane slid out to her feet and retrieved her robe. "You're welcome to borrow some more clothes if you want. Chances are Yancy will want to talk to you before we start shooting for the day."

Ree nodded, waking up bit by bit. The scary loomed closer at the edges of her attention, teaming up with the be-a-screenwriter demands on her time to kill her buzz. "I need to hit the pavement again, try to get a better read on Rachel, how the ritual worked, what we can do to break the curse-backlash thing."

Jane slipped into the robe and leaned back to the bed. She touched Ree's cheek and kissed her softly. "You've got it, hero."

Ree flinched at the appellation. "Save that for when I get MacKenzie off your case." Ree found her clothes from last night and her bag of tricks, arranged in a haphazard pile in the corner.

Ree imagined some horny grad student and her paper.

"Where Are My Pants?: A Psycho-geographic Analysis of Sartorial Shedding in Hook-Up Culture" by R. G. Houston in Damn Kids Get Off My Lawn: An Interdisciplinary Analysis of Twenty-First-Century Youth Culture (New York: Palgrave Quirkmillan), 47-69.

Jane headed for the shower, leaving Ree to her thoughts and her pile of clothes.

Well, you're right and properly in it now, Ree told herself. She checked her phone and saw that Drake hadn't called. Did he go to Grognard's, or had his night gone like Ree's?

Too many things to keep track of. Focus. There was more detective-ing to be done, script management to be done, and she should probably tell her friends she was alive sometime.

There were more Google Alerts for her name and *Awakenings,* which she glossed over and skipped any time they got too gossipy or mean-spirited (which, sadly, was most of them). But one was from a woman who had been a Konrad fan since they were all teenagers and who thought the story sounded interesting. Ree emailed the link to herself and then read it again, boosting her spirits (+2 Morale Bonus to Getting Shit Done).

Ree plugged her phone in to get a charge, as it was sitting at 35%. Since starting down the Geekomancy path, she'd taken to treating her phone even more reverently, since it was both her connection to the rest of the world and the best, most convenient source of magic. It was a Green Lantern Battery and communicator in one. Plus, *Angry Birds.*

Charge, my pretty! she willed the phone while reviewing the scenes they were set to shoot that day.

CHAPTER TEN

The Show Must Go On

There's an unspoken code in show business. People speak it all the time, but those aren't the ones who really mean it. Someone gets sick? The show must go on. Script sucks? Show must go on.

Each show is a living thing; it has its own momentum. Shows are like sharks: They have to keep moving forward or they die. No matter what happens, keep going. Better to go down as the most ambitious messy failure than to just quit and fade away, having never tried.

—Jane Konrad, Actor's Alley, *November 17*

It looked like Yancy'd had a rougher night than Jane. His hair was rumpled and he had bags under his eyes, sipping coffee as he orchestrated the grand machine that was One Tough Mama.

The set crew was dressing the apartment where they were shooting scenes between Allison and her girlfriend, which would actually go before the dinner scene they'd shot two days ago. It blew Ree's mind that actors could keep a whole story in their head and tell it part by part, out of order, while building in a character arc that made sense when viewed in the proper order. The postproduction editors and producers obviously helped, and that's part of why they'd get several different takes of any scene, to have a range, but it was still foreign to Ree's LARPer/gamer/writer brain, where characters tended to develop emergently (which was just the fancy way of saying that she made shit up and hoped it worked).

The PAs were clearly getting to know her, since two steps into the building, Patricia/Vanessa greeted her with a steaming Styrofoam cup of coffee.

"You're gorgeous," Ree said, accepting the cup. The assistant stepped back and started to walk off, and Ree said, "Wait."

The woman turned around slowly, looking like she'd already mentally moved on to the next task.

"I'm very sorry, but I can't for the life of me remember your name."

Understanding flashed on the woman's face, and she relaxed for a second. "Vanessa."

"Thanks, Vanessa," Ree said, raising the cup in salute.

Vanessa nodded and zipped off.

One mystery solved. Now if all of the other ones would be as easy to solve as getting over my pride.

Ree ran a partition in her brain to think up caper-style ways of getting access to Rachel MacKenzie while going over the day's sides with Yancy, making little tweaks here and there.

Yancy liked to get a fresh look at the script each day, to work it around in his mind like a tumbler. He was a great editor—after all, the man had been directing since Ree was a diaper-wearing, lightsaber-binky-wielding toddler.

Not that he'd appreciated it when Ree had said as much in conversation. But he'd grumped with a smile on his face, so all was well.

Ree watched from her still-totally-exciting chair as the shooting got under way.

She failed her Save vs. Charm when Jane walked into the room, as radiant as she'd been at the panel. Most of her mind was busy being entranced, while her Spider-sense was going off, reminding her of the cost.

You shouldn't be doing that, remember? she thought at Jane. *With the night-haunt and all?*

Ree harrumphed to herself. *It's her life. If she wants to burn out rather than fade away . . .*

Then your career gets tanked before it even takes off, and everyone here loses their jobs.

There was some enlightened self-interest involved, but Ree knew she couldn't let Jane go out like Marilyn Monroe or Kurt Cobain. Though neither of them had killed themselves through overuse of magic. *Probably. Maybe. Possibly. Damnit. Magic exists, and it is weird as hell* never ceased to make things that Ree used to be certain about totally up in the air.

Ree started to get up to do something about it, but Yancy beat her to it, launching out of his chair. The rest of the room seemed to be under the same level of entrancement, but Yancy was having none of it.

Deciding that not dog-piling on your maybe-girlfriend was the better part of dating (if not valor), Ree returned to her phone, where she saw she had a handful of direct messages from Charlie.

She'd almost forgotten about putting him on Rachel MacKenzie's trail.

All right, King of the Internet, give me the lowdown.

Charlie being Charlie, he sent the whole report in Twitter DMs instead of an email.

Ree scrolled through the tidbits and links, assembling the picture of a woman who was indulgent in public and aggressively reclusive in private. She made plenty of public appearances and was working as actively as ever, but her personal security had stepped up in the last year, as evidenced by the fact that four paparazzi had been arrested for trespassing on her property since last summer.

So what are you so twitchy about, then? Ree wondered. Judging from the epic smackdown she gave Jane, her Celebromantic magic pool was at an all-time high.

Curiouser. So how am I supposed to get close enough to get her to break the curse or find out how to do it myself? The Midnight Market was coming up that night, so she could pound the subterranean pavement herself, but traipsing around at the Market asking about breaking Celebromantic curses would be about as subtle as sneaking behind the counter to squeeze the HeroClix boxes looking for oversized figures. Not that she ever did that. No siree. Her record of pulling ultra-rares like it was her job was just a nascent manifestation of her Geekomancy. *Yeah, that's it.*

Charlie's deluge of DMs had come to an end, so Ree checked her other messages (sure enough, more trashy Google Alerts) and perked up when Yancy called quiet on the set.

×[×]✕[×]⬡[×]✕[×]×

Yancy cut her loose around noon, though Ree knew there was a better-than-nothing chance he'd call again later in the day if something wasn't working.

She went home for a quick shower and a change to get ready for the long night in Geekville.

The afternoon at Grognard's was mundane enough that Ree could almost forget how weird the place really was. A few clean-cut older folks came in at around four, browsed through hermetically-sealed merchandise, dithered about what to buy, then walked out with a couple hundred dollars' worth of vintage lunch boxes and action figures.

It wasn't until she stopped and thought about what magic ritual someone might do with a 1987 *Transformers* lunch box and three different Starscream figures that the weird came back in.

Grognard was in a particularly surly mood, as Ree had had to jump in and cut him off when the gruff geek started to berate a young Japanese woman in a Magical Girl outfit after she'd wandered behind the bar and picked up a glass case containing a heart-sized device that looked like H. R. Geiger on a Hello Kitty trip. Grognard had been reaching for his shotgun when Ree jumped in between the girl and the gun to say, "Please put that down, for the love of all that is decent and not exploded."

Watching Ree (and probably the shotgun behind her), the woman put the device down and stepped away.

"Why?" the customer asked.

Grognard's voice came out as a growl. "Because if you think the wrong thing while holding that, you'll go from Sailor Perky to Sailor Shoggoth."

The woman face-faulted. But not in the normal way that humans do, even on sitcoms. Her mouth and eyes grew to three times its normal size, scrunching up in terror.

She just chibi-ed out! Ree thought. *Holy crap.* Ree marked one more on a tally in her brain that said *Drinks I will drink tonight because my life is wild.*

She was embarrassed to think about how many marks were already there, since it would probably be enough to blind a mule.

The Magical Girl excused herself shortly afterward, leaving Ree to check in with Grognard.

"Everything okay?"

Grognard shook his head, rueful. "I've seen what that thing can do."

"Then why keep it?" she asked. "Wouldn't everyone be better off if ridiculous things like that just got tossed into Mount Doom? Or someplace worse, like an endless tire fire in Gary?"

Grognard shrugged, replacing the shotgun in its home under the bar. "That thing will make me a helluva lot of money when I find the right person to sell it to."

"Who would that be?"

"Someone stubborn and righteous enough to put up with it. Things like that have a tendency to get themselves free, like The One Ring or possessed items. Lock and key isn't always enough. I keep it until someone comes along I can trust with it."

"So you're waiting for Tom Bombadil to come a-browsing?" Ree asked.

That got a satisfied grunt out of Grognard, who disappeared into the back room.

Ree watched the store from the bar, scanning the room to check drink levels and try to spot anyone whose demeanor said *I need help* or *I wish to exchange currency for goods and services.*

A minute later, with Grognard still in the back, the self-styled "Lieutenant" Wickham walked into the store like she owned the place. Lt. Abigail Wickham (Strength 13, Dexterity 14, Stamina 12, Will 8, IQ 14, Charisma 16—Old Money 4 / Mean Girl 3 / Model 2 / Blogger 2 / Steampunk 1) was a tall woman, standing nearly five-ten in her boots. Her outfit probably cost as much as four months' rent on The Shithole. She wore a velvet-lined suede jacket over a low-cut linen shirt with hand-embroidered blackwork, and layered skirts pulled high for mobility (and for her to show off toned legs and her custom-fitted boots with compact hydraulic pistons running down from the knee).

Wickham had unmockably natural golden-blonde hair, which she kept in a complicated braid and tucked under a military cap. Her goggles were polished gold with red lenses. She wore what seemed to Ree to be a permanent sneer as she crossed the room, walking straight to a stool and setting her rifle against the bar with casual distaste.

"Jack Daniel's Single Barrel, neat," Wickham said, not meeting Ree's eyes. *I hate her so much,* Ree said to herself.

Ree stepped onto a baseboard shelf to reach the bottle, then poured the drink with as much expedience and as little fanfare as she could, sliding the glass to Wickham. "Twenty-five."

The woman snickered, setting down a platinum card.

Ree took the card and started a tab, wishing Grognard would come back so she could relocate to the game section. It wasn't just that the "Lieutenant" was self-important and cruel, it was that she was self-important, didn't make a single bit of her gear herself, looked down on poorer Steampunks, and had posted a two-thousand-word rant on her blog a few months back that had enumerated the many perceived faults of Priya's totally awesome laptop casemods.

But there was no joy in Geekville that night, since Grognard seemed to have properly disappeared. Ree made herself scarce at the bar, taking laps around the seating area to check in on the other patrons.

Ree went to check on Joe, even though she knew he'd be fine, then, as she returned to the counter, Lt. Wickham coughed deliberately, waving her empty glass. *Urge to kill rising* . . . But homicide would complicate her already-ridiculous week, so instead she poured more whiskey, adding a mark to her To Drink tally.

The door chime rang again, and Ree looked up to see Drake walk in. She dual-booted her response, happy to see a friendly face with one partition, worried about the imminent throwdown with the other.

Lt. Wickham turned on the barstool and narrowed her eyes as Drake walked in.

"Well, look what the Cait Sidhe dragged in," she said, a cruel smile on her face. "Where's your kindergarten-crafting lady friend, Drake? Got a paper cut on construction paper?"

Drake stopped in place and sighed.

"Good day, Lieutenant Wickham. It brings me the greatest pleasure to see that your life is still meaningless and unfulfilling enough that you feel the need to tear down other's accomplishments to make your own seem to stand tall by comparison."

Boom! Ree thought, cracking a smile.

"Today I acquired a collection of ray guns, posed for a cover spread, and wrote four thousand words of essay, including a reminder for my readers to avoid that terrible gallery show. What have you done?"

"Science," Drake said, annoyance shadowing his face as he crossed to the bar. The fact that Wickham could make Drake, one of the happiest, most glowingly optimistic people she knew, go to the angry place, should be proof of her vileness by itself.

Grognard's gone . . . Could I get away with a smackdown? How much would we really miss her business? Ree pondered an assortment of verbal and physical recourses while Drake and Wickham continued to spar.

Drake took a position at the opposite end of the bar from Wickham, throwing back his duster as he sat. Ree met him at the seat, presenting him with an ice water. He nodded to Ree and held up the glass. "To your health."

Out of the corner of her eye, Ree saw Wickham glare. The rest of the customers were still locked in their individual worlds, with no seeming interest in the Steampunk Showdown.

When Ree had asked Drake why Wickham was always after him, all the displaced magitechnician had said was that their priorities were catastrophically incompatible. Which, as far as Ree could tell was his way of saying *I hate her.* But Drake was too classy to come right out and say something like that.

Ree, however, was not too classy, but she liked keeping her job. So she locked onto Lt. Wickham in her peripheral vision while talking to Drake.

"How was the art show?"

Drake's smile was even wider than his usual grin. This was a grin sufficiently rakish that it sent shudders of implication down Ree's back. That was an *I got action* kind of smile.

"Quite fabulous. Due to having work in the show, we were able to attend the private showing, which included hors d'oeuvres, music, and a performance of one of the artist's short plays. It is quite a community, Ree, and no small amount of comfort to be once again among people dressed in the manner of my home."

Drake considered for a second. "More or less."

"That sounds awesome!" Ree leaned in. "Did anything else happen?" she asked, making the leading question as clear as she could, Curiosity having since hog-tied Jealousy and left it in the alley.

At this, Drake blushed, picking up his drink and taking a sip, breaking eye contact.

"It did!" Ree said, a little bit too loud for the room.

Drake pursed his lips, drawing back from the bar a shade. "I do not feel comfortable discussing those matters, Ms. Ree."

Ree wanted to push, to figure out just how tangled this love n-gon had become, but Jealousy had slipped its bonds thanks to Self-Restraint (irony!).

"Fair enough. Glad it was fun. You headed to Market tonight?"

"Indeed. Will you be Grognard's purveyor of ale?"

"You know it. Only booth babe gig I could stomach."

Grognard emerged from the back, as if on cue. "If you're a booth babe, then I'm a shoo-in for a Sailor Moon costume contest."

Ree raised an eyebrow. "You saying I'm not pretty?"

Grognard scoffed. "You don't need to fish for compliments. You know as much about the mainstays of geekdom as nearly anybody there. As soon as you can give a full litany of all of the Robins in order, you've leveled out of 'booth babe.' Now come help set up the taps on the cart."

"Roger that," Ree said with a grin. On her way to the back room, she looked over her shoulder and asked Drake, "You headed over soon?"

Drake nodded once, then saluted Ree as he stood.

CHAPTER ELEVEN

Corner of Geneva and Talsorian

Pearson's Midnight Market is one of the oldest in North America, dating to 1963. Watch your step and your wallet. The Midnight Market is officially neutral territory, but squabbles and rivalries often simmer close to the surface.

Local magicians and vendors hawk their wares, and there's something for every discerning magician: a quartz for your summoning circle, an overclocked netbook that can dial directly to Spirit, or a rare graphic novel to complete your ritual.

Be sure to catch the auction, but don't bother bringing cash; all bids are for barter. And watch your back as you head home.

— Not For Mundanes: Pearson

The Midnight Market was a zoning nightmare. Or it would have been if anyone who cared about those codes could ever find the place. Somewhere along the line, the city (or maybe not the city) had built a football-field-sized hall beneath street level, complete with ten-foot-wide pillars and blank-slate walls. Most of the time, it stood mostly empty, but once a month, it served as meeting place, trading post, and town hall for Pearson's magical underground.

Ree had set up the Grognard's Games and Grog cart in its place of honor, at the intersection of Geneva Lane and Talsorian Row. They weren't actual streets, but since the Market had been active for more than twenty years, repetition had become tradition, and tradition had been enshrined. Folks told Ree the customary lanes of traffic had been named for a decade before people started making signs, but now, every intersection sported handmade signposts, with smaller signs attached at various angles, pointing the way to individual carts and booths, both the exits, and the auction area.

The market reminded Ree of a small city convention crossed with the Goblin Market. And it was awesome. Well, when she wasn't ambushed fifty yards outside the agreed-upon neutral ground of the Market . . . like the first time, with Eastwood. *Screw you, Lucretia. My vengeance will be served with a side of dumping-beer-on-your-priceless-lacy-dress.*

But the Market itself was safe, at least tonight. Like usual, her neighbor to one side was Uncle Joe's booth, where he broke open his CCG singles collections to show and sell (alphabetized by artist, of course). Across Geneva Lane, one of the main "streets," was Kuo's Komics, specializing in independent comics and merchandise. Kuo had his head so deep into manga and comics that when he spoke, speech bubbles popped up in front of him—a side effect of decades of genre emulation. He restrained the effect out in the normal world, but according to him, that was like intentionally speaking in another accent—not hard to start, but very hard to maintain.

Across from Kuo was Mirrorshade Designs, the shop of a local technomancer who had come up in the '80s and treated the oeuvre of William Gibson like a lifestyle bible. Some of the devices he sold were older than Ree, but they were painstakingly maintained, most of them in as good shape as a straight-off-the-line iPhone. Apple IIes stood proud beside ancient Ataris, boom boxes, and more.

But Shade's real treasures weren't the refurbished units, they were the kitbash stuff he made himself. Shade restricted himself to parts from '81 to '90, which as far as she could tell was some ritual constraint for his magic. But what he did with them was astonising—cyberware, magical radar scanners, laptops that took thirty-year-old parts and outperformed a retina-display MacBook.

To Ree's left, across Talsorian Row, was Talon's Blades, which looked like a generic Fantasy Sword Shop, complete with totally unrealistic blades and rows after rows of knives. Except Talon's wares were all film and TV surplus, mostly lower-end, each one imbued with a special kick of one sort or another. Some were the knives used by sexy ninja chicks in bad action movies and would fly straight over twice the normal distance; some were holdout knives used by the hero to cut their bonds and would shear through steel cables.

For the last three months, Ree had been ogling a hero copy of the knife Aragorn used in *The Lord of the Rings* while he was fighting Lurtz. But at two grand, ogling was all she could afford.

Talon hopped across the row to order a beer. Patricia Talon (Strength 15, Dexterity 15, Stamina 13, Will 16, IQ 13, Charisma 10—Geek 3 / Blacksmith 5 / Swordswoman 4) was second-generation Scottish Sword Geek, born and raised in the Society for Creative Anachronism. She stood five-eleven in flats (six-one in her stompy boots) and kept her brownish-red hair back and up, a feminine approximation of a bushi's topknot, without the pesky pate-shaving. She dressed in leather over leather, serving "Boffer LARP by way of the biker bar." She wore three visible knives:

one at the hip, another on her thigh, and the third stuffed into one boot, and Ree bet there were another four she couldn't see.

"What gives, Ree? It's dead tonight." Talon was right. It was only eleven, but the crowd was still strangely thin. Ree'd been so caught up in her own drama that she had no idea if something else was going down. Drake had stopped by for a pint of beer with an awkward chitchat chaser, then wandered off to talk gears and gadgets with the merchants over in Clockwork Corner.

Ree shrugged. "No idea. I haven't heard of anything going down. Maybe folks are taking a month off?"

Talon quirked an eyebrow. "You're still new-ish, but the last time this many people 'took a month off' was when a mob of Cinemancers tore through town trying to buy up merch and IPs like we were a boomtown waiting to happen." Talon shook off a chill. "Give me a pint of the Dunkel."

Ree nodded, pulling a glass off the stack and pouring the drink. "Well, there are a lot of film crews here, right?"

Talon shrugged. "Yeah, but it's been like that from March to October every year since Mayor Yu signed the new regs. But most of those crews don't have Big-League Celebromancers."

Talon's look told Ree to expect what was coming next, so she sipped some of her own beer.

"Hear you've been getting close with Konrad. I bet you don't need anyone else to tell you that she's trouble."

Ree handed Talon the full glass. "No, but coming from you, it sounds even scarier. If *you* think she's trouble . . ."

Talon took a drink, then set the glass down on the cart and indicated her ring. "Hey, I'm happily married." Talon's husband was an insurance lawyer, which had originally confused Ree.

But then she'd heard how they met.

"Yeah, to a former Tuchuk," Ree said. The Tuchux were a Gorean society that played with the SCA but weren't really part of it. They dressed in leather and loincloths, featured Dom/Sub pairings with slave contracts, and, according to Talon, were fucking terrifying to come across on the battlefield, despite the fact that they nearly all wore the bare minimum legal armor.

Talon laughed. "Dan never was much of a Tuchuk. He just fell into it with his buddies."

"You still have the best meet-cute ever." The two had faced off in the championship match for an armored combat tournament at Pennsic. She'd beaten him fair and square, and his fratboy-turned-Tuchuk buddies had never let him hear the end of it.

But he'd ended up with a wife and a way out of the Tuchux, so he called it a win. At least, according to Talon. He had mostly retired from the SCA and had never been into the magic world to begin with.

Talon shrugged. "Just think. If he'd ducked that swing, I might never have known him from Adam."

Ree tried to imagine the fight, making a storyboard in her mind, switching between medium shots of the fight and close-ups of their significant glances through the eye slots of their helmets.

"So what else have you heard about Jane Konrad? Or the show Rachel MacKenzie is working on? My sources tell me that MacKenzie has a hate-on for Jane, but I don't know what she's doing about it." Ree didn't feel like disclosing the fact that her "sources" involved sneaking into a closed set; not a detail Talon needed to know.

The magic community in Pearson was tight. But even tight, it was anything but homogenous. She'd tried to build a map of the factions and subgroups and had gotten tired when her graph had gotten more convoluted than the board on *The L Word*. Ree felt like she trusted Talon as much as almost anyone in the Market—not as much as Drake, but more than the average Geekomancer (though since there was no such thing as an average Geekomancer, making the whole thing even more complicated).

Talon took a long swig from her glass. "Haven't heard much.

MacKenzie has the mantle of America's Sweetheart locked up, and Konrad's in a death spiral. Seems to me all MacKenzie has to do is keep clear and Konrad will do herself in." Talon shrugged.

"You might take a lesson from her, Ree. Opportunities are great and all, but this one has disaster written all over it. They don't make Celebromancers like they used to. These days the stars all get their power through sex tapes, online feuds, and reality shows."

Ree shook her head. "That's not Jane. And my loyal streak runs about as long as my stubborn streak." A shiver hit her arms, and she tried to shake it off. Just nerves.

Talon toasted with her glass. "Good luck." Ree raised her own glass in salute, and they both drank. Talon took her pint back across the row when a graying man with a Radio Flyer wagon full of miniatures cases wheeled his way into Talon's booth.

The hall filled out a bit leading up to midnight, and a notable proportion of the crowd stopped by the cart for a drink to nurse during the auction. She'd miss the auction itself while womaning the cart, but the steady trickle gave her the chance to pump more people for information.

"I heard MacKenzie took a *geas* to never wear anything but couture," said Uncle Joe, who collected another Guinness, still thumbing through a stack of cards.

"Last I heard, she's putting everything she has into the divorce," said a short Black woman with an anime-patterned hijab and a broadsword bigger than she was strapped to her back. "They've got the biggest baddest lawyers at it, and no one is pulling punches."

"She's making a bid for an Arcana spot, I heard. Going for Empress," said a small white woman whose name Ree didn't know. She showed up to every Market in a TOS Star Trek communication officer outfit, complete with boots and earpiece.

Ree knew the Tarot, but had no clue how a mortal could become part of/supplant one of the major Arcana. And frankly, she had enough on her mind. Still, she dutifully filed the rumor under *WTF?* and went back to business.

Finnish ass-kicker-for-hire Sven Carlssen neglected to answer her query about Rachel MacKenzie, but he wasn't too proud to swing by for a bottle of imported Finnish Ale (which Grognard stocked for that express purpose). The mountain-sized mercenary didn't seem to harbor Ree any ill will, despite having tried to maim her in the sewer six months ago. Ree, however, had vengefulness for everyone. *A little for you, a little for Lucretia, and a lot for Wickham. One day, I will be the fucking Oprah of Vengeance.*

Luckily, other people had more to say than the Finn.

"I hear she loves to find little out-of-the-way fountains and read. She doesn't take her guards, even uses a glamour to avoid notice," said Shade. Shade Turing, of the Obvious Pseudonym Turings (Strength 10, Dexterity 12, Stamina 8, Will 16, IQ 17, Charisma 14—Geek 4 / Rigger 6 / Cyberpunk 4 / Salesman 3), was a thicker Black man of fortyish, wearing a two-piece royal purple suit and matching mirrored shades. The techie held up a pair of totally outrageous sunglasses. "But with these, you can see through any veil!"

"Nearly any veil," Talon said from across the row. Ree raised an eyebrow, but Talon just shrugged.

Shade smiled through Talon's comment, grabbing Ree's attention again, his drink forgotten. "Nearly any veil! Money-back guarantee, cross my heart and hope to de-rezz!"

He was charming, in a Max Headroom kind of way.

But charms wouldn't get her past a half-dozen Holly-wood toughs and fifty twitchy PAs. Probably. The shape-shifting had worked, just not long enough. And if she could pin down MacKenzie's picnic spot, then it might be her best chance of forcing a confrontation on her own terms.

"But she brings guards, right?" Ree asked Shade.

"Of course. But usually only two or three. And I heard she prefers places without cell signal so she can avoid calls. So, what do you say?" Shade produced a tape from seemingly nowhere.

"Only a hundred bucks, and I'll throw in this Betamax tape of *The Rocketeer*!"

Not that she had a Betamax player, but still! *The Rocketeer* topped Ree's Underrated Pulp Adventure Movies list, along with *The Shadow* and *Dick Tracy*.

Ree checked her wallet. "I don't have a hundred on me. Can I pay you half today and half tomorrow?" she asked.

Shade produced his smartphone, which had a credit card swiper attached. "Baby, I'll take it any way you like."

Ree snorfled a laugh. "Sure, just don't call me *baby* again."

The merchant held the phone out, swiper toward Ree. "Sure thing, sugar."

Ree rolled her eyes as she swiped her card. Shade consulted the phone, and a few seconds later, he passed it to Ree to sign with her finger.

I love living in the future, Ree thought, handing the phone back to Shade. He set the shades on the cart, along with the tape, then picked up his pint of Russian Imperial Stout and toasted Ree as he stepped away.

This is almost sounding like a plan. Assuming I can figure out where she takes her getaways. And assuming I can get past her guards. And that she doesn't just blast me off the face of Earth with Fame-doukens when I try.

Ree got a few more tidbits about MacKenzie from other visitors throughout the auction, but nothing she hadn't already gotten from Charlie's Twitter info-dump.

Midnight Market closed up around 2 AM, leaving Ree to wheel the cart through the sewers back to Grognard's. It wasn't a long trip, and it stayed clear of all of the known monster dens, but it was still one woman and a cartful of expensive beer.

Well, one woman, one man, and a cart. Drake had lingered at the Market for seemingly no better reason than to escort her back. *For a guy who's dating one of your best friends, he's awfully chummy*, a voice in her head nagged as they made their way through the poorly lit, could-be-romantic tunnels.

As Ree started to turn the cart around a corner to get on the last stretch to Grognard's, all the lights in sight went out at once, like someone hit a switch.

"Oh, bother," Drake said.

Well, frak me, Ree thought, reaching for her lightsaber.

CHAPTER TWELVE

Nothing Good Happens after 2 AM

Traveling in Pearson's sewers is a terrible idea. Unless you want to avoid the gangbangers on the west end, if you need to get to the Market, Grognard's, or any of the other dozen hot spots built under the Pearson that most people know.

So basically, you have to do it, even when you don't want to.

Walk quietly, carry plenty of ammunition, avoid the gnomes, and whatever you do, don't let your light go out.

—Eastwood, personal correspondence with Branwen nic Catrin

R ee's lightsaber lit the tunnel in a pale-blue light, revealing hundreds of tiny shadow-bat things that looked disturbingly similar to the not-so-friendly fauna from *Pitch Black*.

She waved the lightsaber, trying to get a better look at the creatures as the light passed over them. They shied away from the light, clinging to the walls and hovering in the air on hummingbird wings.

"The fuck?" Ree asked.

"I'm afraid I have no idea, Ms. Ree," Drake said, his voice thin, tense. Drake touched something at his neck, and light spread out to his front like a wearable flashlight.

"Lucretia? Is this one of your tricks?" Ree shouted, making a guess as to who might be responsible for her current probably-going-to-die predicament.

There was no answer, just the sound of claws on stone and wings flapping in the air. The creatures clustered together, forming a near-solid mass.

That's not good, Ree thought. And then, of course, they charged.

Ree cut a swath through the creatures, jumping to the side as they hit. She avoided the majority of the attacking swarm, only taking slashes and bites along her legs and abdomen. The pain hit her like a splash of still water pushed off of an awning. But she gave as good as she got, a handful of creatures hitting the sewer floor in smoking pieces.

Drake's rifle fired several times, green light from the blasts mixing with her lightsaber's blue. More creatures fell, but the mass continued, rolling off the wall and coming at Ree again.

Fucking Swarm rules, Ree thought, biting back the pain. The saber and Drake's gun wouldn't do nearly enough damage to keep them alive for long. The light seemed to deter the creatures a bit, but she needed bigger guns.

"On me!" Ree said as she bolted behind the cart and pawed for the panic button that Grognard had installed. The creatures swarmed over the mobile bar, carving gashes into the wood and doing their best to shred it to kindling. Ree knocked over glasses and spilled bottles as she searched, trying to avoid the shards of now-broken glass. She reached out with her legs and hooked them around Drake's waist as she depressed the button.

There was a thick *whoom* sound, and Ree felt a burst of energy push out, washing over her and knocking the creatures back and away. A dome of energy rippled around the cart at a diameter of about ten feet, and the claws and bites of the creatures strained against it.

Grognard had enchanted the cart with a circle of protection, fed by a small gas oven that used Land cards from *Magic: The Gathering* for kindling.

"With a full deck, it should last about five minutes, less for every bit of constant attack. Pray you won't need it," the bald bartender had told her the first night he sent her out to Market.

Ree looked back from the mass of creatures to Drake, who stared around with wide eyes. "Quite remarkable!" he said, shifting his weight to sit up. "If you don't mind, Ms. Ree." He looked down to her legs, which were still vise-gripped around Drake's midsection.

"Sorry," Ree said, letting go with her legs and finding her own feet, careful to keep the lightsaber clear of the cart, any body parts, and the dome of energy. The lightsaber was still their brightest source of light and omnidirectional, unlike Drake's shotgun-spray amulet.

Ree stood, inspected the cart for damage, and pronounced it fit to haul ass. She called Drake over, and the two of them pushed the cart, Ree on the right, holding the lightsaber off to the side for light. She'd be better off getting out her actual flashlight, but a flashlight wouldn't do her a fat lot of good if the circle of protection gave out before they got back to Grognard's.

She couldn't call the store for help, since the store's cell signal extended about three-and-a-quarter to five feet beyond its sewer entrance, despite Grognard's best efforts. So all they could do was book it back to the store. That and pray.

"It's not far," Ree said, as much for herself as to encourage Drake.

Drake strained against the cart, which wobbled like a drunken kitten, thanks to a cracked axle. "I am doing my right best, Ms. Ree." He had a determined look on his face, along with scratches and bruises, including a welt that was swelling his right eye shut, half-blinding him. Ree knew she was probably just as bad off, but that was pretty far down her list of worries. Said list had gotten so big it no longer fit in the overhead compartment of her short-term attention.

More than a hundred feet down the tunnel, Ree saw lights on, including the blue bulb that signaled the store entrance.

The creatures continued to slam into the sphere, their impact like heavy rain on a windshield. If rain had teeth, claws, and off-white eyes.

Inside the bubble, the air wasn't circulating, instead recycling the smells of sweat and fear from the two of them, and the sharp scent of burning cards.

"Almost there!" Ree said, pushing harder, trying to keep the cart steady.

The left wheel, closer to the sewer side of the ledge hit something, making the whole cart lurch. Ree held on to the right side, but as it bounced back to the concrete, it veered left, the desperate momentum she and Drake had built carrying it straight off the side and into the river of sewage in the middle of the tunnel. And this with the blue light of Grognard's and the promise of safety less than eighty feet away.

With the cart thus felled, the protective circle filled out, creating a full sphere. The lightsaber slipped from her hands and reverted to its prop form, rolling around in the base of the sphere.

"Goddamned monkey fuck!" Ree shouted, pitching with the cart as the sphere bobbed up and down in the muck. In the faintest blue light, Ree saw impressions of the creatures pressing at the edge of the bubble, teeth chittering with anticipation like a tomcat eying a wounded bird.

But this bird is no fledgling, Ree thought, pawing through her bag, taking the moments to search for the flare she'd buried somewhere near the bottom. Ree stood and held up the flare, her feet making waves of energy on the shield.

"What now?" Drake asked, balanced on the curve of the sphere like it was a mountain slope, his rifle gripped in his left hand.

The shield held for the moment, but Ree didn't want to bet that Grognard had designed the stove-crucible-magic thing to take this kind of abuse. Ree looked to the blue light, hoping that just maybe, Grognard had stayed late and heard the crash.

"Fuck," Ree said, thinking.

"I do not imagine that is the plan?" Drake said, managing a half-rakish smile.

"Perv." Ree answered his grin by sticking her tongue out. She waved the unlit flare at his rifle. "Do you have a flame-thrower setting on that thing?"

Drake's eyes went wide for a moment, but he reached into his coat and pulled out a red-orange crystal. He pulled a slide and removed the green crystal, replacing it with the red. "This will not last long, I'm afraid. The rate of energy consumption removes the possibility of a sustained gout."

Ree scanned around and noticed that the sphere of energy had gotten tighter, the creatures pressing in. Ree dropped to the shimmering floor of the wedged-in sphere and found the edge of her lightsaber, snatching the prop back up and holding it ready in her right hand.

"I don't think we have time for a better plan." She didn't have the right cards on hand to get them both to safety. For a sideboard that big, she'd need to carry around whole folders like Uncle Joe.

"When I drop the shield, you blast a path in front of us, and we make a run for it," she said, speaking to Drake but keeping her eyes on the creatures.

She waited, hoping for a shift in their tides that they could use, but the waves were too close together, the creatures relentless in their assault.

Persistent buggers, aren't you?

"Ready?" she asked. Drake had shifted his weight onto the cart, which would be the only solid ground once the shield disappeared. She joined him, then said, "Go!" as she pressed the button.

All at once, the dome vanished, Ree's lightsaber ignited, the beam passed through the tip of the flare, lighting it as well, and Drake opened fire, his rifle throwing a cone of flame ten feet long and five feet wide at the end. Ree and Drake jumped off the cart and onto the walkway.

Ree spun the lightsaber and flare around her as she cut a defensive pattern over herself and Drake, turning as she dashed forward, trying to cover all angles of attack. The two of them moved in concert. Drake fired belches of flame from his rifle as the creatures massed and pressed the attack, then lowered his weapon as Ree's blade spun around through the space he'd just occupied.

"Run!" Ree said, letting Drake outpace her. She turned and spun the lightsaber in a figure eight behind her as she sprinted.

The creatures followed on her heels like collections agents from hell, even as the flame and saber cut them down by the dozen. Ree felt cuts accumulate on her arms, legs, and back, but ahead she saw Drake throw open the door, granted access to the warded door by virtue of his membership in Grognard's list of trusted clients.

Drake said, "Slide!" and without thinking, Ree dove to her side as Drake fired a blast through where she'd been, burning off a cluster of the creatures. The two of them scrambled inside, pulling on each other. Ree hauled the door closed, endlessly glad for the part of the enchantment that rendered the door nearly weightless to members and staff.

The door slammed closed, and Ree pawed for the drop latch. Once it slammed into place, Ree found the light switch to illuminate the room.

Grognard had clearly gone home, as the place was already spotless, and totally empty.

Ree deactivated her lightsaber and slumped to the floor.

Fuuuuuck, Ree thought as she gasped, catching her breath.

Her lungs burned like a brush fire doused in kerosene.

She looked to Drake, who had dropped to one knee, panting.

"So what in the name of Riddick was that?" Ree asked.

Drake raised an eyebrow. His gaps in pop culture knowledge were closing, but slowly.

"I haven't a notion, Ms. Ree. But well done, nonetheless. With less astute company, I imagine I'd be being digested presently."

"Part of you looks like it was already," Ree said, seeing the man's many wounds.

"Well, there is that. I'd say a trip to Dr. Wells is in order, except . . ." Drake trailed off, waving to the door.

Ree nodded. Except the doctor was back out there, through the tunnels. Or an amusingly tricky trip through the basement of an Armenian and Turkish apartment building.

Grognard had a full medical kit in the back room, and between the two of them, they patched up the worst of their cuts and bites. When all the gauze was said and done, Drake looked like he'd joined a Fight Club populated by goblins, but he wasn't going to bleed out any time soon.

Ree didn't look any better. "Okay, we can take the easy way out here, but I've got to leave a note for Grognard to try and lessen the chance that he'll rip out my liver and use it to strain his next batch of stout."

Drake nodded, draping a towel over a stool to keep the blood from staining it as he took a seat.

What the fuck is going on with all this random monstrosity? Did the universe's GM get a new Monster Manual or something? Ree pushed aside the implications of the universe running on game supplements as she searched through papers at the bar to find something she could write on and not spoil an artifact or mess up Grognard's byzantine organization system.

Moving a stack of paperwork, she noticed a gold-plated pocket watch with a sticky note attached to it. The watch had a classic look, analog numbers, burnished metal, and a manual winder.

The handwriting on the note was Eastwood's.

Kid,

I hear you've been tangling with Celebromancers.

Thought this might come in handy.

Turn it to 12:16 and Andy's your uncle.

—E

Ree examined the watch, looked at the note again, then smiled knowingly before stashing the watch in her coat.

Finally discovering a piece of real, honest scratch paper, she started her note to Grognard. She didn't even try to sugarcoat the situation, since Grognard wouldn't have any of it.

She even left out her suspicions of who might have been responsible (Lucretia), or what she was going to do to whomever was responsible (description not suitable for professional fucking discourse).

After sticking her note to the cash register, Ree did one more walk around the store, seeing if there was anything she could tidy or take care of to feel like she'd gotten something useful done, given that she had just lost hundreds of dollars in cash, several hundreds more in product, a three-thousand-dollar handmade cart, and Grognard's totally awesome if ultimately-insufficient shield device.

And on top of that, I left the goggles and tape in the cart. Another $100 down the drain . . . literally.

Not my best day on the job.

She plucked her phone out of her pocket as she walked back to leave with Drake, and saw that she had three voice-mails and ten text messages from Jane, Yancy, and Danny. Ree stopped in place as she flipped through the texts, Instant Worry cooking in her stomach as she put the picture together.

But wait, there's more. Ree was almost afraid to listen to the voicemails, but listened anyway.

Ree worked her way down the list, then said, "Fuuuuck," as she set down the phone.

"What is the matter now?" Drake asked, concerned.

"I think someone's been having an even worse night than us."

CHAPTER THIRTEEN

Nightmare on Douglas Street

Another round of libel charges have been filed against Plugged (A Cosmic subsidiary) due to stories posted by its editor and creative director, Alex Walters.

Cosmic attorney Jessica Charles says the claims are baseless and that Cosmic has moved to have the charges dismissed as the last four rounds have been.

The plaintiffs (all Tower Media Agency clients) have asked for Judge Oswald Smith (who presided over the previous cases) to recuse himself, citing conflict of interest. Smith has recently come under fire for his wife's undisclosed holdings in various Cosmic subsidiary companies.

Walters is currently in Pearson, Oregon, covering the Cosmic production Blog Wars, *starring Rachel MacKenzie. When asked for a response, Walters deflected questions and began speaking about the latest exploits of fallen-from-grace star Jane Konrad.*

—SpiceOfLife.com, May 17

The first message was from Jane. She sounded out of it. In a normal world, Ree would have thought the star was drunk dialing her, but in her new world, Ree guessed she could pin it on the magic, carried away again like she'd been at dinner and dancing.

The second was from Yancy, also asking her to come over. He said Jane was restless, and it had been all he and Danny could do to keep her from going out.

The third message was also from Yancy, an hour later, saying that Jane had vanished from her trailer, the set area, and the surrounding blocks.

Fucking Carmen Sandiego *bullshit*, Ree thought.

"Feel like turning the city looking for a superstar?" Ree asked, feeling the weight of hours on her shoulders, along with a dulled undercurrent of pain.

Drake took a long breath, then said, "Certainly. Ms. Konrad, I presume?"

Ree nodded. "She's flown the exquisitely appointed coop."

Ree opened the app that held all of her media playlists. No way she'd be able to run Jane down just by walking the neighborhood, not if she didn't want to be found.

She pored through her videos as she led Drake out the office building entrance to Grognard's.

Batman? That wouldn't last. *Sherlock?* Maybe, but she'd need to spend time inspecting the scene, which would leave her with less energy to use the skills after leaving the set. One of the earlier X-Men movies might work, but she didn't have a Cerebro prop, so the range would be really short. Plus, she didn't relish the idea of trying to learn how to filter telepathy under pressure.

Buffy's "Earshot" told her that was a terrible idea.

What she really needed was a tracking prop. Maybe one of the props from the *Dresden Files* TV show was on the market.

Or she could dedicate herself to enjoying the short-lived show *Finder*.

"Where do we start?" Drake asked, breaking her train of thought. Ree looked up and saw that she had stopped to ponder in a lane of traffic. Since it was after 2 AM, there weren't any cars on the street, but there were a few going by the cross street.

She hurried forward a few steps onto the opposite sidewalk, then went back to thinking.

"Can you whip up a tracking device?" she asked.

Drake's head bobbed as he considered. "I should be able to adjust one of my existing devices, but I'll need something to calibrate: an item of Ms. Konrad's, or something with a strong semiotic tie."

Ree laughed. *Well . . .* "You could use me. I've spent a lot of time with her the last couple of days."

Drake raised one eyebrow, considering. The humor of the motion was accentuated by the fact that he almost certainly had no idea who Mr. Spock was or why that gesture was funny to her. "Possibly, but another item more singularly associated with Ms. Konrad would make it easier to pinpoint the aetheric wavelength."

"Would clothes work?"

Drake nodded. "Certainly."

Ree hoped Drake would be caught up in the hunt enough to not want to put things together.

What if he did? He's a big, if totally weird, boy.

Not important, she thought immediately after. *Priorities.*

"Then we make a quick trip back to my place, and we're off. Plus, that way I can change and restock."

No matter how short the trip through the sewer, Ree never felt fully human again until she got a shower. Not for the first time, Ree was very glad she didn't pay her water bill.

⬡

After the trifecta of shower, coffee, and Geekomantic weaponry restock, Ree was ready to go. By the time Ree plucked Jane's shirt out of the laundry, Drake had started his calibrations on a handheld astrolabe.

Ree tiptoed back out of her room, wearing a fresh set of black-on-black with an older pair of faded jeans that hung a bit loose on her (all the better to jump-kick you with, my dear).

"How goes?" Ree asked in a whisper.

Drake nodded, standing with the astrolabe, leaving the shirt on the table, neatly folded. "We may proceed at your leisure."

"Did you want some tea?" she asked.

"I will be fine, Ms. Ree. Thank you."

"You sure? Sandra has some wicked oolong," Ree said.

Drake smiled his smile of polite refusal. "No, thank you. Shall we away?"

They made their way back to Jane's trailer, and after feeding it (not literally) a semiotic anchor (Drake's words, not hers), the astrolabe was ready to go. The trail led them several blocks to the north, then east, heading into downtown. Ree watched most of an episode of *Buffy the Vampire Slayer* ("The Harvest") on the way over, and felt the energy of the magic zipping through her veins like quippiness caffeine.

She and Drake got more than a few odd looks from clubgoers, homeless people, and one police officer on the night beat. Ree thought the officer might have been one of the cops she'd met the night after the first attack, but when she was about to stop and ask, Drake took a sharp turn and said, "This way! The signal has become stronger in a most inexplicable manner!" and so she followed.

Drake lead them down Third Avenue, then paused in front of an active construction site, fenced off, yellow cranes and plows lit at odd angles by the streetlights, looking like a twentieth-century elephant graveyard.

"Here?" Ree asked.

Drake puckered his lips, then said, "So it would seem. The astrolabe says she is less than one hundred feet straight ahead."

Ree looked up and down the street. "We should go back and get that beat cop, have her help. I'm not excited about the idea of breaking and entering while she's in the neighborhood."

"I'm afraid that the extranormal matters of our situation would come out all too easily, Ms. Ree."

"Well, I'd rather have her on my side than slapping cuffs on us for an overnight visit to the lovely accommodations of the Fifth Precinct lockup. We'll just rely on the Doubt for this one." Ree turned and jogged back to where she'd seen the beat cop.

"Officer!" Ree called as she spotted the cop.

The woman turned and looked at Ree. "Yes?"

Ree looked both ways and then crossed the street, amused by the fact that she was jaywalking in front of a police officer.

"I'm Ree Reyes, I think we met at the *Awakenings* set."

The officer looked at Ree again, then nodded. She was just a couple of inches taller than Ree, was solidly built, and moved with smooth confidence. Her thick hair poked out from the sides of her hat but didn't obscure her vision.

"Yes, Ms. Reyes. What's the problem?"

"Jane Konrad is gone, and we have good reason to suspect she went into the construction site around the corner, and I thought it'd be a helluva lot of a better idea for us to tell you than to tresspass ourselves."

Ree waited while the officer considered. She shifted her weight to the other leg, then scanned the street. Apparently satisfied, she leaned into her radio, saying, "This is Washington, Badge #71359. I have a lead on Konrad. Proceeding on foot to the construction site on Third and Harrison, over."

The radio crackled, then there was a response in a bored female voice. "Stand by. We're sending another unit. Over."

Ree looked at Washington. (Was it Lieutenant Washington? Sergeant? Ree had never bothered learning the police visual ranking system . . .) "If she's in trouble . . ." Ree said, trying to catch the officer's attention.

"No good, dispatch," Washington said. "I'm proceeding on foot. Get the property manager on the line and tell them I've gone in. They should send somebody down."

"Washington!" the dispatcher said, but Washington turned a knob and dropped the volume to a whisper.

"You follow me, keep back ten feet, and don't talk unless I ask you to."

"Yes, ma'am?" Ree said, taken aback at the officer's Chaotic Good inclinations.

"Is it sergeant or lieutenant or?"

"When I ask, you can call me officer."

Wow, touchy much? Ree thought. *So she leans chaotic, doesn't want to wait for backup, but also doesn't want to talk?*

Ree wondered. *Then again, for all she knows, I'm a stuck-up Hollywood type. Give her respect, and maybe she'll return it. As long as she gets the job done and doesn't arrest us.*

Ree lead Officer Washington back to the construction site, where Drake had activated a glamour to make his totally illegal rifle appear as a walking stick and make most folks gloss over the obvious bits of his outfit. She could see the glamour like a transparent overlay, since the Doubt didn't do jack to her anymore.

"Good evening, Officer," Drake said, nodding to Washington.

"Who are you?"

"A colleague of Ms. Ree's." *Take the formality down by a notch or three, Drake. Even brusque cops aren't that old-timey.* Not that he could hear her, but she hoped he could read her body language, which she was trying to use to say *Play it cool.*

Washington passed Drake and pulled out her flashlight, looking the construction site over.

"And why do you think she's here?" Washington asked.

"She likes to be able to see the skyline," Ree said, almost before she knew it. Ree was surprised to remember that it was true. She'd said so during their dinner at Yoritomo's.

"Movie stars," Washington said, chuckling.

The officer kept walking, reaching the ten-foot-tall fence around the site. She eyed the fence, then holstered her flashlight and started climbing.

Ree looked to Drake, who shrugged, a motion that still looked too casual on him, even with his toned-down look.

"After you," he said. Ree handed her bag to Drake and then jumped up onto the fence, very glad that the construction company wasn't a fan of barbed wire.

Ten feet up, she could do. The ten stories up she might have to go in that building, with no walls and unfinished floors, that would be a whole different barrel of terror. Strangely, facing down atavistic fur-suited werewolves, flesh-eating gnomes, and Dork Lords of Hell had not cured her fear of heights.

She climbed up and over with magically-enhanced ease, lowering herself halfway down the other side before dropping to the ground. She'd have done a backflip over the fence, but she got the feeling she might need to save the magic for what would come next.

Ree looked away from the building and to Drake. "Toss me the bag?"

Drake nodded, keeping eye contact as he lobbed her bag over the fence. Ree caught it easily, between her *Buffy* magic and the fact that the bag wasn't as loaded down as it sometimes was. Taking her laptop into the field would really probably only ever do one thing: make her shop for a new laptop. She'd been considering Shade's rigs, but their toughness came with bulk and weight. She'd just have to trust her phone for the on-the-go power-up.

Which she had been planning on doing, except Washington was already booking for the building even as Drake was swinging one leg over the fence, trying to keep his jacket and rifle from tangling.

Washington was halfway across the ground level when Drake touched down, so Ree tapped into the *Buffy* magic and started dashing after her, moving like she was on a walkalator. She ate up the ground, closing in on the half-done building.

The building's walls were unfinished, and the soon-to-be-mega-office ended at the tenth floor, with a half-dozen girders poking up to suggest a roof yet to come. Orange floodlights illuminated the site from the ground and each floor. Washington stopped at the first-floor stairs, lit in forced profile by the light in the far corner.

Ree slowed to a stop ten feet out, and turned back to see Drake jogging over, his rifle unslung. *Careful, Drake,* she thought, wishing once more for projective (and only projective) telepathy.

Note to self: Research a show for telepathy. But one where they have good control and less of the maelstrom of a zillion voices.

"Keep a half flight back, and let me clear each floor before you come up and start making noise. Do you have flashlights?"

Ree produced a Maglite from her bag and clicked it on, the six-bulb light cutting through the dark like a laser. Drake pulled a foldout lantern from his jacket, snapped it together, then turned a knob to start the gaslight.

Ree laughed, which made Washington give her a suspicious look.

"He's just endlessly useful, isn't he?" Ree said.

Ree thought she heard Washington say, "Weirdos," under her breath as she started up the stairs. Ree turned to Drake and said, "Let's try not to freak her out unless something woogy shows up."

"*Woogy?*"

Ree laughed. "One day I'll get you caught up to modern lingo."

Drake shrugged. "And to think that I considered The

Queen's Tongue a deep language in my time. It seems there are fifty new words every day I could never have imagined in Avalon." Drake said this with a somewhat bittersweet smile, checking his rifle again, which looked very odd as Ree saw it both in reality and in the glamour, where Drake looked like a man playing pretend with a cane.

They followed Washington up the stairs as the police-woman cleared floor by floor. Ree knew without knowing that they wouldn't find anything until they got to the top floor. *Laws of dramatic narrative, y'know. No one stops a bomb before the clock reads 00:01, sibling enemies get more powerful one by one as you meet them, the big boss is always on the top floor of the tower, and so on.*

True to form, Washington didn't twig to anything until they got to the top floor. As the officer scaled the last flight of stairs, Ree poured on the speed and caught up, passing Washington on the top floor and turning left immediately, following her gut.

She didn't think she'd acquired the Vamp-sense from *Buffy*, but she'd learned to follow her gut (unless her gut was threatening to move out and find a new home in a less self-destructive body, then she denied it thrice and thrice again).

They were now high above the rest of the neighborhood, with a great view of downtown, the court building, and the Sky-If-It's-Falling-Scrapers. The drop-off was far away enough to keep her from freaking out right now, but she got the feeling she'd be seeing the building's edge before the night was through.

Right on cue, Ree spotted Jane in the corner of the build-ing, retreating from a shadowed figure. The figure looked like a moving glass case enclosing gray-black smoke, which moved and shifted like breathing lungs.

"Over here!" Ree shouted, signaling Drake and Washington and drawing the figure's attention all at once. There wasn't time to explain anything to Washington or negotiate, not with the fear she could see in Jane's eyes. The woman was a professional actress, which meant when she emoted, you could see it a hundred feet away. And unless she was putting in an Oscar-worthy performance, the star was Failed-Sanity-Check terrified.

The figure turned, but Ree didn't see a face, just more contained smoke.

"Put your hands up!" Washington said, her voice unsettled but not broken. The figure didn't move.

Ree saw Drake circle out to flank, his rifle/cane up and ready.

The illusion would likely break as soon as he fired, but it was past time for disguises. *Washington can arrest me if she wants once everyone is out and safe.*

Closing within fifteen feet, Ree drew a *Deep Space Nine*–era phaser and trained it on the figure. The whorls and waves of smoke moved quickly, but the figure's head didn't shift even as they flanked it.

"Get back, you two," Washington said.

"Sorry, Officer. Unless you're secretly a Black Cat cop, this is outside your realm . . ." As Ree cracked wise, the smoke figure launched forward, ripping Ree off her feet with one arm, dangling her a good two feet higher than her height justified.

Oh, crap. The figure was just as strong as before, its grip as tight as an ogre's. Ree fired the phaser at the creature's face, and it staggered back. With the figure distracted, Ree used the fading *Buffy* magic to rip herself free. She fell, she hit the deck hard, and her glasses slipped from her face.

Shitshitshitdamnfuck. She heard them bounce and rattle, so they couldn't be far out.

But without her glasses, Ree had worse eyesight than a myopic bat in a discotheque, and the *Buffy* magic didn't do anything for her vision. Ree tried a sweep kick, a desperation move to unbalance the figure and give her time to recover the glasses. *Good luck,* she thought, but she didn't let doubt and worry stop her. She guessed where the figure's legs should bend, and prayed for luck. She connected, but the leg didn't give. She saw a lighter-than-the-night blur coming for her, then a greenish flash. She heard a roar of pain, and the blur moved away. Ree rolled to put more distance between her and the creature.

With uncorrected vision, all Ree could see were dark patches and slightly less dark patches. She tried to paint a picture of the roof in her mind as she scrambled to her feet. Her jacket had a few more weapons and her stack of cards, but with the friendly-to-monster ratio on the roof three to one, firing at random was off the blurry table.

Ree backpedaled, keeping her hands up to defend herself, holding the phaser at the ready. "No glasses! A little help!"

She tried to focus on her sense of hearing and spatial awareness. Should have watched *Daredevil*.

"He is ten feet in front of you. Head right, and watch the pillar!" Drake said, his voice strained.

"Faster, Ree!" Washington added.

Ree scrambled faster, her gut turning like a washing machine.

Her danger sense was going bugfuck, and it was all she could do to keep moving.

Dear Future Ree,

If you survive this self-inflicted heroic quest, you are going to put money aside and buy yourself some goddamned contact lenses, and then you are going to wear them whenever things start coming up Murphy.

Love,

Contactless and Panicked Past Ree

Ree felt the strong hands grab her jacket, and the black in front of her wavered as she felt the comforting cement floor leave her behind.

"Help!" Ree called as Smokey lifted her up again. She felt both hands grab ahold of her, and then she tried to go limp, preparing for the impact, which would probably break her spine or neck or something else generally considered vital.

As Smokey brought her down, its grip slipped. Ree fell, landing on her side and tried to roll with the blow. Something in her shoulder tore, and she went slick with blood. She rolled sideways, turning over several times before she got her arms down to stop herself.

"Hold on, Ree!" Drake yelled. Ree heard the sound of boots on concrete, a brief bright flash, then an empty yell, like an amplified bass drum.

She staggered to her feet, the phaser gone somewhere between her trips to the concrete.

Ree grabbed mental hold of the *Buffy* energy and muted the pain, trying to regain her composure and keep herself from dropping due to the bonfire of pain in her shoulder.

Ree heard a thud, then a smack. Another strong hand, this one smaller, wrapped around her elbow, and pulled her to one side.

"Quickly!" said a voice. Washington's.

"What's happening?" Ree asked, her ears hot. *Definitely contacts.*

"Your friend is going toe-to-toe with a shadow monster, and neither of you seems to be surprised. So . . . that's weird."

"I can explain later. Where's Jane?" Ree asked.

"Still where she was. I'm taking you to her. She has your glasses."

Hallefuckinglujah.

Ree speed-walked, turning with Washington's not-at-all-subtle steering.

"Here you are. Any tips on taking this thing out?"

"Ree!" This was Jane's voice, rushed, breathless. Ree felt something press into one hand. She ran a finger over it. It was her glasses. She brought them to her face as Washington let go of her other arm.

Her left lens was cracked just inside the frame, but she

could still see. True enough, Drake was in melee with the creature, dodging and weaving. He held a kukri in one hand and used his rifle as a defensive cane with the other. The creature's smoke had settled a bit and moved about less.

Is that bad or good? Ree tried to decipher as she searched her jacket for weapons or healing-y things, eager to get back in the fight.

Her right arm was numb from shoulder pain, so getting back in the fight would actually be a terrible idea, even with her remaining *Buffy* magic. But Drake was no knife fighter.

Right on cue, Smokey connected with a haymaker and sent Drake flying.

The man-out-of-time slid off the edge of the roof, catching himself and dangling with all of his weight on one arm.

No time.

"Fire!" Ree shouted to Washington, who popped off three quick shots from her service weapon. Smokey staggered forward with each impact, then turned to face Washington as Ree ran to Drake.

"Hold on to the rifle," Ree said as she closed on Drake, his chin resting on the concrete. She squatted down and grabbed the rifle with her good arm, leaning back to pull the adventurer up.

"Jane? Help?" Ree asked through gritted teeth as Drake tried to reach a leg up onto the concrete floor.

Ree felt her grip slipping, and tried to bring her right arm over to help. Her shoulder screamed in pain, but she kept pulling, her eyes locked on Drake's face: strained, eyes wide, lips curled in a determined snarl.

Her foot slipped forward an inch, and the dull roar of panic grew a few ticks louder in her mind. Her eyes zoomed past Drake down, down, down to the ground, far enough down she knew she'd die if she fell. She'd be helpless for several long, weightless moments, long enough to lose herself in terror before splattering on impact. Her grip faltered, and she had to catch the end of the rifle stock while she regained control of herself.

She stumbled to the ground, hitting her tailbone as she tried to keep traction.

Slim arms wrapped around her waist, and Ree felt Jane pulling on her, the woman's weight all the way back. Ree heaved again, pushing with her feet, trying to keep the pull constant on the rifle.

"Come on!" Ree shouted to no one in particular, then narrowed her eyes and breathed out hard, dive-tackling the fleeing super-heroine energy and hog-tying it to one last feat of strength.

She pulled with all of her might and some of *Buffy*'s, and one of Drake's boots hit the pavement. She kept pulling, pain washing back over her until her companion-in-arms hauled himself up onto the lip of the concrete floor.

Ree huffed out, "Good!" and fell backward, dropping to the floor, Jane behind and beneath her.

"Oof!" the star said, and Ree winced as she imagined the impact.

But when she saw Smokey hit Washington with a round-house punch, she put aside comfort and jumped back to her feet.

She Roadie Ran along the roof and snagged the phaser off the ground, then took a knee and aimed with her off hand. The phaser cut a red line through the air, which hit and dissolved within Smokey's form. The smoke slowed, growing more still.

"Over here, Smokey! Only I can prevent forest fires!" *Okay, not my best*, Ree admitted. She blamed the shoulder and the glasses and the general shittiness that had been her day. "Get out of there, Washington!"

The officer wrestled free and stumbled back several steps, clutching her side. Ree kept firing, adjusting the beam as Smokey crossed the roof at Ludicrous Speed.

"Why won't you go down!" Ree shouted, fumbling with her right hand in her jacket for an endgame.

She held her cards up and dropped the phaser when she saw her prebuilt combo.

Good ol' Channel/Fireball. Ree held on to the top two *Magic* cards, letting the other cards flutter to the ground over the now-inactive phaser. She stared down Smokey, now just ten feet away, and focused her will forward as she tore the cards. A crimson-and-orange burst shot forward like a cannonball, hitting Smokey dead-on. The blast knocked Ree on her back, calling up a fresh wave of shoulder pain on top of the bonfire-in-front-of-your-face heat and the instant migraine from using Channel to pour her own life energy into the blast.

For a moment, it was all Ree could do to breathe. She took air in and looked up. Smokey was gone, wisps of black-on-black smoke dissipating under the floodlight.

"Hot damn," Ree said, sighing with relief.

Ree savored the lack of imminent doom, threat of death, or dealing with heights. Three other sets of lungs breathed heavily beside her: Drake's, Jane's, and Officer Washington's.

"Jane, Drake," Ree said, waving weakly by means of introduction. Drake gave a deep bow of the head, not bothering to stand. *He can be taught informality!* Ree thought, a smile breaking on her face.

"Drake, Jane. Jane, Officer Washington. Officer Washington, Jane."

Officer Washington looked at the space where Smokey had been. "Is someone going to explain what the hell just happened here?"

Ree looked to Drake, then to Jane. Drake looked impassive, and Jane shrugged. *I guess that leaves me.*

"We're not totally sure ourselves. And here's the thing, Officer. There's a good chance that in ten minutes, you won't remember what happened here, or this conversation. So I figure I've got about a 50/50 chance of needing to even bother, as long as we leave this half-built death trap in a hurry and make our way back to the set."

Officer Washington snorted, her face smacked with disbelief. "Like hell. That thing is going to be headlining in my nightmares for weeks. I'd say it'll be a nice change from the meth-heads and Krokodil junkies, but those I at least understand."

"Krokodil?" Jane asked, her eyebrows furrowed. She looked tired.

Not like I don't, Ree thought. But Jane's tired carried the descriptor *haunted*, while Ree imagined hers was more *harried*.

Officer Washington shook her head. "You're better off not knowing."

Ree nodded. "Some things cannot be unseen. 4chan, Two Girls One Cup, and Krokodil."

"I still haven't gotten an explanation for what happened," Washington said.

Ree wobbled to her feet, then thought better of it and sat down again, her vision going starry. "As near as I can tell, it was some magical being targeting Jane, either a manifestation of a curse or being commanded by the same. But that's about all I know, since it's only the second time I've seen the thing. So, are you a Black Cat or what?" Ree asked.

"I don't follow," Washington said.

"*Dresden Files*. The Chicago cops who deal with supernatural stuff were called Black Cats back in the day. Why didn't you lose your shit when you saw Smokey here?" Ree gestured to where Smokey had been.

"Training, I guess."

"Right good training, I say," Drake said, looking impressed.

Washington shrugged. The gesture humanized her, softened the single-minded-ass-kicker persona Ree had pegged the cop with. "Will it come back?"

Ree hauled herself back up to her feet, pushed through the strain in her vision, then scooped up her scattered cards. "I have no clue. It seems unlikely, at least tonight. Last time we scared it off pretty easily, but this time it was pretty Terminator-y."

Rummaging through her bag, Ree found the right baggie and

grabbed several *Descent* healing potions. She ripped one with her teeth, and the energy washed over her like ice-cold water.

When the cold receded, so did the pain in her shoulder. She held a potion token out to Drake, who looked at it and shrugged.

"I can't use those."

Ree tucked it back in her baggie. "Fair enough." She turned to Jane. "Are you okay?"

Jane got to her feet, and wiped the tears from her eyes. "I'll be fine. How did you know I was here?"

Ree nodded to Drake. "My friend here had a whoosa-mawhatsit. And I remembered what you said about liking a view."

Jane smiled. It was a small smile, a tired smile. But it was something.

CHAPTER FOURTEEN

4-Top

From: Alex Walters
a.walters@cosmic.com
To: PTB@cosmic.com
May 25, 4:17 AM

Subject: Override Request (was Re: Starlet Containment)

The Cameron solution has failed to yield results, as previously indicated. Requesting approval to break subtlety policies in order to seal the deal.
I've pulled a half-dozen critters out of films and sent them after the has-been's guardian, but this Reyes chick is a Leading Lady Geekomancer, with her own gang of Scoobies.
I want to have this BS cleaned up before I have to go back with MacKenzie for the divorce trial.

—AW

ˣ×ˣ⊗ˣ×ˣ

Ree, Drake, Jane, and Washington sat around a table at a twenty-four-hour Starbucks, which was empty except for the one bored-looking barista and an unsettled-looking homeless man nursing a short coffee in the corner, his life stuffed into a laundry cart.

Ree was halfway done with a cappuccino, Drake sipped tea, Washington was on her second cup of coffee, and Jane drank hot water. The whole scene reminded her of the after-credits bit in *The Avengers*.

Except no shawarma. I could murderate some shawarma.

"Shouldn't you be on shift or someting?" Ree asked.

"I'm taking witness statements," Washington said, raising her cup with a grin.

"But of course. Would that all chats with the constabulary might be so pleasant," Drake said.

"You can drop the act, Ren-Faire," Washington said.

"Not likely," Ree said. "He's a lifer."

Jane leaned into Officer Washington, both hands on her mug.

"Are you going to report this?"

"I pretty much have to, someone of your profile," Washington said. "Word has likely gotten out, and if we try to cover it up, there will be seven kinds of pushback."

"What would you report?" Ree adopted a nonchalant voice. "A mysterious figure of moving smoke that hit like a T-800 pursued movie star Jane Konrad onto a construction site, where it was subdued by a screenwriter, a Ren faire actor, and a young Pearson PD officer. Case closed?"

"This isn't the only weird thing to come across the dispatch, you know," Washington said. The fact that she hadn't forgotten the whole fight meant there hadn't been enough time, there hadn't been enough social or psychic distance from the event, or maybe the cop just wouldn't forget at all.

Could police training inoculate someone against the Doubt? If it did, you'd think either a lot more cops would end up dead or everyone would think they were crackpots when they tried to tell the mayor.

"Weird like what?" Ree asked.

"Mob deals gone strange, odd drugs with inexplicable side effects, dead-end missing persons cases that just feel wrong. Every beat cop and detective I've met has at least a few weird stories. And now I've got one more."

"Intriguing. In my homeland, there was no effort to cover up the marvels and terrors." Drake stopped to smell his tea, his eyes flashing through memories from an indeterminate past. "Though the powers that be may have just given up when the first of the torture ships crested over the horizon and began shelling the capital."

Jane and Washington looked at Drake like he was from Jupiter. *Well, not Jupiter, but close enough.* Ree tried not to explore the implications of her claim and moved on.

"So what's with the props and those cards?" Washington asked. "There's no way personal laser weapons have been invented without people finding out."

Ree looked to Drake, who shrugged unhelpfully, then turned her head back to Washington. "Off the record?"

The cop shook her head, rueful. "I'm going to have to pull some major Scully on this report as is. I don't need it getting any more complicated than necessary."

Ree raised an eyebrow at Washington, pondering, then began.

"There are many styles of magic. Drake has his techno-mantic Steampunk—"

"Though mine is more properly a science," Drake said, cutting in with a smile.

They'd had this discussion more than once. By this time, Ree knew he was just giving her crap.

Ree nodded, conceding the point. "But mine works off of fandom. What's your favorite movie?" Ree asked.

Washington cocked her head to the side. "*Die Hard.* Why does that matter?"

"Good choice. I love *Die Hard*, too. If I watched *Die Hard*, I could use magic to focus on how tough and inventive John McClane was, and I'd get some of that toughness, that inventiveness. I'd get to bring some of the action-movie physics he lived by in *Die Hard* into this world, be able to fight on when I should be moaning on the ground, maybe even get a flash of insight just in the nick of time, complete with a snappy one-liner."

Ree took a sip of her blissfully consistent cappuccino. "Every movie or show has something I can use, but only if I have a personal attachment to it. If I watched *The Expendables*, all I'd get is a headache, because I hated that piece of crap and have no desire to make any kind of connection with it."

Washington shook her head. "Never saw it."

"Don't. But that's the gist. Props and one-offs like those cards work a bit differently. They draw on the collective love and nostalgia from around the world. The combined nostalgia of all the Star Trek fans makes this phaser prop a real phaser, but only in the hands of someone like me. Make sense?"

Washington's eyes were wide, looking to Drake, then Jane, and back to Ree. "No, but I'll take your word on it. As far as I'm concerned, we chased a perp off and weren't able to pursue."

Ree nodded. "So you keep the weird stuff under wraps, we get Jane back to the trailer, and we're good?" Ree asked, begging the universe it would be that easy.

Washington leaned back in her seat, setting her cup down. She started listing off items on her fingers. "That's the start, but we're going to put a police detail on the set, the detectives will come back for more questions, and one of you is going to fill in the department—and by the department, I mean my captain—about what exactly is going on in this town. If your police force doesn't know what's going on with the magic and weird-shit community, we can't exactly protect you."

Ree stared into her cappuccino, hoping it would give her answers. She took a sip and waited for inspiration.

Nope, only caffeinated deliciousness with a hint of hazelnut.

"It's not going to be that easy. The magic underground is so complicated that it makes season six of *Lost* look like season one of *Lost*," Ree said.

Thankfully, Washington nodded. Jane laughed. And Drake just shrugged.

"So we can go, then? I could sleep for a week," Jane said.

"You think it'll be safe?" Ree asked.

Jane nodded. "Unless whoever it is can conjure another of those things right away, I should be fine."

"Then let's get to it." Washington stood, downed the rest of her coffee in one gulp, then moved for the door.

"Thanks, Mary," she said to the barista, who nodded.

"Later, Von."

Ree stood and hustled two quick steps to catch up. "Von?"

"Yvonne. My first name."

"And what is your rank? It seemed like you were jerking me around earlier."

"Just officer. Though after this, we'll see." Washington's eyes sparkled with ambition. Ree recognized the look from Jane's eyes, and from her own.

Three women driven by stubbornness and ambition, and a man driven by righteousness and curiosity.

What could possibly go wrong?

⊗

Ree left Jane at her trailer and caught a cab home, where she unlocked the door as quietly as she could then relocked everything behind her and snuck to bed. The cappuccino having barely made a dent in her fatigue, she hit the bed like deadfall.

And woke up to the sound of knocking.

"I don't want any," Ree mumbled. She clawed for her glasses, finding them and bringing them to bear to see Sandra in the doorway, wearing a towel around her torso and another one around her hair.

Sandra Wilson (Strength 15, Dexterity 13, Stamina 13, Will 12, IQ 17, and Charisma 13—Geek 3 / Scholar 3 / Dancer 1 / Teacher 1 / Waitress 1 / Chef 2 / Professional 1) was six feet tall and change, and built like a Themysciran from the George Perez era.

On the days that Ree felt down about her own looks, having a roommate like Sandra did not help. But she was kind, funny, financially stable, and giving to a fault.

"What's up?" Ree asked.

"It's eleven. Are you getting up at all today?"

"Do I have to?" Ree asked, trying to remember.

"I haven't seen you in three days. Is everything okay?" Sandra asked.

"This pilot is kicking my ass. And work was absurd yesterday." Like Charlie, Sandra thought Ree worked at a private catering service, since *magic gamer bar/hangout* wasn't exactly going to fly without a lot more explanation.

"Well, do you have time for brunch with the gang?"

"Only always," Ree said. She ignored the voice in her head that said she needed to be making plans, checking sources, and replenishing her armory. She'd promised herself that she wouldn't let the hero gig ruin her life, and damned if she was going back on that. The Rhyming Ladies had always been there for Ree, as long as she'd known them. Plus, *brunch* was code for "societally-approved opportunity for gorging on both breakfast and lunch foods."

Ree rolled out of bed and stretched, noticing she was still wearing last night's clothes, burned shoulder and all.

You don't notice the weird, Ree willed at her friend while trying to act nonchalant. *You want to get brunch.* "Let me get a quick shower, and I'm game. Where are we going?"

"Anya and Priya are meeting us at Top O' the Morning." Top O' the Morning was an intentionally kitschy Irish brunch place that took the Applebee's approach to interior decorating, narrowed the focus to gaudy Irish cultural artifacts and served it all up with a heavy dose of snark. It was Ree's kind of Irish joint.

Ree hauled herself into the shower and started daydreaming about the chocolate chip pancakes, the local sausage, and the heavenly scrambled eggs. The restaurant also served a fine selection of beers, ciders, and hangover cocktails, which they had over nearly every brunch place in existence.

A few minutes later, she had done her best to wash away the night, popped a handful of painkillers for good measure, and packed herself a small badass bag in case there was trouble.

She delayed just long enough to watch a few minutes of the *D&D* cartoon to pull a quick *Mending* on her glasses, and then set off for brunch.

×✕×⬡×✕×

Top O' the Morning was filled to the brim with brunchers: the sickeningly cute young couples, college students sobering up after a wild night, and, of course, Ree Reyes and the Rhyming Ladies. Despite all of her efforts, Ree had failed to get them to be a band.

When she and Sandra arrived, they saw that the other half of their quartet was already there—and seated. Ree wasn't sure who Anya and Priya had killed to get a table for four, but Ree would gladly help move the bodies.

Anya stood from the table to wave them over. Anya Rustova (Strength 7, Dexterity 12, Stamina 15, Will 15, IQ 16, Charisma 15—Musician 5 / Geek 2 / Scholar 4 / Opera Diva 3) was six feet of bombshell in a five-two figure. Today she was wearing an elaborate folded-over-itself pearl necklace and a leopard-print shirt, in concession to her Russian fashionista heritage.

Ree's heart split in two when she saw the fourth of their merry band, Priya. Priya Tharakan (Strength 8, Dexterity 13, Stamina 12, Will 14, IQ 17, and Charisma 15—Geek 3 / Professional 3 / Seamstress 4 / Steampunk 3 / Goth 2) was not your stereotypical Steampunk—she wore black on black on black, instead of the subculture's default brown. Today she had a black turtleneck, a broad black belt bedecked with gears, and a pair of pour-yourself-in black skinny jeans.

She looked marvelous, especially because of the big smile on her face. Which made Ree think about Drake, then Jane, then how ridiculously high school the whole thing had become. But that was a matter for another conversation.

She's happy, let her be happy. You cannot handle a boyfriend and a girlfriend. Seriously, no.

"Thanks for grabbing the table," Ree said as she leaned in to hug Priya. *Gals before datepals*, she thought, affirming her choice.

Then her stomach grumbled, which gave her much better things to think about. Ree hugged Anya and then took her seat while the restaurant bustled around them.

"What's got you so happy?" Sandra asked as she wiped the condensation sweat off of her water glass.

Again, Ree was split in two. She mirrored Priya's embarrassed smile while jealousy danced a traditional seis in her stomach.

"A gentleman caller has not only survived the *Are You a Axe Murderer* date but has served as eye candy at the gallery show," Anya said, jostling Priya with her elbow.

Priya's cheeks were rosy, beaming with the happy of infatuation.

Ree reconsidered her choice to not order a drink. She already had a cocktail of emotions swimming around her stomach, why not a real one?

Their server, an Irish guy with hair curly enough to be a Hobbit came by and took Ree's order for a screwdriver and Sandra's for coffee.

"So, how did it go?" Sandra asked Priya, continuing.

"Good. It was good."

"Good? I can't sell good. Give me copy, woman!" Anya said, affecting a J. Jonah Jameson voice and mock-shaking her friend.

Normally, Ree would be the one doing the JJJ routine so Anya could play Robbie, but cognitive dissonance and fatigue forced her to sit this one out.

Priya let slip that Drake had slept over, but nothing had gone past second base—per his insistence, rather than hers. Sandra called foul and told her to run, but Anya disagreed. When asked to tiebreak, Ree abstained, claiming that since Drake used to visit Zombie Café, she should stay neutral.

The banter and gossip continued throughout the meal, and rather than evading the awkwardness by drinking, she zeroed in on her heaping mound of pancakes, trying to focus on the normalcy and calm that came with her friends instead of the big bag of awkward that was the rest of her life.

Charlie came through again with two MacKenzie sightings less than five minutes apart, dated to half an hour before Ree left the brunch.

Enriched by chocolate chip pancakes and only most of a screwdriver, she excused herself while the ladies chatted a bit more. She hustled home assembled some war tools, and sat down for her media charge-up.

Smart money said MacKenzie would be at the park for the better part of the afternoon, so she should have enough time to get her genre magic working to pull off the plan she'd been cooking up ever since the Market.

Ree sat down with a mug of coffee, her Force FX lightsaber in her lap, and pressed play on *Episode IV*.

All right, MacKenzie, you have no idea how pwned you are about to be.

CHAPTER FIFTEEN

Sunday in the Park with George (Lucas)

America's Sweetheart Rachel MacKenzie is fresh off her Golden Globe win and filming another drama, this time alongside action veteran Julian Douglas.

Rachel made a splash with Downtown Girl *then built her reputation working with sitcom geniuses Isabell Grant and Xavier de Cruxes. After a standout performance in the ensemble* Thanksgiving, *Rachel has gone from hit to hit. But will her upcoming divorce throw a roadblock in Rachel's seemingly sure path to becoming an all-time star in the firmament of Hollywood?*

—Vlada Janczuk, StraightDope.com, May 19

Ree arrived at Miner Park just after 3 PM, which made it all too easy to get lost in the crowd. She knew this park, knew where people went boating, where they picnicked, where they hid to get naked, and the one place where someone could be truly alone, as long as that someone had bodyguards to enforce it.

She spotted the first bodyguard fifteen feet off the path, near the western edge of the park. He wore a black hoodie, but underneath the hoodie was a starched white shirt, and his shoes could have walked right off of Fifth Avenue.

John Williams's music played on loop in her mind, the energy of her boundless love for Star Wars taking musical form as soundtrack for the coming ass-kickery. *How awesome is this?*

Was it like this for you, too, mom? Did you have your own London Symphony Orchestra in your head when you went a-Jedi-ing?

Something else she wished she could ask her mother.

Ree spotted a guy she recognized from the set.

But for now, you are first, my un-Sith friend.

Throwing back her (brown) hoodie, Ree caught the bodyguard's attention. The man raised his hand, stepping forward.

"I'm sorry, ma'am, this part of the park is closed."

Bullshit, she thought, but kept the invective in. Instead, she passed her hand in front of the man's face and said, "You need to go get a coffee."

The man's eyes glazed over, and in a monotone voice, he said, "I need to go get a coffee." The bodyguard looked right past her and walked back toward the path. The nearest coffee hut was a five-minute walk away, on the opposite side of the park. *Boom.*

Ree guessed where Rachel would be luxuriating, and cut wide, moving through the outer brush of a copse of trees, looking for the other guard. Ree figured she'd have at least two, maybe three with her, and the more she could neutralize before confronting MacKenzie, the fewer moving parts in play, the lower her chances of this turning into a written-by-Jared-Sorensen-style Fiasco.

She spotted the second guard pacing around an old pine tree, checking his phone.

Your lack of professionalism is your weakness, she thought in her best Luke Skywalker voice.

Ree thought of the scene where Obi-Wan snuck his way to the tractor beam controls as she tried to mask her movements.

The soundtrack still loomed large in her mind, the volume only having dimmed from a 9 to about an 8 after her mind trick. She was still figuring out some of the fine details of Geekomancy, but it meant she still had pleasant surprises now and then.

Note to self: Watching Star Wars from infancy means you get more bang for your watching buck.

As she watched, she realized the bodyguard was far enough out of the way that she could afford to do . . . this.

Ree pulled out a blaster rifle prop used by a storm trooper and set it to stun. She waited for the guard to turn and face her, just because it was fun, then squeezed the trigger. A zwap sound accompanied the blue circles of light, and the guard dropped to the ground, his phone bouncing along the ground. Ree retrieved the phone, stripped the battery, and slipped it into her hoodie.

Two down. Now, is there a third?

Ree stopped and reached out with her mind, trying to sense the other minds in the area. As soon as she concentrated, she was hit by a wave of sensation, like she'd turned the TV on with the volume left on max. She stumbled back, her concentration broken. The music dimmed to a 6, and Ree wrote that approach off of her Usable Tactics list.

Since ESP was out of the question (Ree stopped to marvel at how awesome a thought that was), she continued with the sneaky-sneak approach, this time unassisted, and tried to watch for snatches of black clothing or fancy shoes as she circled back through a populated area, with picnickers and slightly-too-much-PDA-ers to a bend where the lake fed a river down and to the east.

Ree stepped along the edge of the river, keeping her eyes peeled. By her best guess, she'd come nearly three-quarters of the circle around toward the path where she'd started picking off the guards, and called it good as her inner orchestra faded down to about a 5, moving from "Binary Sunset" to "The Imperial March."

It's go time.

Ree picked her way through the brush, trying to give herself the densest cover as she approached. She came in from the east, hoping MacKenzie would be facing the sun.

Another gentle push of magic to guide her silently through the trees . . . and she saw through to Rachel MacKenzie's hideaway.

America's Sweetheart reclined on an alpaca blanket, wearing a yellow floral-print sundress. As Ree suspected, she faced the sun.

Ree knew she only had a second or two before MacKenzie noticed her. She scanned the glade to make sure there wasn't another bodyguard lurking, then stepped into the clearing and activated her lightsaber, saying, "Are you ready for your close-up?"

Rachel flipped over, pulling her sunglasses up to look at Ree.

"What the hell?" she said, then sat up and reached for her bag.

Ree had no idea what was in her bag but didn't feel like risking it. She reached out to Rachel's bag and became the envy of thousands of geeks (including Silent Bob) as the purse leaped from the blanket and into Ree's outstretched hand.

That's so cool! Ree thought, trying to keep her serious face on as she stared MacKenzie down, dropping the purse to the ground.

MacKenzie stood, one hand out to her side. The superstar drew her glasses down with her other hand. Ree had never seen Celebromancy used offensively, but she wasn't prepared to write anything off. Hence the purse sitting at her feet.

"What do you want?" MacKenzie asked.

Ree took another step forward, the lightsaber humming in concert with the fading music in her mind. She didn't have much Jedi power left, so she'd have to use it carefully.

"I want you to dispel the curse you placed on Jane Konrad. Now."

Rachel smiled an insincere smile. "So it was you impersonating the reporter. Not many magicians in town that can pull off that level of mimicry and also give two shits about Jane."

"One is enough. So are you going to do it, or are things going to get messy?" She waved the lightsaber just enough to make the familiar *whmm* sound.

Rachel took a single sultry step toward Ree, her hips moving as if in slow-mo.

"Why don't you put those toys down so we can talk like reasonable adults?" The woman oozed charm, and Ree had no doubt she was running the same Majesty-esque effect Ree had seen Jane use at the panel.

Ree steeled her mind against the charm and built a wall of grit, anger, and the ambient awesomeness of her arsenal.

"Why don't you stop right there before I stun you into next Friday? I have lots of tricks, and friends in the local police department. All you have is a pair of unconscious and absent guards."

The star chuckled. "Good thing I brought three guards."

Ree heard movement back and to one side and turned just in time to see a big bald white man fire a shotgun at her face.

There were lots of ways that Ree would have ended up dead.

If she'd chosen another film or TV show, or if she'd used up all of her power on showy displays.

Luckily, she had just enough magical oomph left to use Force Speed and race to the side, dodging the spray of pellets.

Ree raised the blaster and returned fire, not willing to cut a man down for doing his job. The bodyguard ducked behind a tree, and the stun waves rolled past him. He popped back out and fired again, aiming at Ree's center of mass.

Running on magical fumes, Ree dodged again, but with less speed. Several pellets hit her like razors, shredding her hoodie and leaving her with a handful of painful lesions. Ree stumbled back, then fired with the blaster again, reconsidering her pacifism.

The bodyguard ducked back behind the tree, but she saw the man grimace as the wave rolled over him. As she closed on the guard, Ree deactivated the lightsaber and slid it into her hoodie's pouch, exchanging it for an extendable beatstick. She snapped the baton open, then jumped forward and swung. The guard blocked with his shotgun, but while he was blocking, he wasn't shooting or reloading, which Ree took as a win.

But of course, while she was fighting the guard, Rachel was probably getting away. Ree feinted a low reverse with the baton, then dove forward to strike the bodyguard in the nose with the butt of her club. He took the shot and went down in a heap. She spun in place, buzzing with pain and adrenaline.

Rachel MacKenzie was at the edge of the clearing, heading south through the brush. She'd be back on the path in moments, and Ree would be nothing more than a crazed fan assaulting a superstar.

Shit shit shit. This plan was really cool in my head. Where the hell had that third one come from? She should have spotted him.

No one said Celebromancy could detract attention as well as attracting it.

Unless Rachel was the distraction.

Motherfucker.

Ree fired the blaster again, but Rachel had broken the tree line, and the blast dissipated among the trees.

"Help! Help me!" Rachel screamed, her voice muted by the foliage.

Oh, fuck this. Ree realized there was no way she was going to pull this out now. She'd lost control of the situation, and needed to tend to her bullet wounds, pronto. If she pursued the superstar, she'd just get herself arrested.

Ree turned hard on her heels and started running north, her fastest way out of the park. She stunned the guard with one more blast, just in case he was playing possum.

It was time for her to GTFO. Ree poured on the speed, threw up her hoodie, and cut through the brush with the lightsaber, using the weapon like a science fantasy machete to clear her way.

I am soo screwed, Ree thought as she checked over her shoulder on the way out of the park. She deactivated the lightsaber and stowed the blaster in her hoodie pouch, then tried her best to look like a normal jogger, despite the blood and tears on her hoodie and the wounds on her arm.

She kept up the *oh, shit* pace for several blocks out of the park, holding the jangling props in the hoodie's pouch, and then slowing to a quick walk to put more distance between her and whatever security/police/beatdown Rachel MacKenzie could bring to bear.

.×[×]⊗[×]×_×

Ree went home first, using another *Descent* potion and hoping that the police wouldn't beat her there. She changed and started pacing her room with urgency.

What's my next move?

She had to slow herself down to focus, clear her mind, and push back the loop of self-deprecation that had been running in her head all the way from the park, yelling at herself for not being careful enough, going off half-cocked like a kid on a damn-fool idealistic crusade.

For at least the second (third?) time in a week, Ree wished she'd stolen Eastwood's Psychic Paper. It'd be a big fucking stretch to use it as a get-out-of–jail-free card, but she wouldn't pass up any help.

She pulled out her old set of glasses, which were even larger and chunkier than her current pair, hopefully chunkier enough to look different. She stuffed her normal glasses in the hoodie and topped off the look with a brown fedora from Goorin Brothers.

She tied her hair in a quick braid and pinned it up under the hat.

There. That should be a different enough look to help her move around without as much worry.

So, options:

Calling dad won't help, though he would happily hop on a plane and take on the Pearson PD by himself if I asked.

The cops will go to the set as soon as they get more info about me, so that won't be safe.

Zombie Café's out, too. I couldn't put Bryan in that much heat.

Grognard's is probably the safest hideout, since it's off the street.

But I need to warn Jane that things went south. And Drake should know not to come looking for me.

But if she went to Grognard's, she'd also have to deal with her boss's wrath over the fact that she'd gotten thousands of dollars' worth of equipment broken.

So, Grognard or the cops, who was she more afraid of? Ree chuckled at the question, but it was all nerves bubbling over.

Ree pulled out her phone and dialed Jane's number.

Please pick up.

The phone rang once, and Ree bent open her blinds to look down the street for squad cars. It rang again, and Ree started tapping her feet. "Come on, Jane."

The line picked up during the third ring. Jane sounded positively electric. "Hello?"

"Thank Jeebus. Have the cops come by?"

"Are you all right?"

"I fucked up bad, Jane. And if Rachel is smart, I've probably got an APB out for me right now."

Ree swore she could hear Jane's smile. "Not anymore, hon. I took care of it."

A beat passed as Ree tried to process. "Shubba-what-now?"

"It's taken care of. A detective came by with two squad cars of backup, but I handled it. You should be fine."

"I repeat—what?"

"Celebromancy is a lot more than instant makeup and playing to the room. But you should come by so we can talk."

"And I won't get surrounded by a bajillion cops along the way?"

Jane laughed, her energy infectious. "Of course not."

"And you're not saying this because the cops are there making you be the bait so they can bring me in?" Ree asked, thinking of the dozens of TV episodes she'd seen with just such a move.

"I'm alone, and even if you were still a fugitive, which you aren't, I'd be tempted to mind-whammy you into coming over so I can tear off all your clothes that much faster."

Gulp. Jane was a good actress, but if Jane could dial in that much sultry without meaning it, Ree would eat a month-old croissant from Zombie Café.

Pack a teleport card just in case, she thought, scratching her paranoia. She walked back to her room to the card supply and said, "I'm on my way. And thanks."

"Think nothing of it, my raven-haired beauty. Be careful."

Ree built herself an Escape-from-Cops sideboard with a couple of teleportations, some cards from *Netrunner* to beat a trace, and some kung fu from *Marvel VS.* for good measure. She slipped the sideboard into a breast pocket of her jacket, double-checked her basic disguise, and then headed out.

⋅✕ˣ✕⊗✕ˣ✕⋅

Ree managed to get across town on a bus without being cuffed, flagged down, or otherwise arrested, so by the time she got to the trailer camp, she was ready to accept the half-reassuring possibility that Jane had actually magic-ed the police off her trail.

It was only half-reassuring because, while it made one problem go away, Ree could guess how much magic it had taken to pull of something that big, and now it was going to be a matter of time before the other Gucci dropped. And if the Smokinator came back tonight, Ree didn't like their odds, even with Danny, herself, and a troupe of mundane bodyguards.

One of said guards met her at the edge of the camp. He was a tall blond with a look that spoke to Northern European ancestors. He held up a hand, giving her the once-over. "Hold on there, sir."

"Sir, really?" The question came out more snippy than Ree intended. She double-checked her outfit and acknowledged that she wasn't exactly exuding femininity at the moment—yes, short hair plus fedora—but still.

Ree softened her tone, pulled off her hat, and started again.

"Ree Reyes, I'm the writer? Jane Konrad is expecting me."

Ree let her brain narrate while the guard called someone on his phone. *Little did she know that it was not the police who would be the challenge but a none-too-perceptive hired guard. Intrepid adventurer Ree Reyes evaluated the statuesque sentry, gauging whether she would need to use the Five-Point Palm Exploding Heart Technique. Instead, she settled on the Indignant Name-Dropping Style, hoping to spare the guard his life.*

The guard put away his phone and nodded to Ree. "Go ahead, Miss. Sorry about the confusion."

Stepping past the guard, Ree chewed up the pavement between the entrance and Jane's trailer. If Jane was high on magic, who knew when the crash would come or how bad it would be. Ree had dated some potheads in college, but no one who more than dabbled in the hard stuff. The way Jane was hitting the Celebromancy was approaching full-on season six Willow, and Ree prayed that it wouldn't come to the obelisk-of-death, save-the-world-with-broken-crayon story level. She'd always hated the magic-as-drug analogy, anyway, but judging from the curse, it seemed like Rachel MacKenzie didn't share Ree's aesthetic.

Ree saw Yancy duck out from under a tent and wave her down. He was wearing a tan suit and carried a leather briefcase.

"Ree, a second?" he asked.

She veered left and met Yancy at the tent.

"What's up?"

Yancy set his bag down and checked over his shoulder. There was movement near the sets, but nothing nearby. "I need you to talk Jane down. She said she wouldn't use her power except on the set, and only one take per shot. But when the police came . . ."

Ree nodded. "I got it. That's why I came. Are you sure the cops won't be back?"

Yancy gave a lopsided grin. "This isn't the first thing we've covered up. The press is voracious, and sometimes it's better for everyone involved that news doesn't get the chance to spread." He dropped the grin, and in stillness, he looked tired.

"I hate to muck with people's memories, and I get why she did it, but if Jane doesn't dial things back, I'm going to lose control of this production. And at that point, I'll have to pull the plug in order to protect everyone, you included."

"I get it. Any tips? If she's not listening to you . . ."

Yancy pursed his lips. "We need something to bring her back to Earth first, and then convince her to keep her eye on the long-term, not just the I want it right now short-term. She used to be good at that, but this curse has wrapped itself around her brain, and at a certain point she just starts ignoring me. I'm not her father, and I'm not going to take choices away from her unless she becomes a danger."

Yancy took a breath, his face looking suddenly older. "Do something before it gets to that point."

"I get it. If she blows me off, then we may have to get drastic. But let's keep the doomsaying on hold for now, okay?" Ree said, as much for herself as for the director.

Yancy clapped Ree on the shoulder, and picked up his bag.

"Good luck. I'm off for a meeting to get us a bit of wiggle room on the budget. Without more money, we could bring Jane back on track and still not have enough to pay for postproduction."

The director pursed his lips and thought a moment. He looked like he was about to say something else, but all that came out was "Good luck."

Then he nodded to her and headed toward the parked cars. *No pressure, right?* Ree thought.

Dear Universe,

It has come to my attention that, of late, you appear to be fucking with me a lot more than usual. I'd like to formally request that only one of my jobs go kablooey at once.

If that is almost always my whacky Urban Fantasy life, so be it. In fact, that'd be preferable, since it's easier to compartmentalize and keep my friends out of the epic-level danger. But when my urgent to-do list includes "go into work and get yelled at for failing to fight off a cloud of Pitch Black *monsters," "navigate a love quadrangle with a superstar, one of my best friends, and the most useful magic ally I have," and "talk down aforementioned superstar while she's on a magic bender," a girl can get a little overwhelmed.*

Care to lend a hand?

Thanks,

Ree Reyes

B.A, M.F.A, G.E.E.K.

P.S. A simpler love life wouldn't hurt, either. Not holding out for that one, though.

Ree gave the letter time to process and, fresh out of excuses and distractions, headed to Jane's trailer. Danny sat on the couch, his baseball bat resting against the other corner. He looked only a bit less wrecked than Ree felt, though he'd changed since yesterday.

As soon as she registered Danny, Ree was nearly knocked off her feet by a glomp-attack from Jane.

"Hello, sailor!" Ree said as Jane found her footing, only to be cut off when the star locked her in a kiss. Her lips tasted like strawberries, and Ree let the concerns fall away for a moment, let her world narrow to the gorgeous woman who was nearly knocking her over.

Ree had never considered kissing as something that would call for a Reflex save. Ree kept her footing, but only because the two of them leaned into the wall of the trailer with a totally-not-subtle thud.

A breathtaking moment later, Ree disentangled herself from the star, who was, for some reason, wearing a metallic blue evening gown. It was, of course, gorgeous—a sleeveless over-the-shoulder number that had ruching where ruching should go to accentuate the bust, then hugged close around the waist to flare out down to her ankles.

"Damn . . ." Ree said, indicating the dress.

"You like?" Jane twirled like a Disney Princess. Except that Disney Princesses didn't tend to make bedroom eyes while they twirled in their fairy-godmother-granted dresses.

"Hell yeah. Any reason why you're wearing it on a Sunday afternoon?"

"Why not? I get these dresses for awards shows and premieres, and then I either send them back or they just sit in a wardrobe. I felt like hitting the glam button."

And hit it she had—Jane had Broadway amounts of makeup on, though Ree got the sense that most of it was applied with a wand rather than a brush.

"It worked. But aren't you throwing magic around a little blithe-tastically?"

"Hey, if I hadn't done that whammy, you'd be getting a ride in a squad car, and the nicest clothes you'd be seeing in a while would be prison orange and a judge's robe. Where's the gratitude?"

Was Jane even in there? Or was it just the magic driving? Ree reached out and grabbed Jane by the shoulders as gently as she could. "Of course I'm grateful. But I'm worried about you. I really don't want to go another round with Smokey, and if you miss another day of shooting, Yancy says we're fucked sideways with a rusty spade."

"He didn't say that," Jane said, waggling a finger.

Great, now she's five. Things didn't tend to go very well when Ree was the mature adult in a discussion.

"I embellished. Creative license, don't you know."

Jane laughed, a deep belly laugh. *Okay, that was funny, but maybe not* that *funny.*

The whole scene took Ree back to her college days, complete with the totally sober friend in the corner who was embarrassed to be there, played this time by Danny.

Jane took Ree's hand and started to lead her to the bedroom.

Ree leaned back and stopped their movement. "Not now, Jane. If the curse works anything like it has before, this come-down is going to be killer . . . maybe literally."

"You worry too much. If the comedown is the trouble, maybe I just won't ever come down! I can just keep shooting until we're wrapped, stay awake like in *A Nightmare on Elm Street*, and you can go and save the day, and then everything will be marvelous. See? No problem. Now come on."

Ree reached out and grabbed Jane's hand, locking the magic-drugged woman in her gaze. "Seriously, Jane. If you're too stoned on magic to be reasonable, then I'm not going anywhere near a bed with you."

Jane went to the naughty smile place. "That didn't stop you before."

"No, but this time I'm sober, and I didn't know that a curse-induced Smokinator was gunning for you. Let's sit down and talk this out, okay?"

Ree crossed to the couch and sat, patting the seat next to her. "We can do this. I need you with me, and I need you to focus."

Ree looked to Danny, raising her eyebrows to say *A little help?*

Danny hopped up and helped corral the highly-distracted Jane to the couch.

Start from the beginning. Jane might not be any help, but

one thing Ree had learned so fast is that you never really knew with magic. Even the most rote procedures still had some built-in critical chance for win or embarrassing fail. "Okay, so we need to get the curse lifted, and to do that, we either need to get Rachel to do it or figure out how to do it ourselves."

"I tried that," Jane said. "It sucked. Schemey glam bizzna, sucks."

Great, so she's not even cogent.

Ree stood, went to the door, and leaned out of the trailer. She called, trying to mix urgency and politeness into a one-two punch. "Can we get some coffee in here, please?!" She returned to the couch to see that Jane had splayed out, one leg showing through the tall slit.

What was I doing again? she thought, her ears getting hot.

Focus. Sexytimes later. Jane had the charm effects cranked to max, and Ree nearly had to push her chin up to take her eyes off of the line of the star's legs, the movement of her breath, the crinkles at the edges of her eyes—

Not helping!

Ree sat on the far side of the couch, just past Jane's head. She caressed the intoxicated woman's hair with one hand and sent her smartphone coursing across the Internet with the other.

A quick visit to TMZ showed Ree that Rachel MacKenzie was spotted coming out of the Pearson Crown, the poshest hotel in town, where visiting dignitaries stayed for visits and superstar surgeons held their conferences.

"Okay, so Rachel is staying at the Pearson Crown Hotel," she said out loud, on the off chance that Jane would be useful or Danny would turn out to be a criminal mastermind.

Ree turned to Danny. "By the way, you don't happen to be a criminal mastermind, by chance?"

Danny shook his head. "Kung fu, intimidation, and world-class drunk-sitting are the extent of my superskills. That and crocheting, but that's probably not relevant."

"Crochet, no shit?"

Danny shrugged. "My partner got me into it, and now my son has a small army of doilies."

"You have a kid?" Ree asked.

"His little boy is so cute!" Jane said, leaning her head back in Ree's lap to look her in the eye. "Soo cute!"

Danny smiled a genuine, unguarded smile. He stepped forward and tapped his phone a couple of times. The phone displayed a picture of a thoroughly unamused toddler being held by Danny and an equally-tired-but-proud-looking white guy with blond hair and a wide smile.

And for a moment, Ree forgot just enough about saving One Tough Mama, fighting monsters, and her magic-drunk kinda-girlfriend to say, "So cute!"

Just then, someone knocked on the door. Danny crossed, opened the door, and was handed a coffee. Danny handed the coffee to Ree, who squeezed Jane's shoulder and said, "I got you some coffee. Doesn't that sound like a great idea?" Ree tried to remember her ill-fated babysitting days, or at least, her half-successful interactions with the Blin twins, Luke and Leia.

Jane sat up and took the coffee cup in both hands. She took a sip, then a longer swig.

And if we're lucky, that will help. If not, it'll keep her preoccupied.

Jeebus, if you'd like to help out and give me the sobre and sensible Jane back now, that'd be awesome.

Ree turned back to Danny. "What are their names?"

The bodyguard's grin got wider. "My son is Jonathan. My husband is Laurence."

"So Laurence takes care of him while you're working? When do you get to see them?"

"They're in L.A., so when Jane isn't on location, I see them pretty much every day. It's been nearly a month since I left."

There was a ka-chunk sound in Ree's brain as yet another brick fell into place on her wall of responsibility. It read:

#316—GET DANNY BACK TO HIS TOTALLY CUTE FAMILY.

When she turned her attention back to Danny, his phone was gone.

"Then let's see about wrapping this thing up and getting you back home to your guys. Do you know anything about sneaking into hotels? Like, reverse bodyguarding?"

"Well, I certainly wouldn't want to participate in conspiracy to commit kindapping . . ." Danny said with a smile.

"Of course not. But as a writer, I'm very curious about the bodyguarding business, and I'd love to pick your brain about a hypothetical situation." Ree put quotey fingers around hypothetical, matching Danny's smile.

Danny sat back down, putting his phone away with a grin.

"Ah, of course. Professionally speaking, if I were protecting Rachel MacKenzie, here are the things I'd be worried about . . ."

CHAPTER SIXTEEN

Hypothetical Kidnapping Is the Name of My Leverage Cover Band

The Heist. It's a plot that dates back to the myths of Prometheus and Maui, recurring time and time again.

Whether it's the solo thief or the ensemble, some things remain the same:

1) The Thief—who must test their agility, mental and physical both.

2) The Mark—sometimes unwitting, sometimes armed to the teeth.

3) The Loot—be it MacGuffin, magic, or money, the loot is the ultimate driving force in the heist, something worth staking your life on.

4) The Twist—get in, get thing, get out is too easy.

For millennia we've been complicating the heist in ways both new and old.

Will humanity ever get tired of the heist plot?

Not as long as there are cloisters of power, scarce resources, and the magic alchemy of ambition and courage necessary to cross the threshold into enemy territory.

—It's All Been Done: Tracing the Roots of Modern Story Structure, by Robert C. Lutz, (Grumpy Scandinavian Press) 117.

Hypothetically speaking, Ree hopped a bus across town, giving her enough time to watch an episode of *Leverage*, during which she focused her attention on the delightfully odd thief, Parker (First name or last name? Yes.), played by the marvelous Beth Riesgraf. She probably would have been fine dialing in to any of the crew, picking up on Elliott's awesome fight and fight-avoidance skills, Hardison's hacking (though she lacked a disposable netbook to use his only-on-TV Technomancy), Sophie's confidence-woman acting skills, or Nate Ford's mastermind skills.

But the thieving sounded the most fun. Thanks to a Julie-Newmar-induced crush on Catwoman at the age of six, Ree had always been intrigued by the Cool of the Thief. Her love of the thief had led to playing dozens of rogues over the years, several perfect-stealth play-throughs of video games, and a special bag just for her sneak attack dice, onyx black with metallic red pips. And in the real world, she'd even managed to pick up some lock-picking skills of her own. But Ree hoped that the magic skill from *Leverage* would boost what little tradecraft she had on her own.

Rogue skills, don't fail me now.

Ree knew from hundreds of heist movies and the magic buzzing in her head that she would have three major hurdles in getting to Rachel MacKenzie.

She adjusted her bag as she turned the corner to approach the first biggest hurdle: the front door. The Pearson Crown Hotel, being the top-end hotel in the city, had doormen at the main entrance, and visitors were marked and classified before they could take three steps inside. If Ree didn't look the part right away, she'd be pegged as a variable, and they'd have eyes on her the whole time. Plus, if she was ID-ed coming in, then she'd be back on the APB as soon as Rachel called the alarm.

Which meant that she needed an excuse to be inside. Which meant disguise. Therefore, on the way to the hotel, she retrieved the chef's outfit that she'd worn when she and Sandra took cooking classes together to help Ree learn how to approximate human food and for Sandra to pursue her long-unfulfilled dream of becoming a restaurateur.

Ree didn't have a hat, but it didn't seem to matter. After walking down the alley, she found the back entrance and nodded to a couple of workers taking a smoke break there. Kitchen staff had a big turnover, even at a big place like the Crown, and especially on the bottom of the ladder, so she was betting these two wouldn't care if they didn't recognize her exactly. And they didn't.

Ree did her best to walk with confidence while not bringing attention to herself, her shoulders hunched up a bit in the same way she'd seen Parker do a dozen times on the show while trying to unobtrusive her way through a situation. Feeling a twinge of magic, she opened the door and stepped into the steamy, noisy back end of the Pearson Crown Hotel.

One hurdle down. *Let's hope it stays this easy.*

Continuing her purposeful walk, she passed the main kitchen, where cooks, dishwashers, servers, and an angry chef carried out a culinary cacophony, with rattling pots, gouts of flame, plumes of steam, orders called at Mr. MicroMachine speed. A cluster of smells hit her nose: fresh pasta, seared meat, and soapy water.

The kitchen staff used curses and insults like they were an integral part of restauranteering grammar (and perhaps they were). Ree stopped to listen to them, a small grin breaking her poker face.

"Get me a goddamned steak frites, for fuck's sake, or I will drag your ass out to the front so you can explain to the city councilman why a fry cook with ten years of experience can't figure out how to dunk slices of potato in hot oil when pimple-covered teenagers with their hands down their pants manage to do it in three minutes or less every fucking day!"

The chaotic sounds spiked a bit higher, and Ree heard a guy with an Ecuadorian accent invite the first speaker and Councilman Thompson to blow a Chupacabra in Hell (in Spanish, natch). Ree made a note to of the line to use sometime later, then continued down the hall, having acquired the gossip she needed.

Ree found a room that was unlocked, then snuck into the tremendously useful closet. It was filled with cleaning supplies, a carton of cigarettes hidden in the corner, and a vent.

Oh, vents. Lovely, marvelous vents. But this wasn't the vent she needed. That would come with outfit number three. Ree unbuttoned the chef's coat and stuffed it into her bag, then pulled out outfit number two: an evening gown borrowed out of Jane's closet.

It was a newer dress, from when Jane had gone to the VMAs despite being a walking wreck and twenty pounds under her normal weight.

But Jane down twenty pounds put her at just about Ree's build.

It was still a bit wide in the waist, but Ree hoped that the Push-Up Bra of Thundering Cleavage would cover for the imperfect fit. Said bra had cost her a complete collection of *King's Quest* floppies and many, many, many odd stares at Midnight Market.

Let's hope it does the trick.

Ree pulled a quick change, then produced her makeup kit, unfolded the compact on a shelf, and set about putting on a Pearson Escort look. Pearson wasn't as upscale as L.A. or N.Y.C., so she went for classy but not too ostentatious. The bra would do most of the talking, anyway.

Several minutes later, she checked the look in the mirror one more time to check her hair. She gave a slight tug, and let one curl of hair fall in front of her right eye, just so.

In a normal world, there's no way Ree would have been able to put on a red-carpet-ready look in a hotel basement closet. But thanks to the wonders of *Leverage* magic, she'd done just that in five minutes. Ree made note of the fact that of the cast, only Sophie would have been able to do that quick makeup job, and resolved to use ensemble shows more often for the versatility.

Ree took a picture with her camera (for posterity, because why not). She checked the picture and went over the elements of her outfit one more time:

Red awards-show gown with bustling to highlight the magic bra; Christina Hendricks–level cleavage thanks to said magic bra; full-face makeup with just-that-side-of-gaudy eyeshadow, just-this-side-of-gaudy blush; bloodred earrings (again borrowed from Jane); a black suede purse; and hopefully-not-too-out-of-date Christian Louboutin heels.

She stuffed her phone, lightsaber, emergency deck, and the bag containing the accessories for outfit number three in her thank-God-they're-in-style massive purse, then wiped the room for prints and left the cloth, stuffing outfit number one in the bag.

Time for the second hurdle.

⨯✕⨯⬡⨯✕⨯

Her disguise plus a bit more *Leverage* power got Ree out of the basement without incident, and she made it as far as the rear elevator hallway before someone stopped her. It was a taller Asian woman in a conservative black dress, her hair back and up with a swanky jade clip, who challenged Ree with a "Can I help you?"

Ree turned and smiled, tapping again into the magic, remembering the part in the episode when Parker had to channel Sophie, demure and charming. "Oh, sorry. I got a little lost. I'm supposed to meet Councilman Thompson tonight?" Ree took a long breath, trying to say more with less . . . and to let the magic bra do its thing. "He said I was supposed to be discreet—you know how these men can be."

Ree mentally crossed her fingers that the woman was high enough on the Kinsey scale for the bra to have been worth the bother. For a moment, Ree couldn't breathe as she watched for the woman's response.

At first, the woman looked skeptical, but after a brief but significant gaze at Ree's chest, she said, "Of course. The councilman is in room 719. Do you need me to let you in?"

Ree gave her best Big Smile. "That would be lovely, thank you."

⬡ 12

Ree closed the door of room 719 behind her and exhaled slowly.

The Leverage magic was nearly gone, so she wouldn't have much time to get past hurdle number three: the bodyguards.

Rachel's room was two floors up, so she'd need every bit of magic to navigate the ducts up those two floors to even get to the bodyguards. Ree kicked off the heels and put her "cook" shoes back on, then spotted the air duct she needed.

Any other time, Ree would have taken a few moments to enjoy the lavish furniture, the comically large bouquet on the table, and the doubtless-expensive bottle of Champagne by the bed.

Someone was going to have one hell of a night, but it wasn't her.

Ree reached around to her back, hopped a couple of times as she tried to reach the zipper, then opened up the back of her dress. Ree let the gown drop to the floor and removed the Bra of Thundering Cleavage. She'd have to try it again sometime soon in a less felonious situation. Maybe with Jane, once this was all over and done.

She took the tool kit she'd hidden in the ample space, set it on a chair, then pulled up the top half of the bodysuit (aka outfit number three) hidden under the bottom half of the gown. As she stuffed the bra, the fancy purse, her borrowed shoes and accessories, and the awards dress inside, all she could think was, *Oh, the crimes I am committing against fashion.*

After situating everything in the bag, Ree pulled the cushy chair over to the wall, made sure it was steady, then climbed up to the wall vent. She grabbed the tool kit and opened the vent in a hurry, using some of the remaining *Leverage* magic.

Ree threw the duffel into the crawl space, then shimmied into the vent feetfirst so she could fix it back into place (not perfectly, but well enough that if the councilman came back before she'd made her escape, he wouldn't be likely to notice). Not that he'd be likely to notice anyway because who actually looks at vents when it isn't too hot or too cold?

Once the vent was on, Ree pulled out her phone again, which involved quite a bit of squirming and sliding (should have done that first!). She cued up the same episode of *Leverage* again for one more power boost.

She got about five minutes in before she heard someone at the door. They were noisy, clumsy. Probably the councilman.

And even if he didn't look at the vent, if he heard the show or saw the light, she'd be made in a drunkard's second.

Ree clicked the phone off and slid away from the vent. She looped the duffel strap over her leg because she knew that at some point . . .

There. The duffel tipped off the ledge and started to fall down a hole. Ree curled her leg up and pulled it back onto the vent.

Two floors up, then Rachel's room should be just down the hall. You can do this, she told herself.

Ree grabbed the duffel with both legs, then steered it back over the hole and deposited it over on the other side of the vent.

After one last careful nudge, Ree scooted herself back and let her legs feed down the hole.

Here was where the magic really came in handy. Ree looped the duffel around her front again and positioned herself in the vent.

In defiance of practicality, Ree started to climb up, her hands and knees pressed against the opposite side. This could be done in the normal world, but Ree didn't want to think about how much harder it would be. And she definitely didn't want to think about how far down the vent went, or how tremendously dead she'd be if the magic gave out before she got to the ninth floor.

Wouldn't that be a helluva teaser for a procedural cop show, Ree thought. *Mangled body shows up in the bottom of an access vent, with a $7,000 dress in a duffel bag, expensive earrings, and a black bodysuit. Good luck, Beckett and Castle.*

The vertical shimmy got her up one flight, but the energy buzzing in her head was nearly empty. She only had to get another ten feet up and onto the ledge. From there, she could recharge and keep going.

Ree pushed down on the side of the vent, trying to speed herself up the shaft. Her confidence was fading foot by foot, and when she was half a flight from her destination, the energy fizzed out.

Fuuuuck, Ree thought as she strained against the sides of the vent, keeping herself steady as the universe reset from magic-enabled Heist Movie Easy Mode to Hard. *There's no way she could safely recharge, nor could she reach for any of her other artifacts or tools.*

Ree took a long breath and tried to talk herself up. *You're almost there. You can do this. Just a few more feet. It's like a ropes course, you can do this yourself.*

But then panic came a-knocking on the green room of her mind. *The fuck it's like a ropes course! You're at least a hundred feet up a tiny shaft, and it doesn't fucking matter which cute or dashing or rugged detective finds you and tries to solve the case, you'll still be dead!*

She took another moment to breathe, the air in the vent still with the scent of sweat, then looked up and focused on her destination. It was almost within reach. She just had to push one, maybe two more times up the shaft. Ree pressed with her right foot and slid her right hand up the wall, maintaining pressure. It was far slower than what she'd been doing with the magic, but slow and steady would win the race of not dying in a ventilation shaft.

Ree stretched out with her left, but she stopped a few inches short at the end of her extension.

One more, Ree. She pushed off with her foot, but the shoe slipped.

She fell, hands scraping and sliding down the vent.

Ree cried out, arcing her back and straining with her legs to catch herself. Her hands burned, and she felt friction catch her back on fire as she slid down to just above the seventh floor.

"Fuckmuncher!" Ree growled aloud, instantly regretting the outburst. *Now I get to find out how well sound carries from here. For science!*

Ree tested her footholds and slid herself a couple of inches up, then climbed up the vent with her left arm.

Slow and steady, Ree. Don't get hasty.

Inch by glacial inch, Ree scaled her way back up the vent.

Her legs were burning with the acid of *why the fuck don't you do more cardio?* and her back was screaming *oh, God, ow, I need a fifty-hour hot bath,* but she was making headway. Her legs started trembling, and she couldn't afford to shake them out.

Come. The Fuck. On, she told herself. Her right hand found the vent opening, but she wasn't done.

If she was going to have any chance of pulling herself up into the vent, she'd need to climb even higher so she could get her head and shoulders in without lifting her entire body weight with her arms, which, while more mighty than when she'd started hero-ing, were still not really up to Action-Hero levels.

She hauled herself up as much as she could with her hands and legs pulling and pushing together, then leaned forward, straining against the vent with her tailbone, trying to keep pressure up so she didn't slip back down again.

Okay, think this through. Aside from the pants-wetting terror, the situation didn't map to any of Ree's experiences with rock walls or ropes courses from the leadership course she'd taken as a kid. In this case, leadership meant "self-confidence and making friends." Ree had succeeded at the first, but not so much at the second. She had her peeps already, her cultural affiliation delineated pretty clearly after her going as Han Solo three Halloweens in a row.

Ree thought back to the terror from those early attempts on the ropes courses, about how everything seemed impossible at first. But each time, she'd thought it through, swallowed her terror, and kicked its ass. *No reason to stop now*, she told herself, and stretched her legs straight, pushing herself up and forward.

She re-placed one leg beneath her butt, ready for the last push-off that would (hopefully!) get her waist-deep into the vent.

Visualize the pwn. I will roll a 20, and I will not fall to an ignominious and painful death. I will achieve my goal and be totally awesome even if no one is around to see it.

Ree exhaled and pushed off with her leg, hauling herself forward with her arms and diving forward. She got as far in as the bottom of her rib cage, then wobbled, half in and half out. Knuckles white with tension, she clawed her way forward, flailing with her legs to scoot farther in. Two inches more, and the wobbling stopped. She military-crawled forward, the duffel filling the vent at her back.

Confident that she was in fact not going to fall and die, Ree went limp in the vent, unable to do anything more than breathe for who knows how long. Her bodysuit was slick with sweat, her hair plastered to her face.

Hot damn.

She heard a fake sales pitch in her mind as she panted:

The Hero Gym would like to offer you an exciting opportunity: four indoor climbing courses at the low, low price of eight easy payments of $89.99

(plus S&H).

After training at The Hero Gym, you will be able to face gorgeous Celebromancer villains without looking like a wasted hot mess!

Call today and we'll throw in a carabiner with totally vague utility, a $29.99 value!

Ree pushed aside the product of her loopy brain, accepting her hot-mess-itude. Then again, the sweaty would let her do the Ripley-at-the-end-of-*Aliens* look, which was always a plus. Her bodysuit was about the right amount of not-clothing.

Ree squeegeed her hair off of her face and shimmied forward.

Now she had to find out which room on this floor was Rachel's.

The paparazzi that Charlie had researched from were damned good, but even they couldn't get her room number.

⋅×˟⬡˟×⋅

After what seemed like an hour of skulking around in the vents, she found Rachel MacKenzie's room.

There were three things that made her sure she'd found the right place:

1) The mass of leopard-print suitcases,

2) The powerful scent of the perfume she'd smelled on the star in her trailer back during Ree's short-lived career as a media journalist impostor, and 3) The sight of the bodyguard who had ruined her last run at MacKenzie with a shotgun, now standing in the corner, scanning the room with bored focus.

All right, girl. Go time.

Ree checked the clock on her phone, then cued up *The Matrix.*

She wouldn't need much to get past the guards (hopefully), but having a little kung fu left to intimidate Rachel wouldn't suck.

And this time, she'd know to look for three of them, not just two.

As the film opened, Ree focused on Trinity, empathized with the calm sexiness of Carrie-Anne Moss's performance, the sleek awesomeness of this badass woman in head-to-toe PVC. She felt the power build in her mind, even with the sound turned off, the light shielded from the hotel room by the corner of the duffel.

She might end up having to leave it behind, which would be tons of physical evidence, but if today was nearly endgame, it shouldn't matter.

Keep believing that, kid, a cynical voice in her head said—a voice that sounded like Eastwood. He hadn't been her mentor for very long, but his stern cynicism had apparently made a mark.

Ree focused on the kung fu again, on the wonder of the first time she saw the bullet-cam effect blended perfectly with wire work.

When the scene was over, Ree put the phone away, mind buzzing with energy. The color palette of the world green-shifted ever so slightly, and Ree pulled out her screwdriver to open the grate.

Surprise Shotgunner crossed the room to get a drink of water, and Ree made several quick turns of the screw and grabbed the grate. She aimed, thought of Trinity, and threw.

True to magical form, the vent hit the guard on the side of the head, and he went down in a pile of muscle and silk.

Ree knew she had less than a second, so she fell forward and flipped into the room, the duffel over her left shoulder. She scanned the room, saw the other guard to her right, and kicked a chair at him. The chair knocked him back a step, and in that time, Ree jumped forward onto a table then whooped with joy (internally) as she did Trinity's signature jump-kick. She could almost see herself from outside, the camera panning in slow-mo-groundbreaking-awesome and then jumping back to high speed as she kicked the guard in the jaw.

She dropped back to the ground and looked left into the living room of the suite, where the third guard, the one she'd sent for coffee, took a step back in shock at his companion being Matrix-pwned. His eyes flashed with surprise that quickly gave way to anger. *Great. Looks like he remembers the Jedi mind trick.* Ree imagined getting hoodwinked like that would really leave razor wire in your craw. He set a stance as Ree closed in on him, hands pumping at her side.

The guard raised a large handgun, and Ree crossed her mental fingers.

Dear Wachowskis, please hear me in my hour of needful pwn.

The guard opened fire, and Ree dug deep into the magical reserves, one compound word in her mind: bullet-time. *Wait. Is that one word or two? How do hyphenated words count?*

Later, she told herself as the world slowed to a molasses crawl, the projectiles making ripples in the air. She leaned left under the first bullet, still moving forward. Two more bullets launched out in quick succession, but they were on the same plane, each tracking a bit up as the weapon recoiled. The world grew more colorful, the green filter fading like someone pushed a slider on the control room of her visual cortex.

She'd burned through the magic damned fast with those displays, but it would have to be enough.

Luckily, now she was in range. She dove into a slide-tackle, kicking at the back of the guard's knee with her left foot and scissoring into his shin with her right. The world snapped back into normal speed and the guard stumbled forward. The magic fizzled out in her mind, and the green hues were gone.

Now it's just me and my normal, non-physics-defying self. And my black belts.

Ree let the duffel slip from her shoulders and dove forward onto the guard. He was face-first in the expensive carpet, but the guy still had a hundred and fifty pounds on her, and the extra kick of being pissed off that a skinny-ass girl had mind-whammied him (or so she imagined).

She needed to end this quick, before he could bring his weight to bear. Ree rabbit-punched him in the kidneys, but the blow came in soft, since all she hit was corded muscle. The guard huffed but still turned, roaring like a wounded grizzly. He was slowing down, so she saw his haymaker telegraphed Western Union. She ducked under the blow and threw a tiger fist at his armpit, hoping to hit a nerve cluster.

Her blow connected, but the guard kept coming. And worse, he started yelling, "Red Alert!"

There fucking better not be a fourth gorram guard, Ree thought.

Ree continued to press her advantage. If he got his balance back, she'd be hosed like a sunburned kid at Splashin' Safari.

She switched modes and climbed onto his back, wrapping one arm and her legs around the large man and laying punches into the back of the man's skull with her right. She tore open her knuckles as her fist hit bone.

The guard flopped back, crushing her under his weight. Ree felt millions of nerve endings cry out at once, but they didn't go silent. Instead, they kept complaining, clawing, and clamoring over one another for priority in the emergency-room triage of her brain.

The wave of pain and the pressing lack of anything in her lungs reeled her, but as the man recovered, Ree lost her angle on the vulnerable back of his head. Sighing inside, Ree threw a Hail Mary, a move that was only barely good kung fu, but if it landed, should end the fight.

She shouted, "Headbutt!" and hurled her whole body forward, striking the guard's nose with her forehead.

The world wobbled for a moment, Ree having rung her own bell (and not in the good way). After she reconciled her double vision, Ree confirmed that her opponent was down.

Her vision was still flooded with spots and stars as she checked the room. One, two, three guards down, and no number four in sight. Ree picked up the duffel and kicked open the bedroom door.

To find Rachel MacKenzie pointing number three's shotgun at her head.

CHAPTER SEVENTEEN

Fifteen Minutes Are Up

Celebromancy is a strange style, both complex and simple. Put simply, adoration in becomes power out, but each star's persona is distinct enough that there are as many Celebromancies as there are practitioners.

Heaven help you if you come across a star in their prime. A friend of mine got written out of the memory of nearly everyone who ever knew him after a messy breakup with a star. I only remember him because I was there when he got erased. It's the strangest thing: My only memory of the guy is forgetting him.

I've been working on some protections, since my regular approach of Green Lantern ring is my Ace in the hole failed spectacularly and I ended up spending a weekend wandering the city in an amnesiac fugue. No success so far. I hope the watch serves you better.

Short version: Watch your back.

—Eastwood, personal correspondence with Ree Reyes.
Sent May 21. Never received.

R ee slammed the door closed again and dove back. Buckshot tore through the door but went past Ree on her right.

Rachel MacKenzie's voice came through the hole in the door. "If you get out of here now, I might be lenient and not wipe you from the memory of everyone you've ever known."

"Do you greet all of your fans that way?" Ree asked, scooting away from the door, trying to keep out of the star's eyeline.

"Only the ones that make a habit of assaulting me."

"I just want answers, okay?"

"You're not going to like them."

"I can live with that," Ree said, looking around for something in the room that could take a load of buckshot for her. There were the guards, but she couldn't lift them even if she was willing to use a human shield (which she wasn't). "How do I remove the curse?"

Rachel spat her response. "She brought this shit on herself, you know!"

"Yeah, but does she deserve to die for it?"

A pause. "What?"

That took Ree aback. *Is she shitting me?*

Ree paced the room, raising her voice to call back to Rachel. *Come on, shield* . . . "Are you telling me you don't know? That curse is like feedback mixed with a hangover topped off with a Freddy Krueger Smoke–filled transparent terminator. It's tried to kill her twice, and judging by the amount of power she used today, it'll come back to finish the job tonight. Assuming we didn't kill it."

Did we kill it? That'd be awesome. That thing was ri-god-damned-diculous tough.

She picked up a steel room-service platter and a thick pillow and grabbed the sides of the pillow, hoping the soft-over-hard protection would give her more than a wizard's chance in a melee.

Rachel's voice was softer, uncertain. "It was just supposed to keep her from trying to take my mantle again. I never meant for anyone to get hurt."

The hell? It didn't sound like Rachel was lying, but then again, actress. "Supposed to? You did the spell, right? Shouldn't you know what it was going to do? Since you're a magic-laden mantle-bearing Celebromancer?"

Or is your magic even less consistent than mine? Ree wondered, not at all reassured by the possibility.

Ree waited for a response, but got nothing. After a few seconds, she returned to the door, keeping her makeshift shield front-and-center. She peeked through the hole in the door to see Rachel still holding the gun in front of her, but in a waiting position, not up and sighted.

Waving the cushion and tray like a white flag, Ree asked, "Can I come in? There's clearly some shit going down. I just want to help Jane, I don't have a vendetta." Which was a lie, but only sort of. She'd way rather have a healthy Jane and no vengeance than vengeance a-plenty and a dead Jane. There were other places for righteous fury. Like political discussions, or flame wars about Peter Jackson's *The Lord of the Rings*.

"Don't try anything," Rachel said, the gun lying across her knees on the lush bedspread.

Ree set the tray and cushion down, one eye glued to the gun.

She opened the door and stepped in, one hand up, the other holding onto the gold-plated pocket watch she'd gotten from Eastwood.

This better work, she thought.

As soon as she was full into the room, Rachel straightened herself up on her knees and snapped with a flourish.

Huh?

Ree felt a rush of magical energy as the room flooded with light. She flinched instinctively, but the light didn't hurt, even though it was like she was staring into a six-pack of floodlights.

The light tore at her mind, and for a split second, she forgot where she was, who she was, and what the hell was going on.

She mentally reached for memories, and they pulled away from her, like the fruit from Tantalus. That split second dragged on as Ree's mind flailed for purchase.

But as quickly as the feeling came on, it slipped off and faded, along with the light. Whew.

"What—" Rachel said, dropping her hands.

Gotcha.

Ree pulled out the pocket watch and waved it by its chain.

"I figured you might try to do some kind of whammy, so I came prepared."

On the watch, the time showed 12:16.

"Little trinket I picked up from a friend. He's got a bit of a Warhol fetish. Plan for everything. Your fifteen minutes of fame are up."

Eastwood wasn't high on her Favorite People list after trying to round up the souls of teen suicide victims to get back his beloved (aka Ree's mom). He was obviously trying to make amends, and he'd come through this time. But she didn't forgive that easy. Not him. And not Rachel. And his best solution had only barely worked. *Damn, this woman is a powerhouse.*

The star's facade of confidence fell for a second, and she cursed under her breath, scrambling for the gun. Ree jumped her before the star could bring up the barrel.

Struggling over a gun was a great way for someone to end up dead, but some carefully applied Hapkido made short work of the struggle.

She slid off the bed, held the gun behind her by the stock, and locked her eyes on Rachel, trying to make an Intimidate check. "So how about you tell me how to undo the curse. Is this a plot coupon thing, or do I have to get all of the minor cast members to stumble around reciting a Bob Dylan song?"

Rachel cocked her head to the side, apparently not a Battlestar Galactica fan. "Do you ever speak in English?"

Ree crossed her heart and said, "Uy, ¡Soy Estadouidense! Babosa," in perfect Spanish. "I'm still waiting."

The superstar straightened the sheets and sighed. "First, you're going to need a mirror."

"Any kind of mirror?" Ree asked quickly.

Rachel curled up her face in annoyance. "Do you want my help, or do you want to keep interrupting me every five seconds."

Ree chuckled, then opened her hands as if to say go ahead.

"A mirror with a silver frame, dating back to 1950s Los Angeles. What's important is the material and the location. It has to have been used by a female star, the higher-profile the better. A boudoir is better than a hall mirror. You'll also need head shots of all of the previous America's Sweethearts, dating back to Shirley Temple. I'll write down the incantation."

Ree shook her head. "Even better, you come with me. You could be shitting me, and as soon as I leave, you jet off to California and call the Feds. What guarantee do I have?"

Rachel sat back on the bed, a wicked smile spreading on her perfectly made-up face. "I don't know, what guarantee do you have? My guards will be up any minute, and if I call security, you'll be a fugitive now."

"But why help me if you're so confident?" A part of her mind screamed *It's a trap!* but then again, when didn't it? Paranoia had become a professional necessity. Though her caffeine intake probably didn't help.

"Because I'm a victim here, too."

Ree laughed. A deep, watching-Eddie-Izzard-in-rare-form laugh. "Bullshit."

Rachel looked offended in a most aristocratic way, her nose upturned. It was really quite cute.

Focus. Can't know how much more that watch will stop.

Rachel looked around the room, then closed her eyes and furrowed her eyebrows. The pressure in the room changed, then Ree suddenly felt more alone, like there was nothing outside the room for miles.

"I did the ritual, but it wasn't my power going into it."

"Huh?"

Rachel said. "I don't have much time. He'll notice the privacy bubble within a minute."

So that's what I just felt. "He? Bubble? More exposition, please."

"The bubble's a minor effect. Lets stars get breathers from the attention now again. The 'he' is the paparazzo Alex Walters."

The name rung a bell. "I think I met him at the press panel. Smug hipster?"

Rachel nodded and rolled her eyes. "That's the one. Here's the thing about being a Celebromancer: Your power comes from being seen, known, and thought about. And whoever controls the images people think about controls the power. Walters works for Cosmic, and they have me locked in an exclusive contract, all the way down to controlling public appearances. My contract dates back before the Internet, and their lawyers wrangled it so even my Internet presence is under their control. Most of the power goes to them first, and then gets lent back to me to keep delivering on their investment."

"How the hell does that work? I'm no lawyer, but that seems unconstitutional as hell."

Rachel snarled, then looked down and away, a resigned look on her face. "You make a deal with the devil, you know it's going to come with a price."

Ree thought back to the Thrice-Retconned Duke of Pwn. "Wait, a real devil?"

Rachel looked up at Ree with derision. "No. The studio, doofus. And even if I wanted to break the contract and go solo, Walters has leverage."

"Like what?" Ree asked.

"He has pictures that will hurt my side of the divorce case. If they go public, there's no way I'll retain custody of my daughter. And he's got his own power. He's especially fond of pulling monsters out of Cosmic films and siccing them on his targets."

"Waitasecond." Something clicked for Ree.

Panther-fly. Wyvern. Those sewer things. She knew they were familiar.

"He's a Cinemancer?" Ree asked.

Rachel nodded. "And a good one. One of my costars tried to break her contract, and he sent a doppelganger from one of her Cosmic roles after her until she cracked."

Ree winced. "He pulled a *Gaslight* on her with her own image?? That's harsh." *How terrifying it would be to be haunted by your own image, doubting your sanity a bit more every day.* "So they blackmail you to keep you in line, and they send Alex after you if you break faith? That's why they're after Jane, because she actually broke away from Cosmic?"

"She had a better lawyer from the start, thanks to Yancy. But when they left, Cosmic wouldn't let it go. As she was getting ready to make a bid for Sweetheart, they came to me. I didn't have a choice. If I don't play my part, they'll rig my divorce case, and I'll never see my daughter again."

"So you're willing to let a woman die and a whole production company crumble so you don't get fucked over in divorce court?"

"I get to keep my little girl, for one. You're not a parent, so that you can't understand. And Alex said if I stopped the ritual and helped him deal with Konrad, they'd modify my contract so I get more autonomy, more power, more money, as long as I stayed exclusive with Cosmic."

Ree shifted her weight, checking her phone one more time.

Better wrap this up. "So why are you telling me all of this? How do I know you're not lying?"

"I would kill to protect my daughter, but not like this, not for them. They've run my life for nearly thirty years. If you take them down, I get freedom. Real freedom."

"Okay, that's a good answer," Ree said. "Write down the ritual, and while you're at it, how about the names of the America's Sweethearts. I'd rather not have a woman's life be dependent on me hashing out whether it was Greta Garbo or Hedy Lamarr as America's Sweetheart in 1940 or whatever."

The star scoffed. "Everyone knows it was Garbo, but sure. I'd have thought Jane would go for someone a bit smarter."

"Please," Ree said, dismissive. "Can you tell me the maximum critical hit damage for a multiclass 7th level rogue slash 3rd level paladin using a max-level smite and sneak attack with a short sword?"

That got another blank stare.

"So there. We all have our specialized knowledge. And mine includes being able to kick your ass around this Egyptian cotton bed if you don't hurry up."

Rachel wrote quickly, and Ree checked her phone. *Almost there . . .* The cops would be banging down the door any time now, considering the fact that they were on the penthouse floor and this was that posh of a hotel. The nearest precinct was a five-minute drive away, but Ree didn't know if the hotel security would try to break down a door in response to gunfire. That'd be a hell of a thing. Better to just GTFO before she had to find out.

The star handed Ree a paper that showed a list of names on top, then several paragraphs that read like a mix of *Hollywood Babylon* and a *Mage: The Ascension* spell description.

Ree looked the star in the eye. "And this will do it, no catches, no ifs, ands, or what the fucks?"

"I swear," Rachel said. "Now get the hell out of my room."

"With pleasure." Ree backed out of the room, still holding the shotgun. *No reason to push my luck.*

Ree thought better of stealing a firearm and left it on a marbled counter, making her way to the floor-to-ceiling windows and their southern exposure.

And, time.

Ree pushed the send button on her phone and fetched the balaclava out of her duffel. The sunset was painting the sky in tones from rose to violet, and the beauty of the scene was almost enough to steel her nerves.

Until the door was kicked open and a quartet of officers stormed into the room.

Ah, fuck. Couldn't you have waited one minute? But if Rachel was really committed to helping her save Jane's life, she wouldn't compromise her identity. And the balaclava would do the trick. At least, once she did the other trick.

"Hands in the air!" they shouted. Ree raised her hands slowly, plucking a single card out of the top of her bodysuit, where it had gone slick with sweat. She held it over her head, bringing her hands together.

"Drop it!" another guard said.

Ree smiled and tore the card, a Shadowcat from the 1989 Fleer series. Ree turned in place, hearing a familiar hiss of steam, then saluted the guards and started running toward the window.

"Fire!" the guards said, and they did. Ree saw bullets pass through her in tight bursts, but she didn't feel anything.

Now just have to make sure I can shut it off . . . Ree dove through the bullet-cracked glass out into the colored sky of twilight . . .

And right on time, she saw Drake Winters in his aerothopter, hewing close to the building, climbing as he approached. Drake poured on the steam (literally), and Ree focused on shutting the magic of the card off as she reached out to grab the side of the magitech vehicle. And all the while, she tried not to look down.

Ree slammed into the side of the aerothopter, and the vehicle wobbled with the impact. It was all pipes and engines, no hull to speak of. Drake offered a hand, which Ree flailed for, trying to partition off the large portion of her brain that was screaming in pants-wetting terror. She could tell the magic wouldn't last long enough for her to hit the ground still insubstantial and climb up.

It was a leap of faith or nothing.

Her hand found Drake's, and they both pulled. The aerothopter wobbled again, but she got a leg onto a hot pipe. She felt a blister rise on her skin as she pushed off of the pipe to clamber into the passenger seat of the aerothopter, such as it was.

She adjusted the duffel bag behind her to form a rough seat cushion. "Great timing, as always. Let's blow this popsicle stand."

Drake chuckled. "I trust you mean for us to leave, Ms. Ree?"

"Of course I mean for us to leave. Did you see the guys with guns!" Ree waved an arm in a vaguely hotel-y direction.

Ree turned herself around to sit in the uncomfortable bucket seat and caught the police standing by the cracked windows, watching with bewilderment.

"Seeya!" Ree said, waving to the police as Drake urged the aerothopter west, away from the hotel. In a minute, the Doubt would wipe the aerothopter from their minds or recast it as a helicopter, or maybe they'd remember her basejumping to freedom. As long as Rachel didn't give her up, the guards didn't know her face, and they wouldn't be able to follow her. *That would have to do for now. Plus, once she broke the curse, Jane could cover it all up again, couldn't she?*

Drake steered the aerothopter through downtown Pearson, and Ree did her best to find a comfortable position to be a puddle of exhaustion.

"I owe you one, man," she said as they flew toward the sunset.

"I do admit, when you first told me of the plan, I knew that it might be one of the most daring escapes I've ever had the honor of participating in. Though there was the time when the Mistress and I liberated the prize griffon from the aerie of the Duke of the Northern Sky. Quite a spirited beast, that one."

Ree chuckled, because she couldn't bring her body to do much of anything else. "Don't ever change, Drake-y boy. Except learning more pop culture. It'll be years still before you properly appreciate my humor, and I feel bad for you."

"As you wish, Ms. Ree."

Her heart did a triple Salchow into a faceplant. "As you

wish . . ." *That's the second time he's said that. I don't think he means what I think he means.*

Ree pushed the thought from her mind and did her best to zone out as they made their getaway.

Drake set the aerothopter down on a three-story apartment building a few blocks from the university district.

"You sure the cloak covered us all the way back?"

Drake shrugged as he shut down the aerothopter. "Not entirely. But I doubt that the constabulary had resources in place to pick us up once it did wear off, given that we were flying too low for the radar systems and that you'd already done several impossible things leading up to our departure."

Ree hopped out of the vehicle and grabbed her duffel bag before the aerothopter could start to collapse in on itself. When they were both free, the pipes hissed and shrunk, folding in on themselves bit by bit until it was no more than the size of a suitcase, which Drake hefted with a smile.

"What is next?" he asked.

"First step is food. Lots of food. And all of the caffeine. Step two is me going shopping. You're welcome to come along, and I won't even make you wait while I try things on."

Drake quirked an eyebrow at the comment, which made him look entirely too much like Mr. Spock. And with that, the clumsy ice-skater feeling in her chest bubbled back up again.

They climbed down the fire escape, which was close enough to a reasonable thing for two people to be doing, even if one of them was in a bodysuit and the other looked like he was perpetually late for a gears-and-gadgets *Parasol Protectorate* tea party.

The lines anywhere would be absurd, but she had other plans, even if they didn't involve milkshakes.

×[×]⊗[×]×

Turbo's Pizza was packed to capacity, with families and college students crowding every table in the joint. Turbo's was the best sit-down pizza joint in Pearson, famous for the space-jockey mascot Turbo the dog, who graced all of their to-go boxes.

Ree nudged her way through a dozen people waiting in the entranceway for tables. But when Joni, the main hostess, saw Ree, her eyes lit up.

"How's it going?" Ree asked.

Joni gave a polite smile, looking down at her map of the restaurant, smeared with grease-pencil marks. "Busy as ever."

"How's the filming, Ms. Speaking Role?" Joni had a small part in Rachel MacKenzie's *Blog Wars*. It wasn't much, just two lines, but it was a huge step up from extras work, where Joni had been stuck since she got into the acting gig. There were only so many roles for a tiny cute girl if you weren't already famous.

The market was pretty well filled for most roles. In a more reasonable world, Joni should have been a star, but Ree still had hope. After all, she'd gone from frustrated screenwriter to possibly-not-doomed-debut-screenwriter in a matter of months.

Joni beamed. "It's amazing! Rachel is a marvel. She has such range. She can say yes in fifteen ways without blinking."

Ree smiled for Joni's sake. There was no reason to take the idol away from Joni. Not yet, at least.

"That's awesome! Any trouble getting time off from the pizzameister?" Ree asked.

Joni shook her head. "Of course not. Did you see the sign?"

Joni pointed to a sign on the host podium.

It showed a head shot of Joni and a note written in Cole's hand. "Proud home of rising film star Joni Smith."

Ree smiled, this time without reserve. "That's awesome. Any chance of us getting a table for two?"

Joni looked down at the table list, then squinted. "Give me just a minute, we're pretty backed up."

Ree shrugged. "Beggars can't be choosers."

Joni flitted off, an extra spring in her already-springy step.

Ree turned to Drake, who watched the crowd, looking more the transplant from Faerie among the crowd. "We will of course order the marvelous frites, yes?"

Ree clapped her companion on the shoulder. "Sorry, Drake, they're all out."

The inventor was crestfallen, his shoulders slumped. Ree squeezed his shoulder. "Just kidding! Of course we can get the fries. I wouldn't torture you like that."

Drake sighed in relief. "It may seem particularly trivial given the stakes of our pressing engagement, but that dish is like unto none other I've found on this plane. Badass, as you would say."

"I would say!" Ree chuckled, then turned as she heard Joni return.

"Follow me and look like you're important."

"When don't I?" Ree joked, lifting her arm from Drake's shoulder. "After you, wheelman."

Joni led the pair through the packed restaurant, weaving through red-and-white-checkered tables, worn but comfy booths, and stained-glass lampshades. They passed unguarded laughter, the glorious smells of melted cheese and sauce, and the satisfied sounds of noshing.

Ree drank it in as they went, added the feelings and memories to her bank of joy, just in case she'd need to draw from it for some supernatural effort or to dig deep to keep going. Having Drake with her helped all by itself, but Ree tried not to dwell too much on why, deluding herself into thinking it was the reassurance of having someone at her back, and not those marvelously unselfconscious smiles or the way he bit his lip during a fight . . .

Focus.

Joni escorted them past the tables and into the back office, where Cole Lutz sat in front of a pile of paperwork.

The pizzeria owner stood to greet Ree, seeming all-too-happy to leave the papers behind.

Cole Lutz (Strength 10, Dexterity 13, Stamina 11, Will 14, IQ 15, Charisma 13—Cook 4 / Entrepreneur 3 / Pizza Master 5 / Dad 2 / Geek 2) was a well-preserved fiftysomething, with a full head of white hair and a trim build despite basically living in a pizzeria.

"Ree!" he said, wrapping her up in a big hug that smelled of grease and cooked dough.

"Do we care what the health inspector would say about this?" she said with a single eyebrow raised.

"She was just here last week. Take my seat. I need to get back out there anyway."

"Didn't you say those forms were due tomorrow first thing?" Joni asked.

"I recall saying nothing of the sort. Now back to the hostess stand. I wouldn't want to think your star turn has gone to your head," Cole said with a wink.

"You're still paying me more than the movie is," Joni said with equal levity. "I know where my rent money comes from." The small woman turned in place, letting Drake through before she left.

"Drake, right?" Cole said, extending a hand. Drake met Cole's hand, and the two men shook. "Well I'll get out of your hair. Some of the merlot tonight?" he asked Ree.

"Not tonight. Diet cola all the way." Ree turned to Drake.

"Hero fries and a deep-dish?" The adventurer nodded.

"Your taste has not led me astray . . . save for that one unfortunate occurrence with the Taqueria."

Ree whispered, "That was not my fault. How was I supposed to know that the ground beef was still haunted after we banished the ghost?"

Drake matched her smile, mixed with a grimace of remembrance.

"Hot tea?"

Drake nodded, the grimace fading.

Cole slid by the pair of them and left them alone in the office.

Cole's office was narrow, and only barely deeper than it was wide, with haphazardly filed paperwork threatening to cause an avalanche of papercuts at any moment. Ree shimmied deeper into the room and pulled a second folding chair out from a closet, leaving the first one for Drake.

"So now we can talk shop and not freak the diners."

Drake pulled off his duster and hung it from a hook on the inside of the office door.

"Very well, then. What sort of shopping must needs done for our task to be complete?"

Ree shook her head, leaning back in the chair, watching to not go so far she hit her head on the other side of the office.

"Not till I've appeased the fiend."

Drake looked around. "Fiend?"

Ree pointed at herself. "I need some caffeine before I fall over."

Drake chuffed in amusement. "Very well. Shall I regale you with adventures from the farthest reaches of Faerie, speak of my latest invention, or leave you to meditate upon the consequences of chemical addiction?"

Ree put a finger to her mouth. "Shh. Adrenaline has faded, and there's nothing to replace it. I need quiet time until the go-juice arrives."

And so, they waited, Drake with his hands folded in his lap, Ree with her head back and eyes closed.

CHAPTER EIGHTEEN

Deep-Dish Plotting

The titular Grognard of Grognard's Games and Grog is notoriously gruff, reputed to still be carrying grudges from before Chainmail was a gleam in Gygax's eye.

If you ever find yourself on his bad side, your best options are appeasement and abjection. If you can distract him with something rare and shiny, you might get away with your head.

Some visitors claim to have heard strange voices at closing time, but this writer cannot confirm or deny the accusation that they belong to patrons who have crossed Grognard.

— Not For Mundanes: Pearson

The soda brought Ree her second wind (or third, or fourth, whichever it was), and the fries followed shortly after.

Cole wouldn't share exactly what went into the marvels, but it included red pepper flakes, parsley, Parmesan cheese, and garlic, with an aioli dipping sauce to mute the spiciness, which would still build from fry to fry until Ree had to take a break and just drink soda for a few minutes while Drake continued to munch down.

"I must find a way to properly thank the proprietor for this culinary marvel. Do you think he would care to have his ovens upgraded?" Drake asked as he sipped on his tea. Avalon may not have been Britain, but to see Drake drink tea, it might as well be.

"I don't think the health inspectors would like it, though Cole might think it was awesome. Even with the Doubt, the inspectors are likely get twitchy about a souped-up oven powered by magic steam power."

"It is only fit to call my work magic because the physics of this world are . . . limited. I cannot be blamed for your plane's shortcomings, can I?"

Ree saluted Drake with her glass. "Not at all." Ree reached down her shirt and pulled out the notepaper. She set it down on the table between them, next to the fries.

She took a pair of fries, dipped them in the aioli, then started munching as she scanned the paper. "First, we need to get signed head shots of these stars, all the women who have held the mantle of America's Sweetheart back through the early days of cinema. But that's just the base, like the stock of the spell. The real firepower comes from the mirror, which is going to be harder to find. MacKenzie gave very specific requirements."

She licked her fingers, then counted out the details of the spell.

"I need to check in with Yancy and Jane, they might be able to rustle up the head shots and point us at the mirror." Ree stopped. "This is assuming that you want to keep on with this. I know you have other stuff you could be doing, other people . . ." she said, trailing off as her stomach twisted.

Drake blushed a bit, but sat straight. "I am certain Ms. Tharakan will understand. You are, after all, her friend. Even if you have chosen to keep the details of your new calling from her."

"That's a whole different conversation," Ree said, waving the thought away. "But I'm happier with the backup. Either before or right after checking in with Team Show Biz, I need to face the music at Grognard's, and I'd love to have you backing me up."

Drake nodded, munching on some fries. He finished swallowing and took a sip of tea before responding, ever the gentleman even with food-slicked fingers. "But of course."

There was a knock at the door, and Cole ducked his head in with a deep-dish pizza and several plates. "Here you go," he said, moving the fries to set the pie down between the pair. "Ree, there should be clean silverware in a bin . . ."

Ree reached to her left and pulled out two rolled napkins with flatware. "Got it."

Cole nodded and said, "Got to get back to the crowd. Bon appétit."

Ree cut the pie with the knife from her flatware, sawing through the deep-dish crust. She folded the melting strings of cheese back onto the slice as she served it to Drake, who waited with the reverence of a devout man receiving communion. Then she cut herself a slice and only barely let the plate hit the desk before she carved off the tip and took a bite.

The crust was the perfect combination of fluffy and crunchy. This pie had sausage patties, feta cheese, and slices of Roma tomatoes, along with Cole's traditional blend of cheeses and Parmesean-topped sauce.

The two of them spent a few minutes communing with the pizza gods, all conversation forgotten. But Ree continued to think as she ate, wracking her memory to see if Eastwood might have any of the bits they needed, whether she wanted to deal with his random moods to get it, and exactly how deep of shit she was in with Jane, Drake, and Priya. Even if the thing with Jane was just lightning in a bottle, every extra step Drake took with Priya made it more likely she'd have to tell her friend that 1) she knew Drake and that 2) they'd come about this close to . . . something. Probably. Maybe . . . if she was reading Drake right, which she was only half-confident about in the first place.

Romance confusing. Pizza tasty, Ree decided in her Buffy "Beer Bad" voice, and took another bite.

"How are things with Priya?" Ree asked before she knew what she was doing.

Drake coughed on a bite of pizza, though she doubted it was the food that had caught him by surprise.

"Never mind, it's none of my business," Ree said, letting Drake off of the hook.

Drake's voice was hurried. "She is your friend, as am I. You were only being polite."

"Which is pretty damned out of character for me," Ree admitted.

Her partner in crime grinned. "Let the record state that it was not I who said such a thing."

Ree carved out another piece of pizza. "So noted. While I'm at it . . ." Ree offered Drake a slice, which he accepted, meeting offered food with his plate. Ree cut herself another slice and started carving it up, noting that Drake had opted not to actually answer her inquiry. *Thank the gods.*

"I can call the folks on the set now, and then we can start pounding the pavement. Sound good?"

Drake considered with bobs of his head, then affected an additionally concerned voice. "But it is only in our best interests to be properly fueled for this endeavor. For preparation's sake, I suggest we be sure to fill our stomachs and souls."

"Just don't fill it too much. A third slice of Cole's deep-dish is almost always a bad idea, unless we need to serve as our own ballast for your shiny FAA violation."

"Which acronym is that again?" Drake asked as he carved his pizza with short, efficient movements.

"Federal Aviation Administration. The people who would slap you with a bajillion dollars in fines if they knew you were zooming around the town with an unlicensed helicopter."

Drake smiled. "Ah, them. I have every confidence that they will continue to know as little about me and my device as ever, as long as I am tidy about putting the saucer out on the full moon."

Ree toasted Drake's presumptive Faerie helpers and then set about finishing her dinner. Ree boxed up leftovers and counted out some bills, her food budget much less taxed thanks to craft services and Jane's sugar-mama-ing.

×× ⬡ ××

The cell signal in the alley behind Turbo's was pretty anemic, but she didn't want to press her luck with the Doubt by talking out on the street. Drake stood a courteous ten steps away, seeing to his weapons and gadgets, with the carryout box at his feet by the collapsed aerothopter.

She tried Jane first. No reason in having to ask Yancy about her.

The star picked up on the fourth ring.

"Hello, darling."

"Hey. This is a business call, sad to say. I have the ritual for the countercurse, but the shopping list is pretty specialized. Think you and Yancy could pull some strings?"

Jane's voice raised a register and a dozen decibels. "Fantastic! Thank you, thank you, Ree! Finally, finally this will all be over."

Ree heard the creaking thud, which she took to be someone jumping up and down in a trailer. A second later, Jane spoke again, her voice calmed down again. "I'm sure we can put everything together. I still have a few markers to call in. Well, two. But Yancy's credit line runs deep, even after taking care of my . . . rough spots."

"Awesome. Got a pen?"

Jane laughed. "I memorize soliloquies for breakfast, hon. Lay it on me."

Ree rattled off the list and related the details of the ritual.

Jane hmmed and uh-huhed through the list, then inhaled slowly when Ree mentioned the mirror.

"That one is going to be a bit harder. Those are in high demand, especially with people trying to replicate the success of *The Artist*." Jane pronounced the capitals, which Ree logged as specifying the film rather than the generic term.

"Any leads? I'm already racking up a nice rap sheet, might as well add to it."

Jane cut in as soon as Ree finished the line. "What did you do this time?"

"Impersonating a chef, impersonating a high-class escort, getting your dress messy, four charges of assault, intimidation, resisting arrest, and jumping out of a ten-story building. The last one isn't a crime, but it was about as inadvisable."

Jane sighed in what Ree took as amusement. "I love how you classify mussing my dress as being worth mentioning in that list. I told you to take it."

"Still. The dress was the shit. Even looked good on my stick figure."

"Hardly. I prefer to think of it as a runner's physique."

Ree shook out her legs. "Tell that to my calves. I had to climb up two stories in a vent. I think there's more lactic acid in my veins than blood." Ree looked to Drake, who stood at the ready, fiddling with a gauge on one of his still-unexplained gadgets. "So, yeah, any hints on the mirror?"

"Nothing yet, but I'll check with Yancy. When we find something, we can get it overnighted."

"Or we could skip town to avoid the smoke assassin and do everything from L.A.?" Ree said, totally not just looking for an all-expenses-paid trip to SoCal. Not at all. Nor was she certain that running would actually do anything to deter the smoke-monster, since it seemed part and parcel of the curse.

"Nice try. You'll need Yancy and me for the ritual, and we can't leave the production without word getting out."

Ree smiled into the phone. "Even with your incredible power?"

"I thought you wanted me not to use my magic until the curse was lifted?" Jane said with a tone of gotcha.

Drake continued to fidget as Ree talked. "Touché. I'm going to hit up one of my suppliers. Drop me a line when you know more about the shopping list?"

"Of course. Will you be out tonight?" Jane said, the follow-up question implied.

"Almost certainly. But I'll be in touch soon. We'll put this to bed soon."

"My thoughts exactly," Jane said with a hint of wicked in her voice.

"Good night, everybody!" Ree said at an inside-voice-shout, then hung up.

Ree slipped her phone back into her jacket, then looked to Drake.

"One more ball in the air. Now it's time to face the Female-Fronted Metal." Which was all Grognard would listen to: Nightwish, Within Temptation, Lacuna Coil, etc. That and the Canonical Soundtracks of Geekdom™.

Drake nodded, adjusting the strap on his rifle. "It is only right that we take responsibility, as I wager that those light-fearing beasts are unlikely to carry insurance or appear in a court of law." Ree laughed, clapping Drake on the shoulder as she led the way to the street.

⋅✕⋅⊗⋅✕⋅

Grognard's was moderately busy, with a noisy six-person game of *Vampire: The Eternal Struggle* (half of the players using the original pre-name-change cards) running in the bar and a four-thousand-point *Warhammer 40K* tournament that, judging by the accumulation of empty bottles of the Dew and discarded bags of chips, had been raging since sometime last night.

Ree slinked in as best she could, but no one entered Grognard's without him knowing it. She didn't know if it was actual magic or if the man just knew the shop like it was part of his own body.

Either way, as soon as the door closed, she saw Grognard lock her in his gaze, then nod back into the office.

There was no mistaking the gesture.

Ree turned to Drake and said, "I hope you've put your affairs in order. I'm sure Priya will say something nice at our funeral. Something with imagery," she added, happy to steal a line from *Firefly* whenever possible.

The odd couple walked past Grognard into the office. The owner nodded to someone in the bar, then closed the door.

Then, because sometimes Grognard was a cruel bastard, he waited. He stood inside the door, arms crossed, beer-stained black sleeveless shirt showing oft-sunburned shoulders with faded tattoos.

And then, he waited some more. Ree fidgeted in the chair, her mind running through possible rhetorical frameworks of out-chewing that Grognard might use:

There was the *I'm very disappointed* style that her dad broke out when she'd been careless, or maybe he'd stick to a simple *You're fired*. He might even go for a more *The Office*–style extensive litany of her failures, or maybe a mobster-esque speech about how he treated her like family. And somewhere in there, she had to try to ask for help getting materials for the ritual. *Good luck with that*, she thought.

Grognard put Ree out of her misery. "So. You're not dead, which is good. But my cart is ruined, along with a keg's worth of brew. That is bad. So why don't you run the story by me again to make sure I wasn't misreading your note." He spoke in a tone that made it very clear he knew he wasn't misreading.

Ree started with Drake and her leaving the Market, then talked through the entire run-and-gun encounter, with Drake piping in to add his side of the story.

When the story was over, Drake added, "I may not be able to pay for the damages immediately, but you have my word I will do everything within my power to settle this debt."

Grognard pulled a bottle of Bärenjäger out from behind a shelf that she had thought was just full of paperwork, then took a long drag.

"Well, that little escapade cost me several thousand dollars and six months' worth of ritual time." Grognard paused for a second. "But you're both alive, which is the important part."

Tension drained from Ree's shoulders and back like someone had let out the air. She exhaled and relaxed.

"Because if you were dead, you couldn't work off the losses. Three thousand each, by my estimation."

Feeling like an anime heroine, Ree face-faulted.

Grognard chuckled. "You've got that big-time screenwriter money now, right? So you can afford to work off your debt for me for the rest of the year."

Drake cut in. "I would be happy to compensate you with goods or services."

The big man then turned to Drake. "I'll take both. There are always too many dishes on weekend nights and during tournaments. And when your hands dry out from looking like a California Raisins reunion cruise, you can help me design the new cart. I've got some ideas that will make sure shit like this never happens again."

Grognard stopped and looked at each of them in turn. "Get it?"

Drake nodded, and Ree said, "Got it."

"Good." Grognard opened the door back to the bar. "You can start now."

Drake took off his coat and rolled up his sleeves, looking back at the mountain of dishes and glasses cresting out of the sink like the Great Pacific Garbage Patch.

Ree waved to Drake and grabbed the serving apron from the locker that Grognard had allotted her, leaving her jacket behind.

She had a million and one better things to do, but if she didn't at least make an effort to mollify Grognard, she could kiss her flexible-hours-with-a-clued-in-boss job goodbye, and that sweet screenwriter money was a one-hit wonder unless the show got picked up to series.

So she put on her stolid server face and made the rounds, taking arcane cocktail orders from the *V:TES* players and delivering pitchers of beer and fresh pint glasses to the 40K-ers, watching as Greg swooped down from the high ground with a fleet of Ork Bikes to cut a swath through the advancing Tyranid horde.

Ree filed the idea of Bikers vs. Aliens away in the part of her brain that knew that terrible concepts didn't stop something from being saleable. Case in point: *Battleship* the movie.

Janet at the *V:TES* table ordered a round of mochas as part of what seemed like a bargain to get Rachel's Bruja to protect her squishy Tremere, so Ree made her way to the espresso machine.

Ree lost herself in the familiar routine, the memory of thousands of lattes made across her food-service history. Ree let her mind wander as she steamed milk, touring through her memory of the last several Midnight Markets, trying to recall if she'd seen anyone with a mirror that might fit the ritual bill, re-filtering gossip and bragging with her new priorities.

Ree had learned to store things away for future consideration whenever possible, but her memory was far from eidetic. She was pretty sure that most of her memory hard drive was filled up by trivia: movie quotes, monster stats, and card game text.

The pie chart of her brain probably read something like:

Geek Trivia: 53%

   Comics: 18%

   Movies/TV: 15%

   Games: 11%

   Literature: 7%

   Anime: 2%

Everyday Knowledge: 18%

Taekwondo/Hapkido: 6%

Sarcastic Barbs: 12%

Job Skills: 11%

Luckily for her, that Geek Trivia converted directly to her magic, like an Obsession Skill in *Unknown Armies*.

The machine made a strange clunking sound while she prepared the mochas, which she logged to get to later.

Once the drinks were done, she returned to the cadre of card floppers with a trayful of mochas, setting them on a foldout stand by the table. She passed out the drinks, which were received reverently and slurped noisily, then placed in between clusters of sleeved cards and glass beads.

She popped in to the back room to check on Drake, who was humming something that sounded like a sea chantey, up to his elbows in suds and dishes.

"Doing all right?" she asked.

Drake turned and gave an unguarded pleasant smile that lit up his flushed-with-effort face. *Oh, if only I had any capacity to pull off polyamory.* Her one trial run had gone disastrously wrong, and Ree had identified herself as the problem, which took it off the table until she could reliably both communicate well and not be jealous as fuck when she saw people whose bones she wanted to jump getting attention from other people.

She returned the smile in brief and slipped back into the main room, laughing at her all-too-predictable responses.

When she was a teen, Ree thought that being an adult meant growing past the silly feelings of awkwardness around people she liked, learning not to put her feet in her mouth, and so on.

In reality, it just seemed to be a case of accepting your habits and contextualizing. So instead of continuing to stew in the bowl of butterfly soup in her stomach, she set about cleaning the espresso machine.

She pulled out the portafilters, disassembled the front of the machine, and found that one of the nuts connecting an internal pipe was loose (testing with hot pads so as to not give herself second-degree burns). She pulled out Grognard's set of tools and tightened the nut, then reassembled the whole thing and steamed up some soy milk to make sure everything was fine.

Since it was, she made herself a victory chai, with a bit of vanilla to give it an extra kick. She'd be up well past midnight again, so a steady stream of caffeine was essential.

The *V:TES* game wrapped up around 11 PM, and Ree took the opportunity to rescue Drake from the back room, where Grognard had put the adventurer to work in cleaning the silos and tanks for Grognard's brewing.

"You'll be back tomorrow," Grognard said, not a question, just an assertion of understood reality.

Ree nodded, wondering if it'd be worth getting injured over the next day or so to call off from work and give Grognard's anger a chance to settle a bit more. Probably not worth the medical bills, though. She'd already borrowed more against her credit asking about a mirror for the ritual, though Grognard had only been able to give vague possibilities. Golden Age of Hollywood was really out of his area of expertise.

She and Drake took the office exit, still avoiding the site of the cart's demise. Grognard had mumbled about extending the wards on the store, but that would be as big a project as making a new cart, and not being at the Midnight Market would cost him thousands of dollars in lost business every month. So it would have to wait.

The pair stood under the orange-yellow light of the streetlamp, Pearson being one of the cities that had jumped on a more energy-efficient but totally ugly set of bulbs. They cast the street in a sci-fi light, everything one shade off of normal, even though Ree had lived with them for years now.

"I've got to get to the set, in case something else comes for Jane. Rachel wasn't forthcoming about the hows of Smokey the Terminator."

Drake shifted his weight, clearly wanting to say something.

He hesitated, then settled over his left leg and asked, "Do you need assistance?"

She wanted to say yes, but knew that inviting him would have a x3 Awkward multiplier with Jane. Danny would be there, and the security.

"I think we'll be fine. Go rest up, since tomorrow we get to scour the city from top to bottom for the right mirror."

Drake nodded. "I believe that a hot bath and a good night's sleep are in order. I will be available at your earliest convenience tomorrow, and do not hesitate to call if events transpire this evening."

Ree made a focused effort not to instantly throw out the dirty joke that came to mind. "Sure thing," she said instead.

Drake gave an exaggeratedly deep bow, then rose with a smile. He was still of his time and place, but they'd become familiar enough to make jokes about their many differences.

Ree watched Drake walk off, wind picking up the edges of his duster and running its fingers through his close-cropped hair.

She sighed, and then checked her phone vs. her memory of the bus schedule. She fetched her earphones and cued up an episode of Buffy to calm herself down and prepare a power-up in case things broke bad at the set.

The bus trip to the set took the better part of an hour, far off the prime time. She was joined by a thin assortment during the trip: some college kids that hopped on for three stops, talking in booze-thick voices; a man sitting in the back corner with a bundle of plastic and paper bags who worried at his mostly-gray beard; and a no-nonsense woman in business black who spent the whole trip with her face lit by a seven-inch tablet.

Ree had her own twenty-first-century flashlight mood lighting, wrapping herself in the comfort of "Chosen," feeling the burden of power along with the ever-harried heroine. *At least I don't have to fight in heels for the ratings*, Ree thought, though she knew that she could if she had to, another gift of the genre emulation magic.

She reviewed her agenda as the bus reached the last stop before hers, making sure she was remembering everything.

Ree tugged on the call wire as they approached her stop, rising as the bus slowed to a halt on the empty street. She saluted the driver and hopped off, seeing the stand-up floodlights that One Tough Mama had set up throughout the trailer campus.

It was an odd feeling, heading into a situation not knowing if it was going to end with smooching, fighting, or both.

I have a weird life, she thought.

No shit came her brain's response.

A bored-looking guard stopped her at the edge of the campus, standing underneath a pop-up tent. He waved a flashlight over her face and then waved her through.

Her night-vision completely shot, Ree blinked the light out of her eyes and continued on to Jane's trailer. There was another guard posted at the door, the same guy who hadn't recognized her earlier in the day. This time, he nodded and knocked on the door in the shave-and-a-hair-cut pattern.

The door opened from within, revealing Danny in a leather jacket, baseball bat in his arms. Ree saluted casually and stepped up as he moved out of the doorway.

"How are you holding up?" Ree asked.

Danny took a long breath. Up close she could see the bags under his eyes, the tension in his shoulders. "I got a nap earlier today when we had a full house. But it looks like it's going to be another long night."

Ree spoke in a lower voice. "How's she doing?"

Danny pursed his lips, a restrained wince.

"That bad?"

"She'll be very glad to see you," he said. "We've got the trailer covered from all angles, and a pair of squad cars around the corner. We're as ready as we can be without putting up barbed wire and putting machine guns in people's hands."

"All of this over a popularity contest."

Danny shook his head. "I never thought it'd get this bad. Jane says you have a plan, though."

"Ish. We need a lot of stuff still, and once that's done, we still have to track down the jackass who got the whole thing rolling."

Danny cracked his knuckles, shaking his head. "Walters. I never liked him, but I thought it was just because he was a smug prick."

"That's a perfectly good reason not to like him. But now we have a reason to kick his ass if he shows up."

Danny chuckled. "You have great anger."

"Was that a Yoda condemnation or a compliment?" Ree asked.

The bodyguard shrugged.

Ree scanned the room, reminding herself how she would take cover, gain ground, or flank someone in this room, then headed toward the back room.

"Jane?" she called, announcing her presence.

The door to the bedroom opened, revealing Jane in her silk robe over a pair of tights and a loose shirt. If Danny had bags under his eyes, Jane had suitcases. Ree closed the door behind her as she scanned the room.

Someone had ridden a whirlwind through the bedroom, turning out closets, spewing books and magazines all over the bed and the floor. Nothing was in the same place it had been, including the bed, which had been pushed up against the corner of the room farthest from the window.

Jane wrapped Ree up in a full body hug, leaning into the erstwhile heroine.

"I can feel it coming, Ree. You were right, and I knew it, but I didn't care, and now it's coming."

"What, Smokey?" Ree asked.

Jane sobbed into Ree's shoulder. "I don't know. But it's never been this bad. I can feel the magic trying to empty me out from the inside. I close my eyes and all I can see is that thing straddling me, its hands around my neck."

Guilt hit her like a sledgehammer to the gut. *Well, shit. And here I've been kicking around noshing on pizza, treating this like a scavenger hunt.*

Ree squeezed the star. "It's going to be fine. We've got this place locked up tighter than Amazon's sales numbers."

She ran a hand through Jane's hair while the actress trembled in her arms. The Buffy energy continued to buzz in her mind, enforcing her desire to protect this woman, Danny, and the cast.

But she didn't have anything to fight, just a big emotional mess and a sense of a monster-sized other shoe about to drop. She stayed like that for a long moment, holding Jane tight, trying her best to fight off the demons just through her presence.

You know we're screwed when I became the emotional rock in the situation. Her ex Jay would laugh his ass off at this. *Well, fuck him anyway,* she thought. *It's not my fault he's a heartless sod.*

When Ree heard shouting from outside, it was almost a relief. The noise came from the far side of the alley, near the office building set.

Ree hugged Jane tighter, then untangled herself. "I'm on it. Stay here, okay? I won't let anything happen to you. Nothing."

Jane pulled herself together and stood to her full height, putting on a noble bearing only a bit marred by the puffy eyes and tears. "Kick its ass."

"Yes, ma'am."

CHAPTER NINETEEN

Shout It All Out

Cosmic Studios has announced this to be The Year of Creatures. The film juggernaut is re-releasing its Classic Creature Cinema Series on Blu-Ray, starting with The Orcs Return on April 17, and continuing with De-Evolution on July 18, Dragonstrike on August 23, and Panther-Fly on September 12, with more to be announced.

—Plugged.com, January 17

Ree booked it out of the trailer, through the short hall, and then down the stairs as fast as she could, the trailer door slamming against the outside wall. Ree stopped at the base of the steps to look, and the door guard pointed.

"There. It sounded like Grant."

Not that Ree knew who Grant was, but the direction was enough for her to bolt toward the noise, dipping into the energy of Buffy for a boost. She hurdled metal fences, dodged huddled extras, and tore down the pavement until she passed the last trailer and turned to see.

Monkeys. Well, apes, really. But her mind went to Giant Freaking Monkeys. And these weren't normal gorillas. The same hairs on the back of her neck were on end that danced a jig when big-time Magic was going on. So, magic gorillas. Maybe summoned, like the other creatures Alex had been sending her way. Hopefully not demon gorillas.

One particularly large gorilla was hunched on the roof of one of the carts used to shuttle personnel and props around the campus. It howled to the sky, hammering its chest with its fists, while another two were cornering a cluster of crew and extras in one of the three-sided tents.

"Ook ook," Ree said, grabbing the apes' attention. One of the two turned to face Ree, as did the roof-rider.

The roof-riding gorilla bounded down and landed in a crunch of corded muscle in front of her. It looked . . . bigger in person than on TV or fifty feet away like she'd seen them in the zoo.

Ree took a step back, which the gorilla took as an opportunity to charge.

Doubting even Buffy-level strength would stop a gorilla head-on, Ree jumped the charge, clocking the gorilla upside the jaw with a kick as she went. The gorilla stumbled and fell under her, and she saw a second one following close after. She dodged forward and left this time, diving under the gorilla's long arms to strike the beast under the armpit.

Need weapon, stat. Ree reached into her bag and pulled out the lightsaber, glad that she hadn't used it since yesterday and would be topped off full of power.

She ignited the blade, and the gorillas took pause when they saw the glowing blue sword.

"That's right! Kicking it Old Republic-style, Grodd," Ree said.

But it was still three on one, the third gorilla joining its companions.

"Get out of here, I'll take care of them!" Ree said to the cast and crew. Crew members dragged off a fainted actor, but the gorillas ignored them, instead moving to circle Ree.

"Who wants it first?" Ree asked, turning constantly to keep them all in her field of vision.

One of the gorillas obliged, so Ree turned and chopped down through its outstretched arm. The arm hit the ground with a wet thump, and the gorilla roared, reeling back. The other two charged as one, and Ree jumped, sweeping the lightsaber down to ward them off. Ree landed on the roof of an uncrumpled cart.

Now she had the height advantage, and the gorillas' heads were in snicker-snack range. She took a swing, but the gorillas were out of measure. Instead, the gorillas hunkered down and bullrushed the cart.

Ree started to jump off, but lost her footing. She turned the drop into an attack, cutting deep into one gorilla's back. The one-armed gorilla tackled Ree from the left side, knocking her out of the air. The creature landed half on her as they tumbled to the ground. Ree turned the lightsaber on it, and it went limp.

She heard the bubbling of dead monster moments later as she stood, which took the *Am I killing endangered animals?* worry right off of her plate. She had been about 95% sure already, but to her knowledge, no normal breed of gorilla dissolved into ichor upon death. She would have remembered something like that from Bio class.

That left only one gorilla, which she held at bay with her glowing blade. The sewage-and-blood smell of the monster's remains reached her nose, mixing with the rubber and asphalt of the lot.

I've got this, Ree thought as she prepared to dart forward and finish off the last creature.

Then there was an earsplitting cry from across the campus, followed shortly by a BOOM!

Looking past the gorilla, she saw a plume rising into the air, smoke curled around flame.

"Fuck!" Ree said, diving forward, spearing the gorilla through the chest, and then continuing on. She poured the Buffy magic into her legs again, moving with Captain America speed.

She saw the silhouette of something large moving through the air and heard another scream.

Shit. Wow. Fuck. It was a dragon. A "No shit, there I was" dragon, blood red and looking like it had just winged its way out of *Sucker Punch*, soaring through the now-upturned floodlights.

The dragon shot out another breath attack, and Ree leaned to her right to move away from the blast. She grabbed a guardrail and swung herself around to come at the dragon's side.

Except that it was twenty feet up. And that everyone around her was running around in full Dragon Panic Mode.

Ree looked to the lightsaber in her hand, then up at the dragon. Wrong tool for the job. She deactivated the blade, stuffed it back in her bag, then rummaged around for a better weapon.

Sonic screwdriver? No. Phaser? Maybe. Ree's hand ran over wool, and she started cackling. Ree pulled out a quilted cap and pulled it on.

But this was not any cap, no, it was a quilted version of the iconic helm of the Dovakiin from *Skyrim*, seen in all the covers, signage, and pretty much anywhere that the game was promoted, including viral videos that had bred like bunnies across YouTube.

Ree looked up to the dragon, then bellowed the most famous made-up words of the year.

"FUS RO DAH!"

Ree heard a swelling of music as the Dovakiin theme filled her ears and the wave of force shot up toward the dragon. The force knocked the dragon sideways in the air, forcing the creature to turn and buffet its wings to regain its balance.

But once it did, it turned and focused on Ree.

Ree dashed behind another trailer, hoping people had already evacuated the giant hotbox. She felt a wave of heat as the blast hit the trailer. The vehicle wobbled, but didn't roll over.

Ree fumbled in her bag for a ranged weapon to go along with the cap. She could theoretically try one of the other shouts, but only "Fus Ro Dah" had hit even the gaming mainstream. Any of the other ones she could use wouldn't have a sliver of the ambient energy to pull from.

If only *Community* had actually shown the Rod of Dragon Control in their D&D episode. The D&D movie had one, but that film was so reviled that its prop might not even work on a hatchling.

As she ran, Ree counted down the recharge on the shout, hoping she'd get another use before the dragon cornered her.

She probably couldn't get any blasting magic out of the cap, so she'd need another weapon, since even shout-assisted, going into melee against a dragon seemed like an exceptionally bad idea, especially without armor. She reconsidered the phaser, plucking it out of her bag despite its being not as sexy as some options. Hers was pretty low-grade, just an old plastic toy.

She raised the phaser and fired at the dragon's flank, the beam zapping up and connecting just above the haunches.

Said creature did not budge.

"Figures," Ree said, doubling back behind the trailer again as she looked for another option. The phaser wasn't an original prop, wasn't even one of the more respected and beloved replicas. A run-of-the-mill plastic toy just didn't attract that much nostalgia, and no nostalgia, no oomph.

She did have a trio of batarangs, and her stock of CCG expendables included some ranged attacks. Plus . . . she could improvise.

Ree eyed a stand-up light and hoped that Yancy would forgive her. She pulled the light down, then took a long breath, focusing on applying her Buffy-strength. She twisted the pole between her hands, then slammed the twisted joint into her knee. The pipe cracked, leaving Ree with a tip-heavy pole with a broken light (complete with sparks of dying electricity) and a six-foot metal spear. She peeked around the corner of the trailer just as something gigantic went crunch above and behind her.

"Eeep!" Ree shouted as the dragon chomped down at her. She fell backward, throwing the makeshift spear out as a stop-thrust.

The dragon aborted its attack, then batted her spear away with its snout before lancing down for another bite. Ree rolled with the spear, dodging the bite.

"Danny!" she called, desperate for backup. Even Buffy hadn't gone one-on-one with a dragon. (Angel had, but unless it was in a book or comic she'd missed, neither of them had beaten one).

She got her footing again and danced with the dragon for a while. It would reach out to bite, she'd counter with the spear-pole, and then they would both jockey for position. The trailer crumpled under the creature's weight, collapsing in rending groaning stages. The mundane security was nowhere to be found, and Danny hadn't shown up yet, likely sticking close to Jane.

The dragon unleashed another gout of flame, which Ree was expecting. She dove as far as she could, keeping the spear in hand. She couldn't risk throwing the spear, since her lightsaber didn't have half the reach. And if 3.X D&D had taught her anything, it was that reach was crucial when fighting Huge or larger creatures.

Ree judged that enough time had passed for the shout to recharge, and waited for the dragon to start another breath attack. She inhaled and then, as the dragon opened its mouth to breathe flame, she bellowed:

"FUS RO DAH!"

The first whips of fire cut at her face and the smell of sulfur hit her nose like a pile driver, but the shout pushed them back into the dragon and knocked it off of its perch. The dragon had to billow its wings and take off once more.

Now.

Ree aimed for the neck and tossed the spear with the running-on-fumes remains of her Buffy strength. The golden floodlights glimmered off of the pole as it dug into the creature's neck, just above the left shoulder.

"Woot!" Ree jumped, pumping one fist in the air.

The dragon wavered in midflight, pecking at the spear like a bird cleaning its breast. It grabbed the spear in its maw, pulled it out, and tossed it in her direction.

Fucker has good aim, Ree thought as she hit the deck. The spear punched through a nearby tent and pierced a craft services table.

Ree looked up to see the dragon climb several stories. It started circling the campus, like it was looking for something.

She cupped her hands and yelled, "Hey, Puff! Where you going? Running away back to Honah Lee?" The dragon did not respond.

Ree dashed by Jane's trailer, trying not to focus on it, in case the dragon somehow didn't know which was which. She shouted to the area. "Status report!"

"Status is we're being buzzed by a fucking dragon!" said one of the guards, his voice cracking.

"Anyone hurt?" she asked, keeping in motion, one eye still on the dragon overhead.

Any response was lost in the sound of another gout of flame.

She felt a splash of pain across her back, then smelled smoke.

Ree stopped, dropped, and rolled, tearing the cap off of her head and flailing with a distinct lack of grace. She rolled up to her knees and saw the dragon swooping down to finish her off.

To: Julio Reyes
jreyes62@hotmail.com

From: Ree Reyes
rreyes@gmail.com

Sent: 9:57 PM, May 25

Subject: We Regret to Inform You

Dear Dad,

I know you're going to be distraught and all, since I'm dead now, but at least I died FIGHTING A FUCKING DRAGON! How amazing is that?

Love from beyond the grave,

Your doting deceased daughter

Ree heard a boom, and the dragon's snout snapped to the side rather than biting down on her head. Ree turned and saw Danny with a shotgun, advancing on the creature, pumping and firing with military calm.

Badass! Ree thought as she scrambled back and to her feet, drawing the lightsaber to give herself a fighting chance.

The dragon's tail hit her like a foot-wide whip, sending her reeling and rolling. She thudded against the side of a trailer, watching Danny continue to advance until the shotgun was empty. Then he pulled out a pistol and reversed direction, firing slow, deliberate shots as the dragon closed on him.

If he's out here, that sure as hell better mean Jane is fine inside . . . Ree thought, wondering just how much the dragon's fire was turning the trailers into microwaves.

But as it went after Danny, stomping tables into kindling and rending through fencing, it didn't come after her to finish the kill. Ree shook the stun off, thumbed the lightsaber on, and rocked herself to standing again.

She wobbled on her feet and stuttered back a step.

Did anyone get the number on that tail? Ree blinked until the three dragons tearing at Jane's triple-trailer merged into one, and she knew where to aim. Ree drew a batarang from her bag, then wound up to throw. "This is me Tanking!

Tank-a-licious! I'm much tastier than them! Spicy Latina right here! Caliente!" Ree threw out whatever came to mind, her mind still fuzzy.

The dragon turned and belched fire at her with that look of disdain only a reptile could manage.

Ree dove to the side, and the world kept spinning when it should have settled into focus once more. Less than a year in the hero game, and she already had a growing collection of concussions and/or concussion-like injuries. Dr. Wells promised that the tenth one came with free permanent brain damage.

Ree found her balance again, then strafed forward and to the right, copying a page from *Skyrim* and attacking at the dragon's flank. When playing the game, she'd found it best to keep far enough forward to avoid the tail and far enough back to avoid the bite. It was the Scylla and Charybdis of dragon-slaying, and far easier said than done.

Ree slashed into the dragon with the lightsaber, leaving glowing gashes in its scaly flank. The dragon lashed out in pain, slamming her with its wings. Ree hit the deck, then jammed the lightsaber into the dragon's belly.

As it moaned a death knell, the dragon collapsed on top of her, its neck falling across her chest like a tree.

The air went out of her lungs like a bellows. Her arms were pinned, the lightsaber pressed to the pavement. But the dragon wasn't moving, so it seemed like the only danger was having her lungs cave in.

Small victories?

Ree wheezed, trying to speak. But since her lungs were desperately trying to exist in the same space as a burned corpse, nothing came out. She kicked her legs, trying to work herself free. And if someone noticed the flailing and came to help, that wouldn't hurt, either. But if they were smart, most everyone should be blocks away already.

Her already-foggy head got foggier as she failed to get new air into her lungs. She flailed harder, trying to get the lightsaber to cut through dragon, concrete, or something to help her get free.

She saw a shadow pass through her vision, then heard metal hitting concrete. There was a grunt, and then the weight lifted from her chest. It took several more wheezes for her to get her lungs to remember how to accept oxygen, but they did fill. Ree sat up, her vision covered with scattered white lighting.

Danny stood above her, backlit by the few remaining floodlights. He set down the spear, which he'd just used to lever the dragon's neck off of her. The bodyguard held a hand down to her, which she took.

Back on her feet, Ree evaluated the desolation. The trailer campus looked like it had been hit by a fire-nado.

She smelled burned metal, roasted concrete, accented by charred kindling. People emerged from their hiding places, some faces ash-white with fear, others soot-stained by the fires.

As she took a step toward the crowd, she heard a deep popping sound and felt a wave of ichor wash over her legs, sending chills up her whole body. *Eeeugh.*

The dragon's remains covered the concrete, spreading out all the way to the street.

And now my pants are ruined, too.

Yancy emerged from one of the trailers and took charge. "The fire department is on the way! Everyone stay calm, and we'll be fine. If you inhaled smoke, go to the props tent. If you were burned, head for the street if you can move on your own. If you can't move on your own, wave or call for help."

Ree joined the triage efforts, helping cast and crew cluster into the appropriate groups for care once the firefighters and EMTs arrived. Ree didn't relish the idea of trying to explain a dragon attack in normal-people terms, but arson would probably have to suffice. That was, of course, assuming the Doubt could cover up something this big.

And the ichor would be dissolved by the time the emergency responders arrived. Hopefully. Except for the stuff that had gotten on her. That tended to stick around until she air-blasted it off. The universe seemed to have a vindictive streak that way.

When the responders arrived, Ree let them take charge and found her way to Jane's trailer. If she let the EMTs look at her, she'd spend the whole night in the hospital, and she had better things to do. Plus, this might have just been the first wave, as terrifying as it was to consider.

Danny had taken the post outside the trailer, his armpit holster showing. The shotgun, however, had apparently gone back inside. The trailer had several rents along the side and a yard-wide dent in the living room corner.

"You okay?" Ree asked.

Danny nodded, his eyes wide. "Hell of a thing. When I heard that dragons were real, I never imagined I'd actually see one, let alone fight it."

Ree smiled. "And lived to tell the tale. How cool is that?" Danny returned the grin for a moment, being polite, then resumed his post, scanning the charred filming campus. Shooting would be indefinitely postponed, if not canceled entirely. The insurance claim would get held up for years, if it even went through.

Ree climbed the steps and opened the door. The inside of the trailer looked like it had been through an earthquake, dishes shattered on the floor, table upturned, papers and Blu-Ray cases strewn across the floor.

"Jane?" she called out as she leaned into the hallway to see down the hallway to a closed door. Ree went to the door and knocked. "It's me. Are you okay?"

The moment of stillness sideswiped Ree, her equilibrium skipping like a laggy video game. She leaned against one wall and focused on her breathing. Her after-action sleep tally had to be up to about thirty hours by now. *But if the production was scrubbed . . .*

Ree was saved from thinking through those consequences by the door opening to show a visibly shaken Jane, clutching a baseball bat like a three-year-old hanging on to her binkie.

At the sight of Ree, Jane's whole body relaxed. The bat drooped to hanging by her leg, and the star wrapped Ree up with her fee arm. "Me? Are you all right? It looks like you've just been to war."

"I killed a dragon. A for-realz dragon. How cool is that?"

The two of them walked over to the bed. Ree flopped onto the lush sheets and was out before she could say comfy.

CHAPTER TWENTY

Schrödinger's Disappointment

WTF RT @PearsonPatriot Large explosion reported at Douglas and 2nd. Emergency responders are on site.
—@Fugu__Ken, Twitter, May 26, 1:17 AM

@Fugu__Ken I heard it was arson. Something to do with J-Rad's crappy new show.
—@MaddowsWife, Twitter, May 26, 1:21 AM

@Fugu__Ken @MaddowsWife Three people were DOA at Pearson Heart. Not time 4 snippiness.
—@BaliAli, Twitter, May 26, 2:13 AM

When she woke, Ree was sore in her everywhere. She popped and groaned as she stretched, and felt a warm presence beside her. There was light from somewhere, and she cracked open her eyelids like ancient vaults.

"How are you feeling?" Jane asked from beside Ree.

"Like death left out overnight during a blizzard."

A hand ran through Ree's hair. "You've been running pretty much nonstop since what, last week?"

Having found a comfortable position and not ready to face the world again, Ree dug in where she was. "Mmm-hmm."

"We've got everything except the mirror, and that should arrive by courier today. We're going to shoot for tonight for the ritual."

Ree grumbled at the talk of real things, flipping over from facing Jane to facing the wall. "So I can keep sleeping, right?"

"Yancy wants a word about the production." She waited a beat. "I'm pretty sure he's going to call it. We can't recover from this kind of damage, not right now. If the insurance claim comes through, we might be able to recoup costs, but we'll miss this pitch season."

"Fuuuuck," Ree said, feeling her professional ambitions go up in smoke. She pulled herself upright, seeing that she'd been undressed and cleaned. Holding a sheet up to her chest, she asked. "Clothes?"

Jane nodded across the room to a folded pile on a chair. "I had them cleaned. They still smelled horrible. So I picked these out for you." Jane handed her another stack of clothes, including a pair of dark-wash jeans, a vintage-design *Galaga* shirt, and a baby-blue sweater. "I wanted to have those burned, but I figure that's your call, not mine."

Ree creaked and stretched her way to standing, then dressed, already starting to mourn her poor close-but-no-cigar-it's-already-burned-because-dragon TV show.

"Can we get coffee before we hear about how screwed we are?" Ree asked.

Jane smiled a weak smile of sympathy. "Of course, hon. And for you, I won't add Bailey's to mine."

"Friends don't let friends drink and thaumaturge," Ree said, picking herself up.

Since the craft services tent had been melted and then impaled during the fight, Danny accompanied them to a nearby café to get a triple cappuccino (for Ree) and a skinny half-calf latte (for Jane). Danny had water.

Ree walked slowly on the way back, savoring the drink. Her senses unfolded with the caffeine, the mothballs-in-the-mouth flavor and the fuzz around her vision receding as she made the proper obeisance to her Caffeine Overlord.

Until she went to talk to Yancy, she still had a pilot in production, in the same way that Schrödinger's cat was alive until you looked. There would be other scripts to sell, and maybe she could even find a way to resell this one once the rights reverted or whatever. But what was supposed to have been her big chance would become, as soon as reality hit, a hellaciously inauspicious start for her writing career.

Eventually, Ree gave in and they got to the tent Yancy had taken up as his new office, given that his trailer was in two pieces and upside down at the moment. The mood on the shooting campus felt like what Ree imagined it would in a battlefield, the kind where a day later the losers dragged away the bodies of the dead while trying to deny the fact that they'd just lost the campaign.

Yancy was unshaven, with a tie loose around a soot-stained shirt and pants. He managed a weak smile as Ree and Jane approached.

Ree's hands shook, and her voice caught in her throat as she tried to get directly to the point. The words died in her throat.

"Good morning," Yancy said. He lifted a pair of foldout metal chairs and handed them to Jane and Ree. "Will you sit?"

They sat, and Ree found her voice again. "Are we screwed?"

Yancy and Jane shared a look, and let the words sit heavy in the air. Every millisecond that passed let more hope out of Ree's lungs. She'd pulled open the box, collapsed the waveform.

Fucking dragons. When I find Alex Walters, I'm going to shove my collector's edition of Skyrim *down his throat and Fus Ro Dah him off of Mount Rainier.*

Another moment later, Yancy sighed. "We can't finish. There just isn't the money. We might be able to get insurance to recoup some of the costs, but by the time that comes through, we'd have to set up a whole new production for the remainder of the shoot, do ADR, and even with that, we'd be behind a season for pitches. Shooting this on spec was the only way we could do it, and without an order, we're dead on arrival."

"How much do we have? Could we splice together a half episode, maybe run some of it as a webseries to drum up support?" Ree said, knowing that she was reaching but not giving a fuck. She'd put months of her life into this; it was supposed to be her big break. "Even a sizzle reel to go to companies? You've got more than most companies have when they pitch, right?"

Yancy nodded. "Sure. But with the curse, Jane's reputation was a liability rather than a blessing."

Jane's already somber look dropped even more at Yancy's words.

"What if we take my name off of it?" Jane asked. Ree did a double take.

Jane continued, "It's a good concept and a damn fine script. You cobble together what we have, and we go in with the concept and a proof of concept on the scenes we've got. We don't have to go to square one, and you get a fair chance at launching the show." Jane was looking directly at Ree, tearing up.

"That's crap!" Ree said. "You're awesome in this. And we're going to kick the curse's ass anyway. After today, it's just you. No magic bullshit, no Smokey, just Jane Konrad and the Comeback Express."

Jane shook her head. "The curse isn't the problem. It's me. No network is going to take a risk on me until I've done something and seen it through. Even spinning this," Jane said, indicating the destroyed set, "as an accident doesn't change the fact that I'm baggage right now. And it doesn't make any sense to just toss the whole thing out."

Jane looked to Yancy. "We knew this was a Hail Mary. It was the only way I could manage my own comeback without my agent sorting through hundreds of scripts to find the one we could spin right to be my way back in. I'm more than an actress, and One Tough Mama is more than just my vehicle. Cut what you can, and we'll start reaching out for pitch chances."

Ree's stomach roiled, and not at the coffee. She stood up and kicked her chair over. "Motherfucker. I'm going to kick Walters's ass so hard he ends up in a parallel timeline where smear journalists are drawn and quartered on sight."

Jane reached out to touch Ree's arm. "We'll get him later. And I can help you do it once we've broken this curse."

Ree stopped, considered Jane's words, but decided to keep fuming instead. "Yes, but I'd like the record to show that step two of that plan should happen as soon as fucking possible."

Yancy said, "So noted. For right now, we get ready for the ritual and hope that nothing else explodes before tonight. But before that," Yancy held up a hand to say wait, then pulled something out from underneath a table. It was a director's chair.

Scratch that, it was her chair. Yancy unfolded it enough to show her the REE REYES, WRITER printing on the back.

"A souvenir of your first show. I'm sorry that this might be all you get to take away from it."

Ree took the chair and laughed, something inside her cracking. And somehow, something got in her eye. That was it, definitely not tears. "Thanks." Ree looked at the chair, then surveyed the wrecked set campus. *This is really it. The dream's over, now it's all cleanup.*

But she wasn't at all convinced that the monster attacks were actually done. She saw no reason to be anything but paranoid, especially while the curse was still active and her career anxieties had exploded beyond her wildest nightmares. She set the chair down and looked for something to do. (Ideally, someone to punch, but no reasonable targets presented themselves.) She checked her phone and weighed whether it was too early to call Drake. Or if maybe she could get more sleep. Not that the latter was likely, considering the zebra mocha of caffeine and adrenaline coursing through her system.

Ree started to head off-set to make with the preparations. Jane caught her on the edge of the campus.

"Before you go, before the magic goes down, I just wanted to say . . ." Jane caught herself blushing, then tucked a stray lock of hair behind her ear. "I wanted to thank you. For believing in me."

Ree cocked her head, a bit surprised.

"Yancy has always believed in me, and the crew here. But you saw me as who I should be, not who I was letting myself be under the curse. It would have been easy for you to give up or walk away, but you didn't. So thanks."

Ree hrmed internally for a moment, guilt bubbling up as she remembered the times she'd doubted the star. "That sounds a lot like we're about to go down with the ship talk."

A shadow of thought passed over Jane's face. "Maybe, maybe not. But I wanted you to know how much I appreciate all you've done."

"It hasn't been all work," Ree said, running the back of her hand along Jane's chin. Jane leaned into Ree's hand, wrapping Ree up in her arms.

The calm before the storm feeling came back, and Ree held it at arm's length with the warmth from Jane's embrace. One way or another, it'd be done after today. Unless the mirror didn't show up. But how funny would it be for them to make all of the final preparations and then get delayed because of a screwup by UPS? She chuckled, then the chuckle grew into a full-belly laugh. The women disentangled as the laughter spread up and down her body, nervous energy fueling the Alanis-Morissette-ironic thought.

"What's so funny?"

"Just thinking," Ree said, trying to get the words out between laughs, "about how screwed we are if the mail doesn't show today. If we win, the UPS person will be partial hero of the day."

Jane joined her for a moment, then said, "Honey, the mirror and reel are on a chartered flight with armed guards. I'm not taking any chances."

"Except for the giant half-understood ritual we got from the woman who tanked your career."

Jane snort-choked on her drink. "Other than that, yes."

"Just trying to stay grounded."

Jane shifted her weight, cocking out one hip. "Says the woman who gets superpowers from wish fulfillment."

"Et tu, fame-girl?" Ree responded with a grin.

Jane nodded. "Fair enough. Where are you headed?"

"To get the cavalry."

The cavalry, as it turned out, was pretty much just Drake.

She could have called Eastwood and guilted him into coming, and maybe sweet-talked a few folks from the Market, but Ree knew she was already headed for a dangerously unpredictable evening, and she didn't want to have to herd cats while . . . doing whatever it was that she'd have to do.

She got home around nine and made her rounds to prep for the day. She ignored the growing stack of mail (largely bills) on the front table, labeling them mentally as Tomorrow Ree's problems. Or more accurately, Ree When She Is Human Again After Sleeping Off This Adventure's problems.

Shower achieved, Ree pulled open her closet and set about assembling her Battle Gear(™). First, she cued up a Two Steps From Hell album to have suitably epic music for her Hero Armors Up scene.

Then she put on her base outfit: well-worn jeans (the one pair left not covered in ichor or blood or ripped to hell) and T-shirt over undershirt over bra. She bound her hair back with a hair tie, then added her Wonder Woman clip. She searched her box of contacts, but as she'd suspected, the only ones left were two years out of date and had already been worn several times. The daily ones itched the hell out of her eyes, and anything better was usually too expensive. If she hit it big with a script (which seemed unlikely at this point), she'd promised to get herself LASIK.

Her base outfit in place, Ree pulled out the buff jacket

she had on seemingly permanent loan from Drake, which had the tremendously handy property of adjusting to fit her perfectly and the even cooler self-repair property that kept the jacket from quickly becoming an accessory only fit for Steampunk Frankenstein's monster (since normal Frankenstein's monster is Electropunk, natch).

Then she assembled her weapons: her Force FX lightsaber, her blaster rifle, the phaser, a pair of arnis canes, the jian on loan from Drake, her batarangs, a knife, some inexpensive prop guns, a Ridiculous Fantasy Sword(™), and a boffer sword.

They wouldn't be in public, so she could pretty well go all out.

She set the jian, the lightsaber, and the phaser in the probably pile, slid the batarangs in one of the buff jacket's pockets, and set the knife next to her big, stompy boots.

Weapons decided, she pulled out her card boxes and skimmed for a few minutes to fill up her sideboard, focusing on direct damage spells and a bit of crowd control, in case Walters had another wave of nasty in store. It seemed like his flavor of Cinemancer resembled nothing so much as a Summoner from *Pathfinder* or *Final Fantasy Tactics*.

Ree's phone chirped with the theme to *Steam Boy*, her ringtone for Drake. She plucked the phone from its rumbling path off of her bed and answered, "Hey, thanks for calling back. How's tricks?"

A beat. "Rather the same as always?"

Ree chuckled, hearing another whif sound in her mind. "You still in for the big shindig today?"

"Of course. Shall I bring weapons, more weapons, or all of the weapons? I have a new hand-cannon I'd rather like to field-test."

"How likely is it to blow up and kill us all?" Ree asked.

Ree heard Drake doing math under his breath. "Not at all likely. Current estimates put the chance under one tenth of one percent. As long as I don't use the highest setting."

She flashed back to Drake's hand-scrawled note on the

gun's gauge. "Good enough for me. Come loaded for bear, but I don't actually know that there will be fighting. It just seems pretty likely given Alex's previous record of spamming monsters whenever he can."

"How does one spam monsters? Also, what is spam?" Drake asked, confused.

"I'll explain later," Ree said. "You coming?"

"Understood. Where and when?"

"The movie set, noon? If you get there early, you can hang around on guard duty if you like, but the things we need aren't scheduled to arrive until midafternoon."

"Certainly."

"And Drake?" Ree added.

"Yes?"

"Thanks. You've always been there for me, even when I didn't know I needed it. I just hope I'm not getting you in over your head."

"That, my dear, is why I have telescoping boots."

"Really?" she asked.

This time, it was Drake who laughed. "And on this day, we shall mark the calendars. That was a joke, Ms. Ree."

Ree matched Drake's laughter. "Awesome. But still, thanks."

"I live to serve," Drake said.

"Don't. The wages suck. Live for awesome. The pay isn't any better, but the sightseeing rocks."

"Well put. Until noon, then."

"Seeya."

Ree disconnected, then dropped the phone on her bed as she finished packing up. She sheathed the sword and brought it with her to the living room.

And now, choose the form of the power-up. She had between three and five hours before the mirror was scheduled to arrive, if she stayed and kept powering up until she got the call from Jane or Yancy that they were ready to get started. The question then was, what to marathon for Real Ultimate Power?

There was the basic stuff: *Buffy*, *Angel*, and *Supernatural*, for general monster-fighting awesomeness. Then there were the ones for Action-Hero physics: *Cowboy Bebop*, *Terminator*, *The Last Action Hero*. She could go more flashy with something like *Slayers*, or the X-Men cartoon for some elemental power.

Hmmm. Terminator had good bodyguard resonance, but it would be really cool to throw fireballs and crap without having to burn cards.

She scanned her shelves again, while running through her mental tally of films on her hard drives. A moment later, she had a tickle of excitement. *What could possibly go wrong?*

Ree plucked *Spider-Man* and *Spider-Man 2* from the shelves and popped the first one into her DVD player. She'd heard a few Cinemancers swear that their magical buck went way further with HD transfers, but Ree wasn't in a position to upgrade her collection more than one or two films a month, especially when she valued breadth over depth, still being at the start of her career.

As she watched, Ree brought up memories of her favorite Spider-Man comics, the video games she'd played, the wild joy of swinging through the city and punching bad guys up and down Manhattan. She keyed in to Ben Parker's motto, "With great power comes great responsibility," the saying that had become synonymous with his nephew's career as a hero.

She was halfway into *Spider-Man 2* when her phone rang, showing Jane's number. She paused the film, but the Danny Elfman score in her brain kept going. "Ree Reyes's House of Heroes," she answered.

"What?" Jane asked.

"Sorry, I've been watching *Spider-Man*, so the Quip is strong with me right now."

Jane chuckled. "Awesome. We've got the mirror, so we're setting up now. Your dashing friend is here trying to help clean up, but I distracted him with some proper tea I picked up at the last London premiere. He said it's something about the bergamot that makes it good. Also, he brought a scary handgun. Do you know anything about that?"

"Oh, yeah! It'll be fine. As long as he doesn't get mopey and start talking about his Mistress, we'll be fine."

"Mistress?"

"It's a long story. I can be over in about fifteen minutes, traffic permitting. I could web-sling my way there, but that would be a waste of energy despite being outrageously cool."

"I've got a car headed over for you. That way you don't have to haul your arsenal through a crowd." Jane stopped for a moment. "You can web-sling?"

Ree made the iconic web-shooter hand sign, saying "Go web go!" and saw a blob of webs shoot out and form a thick net in the top corner of the room, above the TV.

She'd been circumspect about organic web shooters at first, unhappy that Peter's inventiveness was undercut by incorporating the webbing into the mutation. But damned if she wasn't grateful now.

"I sure can!"

Another chuckle. If nothing else, she was keeping Jane's spirits up. "Well, tiger, get your web-slinging ass down here and let's end this thing."

"Yes, ma'am." Ree hung up the phone, gathered her arsenal in the living room, and kept watching until she heard a trio of honks from a car horn.

If only there were Whispersync between my DVD player and my phone . . . she thought as she headed out the door. *Dear technology gods . . .* The thought trailed off as she threw on the coat and took her battle-ready self down to the car, Elfman's score booming in her mind.

Let's do this thing.

CHAPTER TWENTY-ONE

Showdown at Sunset Boulevard

After the Carmine Wharf incident, and per the request of special consultant Mr. Eastwood, I am allocating additional funds to the Special Weapons and Tactics division for personnel, equipment, and training.

The division will take responsibility for squad-level responses to threats to the city.

This aspect of SWAT will remain undisclosed to the public, and all efforts must be taken to avoid exposure, lest a public health and panic crisis threaten to bring down our great city. Mr. Eastwood will be on retainer to assist in educating the officers on more esoteric matters.

God go with you.

—commissioner of police D'walla Richards, in a private memo to SWAT commander Hank Kanagawa, November 23, 10 years ago

There were three squad cars parked around the perimeter of the filming campus when Ree pulled up in the black town car that Jane had sent.

"Couldn't have shown up yesterday, could they?" Ree asked.

Not that the shotgun shells had done much more than annoy the dragon yesterday. And none of them needed more dead bodies on their conscience. Really, the only people who ever did need dead bodies on their conscience were killers, not the hapless fool heroes who were trying to protect people. The really bad people didn't tend to do the whole guilt thing, so it mostly affected the poor schmucks trying to make a difference in a grayscale world.

Less internal monologue, Ms. Parker, she thought, shutting the door. She approached the police cordon, wondering if she was going to have to explain her sword.

Except that the woman who greeted her at the cordon recognized her. "Hello, Ms. Reyes. Looks like you're ready for a fight." It was Officer Washington, this time decked out in SWAT gear and holding a shotgun over her shoulder to match Ree's sword. Washington raised an eyebrow when her gaze settled on the sword.

"What, this?" Ree said without thinking. She gestured to her sword and said, "Walking stick. It's like the katana umbrellas at ThinkGeek. Purely decorative." *Good old Peter Parker, always putting his wit in front of his brain.* She concentrated, trying to keep the magical energy in hand. It was hard, since she was practically bursting with excitement derived from decades of loving and identifying with Spider-Man.

Washington smiled, then waved her past. "Leftenant Anachronism is already in there."

Nice one. I'll have to keep it on file, Ree thought. "Let's hope that you have a really boring day," Ree said.

"Most days are," Washington said. "Not that I mind. Active imagination, don't you know."

"You didn't tell me you were on SWAT."

"Before today I wasn't. Turns out there are more clued-in

people in the department than I knew. Get settled, then let me introduce you to the captain."

There were a dozen SWAT troopers by the building, sitting in wait under one of the mostly-intact tents, riot shields stacked up against the wall like Roman scutum.

That display alone put the stake through the idea that the Pearson PD was anything but clued in as to the weird. The officers nodded to Ree as she walked by, also choosing to ignore the hundreds-of-years-out-of-date sword she carried.

She pondered stopping to talk with the officers, maybe try to get some answers out of them. Were they a full-blown Black Cat/Special Investigations/Initiative kind of squad, or just a SWAT team where the S in SWAT was even more special than expected?

Danny stood guard with the rest of One Tough Mama's security at the door to the warehouse set, loaded to the teeth. *It's like* Attack the Block *meets* The Artist . . . Ree thought, her mind's Hollywood-Pitch-O-Tron kicking on.

Inside, Jane and company had changed the set dressing to make a small theatre viewing area against an interior, the mirror set against a wall and two projectors fifteen feet back into the main room. One was an old-style multireel projector, the other was a portable joint connected to a laptop computer.

The mirror was easily eight feet tall, in a shining silver frame with metallic roses and thorns encircling the mirror's surface.

A dozen photos ringed the inside of the frame, head shots of Hollywood sweethearts from Rachel MacKenzie through Audrey Hepburn, all the way back to Shirley Temple.

Off to one side, Drake stood at the ready, decked out in full adventurer mode, goggles and all. His rifle was slung over one shoulder, and he held the Hellboy-sized pistol in his hands, the weapon approximately the size of his head. He'd prepared, though, and wore an equally heavy-duty wrist brace, complete with gears and pistons.

Ree scanned the room, seeing the nervous techs and PAs

dressing a set, decking the wall out to resemble one of the grand old theatres in L.A., a three-hundred-square-foot version of Grauman's Chinese Theatre. Sure, some of the wallpaper was scorched, and the candelabrum they'd hung up was missing three of its arms, but Ree guessed the effort and the base trappings were all that was needed, and the best they could do in a rush.

Yancy emerged from behind one of the false walls, wearing a freshly pressed suit that was old enough that it jumped clear past retro to pure vintage. He wore wide-rimmed glasses and had his hair slicked back and parted to the side. The net effect turned him from a late-twentieth-century director to a midcentury would-be contemporary of Cecil B. DeMille.

But his transformation paled to the marvel that was Jane Konrad.

The star came out of nowhere, and as she walked, a phantom spotlight followed her even before the lighting team picked her up. She wore a revelation of a dress, an all-black throwback to the Golden Age with matching gloves that reached past the elbow, making her the spitting image of Rita Hayworth.

It didn't look like anything she'd seen in the star's closet, and given the rays-of-the-sun-level of magical energy rolling off of Jane, it seemed as likely as not that the dress itself was spun from pure magic, the star wreathing herself in the adoration of her fans made manifest. Her hair was curled and pinned in a walking waterfall of curls, shimmering like rubies.

Ree discovered that her mouth was open and consciously closed it with a soft click of her teeth.

Be still, my machine-gun heart.

The room was silent as Jane crossed to Ree. The woman's beauty glowed even brighter as she approached, and Ree raised a hand like she was blocking out the sun.

"Holy crap, Jane. You could put someone's eye out with that."

"That's the idea. Let's see Alex try something today. I'm

pretty sure that right now I could upstage Justin Bieber in a stadium full of ten thousand preteen girls." Jane turned to Yancy. "Are we all set?"

Yancy looked up, not meeting Jane's eyes, either. "Very nearly. The police are handling first response, and we get anything after that. I want to send the rest of the crew home now, keep anyone else from getting hurt."

"That includes you," Jane said.

Yancy shook his head. "Not going to happen. I'm seeing this through. And you need at least one assistant during the ritual. Ree's good, but if Alex sends another attack, she'll be busy."

"What's with the second projector?" Ree asked.

Jane smiled. "The tools on the table are old, the traditional trappings of the working actress. But celebrity has gotten a lot more complicated since Norma's time, and so has the magic.

"I put the word out on Twitter, Facebook, and my blog that all my fans should watch and live-tweet their favorite movie of mine, and I'll donate a dollar for every tweet with the #Jane-Day hashtag for the next two hours to my charity, Open Arms."

"And aside from getting you to spend money you don't have, how does that help?" Ree asked, trying to process what Jane's reference to Norma meant.

"When we start the movie, we'll also project the #JaneDay feed. Every tweet of attention will be a bit more fuel, pooling the collective positivity and attention to power the ritual."

Ree whistled, thinking back to the Twitter feud that had gotten Jane into this mess, but also remembering similar campaigns by other stars. A single call for retweets from Neil Gaiman, Justin Bieber, or Lady Gaga could snowball into dropping the entire Internet on an issue. That'd be a lot of attention, even in Twitter-sized chunks. "Wow. But didn't the last thing you did with Twitter backfire?"

"This is a bit different. Plus, the Twitter part wasn't the problem. I know it will work, I just need you to buy me the time to finish the ritual without Alex or Rachel screwing things up."

So there it was. Ree imagined the here's the plan scene in her mind from a Spider's-eye view. The SWAT team was spaced out around the building, covering the entrances, backed up by Danny and the company security. Inside, it'd be her and Drake.

Not much, but it would have to be enough. Plus, she'd gone toe-to-toe with a Dork Lord of Hell, and how much could Alex have left after sending a fucking dragon their way?

Famous last words, girl, said her worried voice.

But, *Spider-powers!* responded a bouncy voice, her inner twelve-year-old who thought being Spider-Man was the coolest thing ever.

Ree helped finish up the preparations and watched as the last of the crew packed it in. And because the universe couldn't resist a little atmospheric foreboding, a rare Pacific Northwest thunderstorm rumbled its way in.

Jane stood in front of a table, a strange assortment of foci in front of her. But if dice, old modules, and action figures worked for a Geekomantic ritual, it only made sense that a Celebromancer working big magic would use lipstick, a marked-up script, one of her awards-show dresses, a 35mm film reel, and a makeup set laid open around a compact. Jane's glow had narrowed, focused into the ritual tools, which beamed with energy like glow sticks.

"Start the film," Jane said, standing between the projector and the screen. Drake flicked the lights off, and Yancy started the reel. The lights beamed out, casting a Jane-sized shadow on the mirror, the film showing around her. At the same time, the modern projector showed a slow scroll of Twitter posts.

It was hard to read the credits with Jane blocking the screen, but Ree recognized the film as soon as she saw the black-and-white figure facedown in a pool beside a neglected mansion: *Sunset Boulevard.*

Whelp, Ree thought. Not the most encouraging film.

The story arc fit, mostly, but in a totally creepy way. It also explained Yancy's retro getup. He channels Cecil B. DeMille, and Jane taps into Norma Desmond's white-hot desire for a return (never comeback) to the big screen.

A cluster of memories hit Ree all at once. The famous lines, the exaggerated costuming, and the tragic ending.

The symbolism worked for Yancy and Jane, but for Ree, it was more than a little problematic. Norma Desmond never gets back into film, and the manipulation of the screenwriter she hires leads her further into dementia until she shoots him dead after he tries to shatter her illusions and escape his gilded cage.

Ree knew that with Geekomancy, you could focus on one aspect of a film or show without getting all of the side effects of another part, but that didn't stop a shiver from rippling down her spine, draining all the warmth out of her skin.

Ree looked to Yancy, but he avoided meeting her eyes, keeping his gaze locked on Jane.

Oh, that's not good.

Her Spider-sense went off like a string of firecrackers behind her neck. She listened, trying to figure out if something was happening outside or if she was just freaking out about the movie choice. This was Swanson's most famous film, and if hers was the only mirror they could find that fit, wouldn't they have to make do? Jane'd had several chances to screw Ree over, why change her mind now? Right?

While she tried to calm her frayed nerves, she heard gunfire outside. She turned to Drake, who was already heading for the door closest to the noise.

Ree let him go, continuing to scan the room, looking for other intruders. Ree heard a whistle, then a crash that she felt as much as heard. She bounded to the door and swung herself up and out of the door, sticking to the outside wall with Spider powers.

Outside, the SWAT team was clashing with several dozen orcs from the Ralph Bakshi *Lord of the Rings*, which Cosmic had bought out from Warner Brothers. They might not be as fearsome-looking as the Uruk-hai of the Jackson production, but there were at least forty of them, and they were close to surrounding the police.

The squad had dropped into a proper Roman phalanx, forming an impenetrable square of transparent plastic and black armor. The shields turned back the arrows and spears, but the soldiers were pinned down, none of them fighting back.

Let's see if I can't do something about that. Ree sheathed the sword and let loose a double dose of webbing, covering a half-dozen orcs and plastering them to the concrete.

"Forward!" called a voice from the team, and they pushed against the weakened flank, knocking orcs aside and breaking the line open. The orcs moved to adjust, but their lines were thinner now, less constant assault raining down on any point.

Ree jumped into the fray wearing an ear-to-ear grin as she hopped and bounded, cutting swaths across the orc line, moving just too fast for the orcs' counterstrikes.

This is fucking awesome! she thought, instinctively dodging a thrown spear by flipping backward. She nailed a three-point landing straight out of a McFarland panel, save for the sword she held out, ready for another run. The SWAT went on the offensive, pushing the orcs back onto one flank, driving the mob into the walls.

Ree hit the opposite flank with another burst of webbing, and the team polished the orcs off in short order, leaving behind a running river of ichor and Ree's webbing.

After checking for more nasty yet to come, she hopped down from the wall and approached the team.

"You guys are awesome!"

One of the team stepped forward, an older man of fiftyish, with close-cropped black-and-silver hair that peeked out at the temples under his shield. "Thanks for the assist."

Ree offered a hand, "Ree Reyes, screenwriter."

The policeman chuckled, then met her with a hand that would have been big without a gauntlet. "Captain Brandon Chu. Washington said you had some skills." Behind him, the

SWAT team dropped the phalanx formation, some of them pulling water bottles from their harnesses while the others watched the campus. These men and women were rock hard. Ree saw Washington's face behind the visor, and the officer saluted with her truncheon.

"This is your squad?" Ree asked, assuming she already knew the answer.

"It is. I've led this team for going on ten years. What's a screenwriter doing with moves like that?"

Ree gestured like a bad stage magician with both hands. "Maaagic."

Chu grinned, taking a drag from his water bottle. "You going to be able to keep that up?"

The music in her mind had dimmed, but was still going strong.

"For a while. You?"

"We arrived about five minutes after you'd cleaned the clock of that dragon. Shame. Most of the younger officers haven't ever faced down a full-grown dragon; they were climbing the walls on the way over."

Ree gave Captain Chu the eyebrow of circumspection. *Most of them? So presumably some of them have? I may have underestimated this town's weirdness level.*

Chu shrugged. "This job takes a special kind of person."

"True story. Send up the signal if something else shows?"

"Will do," Captain Chu said. "Let's just hope this thing works. My girls are totally in love with *Mermaid High School,* and it's hard to tell a seven- and nine-year-old to stop paying attention to their favorite actress without having to either deal with tantrums or share entirely too adult details about someone's rap sheet."

Ree managed a polite smile, not having been in any sort of position like that and not sure if she was being indicted as part of that rap sheet and associated behavior. She left the conversation and checked inside again, where

Jane was in full-on ritual mode, locked into the film, strobing light like a number at the Grammys. She nodded to Drake, and the two of them changed positions, then settled in to wait, while Yancy stood at Jane's side, her silent assistant.

The only sound in the building was the hum and spin of the projector and the steady drone of Jane's litany, which sounded to Ree like a tabloid and historical survey of the careers of starlets across the years.

And I thought my magic was weird.

A few minutes later, another wave hit the campus, this time it was an even larger pack of apes from the *Planet of the Apes* knockoff film *De-Evolution*.

The apes broke the ranks of the SWAT team, so Ree swung into action once more, getting a smaller pack to chase her around the campus in a Spider-power-enabled re-creation of the scene where the heroine parkours her way through an industrial park to get to the secret formula for reversing the De-Evolution virus.

Captain Chu managed to rally the SWAT team, reposition, and call weapons free, which led to dozens of gorillas dissolving into ichor and the side wall of the office building used for the Awakenings set being shot up to the point of looking like it belonged in *The Walking Dead* or *Children of Men*.

By the end of the second wave, Ree's Spider-powers were nearly depleted. She tagged Danny in for door duty and tried to top off her tank again using clips from her phone, but only got a few minutes before a flood of rats hit the campus.

They didn't have much in the way of area of effect weapons, which meant that Ree had to dig deep into her sideboard, flinging fireballs and acid bursts and ice-rays like a level 20 Wizard from atop a wrecked car. When the wave subsided, the concrete was covered in ichor, and Ree stood in the center of a one-person ticker-tape-parade hangover. She was out of Spider power and nearly out of cards, which left her with her mostly-charged blasters and her swords. Drake had run through three-quarters of his charge crystals, and the ritual was only just now half-done.

Ree wished that *Sunset Boulevard* could have been a tight ninety minutes instead of an intense and lingering hundred and ten, but she cast her quibbling aside when wave four hit. Front ranks of orcs, with gorilla heavy infantry.

She watched the horde push forward, standing on a table to see over the phalanxed-up SWAT team.

"Fall back inside and bar the door!" Captain Chu ordered, and the team shuffled back, forming a pocket inside the door to receive the orcs's charge. A group broke off to one side, so Ree ran to another entrance, shouting to Drake as she went.

"Cover the west entrance! We can't let them inside on two fronts or we're fucked!" Ree checked the eastern door, reinforced with a shelving cabinet. She looked across the building to Drake, who stopped at the western door. He gave a thumbs-up, then continued forward, leading with his hand-cannon.

"Status?" Ree shouted back to the SWAT team.

"This door won't hold," Chu said. "I need you to keep the others off our ass."

"Got it!" Ree pulled out her blaster and kicked over some tables to make herself a low-rent fence for cover.

Something hit the door, and the shelving unit shuddered.

"They're heeere!" Ree shouted to everyone and no one, channeling Heather O'Rourke from *Poltergeist*. Ree set out her phaser and sword beside her, wishing she had a gun duffel to keep the weapons coming.

The cabinet shuddered again, and then she heard wood splinter. The shelf flopped forward, landing just short of her table fence. Ree popped her head over the bench and fired as soon as she established the visiting figure was of the wrong genus to be human.

She fired as fast as possible, trying to plug the door while someone came to back her up (hopefully). But a pair of orcs jumped in at an angle, knocking over the table to Ree's left and opening a path for others to follow. One of the leading orcs jabbed a spear at Ree. She ducked behind the table for cover, then held the blaster over the table and fired indiscriminately, scrambling back and groping for the sword. Her hand wrapped around the leather strapping and she pushed herself to her feet, still firing as she backed up.

"A little help here!" she shouted again, panic not so much creeping as barging into her voice. She parried the orc's spear-thrust as it tried to circle her, then dropped it with a blaster bolt.

She didn't have the time or the space to switch her weapons, so she fired right-handed and parried southpaw. She abandoned all pretense of containment, backing off step by step as a gorilla pushed the cabinet aside so that the monsters could stream in.

Ree broke and ran back to the SWAT team and the ritual space. Orcs and gorillas followed closely enough that she could hear lips smacking in an entirely-too-alarming way. The only question would be whether the orcs or the gorillas would get to nosh on her. She pushed the morbid thoughts back as she saw the SWAT team scattered and half-buried under a mass of orcs, with the gorillas hammering at the small cluster of officers, who had maintained ranks in a corner.

"Drake?" Ree shouted, hoping for backup. The only response was the sound of high-caliber gunshots in a measured tempo.

Sounds like he's busy.

Ree opened fire at head level, confident she wouldn't hit any friendlies, since she'd put a still-untouched Jane and Yancy on her right.

A wave of orcs dropped, but some of their buddies decided to come and get revenge. Ree kept on the move, running across the room as she unloaded. Halfway to the west side of the building, as she passed a stale-crumb-laden craft services table, the blaster made the sound of ultimate sadness, whirring down to nothing.

Ree dropped the blaster and switched the sword to her

right hand, spinning into a double-handed slash that cut through one orc's ax and then its midsection.

Two more filled its place before the orc hit the floor, pressing her with weapons that yearned to one day see the Iron Age but were still plenty sharp. Ree beat aside a spear then lunged to stab the other orc. She ducked under the spear as it came back at her, then rolled under a table and looked down the room to see Drake chased by a gorilla, running full tilt. His face was slick with sweat and blood.

"Incoming!" Drake said, jumping over the table Ree had used for cover. Ree rolled out from under the table and found three orcs waiting for her. Drake dropped the first with his rifle, but two more took its place. The orcs and gorillas closed in on them as rats filled the floor.

"That's enough for now," said a new voice, one that sounded like smarmy dipped in skeezy, with a shady cherry on top.

Alex Walters, Cinemancer Sleaze King of WTF.

The monsters held their ground, surrounding Drake and Ree and circling the projector. There were close to fifty orcs and a half-dozen gorillas besides.

Well, we're fucked, Ree thought, her mind flipping through ridiculous plans and finding nothing that would do better than getting them all killed in a hurry.

CHAPTER TWENTY-TWO

Salome Returns

When push comes to shove and the bullets are flying, the mooks are dying, and the next couple of minutes determine who goes home bloodied but victorious and who gets the economy ticket to the morgue, you better hope that you're luckier, stronger, or better prepared than the other guys. Preferably all three.

And if you can only be one, be lucky.

It's worked for me so far.

Mostly.

—Eastwood, private correspondence with Captain Brandon Chu, PPD, June 22, 3 years ago

Another group of orcs marched Danny and the half-dozen remaining SWAT officers into the room. Behind them came Alex Walters, dressed in an expensive suit that hung off of him like he was a tween wearing his dad's clothes.

And finally, Rachel MacKenzie in her own Oscar-night dress, décolletage on display, with a gigantic brooch, hair done up, and ears sparkling with matching diamonds.

"What are you doing here?" Ree asked, throwing the accusation at Rachel. Her eyes didn't match her movement, like she was distracted, splitting her attention.

Alex cut in. "I invited her to join us for the big finale. I was more than a little offended that you didn't send a car. There are standards to keep in this industry."

"I invite you to fuck off and die in a ditch, slowly," Ree said.

Alex gave a used car salesman smile. "Clever as always. But zingers aren't going to save anyone today, Ree. My bosses have already written the ending; now it's just a question of how I want to direct the scene." The crowd of orcs parted for him until he stood at the edge of the circle surrounding Ree and Drake.

To the side, Jane continued her ritual, and the film showed Norma in her masochistic beauty regimen, torturing herself in preparation for a return to the screen that would never come. At the same time, the other projector showed a fast-scrolling run of #JaneDay messages, fans sharing their love of a dozen films and TV series.

"Oh, great, a muckracker with delusions of auteur-hood," Ree said. "Please tell me you're not a frustrated actor or writer. I might choke on cliché."

Alex showed his teeth in a predatory smile. "Keep on talking, girl. You're just making hot air."

Drake kept his weapon sighted, aiming at whichever orc happened to be closest at any time. Seeing him up close, she saw that the blood on his face came from a gash just below the hairline, which had ruined his goggles and torn into his scalp.

Ree looked to the director and star plugging away at the ritual. "Jane, Yancy, a little help here?"

Jane was unresponsive, just carrying on with the ritual, speaking Norma Desmond's lines along with the film. Yancy handed Jane a makeup brush, then snuck a look back to Ree. He mouthed a word that Ree guessed was *stall*. It lacked the *s* at the end to be *balls*, though that would be applicable, and *call* as in call their bluff didn't sound like a terribly good idea.

Whatever, stall it is.

"So, Rachel . . ." she began. "What's with the change of heart? Earlier you were all I *hate those bastards, but my hands are tied. But I'm no killer, just a jealous paranoid with three-thousand-dollar haircuts.* How much of that was crap, after all?"

But Alex cut Rachel off before she could respond. "Just enough to get you to bring the mirror here, to prepare everything ready for us to finish Act Three. And you've played your part perfectly. Even better than expected." Alex looked at Jane and smiled, and it was almost like she could see his brain smirking inside that ugly noggin. "After you left, Jane, the powers that be made the price for your betrayal very clear. First, you had to fail. Anytime you had a film coming, Cosmic dropped a big fat tentpole film opposite your movie."

Ree's mind flashed through release dates, tried to remember poster lineups in the movie theatres. It was true, Jane's post-Cosmic work had always floundered at the box office.

Alex continued with his Villainous Gloat. "Next, you were allowed a modicum of success, just enough of a groundswell that you'd get too big for your dress size. And that's where Rachel came in. That curse, as you call it? It was my own invention, one of my best. Aside from my stories about your flailing that followed."

Ree looked over to Yancy. His face was pained, and it was like he was trying to not hear Alex as he continued. "And it was great, Jane, because then you came here, tried to start over—like we couldn't follow you? You hooked up with this little Geekomantress, and all it took were a few monster attacks here and there to push you to the perfect balance of failure and success to force you to dig deep and fuel the curse. Jane, you—"

Ree cut in, tired of Alex's monologue. "I get it. You're Schemy McSchemerson, vice earl of Schemeton Abbey. But who are these bosses? Your suit says big money, but if you're anything more than a yes-man lieutenant, then I'm Jennifer Lopez."

Alex crossed to stand beside Jane. The star was sweating, her teeth grit as she struggled, her attentions still on the ritual and the screen. Alex seemed to be ignoring Ree's taunts, but she continued nonetheless: "No response for that, huh? Whose lap do you sit on? I know Cosmic holds the purse strings, but whose monkey are you, really?"

Alex rolled his eyes. "Bored now." He waved a hand forward, and a cluster of orcs pounced. Drake took one of the orc's heads off with his rifle, and Ree cut into another. But there were too many, and the group crushed in on them in an instant. Ree lost her grip on the sword, finding herself grappled to hell. The orcs forced her to her knees, but the encircling forces parted to give her and Drake a view of Alex whispering in Jane's ear.

Ree shouted, struggling against the orcs. "Don't listen to him, Jane. Finish the job, and then we'll clean up here." Ree kept the bluster up but didn't see any way out. Barring a whole helluva lot of backup, if Alex wanted them dead, they'd be dead.

Alex whispered into Jane's ear while the star struggled to maintain the ritual. Her gaze wandered over to Alex, her mask of confidence cracking. A buckshot burst of worry hit Ree.

"Don't stop!" Ree shouted. But when she looked to the other screen, she saw that the Twitter feed had changed. Now there were more than a dozen retweets of messages from Rachel MacKenzie and Alex, ripping into Jane and her fans. The hashtag was contested now, split between the original message and the counterprogramming, a Celebromantic clash of the titans extending to their fan-bases.

Magical energy strobed and boomed at full-on concert levels while the film continued, closing in on the tragic finale. *Next time we do something like this, I'm insisting we use Caddyshack.*

Maybe Bring It On, if we're feeling edgy.

In the middle of the scene where Joe sends Betty away, Alex took a step away from Jane, moving back from his in-your-face approach. His voice changed, becoming softer, less abrasive.

"All right, Jane. We can end this now. All will be forgiven if you do as I say. You can have the mantle, you can have your career back, everything you want. That's worth any price, right?"

Jane turned from the mirror, her body alight with energy. The magic paused, light show frozen in place.

Alex's smirk returned, but his voice stayed steady. "There's two ways this can go, now." He started counting with his fingers for emphasis as he strutted around the room, basking in the attention as Ree struggled. "If you take Rachel out, all will be forgiven. The mantle will be yours, the curse will be undone, and you'll never see me again. But if you don't, if you're too scared, I'll kill Yancy, your girlfriend, her boy toy, and the whole cast. This is your last chance, their last chance. Is this what you want your legacy to be? A career implosion culminating in a mass suicide?"

Rachel looked surprised. "Alex? What the fuck are you talking about?"

Jane looked to Yancy, now restrained by orcs, then to Ree, and finally back to the screens.

Ree bit the hand of the orc whose hands covered her mouth, then spat out blood and shouted, "Forget him! You want to take someone out, take him out! This is all because they're pissed you left!" The orcs closed in, shoving Ree flat on the ground.

"It's your choice, Jane," Alex said. "You can't win this without me."

Rachel puffed herself up, taking center stage. "I've smacked you down before, kid. Don't think I can't do it again." She rolled her hands, and Ree saw energy rolling into the star from the screen as tweets from Rachel's fans dominated the screen.

Jane's eyes filled with something Ree hadn't seen before, something far darker. Jane reached out toward Rachel, spectral hands appeared out of thin air, clawing at the superstar, like a mob of adoring fans. The hands latched onto the star, dragging her to the ground, then pulled her in a hundred directions.

"Jane?" Ree asked, her voice shaking. "What are you doing?" *This was not the plan.*

"Taking what's mine, what has always been mine." When Jane spoke, it was in a mix of her and Gloria Swanson's voice, a tight unison of two voices trying to become one. "I should never have left the spotlight. It was mine by right, by fate. She's just a footnote, and she's deprived the people of my talent for too long."

Houston, we have Zuul.

Rachel tossed her hair back and locked her eyes on Jane. The room filled with thousands of flashes and the sounds of cameras and roaring crowds. Ree slammed her eyes shut to block out the light, but the flashes kept coming. She dug her head into the ground to get her eyes away from the light. She felt staggered footfalls next to her, and got one arm free.

Even better. Ree flopped forward, reaching for the dropped sword. She wrenched free of the other orcs. As she struggled free, she felt dozens of hands climb up and over her body like a wave. A discordant chorus called out, screaming Rachel's name.

Ree nicked a finger on something sharp, then traced along the cold steel until she found the handle. *Well, it's now or never.*

Ree spun on the concrete, chopping at legs.

Ree shouted, "Prison break!" as the flashing lights subsided.

Ree slashed at head level as she backed up, until she felt her leg run into well-oiled leather. "That you, Drake?" she asked.

"That it is, Ms. Ree. I will cover your flank."

"No time for that—just watch my back," Ree said, slashing with abandon. "Chu! Get your people out of here, get backup, whatever!"

Ree heard the sounds of weapons clanging and thudding against plastic riot shields. "Move out! Move! Move! Move!"

Jane and Rachel closed, locked in a Fashion Week version of the Gandalf vs. Saruman throwdown. Jane struck a pose, and another wave of spectral hands hit Rachel MacKenzie, tearing at her arms and legs, trying to bring her to her knees. Rachel tossed her hair in a slow-mo move straight out of a cover shoot, and the hands faded. Behind the two, Alex stood like a hipster version of Emperor Palpatine, his smirk wider than ever.

"You're out of your league, girl," said Rachel. "You want to play with the big kids, be the next Garbo or Andrews, but you won't get your hands dirty like they did. I played ball, did the pictures they told me to. I paid my dues, and now I get what I deserve. And I'm not letting you or anyone else take it from me."

Why do I feel like Hollywood Babylon *didn't even start to scratch the surface of how messed up this world is?* Ree thought as she Great Cleave-d her way through the mass of orcs, Drake at her side. They just kept coming, but she could see the end of the mob. The gorillas had chased after the SWAT team, which was bad news for them but gave her some breathing room.

"Ms. Ree, what is our course of action?" Drake asked while struggling with an orc for control of his rifle. He slipped a hand from the struggle and a split second later, the orc fell in front of Ree, a knife in its side. Drake ducked into a roll to pick up the rifle as Ree swung, baseball-bat-style, to knock aside another orc's spear.

"Clear the mooks, take out Sleaze Boy!" As she spoke, a stray gorilla burst through the hole in the wall and charged them.

Well, shit.

Drake rolled up to his knees and popped off a shot against the gorilla, catching it square between the eyes. The beast dropped like a bag of anvils inches in front of the adventurer, its momentum bowling Drake over into Ree and tossing them both across the floor like so many ninepins.

The world kept spinning for a few seconds after she knew she'd stopped moving, so she turtled up, wishing for one of those SWAT shields.

Note to self: Look into expandable/portable magical shields. Sword and Board is much safer than Open Hand, even if it's not as sexy.

She felt a hot gash open up along her leg, then another across the back of her head. Instinctively, she reached up to her head wound and came back with a chunk of hair.

Fucksticks. Ree tried to focus, jabbing out at a dark mass as soon as she was sure it wasn't Drake. The squeal of pain confirmed her guess, and she twisted the blade, trying to force the creature away as she got her shit together.

Ree bobbed and weaved with the three orcs facing her until one lashed out with his ax. She sidestepped past the strike, slashed at the orc's shoulders, then ran past him, making her way toward the magic slugfest. She reached into her jacket and wrapped her free hand around the pocket watch she'd gotten from Eastwood, praying that it'd last long enough for her to do what she needed.

The irony of her life depending on a gadget from the man who'd been ready to kill to save her mom was not lost on her.

But as far as Ree was concerned, Alanis Morissette could have a field day as long as the watch got the job done.

Ree crashed her way through a four-foot-tall wave of spectral hands, but Rachel pegged her before she could close to melee range. The star unleashed another blinding barrage of lights, but the watch blunted the blow. Ree couldn't see, but kept going anyway. She threw a horizontal kick where Rachel should have been, but it didn't connect. She recovered and sliced low, aiming for knee level. Still nothing.

The lights faded, and she saw Rachel five paces away, standing behind Alex Walters. The paparazzo unbuttoned his blazer and struck a fighting stance.

"Seriously?" Ree asked. The guy was so twig-like he made Ree look full-figured.

Alex laughed. "What? You don't think I got smart after the first few bodyguards roughed me up?"

Ree brandished her sword. "Yeah, but I have a black belt and a sword."

"That's nice." Alex said, his voice uninterested as he quick-drew a pistol and fired from the hip. The bullet hit her in the shoulder, opening a floodgate of pain. She rolled with the force and went to the ground. Ree huffed as she landed, adrenaline helping her scramble for cover as Alex continued to fire. A bullet skipped off the concrete near her head, spraying her face with gravel, and she felt another tear at her leg.

Ree's ears pounded, and her senses reeled, shock hitting from the bullets, the head wounds, and the general beating she'd taken.

Don't pass out. Don't pass out. Must save vs. Shock. Don't pass out.

"A little help here!" Ree called, her voice breaking halfway through help.

Ree heard the sound of a thud, then a crash of bodies hitting the floor. And following that, one more gunshot.

She wobbled to her feet, sword now in her left hand, her right hand curled up against her chest, quickly covering with blood.

Gotta end this soon.

As she staggered forward, she saw Alex disentangling himself from Yancy, whose white shirt was already stained deep crimson from a gutshot. *Holy fuck.* Jane and Rachel were now grappling, lights and sounds of applause licking over them like steam off a block of ice. And she saw the edge of Drake's cloak at the bottom of a pile of unmoving orc bodies.

Ree took another pained step forward, seeing Alex scramble for his gun. He brought a magazine up to reload, but she had the range, and cut down into his wrist. He lost his grip on the gun, which clattered to the ground. Alex clutched his hand close, mirroring Ree.

As Ree contemplated taking a Dark Side point and cutting him down right there, she heard a crunch and a cry, and then sensed another body hit the ground. Out of the corner of her eye, Ree saw that only one gown-garbed goddess was still standing.

Jane exhaled twenty gallons of pain and breath through a bloody mouth and leveled her gaze on Alex. Rachel MacKenzie was a pile of unconsciousness, her nose ripped open, her chest covered in blood.

Alex scrambled back, holding his readily bleeding wrist. He looked to Rachel, but the older star was out.

"It's too late, Jane." His voice was thin, desperate, but as he spoke, Ree felt a jackhammer of force move through the air, the biting critique of the gossip hound revved up to a magical 11.

"Nobody wants you back on the screen. They've already moved on."

Jane wobbled in place, catching herself on the ruins of a table. Ree moved to help her, but her adrenaline had broken.

She collapsed, red crowding her vision. Oblivion was knocking on the door, and it had chocolates.

Ree looked to Jane. Her eyes were still flooded with power and that odd look that resembled Norma Desmond way too much for Ree to be comfortable.

Jane turned to the screen. The tide of comments had turned back to Jane's favor. "It's not enough. It should be done by now."

She looked at Rachel, the fallen star's magic dissipated.

"There's just one last step," Alex said. "Rachel was right about paying your dues. Every Sweetheart before has paid the price, that's the big part you missed. It takes blood. Life's blood. You have to take a life of someone you care about, someone who helped you along the way."

Jane looked to Yancy, who held himself up on a table, a huge gash across his ribs. Then, she looked to Ree, and back to Alex.

Oh hell no, Ree thought. *No way.*

Alex continued. "I don't make the rules, kid, but I do know them. It's not like you actually knew how to do this ritual, right? It's different this time from last time. No one ever wrote it down. Every Sweetheart before you had the right producers behind them, with the . . . institutional memory to help them along their way."

Jane narrowed her eyes at Alex. "I am not a killer."

Alex did his best nonchalant shrug, hampered by his profusely bleeding wrist.

"It's either kill or be killed. With the amount of magic you've used today, what do you think the curse is going to do with you? I'll give you that one for free. Tonight you take a life, or you take your curtain call."

The film pushed on toward the climax, and without an outlet, Jane's magical aura started lashing out, producing lights and random FX. The worry knot in Ree's stomach twisted another half-turn. If the curse wasn't broken, couldn't be broken without the blood cost, then she didn't doubt that the curse could kill her.

And if Jane was going to pay the price, then Ree was the obvious choice. Yancy was like a father to her—he was clearly the Butler/ex-husband Max. But Ree, Ree was the Joe Gillis of this picture.

Gulp.

Alex spat at Jane and continued, "If Yancy there weren't in love with you, you would have plateaued at cereal commercials. There's always someone new, Jane. I've got a dozen stars in the wings, all climbing over one another to be the next Jane Konrad, the next Rachel MacKenzie." Alex nodded at Rachel.

"You and she, you're both replaceable, just a face to put on a poster. It's about butts in seats, about gate, about keeping the masses happy. It's never been about you. If you want to keep them at bay, you have to pay the price."

Ree looked at Jane through bleary eyes and wished she'd passed out. Jane's eyes, those eyes that said so much, could convey the texture of emotion, were a mix of a hundred thoughts. She saw fear playing out over Jane's face, but also hunger, ambition. It was an ugly hunger, and with the blood on her face, the look was terrifying, like that of a starving wolf approaching a rabbit.

And Ree was the rabbit.

"Jane! Don't listen to him! There's no one like you. You built this!" Ree waved, if weakly, at the ruined set. "This came from you and from me. We have stories to tell, stories only you can tell. He's full of shit; he's just trying to save his ass!"

"Shut your mouth, worm." Alex kicked Ree, and she fell over onto her wounded shoulder.

Pain blue-screened her vision, and all she could do was cry out. Her eyes locked closed in pain, she heard Jane take another step, her single stiletto heel clicking on the concrete.

"I will have my return." Again, Jane's voice was twinned by the actress's, despite the fact the film hadn't been hooked up to a speaker. Ree opened her eyes and saw Alex's gun in Jane's hand, wavering. Behind her, the film reached its finale as Norma Desmond threw open the door to follow her false lover.

"Jane, don't," Ree croaked, sitting up despite seventeen kinds of pain.

The star aimed the gun at Ree, rage in her eyes. Ree forced herself to watch, her eyes locked on Jane. She wouldn't look away, wouldn't just wait for the end. She tried to pull herself up to her knees but fell backward.

Is this what it was all leading toward? Was I just some fucking pawn in this Hollywood tragedy, caught by my own ambition like Joe Gillis?

A moment later, two shots rang out: one from the screen, and one from the gun. A huge wave of energy swept out from the screen with the gunshot, along with the smell of burning celluloid.

That's All Folks! Ree thought.

But there was no thud of impact, no blossoming of pain. Ree turned and saw Alex drop to his knees, blood spreading on his chest from a bullet hole in his freshly pressed shirt. His eyes were wide as he looked to Jane with snide disbelief, then fell forward to the concrete.

"Fuck. Oh, fuck, thank you," Ree said. She heard the gun clatter to the ground, then Jane wrapped her arms around Ree.

Jane spoke, the echo of Norma Desmond gone. "I couldn't do it. I wouldn't do it. That's not who I am."

Through the pain and the onset of shock, Ree found the energy for one more sentence. "You're goddamned right you couldn't."

Off to the side, Ree heard a pop. She turned, her vision wavering, and could have sworn she saw a flowing puddle of ichor where Alex had been.

"What the fuck?" Ree asked, her voice weak.

"Don't worry. Just stay with me, Ree."

Ree looked up to the screen one last time. On one side, she saw Joe Gillis floating facedown in the pool. She couldn't make out the words on the other side, but she knew that Jane's fans had rallied, that they'd come through. Or maybe that was the shock talking.

"It's going to be all right, you hear? Just stay with me," Jane said.

Ree's nod was as much loll as anything, but she focused on the star's face, tried to keep the black at bay. She lost track of time, and before long, she couldn't hold it back anymore and drifted off into the black.

Only If for a Night

Production of One Tough Mama's Awakenings *ended early today, following extensive damage from arson late Sunday night. Police are investigating the attack but have not announced any suspects.*

Given One Tough Mama's financial problems, it's not likely that the production will be able to complete principal photography without additional investors.

Before Jane Konrad's personal struggles, One Tough Mama had been on a run of successful independent productions with strong showings through major distributors, including the romantic comedy Green Thumb *with Joseph Gordon-Levitt, the toast-of-Cannes drama* Uriel Falls, *and video-game action sleeper hit* Player Two.

—Vlada Janczuk, StraightDope.com, May 28

Ree woke in a hospital room. At least, it better have been a hospital room, because nowhere else was allowed to smell that sterile.

She was bandaged up like an eight-year-old's mummy costume, gauze covering her head, arms, waist, and legs. She tried to lift her head and look around, but she felt like one of the gorillas had followed her to the hospital and was curled up on her chest.

"Well, that won't work," she croaked, her mouth dry. "Testing, one two." Her voice was low, husky, more Tom-Waits-in-drag than torch singer.

She heard movement to her left, then Jane entered her vision.

The star was still wearing the vintage dress, but her make-up and glamour were gone, leaving the woman's face hollow and wan.

"Thank God," Jane said, leaning in to hug Ree.

"Owwfuckshitalloftheow!" Ree said as the compression lit a bajillion pain receptors on fire.

Jane backed off, and the pain receded like a slow tide.

A cog of thought dropped into place, and she gulped. (Even gulping hurt.) Ree opened her mouth, then pursed her lips, struggling to build up the courage to ask the question and face its answer. "Yancy?"

"He'll make it. The SWAT team had already signaled emergency services and backup. They arrived just after you passed out. Good thing, too. The EMT said another minute and he'd have been too far gone." Jane sighed, and Ree tried one of her own, then gave up as the expected wave of pain hit.

"And Drake?"

"He was just unconscious. He's actually checked himself out. Said he was going to 'manage your affairs with the ladies three.' I hope you know what that means, because I've got nothing."

Yep, that sounds like Drake. "The Rhyming Ladies are my three best friends. Sandra, Anya, and Priya."

Jane nodded. "The doctors say they called your dad. You'll want to give him a ring, too."

Fuuuck. Covering up a hospital visit with the ladies was one thing, but her dad would positively flip the fuck out.

He'd probably already bought a plane ticket.

"How long have I been out?" Ree asked.

"About ten hours. I'm just glad to have you up and talking. Pacing around this room and staying out of the halls to avoid paparazzi was getting old."

"How's Danny?"

"Several lacerations and a broken arm. They found him unconscious against a wall with a double-bladed ax on his lap beside his baseball bat."

Ree stumbled through her mental Rolodex, trying to make sure she'd covered everyone.

"Did the crew get out okay?"

Jane nodded. "Everyone who had survived the dragon attack. Are you going to ask about yourself, or should I just have the doctor come back in and read you the list herself?"

"I'm not dying, right?" Ree asked. Another nod. "I've been putting points into Stamina. As long as this arm heals up pretty soon, I'll be fine."

Something hit Ree, a foggy memory from just before she'd passed out.

"What happened to Alex?"

A shadow passed over Jane's face. "He . . . dissolved. Like those creatures."

So I wasn't hallucinating. Go me. "What the hell does that mean?" Ree asked.

"I don't know, Ree. I just don't know." If Alex was a monster or came from the same place they did, that put a whole new light on a lot of things, not the least of which being that something was seriously wrong at Cosmic Studios.

"Huh. I'll have to dig around for some answers," Ree said, trying to sit up. Another wave of pain hit her like a two-by-four across the nose.

"Take it easy, okay? You've taken a lot of punishment."

"I'll be fine." Ree reconsidered for a moment, looking at the hospital room and trying to do some mental math at how big of a bill she'd just racked up. "Though this hospital bill will bankrupt me. Not like I had much money to begin with."

Jane's face soured. "The hell it will. That's all taken care of."

Ree looked over her wrecked body again. "This has got to be like a hundred grand in surgeries and other crap."

"So?" Jane asked. "I was going to have to sell my house anyway." Ree saw a tear in the star's eye, reminded of how much Jane had already given up to plot the course of her own life instead of letting other people pull her strings. Ree's headache asserted its presence like a poorly tuned metal band doing a sound check. Ree kept a working knowledge of her own headaches, and this one was very clearly the vengeance of the Caffeine Fiend.

"I don't know how to repay you," Ree said. "But if I can ask a little more, I'd kill for a coffee."

Jane chuckled, her face lighting up. Even like this, she was beautiful. Not knock-your-socks-off gorgeous, but Ree was beginning to wonder if there was anybody who was actually that hot in person, sans magic, sans makeup. On her own, Jane was still beautiful.

"So what about the show?" Ree asked.

Another laugh. "Oh, we're fucked. With a disaster like this, no one will touch the project. People are superstitious about dragon attacks and things like that."

"And the curse? Rachel?"

Jane opened her arms. "Gone at the end of the film. I used enough magical energy yesterday to power N.Y.C. for an hour, and I'm exhausted, but that's all. I beat Rachel head-on, Alex is dead, and #JaneDay trended for the whole afternoon. One of the PAs counted the tweets, and my fans buried Rachel and Alex's haters 2-1. If the curse isn't broken, it might as well be," she said, waving the issue off.

Ree tried to sit up to ask again. Jane held Ree down and continued. "Rachel slinked off when she came to, all bullshit smiles and thanks for getting rid of Alex. I didn't believe her for a second when she said that bygones were bygones. But she has the divorce to deal with first."

Ree ticked problems off her checklist, one by one. The Unfuck Writing Career box was still empty, but there was no reason for her to be a sore winner, considering how many other bullets she'd dodged.

Ree pursed her lips. Her stomach auditioned for Cirque Du Soleil as she tried to address the Relationship Sword of Damocles swinging overhead. "So, where does that leave us?"

That got a wistful look from Jane, and a long silence. "I have to go back to L.A., be there with Yancy and his family while he recovers. You could come with us. Try to get funding for another pilot."

Go to L.A., live with a superstar, keep tasting the high life.

Have a real career as a writer. But that'd take moving a thousand miles for a relationship. What if things went bad? I know better than to try and pull a Felicity. And I doubted her, thought she was just using me. That's not a great foundation for a relationship. Ree thought of the Blins, Charlie, the Rhyming Ladies, and everyone in the magical underground she'd come to know.

Eastwood, Grognard, Drake. She couldn't just leave all of that behind, hang up her lightsaber and live by the pen.

Ree saw a flash of her mother, looking haggard and worn in the vision provided by the Thrice-Retconned Duke of Pwn last Halloween. *Eastwood and I still have work to do, and someone needs to make sure he doesn't go Dark Side again in the process.*

She shook her head. "My life is here. And if I went to be a writer, I'd be turning my back on the people I can help."

Jane squeezed Ree's unwounded arm. "Think of all the people you could help as a writer, telling stories that need to be told. You could help millions. And it's not like there aren't monsters and more creeps like Alex in Hollywood."

"One of my friends' kids would be dead if not for me. I have to stay here and look after my people, my city." Her eyes were hot, and she wiped the newborn tears away with her unwounded hand.

Jane's mouth wrinkled as she struggled with something. "You're sure?"

Ree sniffed back the totally unsexy snot that flowed like a leaky faucet whenever she got teary.

"Might be the morphine talking," Ree said.

Jane sighed, shaking her head with a knowing smile. "Oh, honey. You're something else. And it was just a week, after all. I don't like it, but I can understand."

She sounded like she was trying to convince herself, putting on a brave face. Ree did her best to follow suit, even as her mind flashed back to dinner at Yoritomo's, the night at Infinity . . . and other things from nights.

Jane smiled the Making Lemonade smile that adults learn to do when they get used to the world stomping on their heads.

"You're welcome anytime you come to L.A. If I hear you've come down and didn't give me a call, I'll be pissed." And then Jane proved herself a saint and produced tissues from nowhere.

Ree blew her nose, embarrassed at how much it sounded like a trombone. The snot was, for the moment, bested.

"I've seen you pissed; I'm not that masochistic," Ree said, trying her best to grin through the laundry list of injuries. "Can you stay for a while anyway?" Ree went on. "In the hospital, I mean. Of course, you'll go home with Yancy when he's out. Just for right now. I don't want my friends to know about this weird magic stuff I do, and I'd rather not be alone just yet." Ree folded the tissue over itself, looking for a usable spot.

Jane squeezed Ree's left hand, and for the first time that day, there was a touch without pain. "Of course. And it may be a terrible cliché, but I'd like to be friends."

Ree slipped her hand free, not recoiling but simply to make the Ted Mosby struck-in-the-heart motion. Jane stuck her tongue out at Ree.

"Of course," said Ree. "But I reserve the right to keep on nursing my childhood crush."

"Done and done. I do wish you would come down. The women in L.A. are too much. I have to go out to the valley or up to the Bay to find someone who has her act together."

"That's what you get for living in Diva Central."

That earned another smile.

Jane indulged Ree a bit longer, and the two kept talking until Ree passed out again.

Ree was mobile in the morning and accompanied Yancy, Jane, and Danny to the short memorial for the four crew members who lost their lives during the dragon attack. Ree might not be able to make the full ceremony down in L.A. with the families, but she wanted to make sure she had the chance to learn their names, etch them on her memory. If she was Pearson's self-styled protector, then they had died on her watch, for her production, and they deserved to be remembered.

Georgia Summers, the lighting tech who had climbed around in the rigging like she was born to it.

Kalolo Grant, the security guard with the big smile.

Christopher Dean, one of the camera grips.

Vanessa Yen, the PA who had dragged Ree into makeup for the press conference.

Yancy, Jane, and several other cast and crew spoke, each with a story about one or another of the fallen teammates. Most of One Tough Mama had worked together for years, some even decades, going back to film school. They were truly a family.

And for a little while, Ree had been a guest in that family.

After the memorial, Yancy, Ree, Danny, and Jane piled back into the town car, the two heads of One Tough Mama still red around the eyes, while Danny looked out the window, watching the city scroll by. Ree held Jane's hand on the way to the airport, stumbling over how she could help. She hadn't known any of the deceased more than the tiniest bit. So, she did what she could, just to be present.

They rode in silence to the airport as Ree locked the stories into her memory, dwelling for a time on the cost of ambition, the dangers of the absurd world she insisted on making her own. And on the implications of a walking, talking, smarmy mastermind who was also the same kind of not-human as the monsters he commanded.

Thankfully, her dad hadn't hopped on a plane, and she had been able to placate his panic enough, promising a full after-action later that day. She sent Grognard a text during the drive, and his response came within a minute, saying that Drake had already touched base and for her to heal up. She still didn't totally get Grognard (like how he could prefer the *AD&D* rule set to *Pathfinder*), but as far as bosses went, she'd had far worse.

The team stepped out onto the curb, where Ree gave teary, tender goodbyes all around, until it was just Jane and Ree, with Danny keeping the crowds at bay.

"Keep in touch, okay?" Jane said.

Ree nodded, tearing up in an uncharacteristic public display of not-put-togetherness. At least, uncharacteristic while sober. "Sure thing."

"And since he's no longer the competition, I might as well tell you that Drake is wild about you," Jane said with a knowing smile.

"Really?"

"I get that he's all man-out-of-time and such, but there are only a few reasons for someone in his position to be so devoted: he's paid to do it, like Danny, he's family, or he's completely in love with you. Plus, one side benefit of celebrity magic and cultivating desire is that I've got a pretty damned good sense about these things. I saw the way you looked at him, even when I was around."

Ree's ears got hot. *This is not me at my sexiest*, she thought, imagining how she must look: beaten, bloodied, teary, and snotted up.

But Jane still looked at her with that kind but sad look. "The way I see it, you were playing it cool like you tried to do with me. Somebody has to be the one to take the plunge, to put themselves on the line. This one is all you."

Ree chuckled. "This might be the only time that I actually take romantic advice given to me by an ex during a breakup."

That got a full-belly laugh from Jane. "That's probably for the best. Go get him, tiger." Jane kissed Ree on the lips, hugged her very gently, then sighed and stepped back.

"And send me your next script as soon as it's done." Jane turned and winked over her shoulder, and Ree swooned all over again. Though that might have been the battering talking.

She slid back into the chartered car, and it pulled away from the airport, headed back into town.

Ah, Drake. This is either going to be amazing, or we're going to make Buffy and Spike look like a minor fling.

After all, when have I ever stuck with the safe and boring choice?

Acknowledgments

This last year has been a marvelous, smile-so-much-your-cheeks-hurt blur. Countless people have been part of getting my writing career off the ground, and I count myself honored to have had such support.

Above all, thanks to Meg White for her tireless support and her keen eye for character motivation. And for not minding when I have to spend whole weekends holed up tapping away at the keyboard.

Thanks to my mom, dad, and sister for listening to countless hours of shop talk, speculation, and brainstorming about how best to handle my nascent career.

My heartfelt thanks go out to everyone who gave *Geekomancy* a shot, and twice over to those who came back for another round. The absolute best thing about becoming a published author has been connecting with readers and seeing my work come to life in the experience of others. Without readers, I'm just a guy talking to himself and writing it down.

Big props to Annie Corrigan, Anton Strout, Gregory A. Wilson, Bradley P. Beaulieu, Dave Robison, Brion Humphrey, Joe, Revan, Flagoon, FireBird, Mary Robinette Kowal,

Megan Christopher, Chuck Wendig, Alex Bledsoe, and everyone else who welcomed me into their digital playgrounds to talk writing, geekdom, and all things Ree Reyes.

Special thanks to the Codex Writers, especially Beth Cato for her astute first reader response, as well as Anaea Lay, M. K. Hutchins, John Murphy, Rebecca Roland, Grayson Bray Morris, Amanda E. Forrest, Marina J. Lostetter, Lisa Shapter, Thomas L. Martin, Keffy Kehrli, Michelle Muenzler, and Laurie Tom for their comments on the early draft of Celebromancy.

Thanks to Scot Shamblin, Andrew Reyes, Megan Christopher, Meredith Levine, and everyone else that helped me learn about the Film and TV world.

Great thanks to my Angry Robot overlord Marc Gascoigne, as well as John Tintera, Lee Harris, Amanda Rutter, Emlyn Rees, Darren Turpin, Roland Briscoe, and the entire Osprey crew, for their active support of the weird Yankee and his writing career.

Huge thanks to Sara Megibow and the Nelson Literary team for their extraordinary efforts shouting to the ends of the earth about my debut onto the scene.

Last but never least, my most ginormous thanks to my editor, Adam Wilson, as well as Ellen Chan, Julia Fincher, and everyone behind the scenes at Simon & Schuster for helping get these books out and into readers' hands.

2ND EDITION ACKNOWLEDGEMENTS

As with the second edition of *Geekomancy*, the changes here are minor. Some give small tweaks and updates to the Hollywood/pop culture references, others remove harmful or careless language that I've learned not to use since publishing this book the first time.

Some thank yous for this edition:

To the team at Deranged Doctor Designs for their excellent work providing the series' new look.

To CreativeJay for formatting and production.

To the Strange Friends for their support and the joys of collaboration.

To my colleagues on various Slacks and Discords and such as we support one another through ludicrous times.

To Kim-Mei Kirtland, for dogged determination.

To Meg, for dyadic folklore and Seeking The Elden Ring.

And thanks to you, the reader, for continuing with the series.

Baltimore, MD
May 2022

About the Author

Mike grew up reading comics, playing games, and trying to figure out how to make being a geek into a job. Now he's living the dream telling stories full-time.

Mike's books are known for their fun action/adventure vibes with inclusive casting and inventive worldbuilding.

His books include found family space opera *Annihilation Aria*, collaboratively-written epic fantasy serial *Born to the Blade*, and the r/Fantasy "Stabby" Award-finalist *Genrenauts* series.

Mike has been a game store clerk, a bookseller/barista, a sales representative, and was the North American Sales & Marketing Manager at Angry Robot Books.

When not writing, Mike plays video games and makes pizzas from scratch. He is the co-host of actual play show "Speculate!" and a guest host on the Hugo Award Finalist "The Skiffy and Fanty Show".

Mike lives in Baltimore with his wife, their dog, and an ever-growing library.

Follow Mike on Twitter @mikerunderwood.

You can support Mike's writing at patreon.com/michaelrunderwood

Newsletter

Find out more about Mike's books, appearances, get bonus stories and more by subscribing to his newsletter at michaelrunderwood.com/newsletter

Attack the Geek

A side-quest novella in the bestselling *Geekomancy* urban fantasy series—when *D&D*-style adventures go from the tabletop to real life, look out!

Ree Reyes, urban fantasista and Geekomancer extraordinaire, is working her regular drink-slinger shift at Grognard's bar-and-gaming salon when everything goes wrong. The assorted magic wielders of the city's underground have come to test their battle skills via RPGs like *D&D*, *V:TES*, *White Wolf*, and the like. All the regulars are there: her ex-mentor Eastwood, Drake (the man-out-of-time adventurer), and, of course, Grognard himself (her boss and a brewer of beer that act as magic potions). However, it's the presence of these and other "usuals" that makes all the trouble.

A nemesis from Eastwood and Ree's past decides to finally take her revenge not just on those two, but on every self-styled "hero" in the city who happens to have crossed her at one point or another. When wave after wave of monsters besiege Grogrnard's store, if Ree & Co. are going to survive, they're going to have to work together. And avoid the minotaur.

For more adventures with Ree,
check out this short excerpt from *Attack the Geek*

PROLOGUE

There's Something About Saturdays

NOW

A hundred fists hammered at the sturdy wood of the thick front door at Grognard's Grog and Games. Ree pressed her back against the door, her boots sliding on the smooth floor of the concrete, failing to find a good grip. The shop was a total wreck—games, cards, figures, and props scattered everywhere, drinks spilled across the bar, tables upended and shattered. Ree wanted to think that the gnomes couldn't make it much worse, but the "getting eaten alive" part banished that thought pretty fast.

"What the fuck has gotten into those little guys?" Ree asked. Pearson's sewer gnomes were already more like ghouls than the helpful creatures in *David the Gnome* or the curious tinkerers from *D&D*, but this was a whole new level of scary.

Eastwood stood beside her, leaning into the door with one shoulder, cuts and bruises scored across his face and hands.

"Don't know, but we can't hold out long like this. And if they get in, we're *bantha pudu*."

Ree could feel the scraping and scratching at the door, then a louder *thud*.

That was no gnome. Ree took a millisecond to consider what else might be out there, but it didn't really matter, since it probably wanted them dead just as much as the tiny ceatures.

"How we doing back there?" Ree shouted to the back room.

"A short while longer, sad to say!" Drake answered, his voice hoarse.

Ree cursed under her breath. "We're not made of time out here. Either the gnomes have made themselves a battering ram, or there's a cave Troll out there!"

"It wouldn't be a cave Troll. They hate the smell down here. Sewer Troll, maybe," Eastwood said.

"Thanks, Mr. *Monster Manual*," Ree said, short temper unleashing the full power of her snark. "How does this help us not get dead?"

Beat.

"It doesn't," Eastwood admitted.

"Then I don't need to know. Hurry up, guys!" Ree shouted again.

Eastwood nudged her. "Get to a weapon. I've got this."

"That's ridiculous. The door will cave in as soon as I move."

"Trust me. We need to be ready."

"I trust you, but I still think it's a terrible idea."

"I'll take it," Eastwood said, pushing her away from the door.

What the fuck is it about Saturdays? Ree asked herself as she felt the door splintering behind her.